A VERY PECULIAR PRACTICE:
THE NEW FRONTIER

The BBC TV series of
A VERY PECULIAR PRACTICE

Stephen Daker	PETER DAVISON
Jock McCannon	GRAHAM CROWDEN
Rose Marie	BARBARA FLYNN
Bob Buzzard	DAVID TROUGHTON
Grete Grotowska	JOANNA KANSKA
Lyn Turtle	AMANDA HILLWOOD
Jack Daniels	MICHAEL J. SHANNON
Julie Daniels	TORIA FULLER
Maureen Gahagan	LINDY WHITEFORD
Mrs Kramer	GILLIAN RAINE
George Bunn	JAMES GROUT
Daphne Buzzard	KAY STONHAM
Ron Rust	JOE MELIA
Charlie Dusenberry	COLIN STINTON
Mervyn Lillicrap	TIM WYLTON
Sweet	GODFREY JAMES
Eric Middling	DAVID BAMBER
Sammy Limb	DOMINIC ARNOLD
Lord Thickthorn	ROBERT LANG
Harry Pointer	MARK DREWRY
Freddie Frith	CLIVE WOOD
Joan Bunn	PATRICIA LAWRENCE

Produced by KEN RIDDINGTON
Written by ANDREW DAVIES
Script Editor DEVORA POPE
Directed by DAVID TUCKER

Andrew Davies recently gave up his day job at Warwick University to write full-time. His play *Rose*, starring Glenda Jackson, played to full houses at the Duke of York's and was subsequently produced on Broadway and in many other countries. Awards: Guardian Children's Fiction Award (for *Conrad's War*); Boston Globe Horn Award (for *Conrad's War*); Broadcasting Press Guild Award for Best Series or Serial (for *To Serve Them All My Days*); Pye Colour Television Award for Best Children's Television Writer (for *Marmalade Atkins In Space*); Writers' Award of the Royal Television Society (for the TV script of *A Very Peculiar Practice*). *A Very Peculiar Practice* was his first novel for adults.

ANDREW DAVIES

A Very Peculiar Practice: The New Frontier

A Methuen Paperback

A Methuen Paperback

A VERY PECULIAR PRACTICE: THE NEW FRONTIER

First published in Great Britain 1988
by Methuen London Ltd
11 New Fetter Lane, London EC4P 4EE
Copyright © 1988 by Andrew Davies

Printed and bound in Great Britain
by Richard Clay Ltd, Bungay, Suffolk

British Library Cataloguing in Publication Data

Davies, Andrew, *1936–*
A very peculiar practice : the new
frontier.
I. Title
823'.914[F]   PR6054.A875/

ISBN 0-413-15510-2
ISBN 0-413-15520-X Pbk

CONTENTS

RUST

Rust is back from the dead. It was a damn close-run thing.
They found him supply teaching at Chiswick Comprehensive
School. His subject was Personal Development. Rust is not
strong on personal development, either as a life-experience
or as an academic subject. As a life-experience Rust has
found that personal development comes in two important
stages. The first is when you recognize that everybody you
know is either a prat, or a shit, or both. The second is when
you realize that you yourself are either a prat, or a shit, or
both. After that, your personal development is complete.
(Rust is a writer: what sort of writer is this, to use these short
unsavoury words? Rust would have you know that he has
many other words at his command: subtle, poignant,
evocative, resonant words, and he will use them too, when
there is money to be made out of them; but for his personal
thinking he prefers the short unsavoury words. For Rust,
they have an inner core of ineluctable truth. Besides, he is
short and unsavoury himself.)

Nobody had enough time to tell Rust the nature of
Personal Development as an academic subject, but he
hazarded a guess that it was one of those new inter-
disciplinary things, combining insights from Biology and
Theology, two more subjects to which Rust had devoted
little thought. He started off bravely from the biological end,
and told his third-year class what he knew about crabs,

1

genital warts and non-specific urethritis. He was received with grudging respect. Then he told them what he thought about God, which took less time, and was received less well. Then he took part in a lively interchange of short unsavoury words. Then the kids started to take him apart.

He was whimpering quietly to himself in the staff-room when Riddington called.

"Ron," said Riddington. "We want you to come in and talk."

"I said I'd never speak to you again and I mean it," said Rust.

"Come on, Ron," said Riddington. "We go back a long time. We've been to hell and back together. We miss you, Ron. Come on in, eh? Just a talk."

"Give me twenty minutes," said Rust.

At Threshold House, the grinning security men refused Rust access to the car park, though he could see spaces: this was par for the course, nothing to worry about. He took the creaky lift to Riddington's slum of an office. Riddington was hunched up by the telephone, looking shagged out and worried. This was par for the course too.

"Hello, young man," said Riddington. "Wonderful to see you."

Rust is not a young man, but he is probably younger than Ken Riddington. Nobody knows how old Ken is, but he is probably over forty and under eighty. Rust looked at Ken, who was rearranging the complicated creases in his face into a sort of smile, and experienced a twinge of affection, a rare event for Rust.

"Come on," said Ken. "Let's go and see Jonathan."

Jonathan Powell is the head of Series and Serials, and his office is much larger and nicer than Ken's, hardly tacky at all, in fact.

"Good to see you, Ron," said Jonathan Powell, not bothering to get up. "Listen: we're getting a very good buzz about the series. People seem to feel it's got the right stuff."

Rust wished that Powell could be bothered to get the note of incredulity out of his voice.

"You mean it's heaven on wheels after all?"

"Well, not exactly heaven on wheels, no, but we think it's going to be quite a nice little cult thing."

"Oh," said Rust, trying very hard indeed to keep the note of incredulity out of his own voice, but failing miserably.

"You can have your name back on the credits if you like," said Ken Riddington.

Rust thought about it. Taking his name off the credits had been the one heroic act in his life as a writer, the writer's equivalent of pistols at dawn, Larkin's "stuff your pension", Alan Ladd riding off into the stormy night at the end of *Shane*. With that one pure single gesture, Rust had redeemed himself as a writer and as a man.

"Yeah, all right," said Rust.

"Ron," said Jonathan Powell. "We think we'd like another series."

And this is how Ron Rust comes to be sitting in his room at Lowlands University, picking his nose. The Arts Council have renewed his Fellowship in Creative Writing, which is just as well, because Rust has no home. Sodding Carol and her chum have turned his flat in Muswell Hill into a sanctuary for women: no place for Rust to lay his head there, or any other part of his short unmemorable body. He has no money to buy another place. But he does have *some* money now. What with the Fellowship and the promised advance on the new series, Rust feels quite rich, for him. He has splashed out on a fragile elderly Mercedes coupé. He loves it very much but it doesn't treat him very well. He even has enough money for a four hundred quid designer suit. And does he look good in it? Well, he didn't actually buy it. When it came to the point he found he was too cheap and mean to cough up the money. Instead he has bought himself a sixty quid copy in Mister Byrite, and he flatters himself that no one can tell the difference. In this, as in most things, he is mistaken.

Still, Ron Rust feels pretty good, for him. He has his bed. He has his view. He has a bottle of Bells he hasn't even opened yet. The only snag is, he has all this *writing* to do.

3

1

THE NEW FRONTIER

The University of Lowlands, at dawn, is a good place and a good time to think about panic, emptiness, despair, dissolution and death.

That was what Jock McCannon was doing. He was sitting on the flaking concrete of a little low wall that surrounded the fountain in the piazza. The fountain was not working. Very little else was working. The biting Lowlands wind blew torn scraps of paper, plastic bags, fragments of unmarked essays, agenda for unattended meetings, used and unused condoms, fallen hair, grey flakes of sloughed skin, and dust, dust and grit, along the sad abandoned walkways, into the cracks and fissures of the empty towers, into the furrowed creases of Jock's ruined old face.

The university had finally staggered to a point of tremulous stillness. It was out on its feet. It was waiting for the *coup de grâce*. After Ernest Hemmingway had failed to sell his university lock, stock and Science Park to the Japanese, after the Prettiman Report, which had diagnosed unscrupulous chicanery mitigated only by bungling incompetence, after the Vice-Chancellor had departed in disgrace, to a knighthood and insider dealings in the City, it became clear that Lowlands had targetted itself as the first of the brave new sixties campus universities to be closed down for ever.

Most of the faculty, and all of Jock's colleagues in the University Medical Centre, had gone to skulk in distant hovels while they waited for the bad news. Jock had stayed, because he had nowhere else to go. He slept in his old consulting room under his stuffed owl, his stag's head, his signed photographs of Ronnie Laing and the Maharishi, and when these gave him bad dreams, or when the security men became irksome, he lurked off to the deserted chaplaincy, and rolled restlessly in its padded conversation pit (the original chaplain had been into the Growth Movement, and had just ordered a jacuzzi when they kicked him out at the start of the first round of cuts). Lately Jock had been kipping in a series of dank students' rooms, savouring their lingering aura of adolescent hopelessness and solitary sex. He slept fitfully, dreamed constantly, and woke early.

Now he sat by the parched fountain, swaddled in a huge old greatcoat, with two well-filled carrier bags by his side, and brooded on the death of universities. On the death of his career, too: even if Lowlands were reprieved to stagger on for another year or two, even if it retained a medical practice, Jock would no longer be the head of it. He had been retired, retained on a part-time consultancy basis only, and Stephen Daker, the young pretender, had inherited his petty kingdom in the swamp of fear and loathing. But Jock felt in his bones that Lowlands had died and would not rise again, even on the last day. Even the birds had deserted it; no fish disturbed the sullen surface of the lake. No human figure intruded into his distinguished melancholy gaze. Except two nuns. He could see them in the distance, flapping round the rubbish skips like a couple of monstrously swollen carrion crows. Yes, well, thought Jock. There will always be two nuns.

So it was that Jock McCannon was virtually the only witness of the Second Coming, the New Frontier. He was aware of a fresh breeze from the West, a ruffling of the waters of the lake, and he tottered towards the crumbling central complex in time to see a huge black Mercedes glide quietly into the university, crunching smoothly over the empty cans and bottles, and purr to a halt in front of the steps of the Senate House. What rough beast, its hour come round at last, was slouching into Lowlands to be born?

The rear door of the Mercedes opened, and a powerfully built man in a dark-blue suit emerged and leapt lightly up the steps, flanked by two other men wearing dark-blue suits and dark glasses. A woman followed, more slowly. At the top of the steps, the man turned, and stared directly across to the fountain where Jock was sitting. He was a youngish man, little over forty, if that. He was smiling and his teeth were a dazzling even white. And his eyes were a piercing light bright blue, and they were looking, even at that distance, directly into Jock's. In that moment Jock McCannon knew that he had seen the Prince of Darkness.

Jack B. Daniels, the new Vice-Chancellor of Lowlands, looked across the ravaged piazza to the fountain where some old bum was sitting with a couple of carrier bags. His wife Julie came and stood by him on the top step.

"Kind of a little bitty pissant place, wouldn't you say, Jack?" said Julie.

His smile did not falter.

"Sure it is, Julie," he said. "But we're going to make it a paradise on earth."

A few weeks later, Stephen Daker was driving his middle-aged Volvo back towards Lowlands, and feeling very strange about it. He had experienced a mixture of relief and foreboding when he read the official letter from a man he had never met called Charles Dusenberry, confirming his appointment, on a temporary basis, as acting head of the Medical Centre, and hinting at sweeping changes soon to be effected on campus. "Temporary" and "Acting" in the same sentence did not exactly reek of security, and anyway Stephen wasn't sure he wanted to be back at Lowlands, now Lyn had gone. Prettiman's lunatic vision of a merger between Lowlands and Hendon Police College had not materialized. The policemen had been appalled by the short beds, bad food and low moral tone prevailing at the university, and had turned it down flat, pronouncing it no fit place for impressionable young bobbies. And Lyn, back in the Force on a high flier's ticket, had gone with the job

6

instead of staying with Stephen. Gone all the way to Hong Kong, in fact. Stephen tried hard to convince himself that he would see her again, talk to her, touch her, look into her eyes, roll happily about in the pit with her ... stop it, Stephen, you'll upset yourself again ... but reason told him to face the situation stoically. His sexual life was over. He would never love again. What a good job he was so keen on being a doctor. Oh, God. Lyn, Lyn!

He drove into the car park, narrowly avoiding a collision with two nuns in a battered Mini who were exiting at speed through the entrance, and parked the Volvo next to an elderly and fragile-looking coupé of foreign origin. Then he struck out boldly for the central campus.

Things did seem to be changing at Lowlands. A lot of construction work was going on: dusty men in yellow helmets were stripping the gaunt buildings of the yellowing tiles which had been falling spasmodically on the heads of the unwary since the middle sixties. There were more security men about, lounging about in twos, eating chips, most of them, and also some quite new sorts of men, tall men in blue suits and dark glasses moving purposefully along the walkways. Stephen tried saying good morning to one of these. The man scrutinized him searchingly without breaking stride or replying, and walked on. Stephen rounded the familiar corner, hoping against reason to hear the steady thump of training shoes and bump into the soft bulk of his lovely gone girl. No chance. And here he was at the Medical Centre.

"Hold it there, sir," said the security man. "Let's see your pass."

"No, look," said Stephen, embarrassed. "I'm Dr Daker."

"And you haven't got a pass."

"No, look, really. You don't understand," said Stephen. "This is the *Medical* Centre. I'm the *Director* of the Medical Centre."

"Not the Medical Centre," said the security man, pointing at a new signboard. Stephen looked. The notice said: "Cybernetics R and D Extension. All passes must be shown."

"Look," said Stephen. "This is ridiculous. Term starts next week. The Medical Centre looks after three thousand staff and students. Are you telling me it's *closed down*?"

"No idea," said the man. "Only doing my job. D'you think I enjoy this job?"

Stephen looked at the man properly for the first time. He was a short unmemorable sort of man, with an expressionless face.

"I don't know," said Stephen. "Do you?"

"I used to teach Personal Development at Chiswick Comprehensive School," said the security guard. "Yes, sir, I enjoy this job very much indeed."

A few minutes later, Stephen, feeling anger and panic in equal proportions, arrived at Senate House flustered and breathless, but determined to have this out with someone. He was welcomed courteously by strangers in dark glasses who seemed to know his name, and shown straight in to see the Vice-Chancellor, who, he was informed, was very keen indeed to meet him.

As Stephen entered the room, he was startled to see his colleagues, Dr Rose Marie and Dr Bob Buzzard, lounging about in easy chairs and smiling their very different sorts of smiles. Clearly some sort of plot was going on. Perhaps he had been ousted already. Then a handsome, powerfully built man rose from behind a vast desk made of some kind of white metal, and held his hand out.

"Jack Daniels," said this man. His smile was warm, sincere, almost boyishly ingenuous, and his eyes were a vivid light blue. He reminded Stephen of someone but for the moment he couldn't think who it was. "Great to meet you, Steve, c'mon, sit down, let's talk."

"No thanks," said Stephen, feeling absurdly prim. "Er, look, I'm sorry, I just don't understand what's going on here."

Jack's smile broadened to take in Bob Buzzard, Rose Marie, the whole throbbing campus.

"We're making some changes, Steve, that's what's going on."

"Including closing down the Medical Centre?" His voice

8

sounded high and squeaky. Jack Daniels's smile became a rueful boyish grin. He brushed back a lock of hair.

"Bobby, Rose, I guess I don't need any more of your time right now," he said. "Thank you for your input, Bobby. Rose ..." and he took her hand in both of his and smiled deep into her eyes ... "you give very good meeting."

"So do you, Jack" said Rose Marie.

"Steve," said Jack Daniels, when they had gone, "I'd like to let you into some of our thinking about the new Lowlands. We're going for excellence. If we can't win, we're not gonna play."

"Look, all I want to know ..."

"Take Electroacoustics, now they're popping with new ideas, busting out of their playpens, so we give them space to grow, right? Philosophy ... eight old boys with research constipation, nothing in the pipeline, kind of a diddleysquat department, so we take the euthanasia option."

"I see," said Stephen. His voice felt better now. Anger was winning out over panic. "So on those criteria, you're closing down the Medical Centre?"

The telephone rang.

"Excuse me, Steve," said Jack Daniels, picking it up. He listened for a moment, then said: "Honey, I'm in a meeting, could I call you back? ... No, it's a man, honey, it's a doctor .... No, honey, I'm fine .... Honey, I swear to you, there are no roaches in the kitchen. Take it easy, Julie. Julie. Listen to me. I want you to have a shower, Julie, and I'll call you right back .... Sure I love you. Now will you go and have a shower, will you do that for me, Julie? I have to hang up now. I have to hang up, Julie."

He put the phone down.

"That was Julie," he said. "I guess she's having some adjustment problems. Ah, Julie is my wife, Steve."

"I'm sorry," said Stephen, like a prat. "Er – I mean – "

"Steve," said Jack Daniels warmly, "I'm not going to hold back on you. I've decided to go with you guys. I believe in what you're trying to do here. I'm giving you a whole new Medical Centre. I've studied your profile in the Prettiman Report, Steve, I like the quality of your thinking, and I know you're going to pick this one up and run with it." Stephen found himself, as so often, struggling with conflicting emotions.

"Thank you very much," he said. "But, er . . . I don't want to seem churlish . . . but don't you think I should have been consulted about the new centre?"

"Don't be grouchy with me, Steve. I guess I wanted you to enjoy your vacation. I think you're gonna like what we've done. Based it on the facility at Lawrence Livermore. You see," and here he brushed the lock of hair back again, "I'm bringing some very special people to Lowlands. Valuable people. And they need to know we value them, right? So we give them the best."

It sounded very plausible, but Jack Daniels was talking to a man whose background had been Birmingham, Birmingham, and Walsall, a man who bore the scars of working in a town where more people are ill than anywhere else in England.

"Isn't everybody valuable?" said Stephen.

Jack Daniels glowed with warmth and integrity. The blue eyes widened and the white teeth glittered. A strong brown hand closed on Stephen's upper arm.

"Hey, right," said the new Vice-Chancellor. "I love that. That's what I came to Europe to hear. Everybody is valuable. That's the bottom line. With thinking like that, who needs a Philosophy Department?"

It seemed that Stephen could do no wrong. Without letting Stephen's arm out of his grip, Jack Daniels led him to the window, where they both stared solemnly out over the scarred concrete remains of the old Lowlands, the churning mud and scaffolding of the building sites, and the distant lake gleaming in a rare and fortuitous ray of sunshine.

"I have dreams for this place," said Jack Daniels. "I'm not just talking Nobel prizes. I'm talking string quartets. I'm talking human fulfilment, dammit."

Stephen was impressed. He had heard of Plato's *Republic*, of course, but he had never got round to reading it. Clearly he was dealing with a man of culture and vision, qualities not altogether common amongst vice-chancellors in these stringent and beleaguered days. Ernest Hemmingway, Jack's predecessor, would probably have thought Plato's *Republic* was a Greek night club where a man of affairs could unwind, tank up on retsina and ouzo, and fumble about with the waitresses. Stephen turned to look at his new master, who was smiling the boyish ingenuous smile again. Now he knew who it was Jack Daniels reminded him of.

"I guess that might sound a little naive to you," said the Vice-Chancellor. He was opening his heart to Stephen. The man who had come across the Atlantic to save Lowlands was confiding his dreams to a humble general practitioner. Stephen was moved and excited. It was almost like being in love.

"No, no, it's inspiring," he said. "Really. When I first came here, I felt that, well, here was a place where I could really do the job properly. Actually push back the frontiers of health care. Um ... what with one thing and another, I don't think we've achieved that yet."

"We will now," said Jack Daniels softly. "We're going to make the earth shake here at Lowlands."

Bob Buzzard and Rose Marie were walking back towards the new Medical Centre, and Bob was feeling his oats. He had a definite hunch that the long journey up shit creek was over, and that now was the time for a chap to get on with his life. The American chap had been a bit coarse and brash, naturally, but he seemed to have the knack of tapping into serious money, and he seemed to know what to do with it when he got it. No doubt he was also the sort of chap who knew a good chap when he saw one, and as soon as Bob had Jack's confidence he would fill Jack in on the shortcomings of the old fart, the uppity dyke, and in particular the utter unfitness for leadership of Dickie Dado the wet liberal. In the meantime, it was never wise to antagonize the uppity dyke.

"Well, you certainly made a good impression there, Rose," he said, plunging into a pool of wet concrete without even noticing it was there.

"Thank you, Bob," said Dr Rose Marie. "So did you."

"D'you think so?" said Bob, feeling tremendously chuffed; praise from the dyke was rare, bloody rare. "Hard to tell with Americans, isn't it? I mean, they're not fully human, are they? Of course, they don't have proper schools over there. I'm gonna give this my very best shot, thanks for your input Bobby, you give very good meeting Rose, have a nice day . . . absolutely barbaric. Nice fellow, though, in his way. Family man, too. Brought his no doubt frightful wife and all his monstrous kids, how many did he say he had, ten was it?"

"Just four, I think, Bob."

"By God, I wouldn't like four American kids," said Bob. "Still he is a family man, and that counts for something these days. If I didn't have Daphne and the twins, where would I be now? Actually I'd probably be in Saudi pulling down eight grand a month but that's not the point is it? I've often thought you've missed a lot Rose, not being a family man, nothing like it for putting you in touch with life's brutal realities. God sometimes I wish I could just shut *up*."

He stopped and tried to brush some of the wet concrete off his gleaming black Oxfords. Rose Marie was regarding him with clinical compassion.

"Are you all right, Bob?" she said softly.

"Fine, fine, absolutely marvellous!" shouted Bob, who was in fact feeling a bit out of control. Then, unable to help himself, he added: "D'you *really* think he liked me?"

"Why, of *course* he did, Bob," she said warmly. "He recognized an essential kinship with you, something a man can't have with a woman. He called you *Bobby*."

"But not Robert."

Bob Buzzard longed to be called Robert, but hardly anybody ever did, except Daphne of course. It would have been marvellous if Jack Daniels had called him Robert. What was so brilliant about *Bobby*? He stared keenly at Rose Marie, breathing hard, looking even more than usual like a very ambitious Dobermann Pinscher in glasses.

"He saw you as a *brother*, Bob. Jack and Bobby? Don't those names resonate for you?"

"Charlton?" It was a bit early in the morning for verbal intelligence tests.

12

"Oh, *Bob*."

Then he got it.

"What? *Really*? You mean ... *yes*! I *see*!"

Old Mata Hari was a smart tottie. Bob had to hand her that. If she was right about this, the sky was the limit.

"Of course," she went on, smiling gently, "we have to remember what happened to Bobby Kennedy."

Jack Daniels and Stephen Daker were strolling through the trees down by the lake. The Vice-Chancellor had expressed the desire to feel the grass under his feet, and when the Vice-Chancellor wants to feel the grass under his feet, the Director of the Medical Centre has to go along with it. Actually, it was very pleasant down by the lake. The usual dogs were fooling about in and out of the water, barking at the ducks, a couple of nuns were fluttering about on the edge of the wood on the far side, and a short unsavoury looking man whom Stephen vaguely remembered as the Arts Council Fellow in something was sitting on a bench quite harmlessly scribbling in a notebook. The only slightly disconcerting thing was that two of the tall men in dark suits and dark glasses were strolling thirty yards or so behind Jack and Stephen, occasionally murmuring into walkie-talkies.

"I feel so good about this place, you know," said Jack Daniels, sucking deep draughts of air into his powerful torso.

"Er ... what are those men doing?"

"Just the same as we are, Steve. Breathing God's good air. Don't worry about them. They're two of the good guys. They're part of the team."

He took Stephen's arm, squeezing it gently, as if checking that it was made of the right stuff, and looked deep into Stephen's eyes.

"How do you feel about *your* team, Steve? Can they deliver? Have they got the right stuff for us?"

"Yes, I think so," said Stephen guardedly. "With good facilities, I think we could do a first-class job."

Jack was still looking deep into his eyes. "All I'm

saying ... if you want to take any of them out, we can facilitate that. Any or all of them. We want you to be happy with your team."

Stephen experienced a moment of dreadful, delicious temptation. He could get rid of them all at one stroke: never again have to wince at Bob Buzzard's cheerful brutality, lie awake worrying about Rose Marie's Machiavellian plots and unfathomable sexuality, nurse Jock McCannon through his terrifying bouts of dipsomaniac paranoia. But no. He couldn't do it. He had sat with Bob Buzzard, actually holding his hand, after the failure of the dodgy drug trials. He had seen Jock McCannon rise from the dead to save the university from the scourge of non-specific urethritis. And Rose Marie had literally saved his life when John Furie, Pro-Vice-Chancellor and Professor of Biochemistry, had come to his consulting room to beat him to death with a filing cabinet. The team had been to hell and back together. It was a horrible thought, but in a way he, well ... sort of loved them all.

"No," he said firmly. "We've had our differences here and there, but no. I wouldn't want to lose any of them." Jack Daniels grinned, released his arm, and they walked on.

"OK Steve, whatever you say. Now you're moving into Kennedy Hall as resident warden, right?"

"Yes, I am. I'm looking forward to it. That's if you ..."

"Fine. Great. I'd like to develop your role in the university, Steve. Get your quality of caring at Kennedy Hall. I guess that name has special vibes for me. John F. Kennedy. Yeah."

They stood for a moment in silent reverence. Stephen wondered if he ought to bow his head or fiddle with his cycle clips or something. Then Jack Daniels, breathing deeply, raised his eyes to the cold and rook-delighting heavens.

"You ever sense there's someone up there, Steve? Looking down and listening?"

"Er ... you mean John F. Kennedy?"

"No," said Jack, looking at him steadily. "Not Kennedy."

"Er ... God?" said Stephen wildly.

"I'm talking about the Soviets, Steve," said Jack kindly

and firmly, as if explaining something to a child. "Just twenty-four thousand miles up there, a Soviet satellite is beaming signals back to Moscow. And right now I like to think of a guy in Moscow checking out a screen, saying holy shit, they're starting something special there in Lowlands. It's a small world, Steve."

Stephen stared at him. Could he really be serious? It seemed he was. The blue eyes were steady. They had inner certainty. Stephen was dealing with a man with a vision.

One of the men in dark glasses signalled to Jack Daniels.

"Hey, I have to leave you now," said the Vice-Chancellor. He grasped Stephen's shoulder. "Steve ... I believe you have the right stuff for us. Hell, let's go to work!"

And he strode away to the concrete cliffs of the central complex.

The new Health Centre looked quite pleasant from the outside, if you liked those colourful high-tech buildings with all their bits showing, rather like a full-colour representation of an unfinished heart-and-lung transplant operation. It seemed quite appropriate for a medical centre, Stephen thought; and doctors are trained not to blench at the sight of internal organs on public display. He went through the automatically opening doors into the waiting room, which looked like the recreation room of a space capsule, rounded unit seating in soft colours, not a sharp angle anywhere, with soothing music oozing out of the walls. Carmen Kramer the receptionist was already at her post, watching an Australian soap on one of the three TV monitors behind her counter. A little twitchy man with a clipboard and briefcase was wriggling on one of the seats.

"Morning," said Stephen to this man, who produced a sort of high involuntary squeak in reply.

"This is a hospital," said one of the characters in the Australian soap. "Full of sick, sick people. Needing our care, our attention."

"The Medical Centre is *closed*," said Mrs Kramer without turning. "There is *no* point in waiting. If it's an emergency, you can phone the *emergency* number."

15

"Hello, Mrs Kramer," said Stephen. Sometimes he felt he even sort of loved Mrs Kramer. She extinguished the television and turned to beam at him.

"Dr Daker! Isn't this *wonderful*!"

"Yes, it does seem rather wonderful," said Stephen, staring round him. "I can't quite believe it."

"Of course," said Mrs Kramer, "the patients are going to spoil it so. Clashing with the colour schemes, leaving their awful little specks and stains . . . ."

"Mrs Kramer," said Stephen, feeling embarrassed for the little twitchy man.

"Oh, *that*'s not a *patient*, that's Mr Perks from Estates and Buildings!"

The little man jumped off the seat and held out a trembling hand to Stephen.

"Geoffrey Perks, pleased to meet you Dr Daker, trust you'll find everything up to specification."

"Well, as I didn't specify anything," said Stephen rather tetchily, "I'm not sure how I'd know."

"All in here, Dr Daker," said Perks, tapping a thick file. "Think you'll find it all in order, we've really moved heaven and earth on this one. Shall we?"

Mrs Kramer pressed the button that released the security door to the inner sanctums of the health centre, and Perks led Stephen through, letting out another of his involuntary squeaks.

First they went to the Body Lab. Stephen had never heard of a Body Lab, but now it seemed he was in charge of one. It was very impressive, partaking of features of both an executive gymnasium and an intensive care unit. Bob Buzzard was in there already, pounding away on an exercise bike in tracksuit trousers and a horrible yellow vest, with various bits of him wired up to various machines, while Maureen Gahagan, the nurse, stood bad-temperedly by with a stopwatch.

"Be with you later, buddy – can't stop now!" shouted Bob. "This new gear is magic! Just run the whole battery of tests on young Maureen here. Won't bore you with the details. Main findings were nice strong legs, working vocabulary of the average hod-carrier, and strong positive indications for a total brain transplant. Isn't that so, Maureen?"

"Right. That is it," said Maureen, pulling a few plugs out, and ripping the electrodes off Bob's hairy arms. "I have better things to do than stand around being insulted by a pathetic misogynistic overgrown schoolboy with the wit and charm of a building site guard dog, and how's that for a hod-carrier's vocabulary?"

She strode to the door, glaring at Perks, who let out a little yelp, and at Stephen, who tried a placatory smile to little effect.

"Nice to see you, Dr Daker," she snarled. "Hope you had a nice peaceful holiday. And now I am going to listen to my Bruce Springsteen tapes."

"She was absolutely good as gold till you two came along," said Bob. "It's Perks there. Think you sexually excite her, Perks. Well, there's another morning's work gone."

After the Body Lab, Perks led Stephen to Dr Rose Marie's room.

"If you don't mind, Dr Daker, I won't come in with you, it's a bit, well she's rather . . . . Oop!"

Stephen knocked and went in. It was beautiful. The little moulded desk with its VDU monitor was tucked discreetly into a corner, leaving loads of space to be sensitive in. At one end of the room was a small and womblike seating group, at the other a circle of tasteful cushions on the floor. Between the two was a sort of miniature Japanese garden, with Bonsai trees and even a little artificial stream and fountain. It was really tremendously calm and soothing in Rose Marie's room provided that you enjoyed total bladder control. Fortunately Stephen did.

"Rose," he said.

She turned from the plant she was tending. She was wearing her familiar dazzling white coat with, apparently, nothing beneath it, and she was smiling one of her smiles.

"Hello, Stephen," she said, turning a simple greeting, as ever, into a coded message of labyrinthine complexity.

"This is ... beautiful."

"Thank you," she said. "Estates were remarkably co-operative. I think we'll be able to do some really significant work here. But ... forgive me, Stephen ... I do think we should start as we mean to go on, don't you?"

"Well, yes, of course," said Stephen warily. "Naturally. Er ... what d'you mean?"

Rose Marie indicated a tasteful notice. It said: This Well Woman Area is reserved for Women Only.

"Oh, Lord, sorry," said Stephen without thinking, feeling the panic of one who has stumbled into the wrong loo with his cock already halfway out of his trousers. He backed towards the door, then stopped. "But look. You can't do that."

"You mean you're forbidding it?" she said silkily. "As head of the practice?"

"No, of course not. But I mean ... are you saying you don't want to treat male patients any more?"

"I haven't finalized my thoughts on that yet, Stephen," she said. "I'm not a total separatist, as you know. But it seemed the right time to claim a space for women in the Centre. A kind of sanctuary."

"Er ... what about men, Rose? Don't they need sanctuary?"

"Oh, Stephen," she said pityingly. "Men have always had sanctuary."

"Well," said Stephen weakly, feeling as always out-manoeuvred by Rose, "I do think we need to discuss this further, Rose."

"Of course, Stephen. I'll look forward to that."

"The elderly gentleman's in here, Dr Daker," said Perks nervously, pointing to a door. Clearly he did not want to go in there any more either. Stephen could imagine what he was feeling. Bracing himself, he knocked, and went in. It was a small room, high-tech like the rest, but stacked to the ceiling with tea-chests and boxes of Jock's dusty and in some cases smelly memorabilia. J. G. McCannon seemed to be trying to reconstruct a replica of his foetid old cave amidst the alien polypropylene. He turned from his task. He was engaged in hanging Freud in a prominent position on the wall, and as he turned, Freud slumped into a crazy skewed angle, at which he would remain for the rest of Jock's tenancy. Nothing, as we know, is purely accidental.

"Stephen," said Jock, smiling his ruined smile. "My dear boy. You have come back. All is not lost."

"Well of course I've come back," said Stephen, trying to dispel the aura of maudlin that hung about the room. "Raring to go. Er, making yourself at home?"

Jock stared at him tragically for a few moments without answering. Stephen found himself wondering, not for the first time, just how old Jock was. That was something nobody knew. Somewhere between forty and eighty, anyway, and today he looked at least seventy-eight.

"I have no home," said Jock. "I have no kingdom." He waved his arm unsteadily at his chaotic clutter of junk. "These fragments I have shored against my ruins." His watery gaze wandered over the old tea-chests, the stuffed animals, the new desk with its rinky-dinky VDU monitor. He growled low and deep in his throat, and tossed a moth-eaten leopardskin rug over it.

"Their eyes are everywhere," he said obscurely.

"Look, Jock," said Stephen forcefully. "Everything's all *right*. We've survived. The new VC believes in what we're doing. I think. Well he must do, look at all this stuff he's given us. We're going to make it work, Jock."

"Poor wee laddie," rumbled Jock. "Poor little innocent prince."

He turned abruptly, and thrust his head into one of the tea-chests, as if to vomit in it. Then he came out with a stag's head in his hands.

"Stephen: I want you to have this," he said.

"Er, no," said Stephen, alarmed. "Really, I couldn't."

"Yes," said Jock severely. "The old stag must bow his antlers while the young buck goes into rut. Take it, Stephen. Rule my kingdom well."

Minutes of a Group Meeting, 27 September 1988; Dr Stephen

Daker in the chair as Head of the Practice and Medical Director

The first item to be discussed was the Medical Director's new suit. Dr Rose Marie asked Dr Daker whether he was now into Power Dressing. Dr Daker said that he was not. Dr Buzzard enquired whether it had been purchased at a market stall, or whether it had fallen off the back of a commercial vehicle. Dr Daker said that if it was any of Dr Buzzard's business, the suit had been purchased from a remarkably reasonable shop called Mister Byrite. Dr Buzzard argued that a man who was too mean to buy himself a decent suit was the sort of man who would let the team down in all sorts of ways. Nurse Gahagan reminded the meeting that a pig in a Savile Row suit was still a pig. Dr McCannon offered to let Dr Daker have the name of his tailor, if he was still alive. Dr Daker declined. Dr Daker then proposed next business. Carried *nem. con.*

Dr Daker invited comments on the new facilities. Dr Buzzard confirmed that the Body Lab was brilliant and that once it was up and running, no one need see or touch a patient again. There were, however, some early teething troubles. Dr Buzzard furnished as an example the fact that he had given himself a psychometric scan and come out as a borderline psychopath. Nurse Gahagan said that that sounded about right to her.

Dr Rose Marie felt that the new Vice-Chancellor seemed very co-operative and receptive to new ideas, which was more than could be said for the head of the practice. Dr Daker suggested that Dr Rose Marie might consider extending her wonderful work with the Well Woman Centre, and proposed a Well Person Centre. Dr Rose Marie said that that was to completely misunderstand the nature of the problematic. Dr McCannon wished it to be recorded that this was Hell, nor were they out of it, and that the University of Lowlands had sold itself to the Prince of Darkness. The meeting agreed to bear this in mind.

Dr Daker announced that he proposed to initiate a series of staff workshops, exploring more fruitful ways of working with patients, and examining the interactions within the team itself. Dr Buzzard said that this took the bloody biscuit. Dr Daker had only been in power five minutes and here he was telling his colleagues they were a bunch of loonies. Dr McCannon disagreed, and offered his services, as a very experienced psychiatric counsellor. Dr Daker said that this was not quite what he had in mind, Dr McCannon hardly being a detached observer. Dr McCannon said that he quite understood how Dr Daker would wish to spurn and humiliate his former leader.

The routine business included arranging medical examinations for new academic staff. Dr Daker offered to take care of the new chap in Art History, a Dr Grotowska, and Dr Buzzard volunteered to conduct the medical for Mr Greg Trout, who was a new appointment in Mechanical Engineering.

In concluding the meeting Dr Daker assured his colleagues that he understood what a difficult transition this was for the whole team, but that he did feel it would help if all staff could try to approach things in a more positive spirit. Meeting concluded at 3.35 p.m.

After the group meeting, Stephen considered going home to bed and crying himself to sleep, throwing himself in the lake, and writing to see whether there were any upcoming vacancies in his old practice at Walsall. But being a moderate sort of man, he did none of these things, and was sitting at his desk doggedly working through Mr Perks's file when Rose Marie knocked softly at his door and came in.

"May I?" she said.

"Of course, Rose," said Stephen. "This isn't a no-go area."

"Don't be bitter, Stephen," she said. She sat down and leaned towards him, affording him a disconcerting view of the dark valley between her not-to-be-imagined breasts.

"Well," said Stephen. "I can't see how I managed to alienate everyone."

"Really?" she said. "You were strong, Stephen. You've claimed your territory as head of the practice. I admired that. I . . . responded to it."

"Thank you, Rose." Stephen always felt jumpy when Rose responded to things.

"Perhaps especially because I understand the pain you're going through just now." Yes. He was quite right to be jumpy. Resist. Resist.

"No, I'm fine, Rose. Honestly." It didn't sound too convincing.

"You mustn't shut out the pain, Stephen," said Rose in an exasperatingly compassionate tone. "It's part of you now."

"Is it?"

"I'm ... not a man," said Rose, perhaps unnecessarily. She crossed her legs, and uncrossed them again. "But I do empathize. For you, at your age, with a broken marriage behind you ... to be rejected by someone you love so much ...."

"Lyn didn't exactly reject me, Rose. She was offered a good job, and she took it. I thought you'd have approved of that. I do myself, really."

"Don't push away the pain, Stephen," she said. "No ... to be rejected by someone you love so much ... well, I should think it must feel like having your penis cut off."

With a supreme effort of will Stephen managed not to bend himself double and whimper aloud.

"I, er ... hadn't envisaged it quite like that, Rose."

"Oh, I think you have. Deep down in your essential maleness."

She regarded him steadily in his essential maleness for what seemed like about twenty minutes. It seemed to be Stephen's move.

"Well ... thanks very much, Rose," he said. "Er, was there anything else?"

"Yes, Stephen, there was. I'd like to ... give you something."

"Jock felt like that," said Stephen. "He gave me a stag's head."

Rose smiled. "Nothing like that. I've been thinking about what you said at the meeting ... and I'm prepared to offer a Male Sexuality Workshop."

Stephen was touched. "Really? That's wonderful, Rose."

22

"You might feel like participating yourself, Stephen, when it's under way. It might ... help," she said.

"Well, thank you Rose," said Stephen, privately resolving not to go within a mile of it. "I'll certainly think about that."

It was only after she had gone that he started to reflect seriously on what a Male Sexuality Workshop run by Dr Rose Marie might be like.

It was early evening by the time Stephen set out to find his new, large, prestigious, ground-floor flat in Kennedy Hall. It was a pleasant evening, though hardly peaceful, because the paths were full of jolly tanned pensioners on racing bikes, the last remnants of one of Ernie Hemmingway's schemes to turn the campus into a subsidiary of Saga Holidays. They weaved rapidly and unsteadily round him, with many a whoop and shriek, scrawny and substantial bottoms pumping away in unison, and raced ahead of him towards Kennedy Hall. Well, not bad, thought Stephen. Good for them. Alive, in scarlet shorts, and still pedalling at sixty-five. Hope for us all.

By the time he had negotiated the security guard on the door, the foyer was full of them, most of them with glasses of wine in their hands, and some of them dancing to "Brown Sugar" by the Rolling Stones, which was blasting out of a powerful sound system. A purple-faced old chap with mutton-chop whiskers and a glass of wine in each hand rolled up to him.

"You look a bit young for this," said Mutton-chop. "Think you'll stand the pace? Drink?"

Behind a banner that told him he had strayed into "60–75 Singles Club Action Holidays", Stephen glimpsed a small notice with a discreet arrow pointing him in the direction of the warden's flat. He slipped under the elbow of the mutton-chop man, and went down a carpeted corridor. The flat was there. His key turned in the lock, once he had remembered to try it anticlockwise (altered priorities at Lowlands), and he was in.

It was blessedly cool and quiet in the warden's flat. Stephen pushed open the first door he came to. The bedroom. Large, greenish, bland. A good-sized double bed to be lonely and have bad dreams in. There was a blue sleeping-bag spread over the coverlet. Odd. Good-sized bathroom, one of the Lowlands New Brutalist originals, solid yellow brick and white tiles, plenty of good thick pipes, a huge big white bath which would look good with a deathly white arm hanging over the side. Why did Lowlands bathrooms always make you think of despair and death? Oh, come on, Stephen. You're the head of the practice. You're the *warden*. New start, OK? New life.

He walked down the corridor and pushed open the door to the living room. Most of the floor space was occupied by a large dirty sheet spread over the carpet. On the sheet stood a disconcertingly large motorbike in a state of disassembly. Crouching behind it, and looking up at Stephen in some alarm, was a skinny waif-like creature in a scruffy blue boiler-suit. His really rather angelic face was streaked with oil, sweat and grime, and he had a large bruise on his right cheekbone.

"Oh, shit," said the waif. "You're not the new warden bloke?"

"Yes, I am," said Stephen.

"Oh, shit. Didn't think you'd be here yet. Thing is all the other rooms are full of geriatric ravers, right? Got back early, had to have somewhere to kip and work. Madhouse, this place, right? Look, I'll be out in five minutes, no hassle."

The waif had a North London accent and a very sweet and no doubt duplicitous smile. Stephen had been told before of the Lowlands netherworld: dozens, perhaps scores, of people, who lived in and on the university like resident rats, using temporarily empty rooms, haunting the back of the refectory and raiding the stores and delivery vans, eking a modest living and supporting their drug habits by stealing and selling the students' bicycles. Now, it seemed, he had met one of them.

"Look," he said. "How did you get in?"

The waif flashed an Access card.

"Flexible friend," he said. "Look, it's all right. I'm a bona fide student. Sammy Limb. Ask anyone. Here, shake

24

hands." He wiped his greasy hand on the back of his boiler-suit and held it out to Stephen. His grip was surprisingly strong.

"That's it. People feel better when they shake har 1s."

"Stephen Daker," said Stephen, starting to feel out-manoeuvred.

"Nice to meet you, Stephen," said the waif, pressing home his advantage.

"Engineering student?" Stephen indicated the bike.

"No, used to be Mech. Eng., but I switched to International Law, cos I want to take the university to the Court of Human Rights, see. The bike's for work. Express Deliveries? Working me way through college, right?"

"But ... don't you have a grant?"

"Oh, dear," said Sammy, worldling to innocent. "Grant don't go anywhere. Some of us have got expensive tastes, Stephen, need to eat every day sort of thing." He smiled his sweet smile again. "Hey, you don't need this at all, do you? You look dead nackered. You go and get settled in. I'll be gone by the time you've done it."

"Look," said Stephen. "I mean, if I kick you out ... where are you going to sleep tonight?"

Sammy sat down and lit a cigarette. It was all going to be fine. The new warden of Kennedy Hall was soft as shit.

Mrs Kramer was feeling very irritated. Term was still two days away, and already people were cluttering up her lovely waiting room. Only two of them, but that was two too many. The man was not so bad: big, quite clean-looking, polite and terrified. If Mrs Kramer *had* to have men in her waiting room, that was the way she liked them. But the other one was getting on Mrs Kramer's nerves. Thin, dark, female, restless and *foreign*, she was striding to and fro wearing out the carpet, snapping her fingers, looking at her watch, and sighing in a silly overdone foreign theatrical way.

"*Do* take a seat, Miss, er ..." said Mrs Kramer, not for the first time.

"This is compulsory?" said the foreign person. She tapped her watch. "Listen, half past two, it said, the appointment. Now it's two forty-five."

"The doctors *are* very busy, you know," said Mrs Kramer with weary contempt. Really. Some people.

"Maybe they should organize their time better. You think we're not busy people, me and this man here?" She pointed a quivering finger at the big shy man on the couch, who blushed scarlet. "You think we have nothing else to do but lurk about waiting for doctors?"

"I'm sure I have no idea," said Mrs Kramer loftily. Mrs Kramer was frightened of nobody. She had even seen Professor Furie off once or twice, and was certainly going to stand no cheek from this unpleasant little refugee person, who was now actually getting a *cigarette* out of her bag.

"*No* smoking in the Health Centre, please," said Mrs Kramer.

The foreign person turned and seemed on the point of crossing swords again, an action she would regret to the very end of her days, when Dr Daker's voice came over the tannoy.

"Dr Grotowska to see Dr Daker, please."

Mrs Kramer frostily pressed the door release button, and the foreign person went through, smiling at Mrs Kramer in an insulting foreign way.

Stephen had been wondering what Dr Grotowska would look like. English art historians tended to be bald, bland and bow-tied. Foreign ones much the same, probably, with beards, perhaps, and with luck, lots of *Gemütlichkeit*. Little fat paunch pushing out the waistcoat. This chap Grotowska might even bring some nice Viennese pastries with him in a little box tied with a ribbon, present for the nice English doctor; old Schusselbaum from German used to do that. Axed now, of course, with the rest of the German Department, poor old chap. Maybe this Grotowska would turn out to be just like him. Stephen hoped so. Today he had been unable to face the dogshit in the refectory, and he was feeling really hungry. Apfelstrudel . . . Sachertorte . . . even a currant bun would be very acceptable.

He had visualized Dr Grotowska and his wonderful pastries so clearly that he was unable to do anything but boggle stupidly when the door opened and he found himself

26

staring at an anorexic-looking young girl with a face like a fierce little cat.

"Yes?" he managed eventually.

"Here I am," said the anorexic. She sounded foreign. Surely *this* couldn't be . . .?

"Dr Grotowska?"

"Yes."

Amazing. She didn't look old enough to be a doctor of anything. And oh Lord, he'd given Maureen the afternoon off.

"I'm so sorry," he said, getting up. "Silly mix-up. For some reason the form had you down as a man. Er – I wonder if you'd mind making another . . . you see the nurse isn't here this afternoon . . . ." Hopeless. Hopeless. Why was he stuttering and gawping like this?

"And?"

"Well, for a female patient she'd normally be present."

"You can't do this on your own?"

Oh, Lord.

"Yes, of course I can," he said. "It's just that . . ."

"You're scared of women?" Right on the button, of course, with her fierce little face and her sardonic grin. For a terrible moment he was on the brink of a really good blurt, all about what his mother and Angela had done to him between them, and how Lyn had come along and for a while he'd felt really all right, and how here he was back at square one, walking wounded again . . . .

"No, of course I'm not," he said firmly.

"You don't like them?" My God, what had she majored in, interrogation techniques? His forehead was beginning to sweat.

"Yes, I *do*," he said, hearing his voice go squeaky on the last word.

"So where's the problem?" she said, sitting down. "Start the medical."

What with one thing and another, it seemed like a good idea to start the medical. Dr Grotowska, it seemed, was Polish by birth, French by a marriage that was now over, had graduated from the Sorbonne, taken her doctorate at

27

the Courtauld Institute, published on the Iconography of the Male Nude ("this frightens many men") and would now be, if she passed the medical, a full lecturer in Art History in a language not her own, at only twenty-six years old. Pretty high-powered stuff, quite daunting in fact. Stephen beat a rapid retreat into strictly medical territory, and here she answered his questions in a brisk irritated way, as if swatting flies.

No, she had no medical history that he should know about, no, no serious illnesses or operations, no, she hadn't consulted a doctor in the last five years. All right, thought Stephen. He made himself look steadily into her eyes for ten seconds (standard practice) and then said quietly and pleasantly:

"Tell me, have you any history at all of psychiatric trouble?"

She glared at him.

"You think I'm crazy, is that it?"

"No," he said, making a real effort to keep his voice level, "I don't think you're crazy, it's just a question that I have to put to you."

She paused a moment.

"OK, you put it. Good boy. No history."

Like hell, thought Stephen.

"Anorexia, for example, is extremely common amongst intelligent young women. And an anorexic episode in the past wouldn't be a bar to your appointment."

"You think I'm too thin, that's your problem," she said. "I like to eat, don't worry."

"All right," he said. It would have been nice if she hadn't been quite so open about her intellectual contempt for him. How had he managed to land such an awkward bad-tempered customer, and on Maureen's afternoon off too? He took a deep breath.

"Well, I'd like to examine you now, so if you'd like to go behind that screen and strip down to your bra and pants?"

"This is necessary?"

"I'm afraid so, yes. It won't take very long."

"I don't have a bra," she said flatly.

Suddenly Stephen felt absurdly embarrassed.

"Well, er . . ."

"I tell you what," she said. "I'll use my initiative. In here, right?"

Bob Buzzard was having a much more straightforward time with Greg Trout, the Mech. Eng. chap. Couldn't put him through the Body Lab because the colleen from the bogs had gone bananas at lunchtime and blown four of the circuits. But Trout was clearly OK, a big strong lad with everything in the right place. Bob slapped the stetho on the engineer's back.

"What car d'you drive?"

"Morgan."

"Louder."

"Morgan!"

"Clear as a bell," said Bob. "Good cars, too."

"Rebuilt it myself," said Trout modestly.

"Did you, by God? Now there's a useful skill. Rebuild my old BMW if you like, it's falling to bits. Heart next." Bob looked at his watch. "Hell's bells, I'm supposed to be on the squash court in five minutes."

"Squash player?" said Trout. "Any good?"

"Not bad," said Bob. Not bad meant bloody good, as any squash player knows. But Trout didn't flinch.

"Play you for a fiver some time then," he said.

"You're on, buddy," said Bob, and made a fast decision. "Look. This medical's a joke. You're obviously a fine young fellow, so what are we farting about here for? Let's get on with our lives, eh? You take your time and get dressed, and I'll just go and thrash the Lodgings Officer."

He was out of the door and down the corridor before Trout had finished replying.

Dr Grete Grotowska *was* very thin, but her muscle tone was good, and her very white skin had a healthy sheen about it. Not anorexic, then; probably never had been. Just a thin woman. Her breasts were so little that they almost disappeared when she lay down with her hands behind her head, watching him sardonically. He took his time about examining them. Touching women in a medical context was fine; it actually calmed him. He liked being a doctor. He was good at it. He actually loved the gentle impersonal contact, and was able to forget about the sardonic little cat face watching him. No lumps. No irregularities. Good.

"That's fine," he said, drawing down her skimpy little black cotton vest. "And you examine your breasts regularly?"

"Yes I do," she said. "*I* enjoy it *too*."

"You're not making this very easy for me, are you?" he said.

"That's what women are for? To make things easy for you?"

"I'd just like to examine your abdomen," he said stiffly.

"Help yourself."

He examined her abdomen in an atmosphere of grim silence. She was quite tense, but everything was in good shape there too.

"Thank you," he said.

"You've finished already? Not so interesting as the breasts?"

Had she taken a particular dislike to him, or was she like this with everybody? Well, whether she liked it or not, she was going to get a conscientious and thorough medical; that was what he was there for. He was listening to her lungs when he noticed the melanoma half-hidden by the top of her pants.

"Would you just lie down on your back for a moment?"

"What for?" she said suspiciously.

"Just for a moment."

She looked at him coldly for a moment, then did as she was told. Stephen drew the top of her pants down about half an inch. Yes. Probably benign, but you couldn't be sure.

"So that's it," she said, "you want to get my pants off. Why didn't you say this at the start?"

"What's this?" he said.

"My bum, I should imagine."

"No. This . . . mole."

"Well, it's a mole. You're not the first to admire it."

"How long have you had it?"

"I don't know. Long time."

"It's quite large, isn't it? Has it always been this size?"

"I don't *know*."

"Tell me," he said, "has it changed colour at all recently?"

"I don't *know*. You think I spend my time looking at my bum or what? Look, get out of there, I've had enough of this."

Suddenly she had twisted round and was sitting up glaring angrily at him. Their faces were very close. She was trembling and breathing quickly; he could actually feel her breath on his face. He wished very much that Maureen was there. The trouble was, he didn't feel calm himself any more. It was all supposed to be gentle and impersonal, and it wasn't. It was personal. A thin frightened young woman in a skimpy black vest and pants, and a man with all his clothes on doing things to her. He forced himself to remember that this was a perfectly routine examination.

"I really think you should see a dermatologist about it," he said. His voice was trembling. "It would probably be best to have it removed, just to be on the safe side. I can arrange that for you."

"Listen, you don't like my mole, that's *your* problem. There's nothing wrong with it, it's a nice mole." Her face was still fierce, but she had pulled her knees up and was actually cringing away from him. He felt dreadful.

"You're probably quite right," he said truthfully. About eighty-five per cent likelihood, in fact. Maybe he could let it go. "Look, let me just have another look."

"No! You've had your fun!" She started to pull her clothes on. "Listen, I know what this is all about. I walk in here, I'm a woman, you're scared of women, so to make yourself feel better you make me take my clothes off and mess about inside my pants. Yes, easy with a foreigner! Well next time, don't pick Polish, now you know, OK?"

"I really do recommend you to see a specialist about that melanoma," he said, shakily.

"You telling me I have cancer, is that it?" She was still

shouting, but there were tears in her eyes now. "It's not enough to humiliate me, you want to see me weep with terror, yes?"

"No! Really ... this is a dreadful misunderstanding."

"No, I don't think."

She stood up.

"So. Am I free to go now?"

He realized that he was standing in her way.

"Yes, of course," he said.

"OK," she said. But she stood still staring at him for a few moments. It was not pleasant. The University of Lowlands is known as a swamp of fear and loathing, but Stephen had never felt so precisely the object of fear and loathing himself.

Then she walked out, slamming the door.

Greg Trout the mechanical engineer thought Grete Grotowska was wonderful. He had admired her arrogant style in the waiting room, and when she walked out of the Induction Course for New Academic Staff, having first told the mediocre man from Arts Education that she had not come to Lowlands to have her tits bored off by stuffed vests, Trout followed her out and caught her up in the piazza.

"Dr Grotowska," he said breathlessly, "you were splendid in there. I mean you said exactly what I was thinking, except I'd never have had the nerve."

"So? Well, I'm Polish."

Greg Trout was not one of nature's smoothest chatters-up and didn't quite know how to deal with this. Then she said: "Hey. I know you. You had the medical. What was it like?"

"Well, fine."

"No heavy innuendo? No groping in your underpants?"

"Bloody hell, no. Look, what d'you ...? Er, look, you don't fancy a ..."

"Thought as much. I go down here. Goodbye."

"... coffee or something?" said Greg Trout, watching her disappearing back. "I'm so lonely."

To Mrs Kramer's utter disgust, Dr Rose Marie said that she would be happy to see the unpleasant foreign female out of surgery hours. Rose was in fact more than happy, especially when Grete (Rose liked to get on first name terms with women straight away) told her that she was being consulted because she was a woman, and that the subject of the consultation was the head of the practice. She listened to Grete's story with sympathy, concern and well-concealed delight, and agreed to help her prepare her accusation of misconduct. She advised Grete to consult a dermatologist, to establish that there was absolutely no possibility of a malignant melanoma. Then she invited Grete back for supper, and Grete was pleased to accept the invitation.

A couple of nights later, Bob Buzzard was just on his way to the court to give a chap called Schwarzenburger a jolly good thrashing when he bumped into the man with the Morgan, just coming off court with Kelly from Cybernetics. Kelly was a hard man, number six on the squash ladder, and the man with the Morgan looked a bit rough.

"Aha! Trout the engineer!" boomed Bob. "How d'you get on? Win?"

"Just," said Trout.

"Did you, by God? Not just a pretty face then. Tell you what, you and me, seven thirty tomorrow morning, right?"

"Er, yes, fine," said Greg Trout rather vaguely. Bob crashed through the swing doors, and Greg Trout sat down on the bench. Suddenly he felt very odd indeed.

Bob was on cracking form, five one up and really giving Schwarzenburger something to cry about, when some bloody idiot actually opened the door in the middle of a point, a hanging offence in Bob's book.

"Get out of here you bloody peasant! This court's booked till seven thirty!"

"Look, you've got to come," said the bloody idiot, who looked a bit pale and shaky, not surprising, considering he was in imminent danger of being punched on the snout. "There's a chap collapsed in the changing room, I think he's dead!"

"Well a doctor's not going to be much bloody use to him," said Bob, who was really feeling bloody irritated about this. He was on the point of serving when he relented.

"Oh, all right. God, what it is to have a conscience. Come on then, where is he?"

33

An anxious little group stood round watching as Bob checked for a pulse in the carotid artery of the guy who was lying face down on the floor.

"Not much going on there," said Bob. "Yes, I'd say he's snuffed it. Come on, let's get him over."

It took two of the bloody fools to help Bob roll the big stiff face upwards.

"Good Lord," said Bob. "Trout the engineer. I'm supposed to be playing him tomorrow morning. Well, well. Buzzard wins by default."

"These things can be tricky," said Jack Daniels to Dr Rose Marie. "This Dr Grotowska ... hell, I'm not suggesting she made it up, but maybe she just got her wires crossed, you know?" Jack was interested. It was an interesting problem. But there were other vibes about. Jack was a people person; he could read the vibes. There was something else going on.

"I do wish I could agree with you," said Rose Marie softly. She had this kind of soft voice, so you felt like leaning towards her: that way, you picked up her scent and got to see a little ways into her uniform. Neat.

"But that sort of misunderstanding doesn't just happen by chance," she went on. She looked at him steadily, her eyes wide. "I ... I shouldn't imagine *you've* ever found yourself in that situation."

"Well, I guess not."

"No," she said. "When a man is really deeply centred in his masculinity ... a woman always knows exactly where she stands ... one way or another."

"Yeah," said Jack thoughtfully. "I guess you're right, Rose."

When she had gone, he asked Charlie Dusenberry to bring in the file on Stephen Daker. And, on an afterthought, the one on Dr Rose Marie.

At a Group Meeting held on 1 October, it was reported that Greg Trout had died from a heart disease which should, according to Halsey at the General, have been instantly recognized at any routine medical examination. Dr Daker told Dr Buzzard that he could come to no conclusion other than that Dr Buzzard's examination of Mr Trout had been less than thorough. Dr Buzzard told Dr Daker not to be so bloody wet. Dr McCannon pointed out that whether or not the medical had been thorough, there was some comfort for the widow Trout had left in Hull; the poor wee lass would now receive a full university pension. Dr Daker said that that was not the point, and that if there were any legal comebacks from this, Dr Buzzard was going to be on his own. Dr Buzzard thanked Dr Daker very bloody much indeed for his sympathetic attitude, and told him that in his, Dr Buzzard's opinion, he, Dr Daker, was going off his trolley. After the meeting, at which Dr Rose Marie had not been present, she sought a private interview with Dr Daker in which she informed him that Dr Grotowska was preparing a formal complaint about him to the General Medical Council, in which he would be accused of indecent assault.

Early next morning, Stephen was out walking by the lake, wondering whether to throw himself in or not. Nobody, he felt, would miss him very much. Two of his colleagues at least would be positively pleased. He would be benefiting the university: he had demonstrated to everyone's satisfaction that he was a failure as head of the practice. Moreover, he had failed in that part of his job where he had always felt most competent, the individual treatment of an individual patient. On the other hand, it was a chilly day, the water in the lake was said to be only six feet deep even in the middle, and Lyn had taught him to swim; perhaps the matter needed further thought. It was settled, temporarily at least, when he heard a voice behind him.

"Hey! Doc!"

He turned. The short unmemorable figure of the man he vaguely recognized as the Arts Council Fellow in something was sitting on a bench with a notebook and pencil, grinning at him.

"Ron Rust," he said, remembering.

"Arts Council Fellow in Creative Writing, as ever was," said Rust. "They've renewed me contract. They *love* me at the BBC. They want a *second series*. It's not right, is it? Blokes like you and me were made to suffer."

"I am suffering," said Stephen.

"You look all right to me," said Rust. "What's the matter?"

"I've lost my girl friend. My colleagues hate me. I've made a new enemy. I'm a professional failure. And I'm facing charges of gross misconduct."

"Ah," said Rust. "I see. Mm."

He paused and thought for a moment.

"Lovely day, though."

"It's clearing up fine now," said Stephen to the boy with acne, "but come back at any time if you're worried in any way at all. OK?"

The boy went, and Stephen looked at his list. Two more to go. He pressed the intercom button. Then the door opened and he looked up. Black shirt. Black skirt. Fierce little cat face.

"Hello. It's me," she said.

She shut the door behind her.

"No. Look," he said. "You and I shouldn't be talking."

"But I want to tell you something. It won't take long."

"I'm sorry," said Stephen, suddenly very angry. "This may sound rude – no, I don't actually mind whether it does or not. I don't want to talk to you. You can say what you want to say to the GMC."

"No," she said, biting her lip. "I'm not going to do that now."

"You're not," he said blankly.

"I changed my mind."

"Oh, you did? Well thank you very much indeed."

"Look," she said. "I want to say something to you. It's not so bad. It won't kill you. Five minutes?"

He wanted to tell her that what she wanted and what she was going to get were two very different things because that was the way *his* life operated and why shouldn't it work the same way for her, and quite a bit more in that vein, but he couldn't quite manage it. In an odd way he wanted very much to hear what it was she had come to say.

"All right," he said, sitting down.

She took the chair opposite him.

"They took my mole away," she said.

"Oh, yes," he said stiffly.

"And the consultant, she said, OK. Not malignant."

"I'm glad."

And he was glad. Very glad. He disliked Dr Grete Grotowska very much, but the thought of that thin, restless, oddly beautiful body being rather rapidly chewed up by cancer was a thought not easily borne. He found that he was actually smiling. Now that she was back from the privileged ghostly company of the dying, he could get back to disliking her with a clear conscience. She grinned back at him.

"This consultant, she said absolutely right to refer me for biopsy, you must have a pretty sharp GP she said."

He was feeling better by the minute.

"I said, funny, he seemed a bit of an asshole to me. Well, she said, asshole or not, he knows what he's doing."

Stephen, who was experiencing a mixture of feelings, could think of nothing to say.

"I just thought I ought to tell you that," said Grete Grotowska. "Don't expect you get too many compliments. Being an asshole and everything."

She was smiling at him.

"Anyway," she said, "I thought I'd tell you I don't think you're so bad."

"I see," he said. "I don't suppose you've any interest in what I think of you?"

She was still smiling.

"Mm, yes, I have, matter of fact."

"I think you're one of the most unpleasant and aggressive people I've met for a very long time!"

He knew he was being imprudent; he knew he was being unprofessional. It was a very satisfying feeling. But this strange creature seemed absolutely delighted with him.

"You think I'm a rude nasty girl?" she said, her eyes sparkling at him.

"Yes. I do."

"Good," she said. And then, rather shyly, as if offering him a lovely present, she added: "You can see me again if you like."

RUST AND THE BIG GUNS

Rust is sitting in an elegant little restaurant in Holland Park with his agent, reading the menu. Well, all right. If we are going to be brutally honest, the restaurant, though little enough, is not particularly elegant; it is an anxious newish bistro, and what he is reading is a blackboard, written upon by someone whose handwriting is even more neurotic and whose spelling is even more eccentric than Rust's own. Why is he not in Julie's restaurant, that is what Rust wants to know. Julie's restaurant is just round the corner from Rust's agent's. Rust's agent practically lives in Julie's. What is the meaning of this? Can Rust's agent be so embarrassed by Rust that he won't be seen with him in Julie's? Many people are embarrassed by Rust, and wouldn't be seen with him anywhere, but agents have to put up with that sort of thing. It goes with the territory. It goes with the ten per cent. And Rust's agent has ten per cent of some pretty unsavoury people. Some of them even come from Liverpool.

I know what you are thinking. If Rust is as dreadful as all that, what can his *agent* be like? But you would be wrong. Rust's agent looks very nice. He has pink cheeks and blue eyes, and though he often reminds Rust of a sweetly innocent but very intelligent sixth former, he is known in the business as a hard man. He is certainly a lot harder, and brighter, than Rust is. He is wearing what might very well be a four hundred quid suit, and his cheeks are even pinker than usual because he has just come back from the Coast.

"I was talking to Andrew Brown in LA," says Rust's agent.

"Oh, yeah?" says Rust, wondering why his agent should have to fly to the Coast to talk to Andrew Brown, who works in an office in Euston Road, and why, come to that, Andrew Brown had to go to LA to talk to Rust's agent. Silly question, really.

"He's quite interested in your work, Ron."

"Really? Does he want to buy any of it?"

"Well, no, he doesn't want to actually buy any of it just now, but he's very interested in it."

"Oh, jolly good."

"And Sam Goldwyn is looking for a rewrite man."

"Could I be that man?"

"No, I don't think so ... you know, Ron, rewrite men get frightfully buggered about."

That's all right with me, thinks Rust. Everybody buggers Rust about, and since that is his lot in life he would far rather be buggered about by a pool in LA with a long-distance telephone and a steady supply of whisky sours than be buggered about at Threshold House with a plastic beaker of BBC coffee leaking into his lap.

"And anyway, Ron, you're going to be far too busy to take on any extra work just now."

Well, yes, thinks Rust, cheering up a bit. There is that.

There is a short interval, during which a rather beautiful young woman arrives to take their order. After a brief alarmed glance at Rust, she addresses herself exclusively to his agent, and describes in some detail the exquisite salade composée she is recommending for starters, featuring lukewarm pigeon breasts, radicchio, Quattro Stagioni lettuce and fennel fronds, gently tossed in her own special dressing made from fresh limes and honey. Rust's agent listens attentively to all this, then says cheerfully: "Well, we certainly won't have *that* then. We'd better have the game pâté and the fillet steak, rare, and some *ordinary green* salad, French dressing, lots of garlic ...."

"And some sauté potatoes," says Rust.

"I'm afraid we don't do sauté potatoes," she says in a shocked manner, rather as if Rust had asked for roast robin, or a bowl of tinned cream whipped up with Stelazines. (Actually Rust is rather partial to tinned cream whipped up with Stelazines, but we won't go into that now.)

"You do have some potatoes?" says Rust's agent.

"Yes, we do," she admits.

"Well, just go and get someone to sauté a few of them for my guest, would you?"

The rather beautiful young woman flounces off to the

kitchen, reflecting that some people are not nearly as nice as they look. Rust's agent smiles his boyisth, almost but not quite contrite smile at Rust.

"You have to be firm with these people," he says. "You mustn't let them bully you."

"So *they* actually asked *you* for a new series?" says Rust's agent a bit later. Rust has got through a bottle and a half of Beaujolais Primeur by now, and is rather regretting it. They serve it so cold in these wanky places that a chap could catch a nasty chill in the stomach.

"That's right," says Rust. "They're quite keen, actually."

"I hope *you* didn't sound too keen, Ron."

"No, no. I was dead cool about it. I treated the proposal with lofty disinterest."

Well, not *that* far from the truth, thinks Rust. He didn't actually fall on Jonathan Powell's carpet and hug him round the knees, he didn't cover Riddington's face with slobbery kisses. Or did he? No, of course he didn't.

"Good," says his agent. "I'm going to get the big guns out on this one, Ron. I'm going to get you five thousand pounds an episode."

"Is that what Dennis Potter gets?" asks Rust.

"Well, no, it's not quite as much as Dennis Potter gets."

"I want what Dennis Potter gets," says Rust.

"Ron: only Dennis Potter gets what Dennis Potter gets. Five thousand pounds an episode is a very prestigious fee, it's a top BBC fee. It's also quite a lot of money."

Well, yes it is, thinks Rust, cheering up again. If he lives like a monk and sticks to refectory dogshit, using the Arts Council money to keep body and soul together, thirty-five grand would be just about enough to get him back to London, maybe enough to put down a deposit on a dog kennel in Hornsey or thereabouts. A chance to get *on* with his life again. Back in North London ... might even meet Carol again by chance, on the street, down the Indian offy ... hello Carol, I'm back on the scene. Old Rust. Can't keep a good man down. And she'd look at him, wondering, and then that old familiar smile would start at the corners of her mouth ... no it wouldn't. She'd give him a brief stab of hardeye, the way people look at each other at Lowlands, and walk on. God, Rust's belly feels cold. Beaujolais Primeur. He might have been drinking lake water for all the good it's done him.

"Think we could have a bottle of something a bit warmer, or some brandies or something?" he says.

Rust's agent looks at his watch. He is thinking that he gets ten per cent of some much more talented and fashionable writers than Rust, and that it's about time he got back on the phone and started earning it. Then he relents. Poor old Ron has been flogging away for a long time.

"Yes, all right," he says.

Rust will be embarrassed when he remembers the next hour or so, if he remembers the next hour or so. What happens in the next hour or so is that Rust drinks a bottle of nice warm Côtes du Rhône and a couple of brandies, which just hit the spot, and has a really good blurt to his agent, such a thorough blurt that he clears out the rest of the clientele entirely, and sets the beautiful young woman to aggressive chair-stacking behaviour, all of which Rust ignores. First he has a really thorough blurt about Carol and how lovely she used to be, and what she and her sodding chum are like now. Rust's agent has heard all this before, but he listens like a good lad, sipping his designer water and thinking how glad he is that not all his writers have to go through these maudlin embarrassing performances before they can bring themselves to go off and flog the word-processor. Then Rust finds himself talking with passionate intensity about this woman he fell in love with at this wanky conference in Poland. Thin as a rake, no tits to speak of, but a lovely lovely face with a wide mouth always moving, fierce eyes like a little cat, and a funny Polish soft little voice that made Rust almost faint with pleasure, or vodka. There had been a party at this conference, and Rust had held this girl's thin hand and blurted out his whole life to her, and she had listened, she had listened to every word of Rust's blurt, her eyes never leaving his. Then she had told him that she could not be with him any more because he was in love with death, and gone

41

off to bed, first with the German girl who had been Rust's reserve selection, then with a massive Norwegian chap who looked like a tree.

There are tears in Rust's eyes as he remembers the Polish girl. He leans across the table and grasps his agent's hand. Bravely, his agent restrains himself from looking round to see if anyone is watching.

"Am I in love with death?" asks Rust tearfully. "Why don't women like me, Stephen?"

"Ron," says his agent. "You're a writer. You're not the best writer in the world, but you're a true writer. It all goes in the work. That's how it is with writers. They write. That's what writers do."

"But it's like being a cripple or something."

"Come on, Ron," says his agent. "We've got work to do."

As they approach Rust's agent's office, Rust is vaguely aware that there is something funny about his car. He didn't think it had a yellow wheel. He blinks a few times and refocusses. Oh, yes. Now he sees. Brilliant. His car is a cripple too. Some bastard has given him a Denver Boot.

2

ART AND ILLUSION

The rubbish was almost knee-deep, and Stephen was wading through it in his pyjamas. He was looking for Lyn. He had to find Lyn before they found her, before they found her in the rubbish and carted her off to the dump. When he got to the skips, he saw that the nuns had got there before him. They were standing in the rubbish high above him, grinning down at him. There was something familiar about their faces, but he had so much dust in his eyes he couldn't see them properly. He rubbed his eyes. Now he could see. The nuns were Dr Rose Marie and Dr Grete Grotowska.

The grinding roar of the rubbish van was very close behind him now. Terrifyingly, deafeningly close. He turned round. It had backed right up to him. And it was tipping. He couldn't make his legs move. He called for Lyn, but he could make no sound. Then it was on him, it was all round him, it was choking him. He was drowning in rubbish.

He woke sweating and fighting the bedclothes. Somewhere in the distance he could hear the sound of the rubbish van trundling away with the leavings of Lowlands. He looked at the clock. A quarter to seven. Not a bad night's sleep, for him. When he had got his breathing back to something like normal, he tried putting his feet out of bed. Someone was coughing in his living room. Who the hell could that be? Then he remembered. Last night Jock had arrived with two bulging carrier bags, a bottle of Bells and two mutton vindaloos, announcing that he had divined Stephen's deep-felt need, and had come to stay with him as long as he was needed. Stephen had protested that Jock was not needed at all, but that had made no impression on his former leader. Oh, well, better go and see the poor old sod.

Dr J. G. McCannon, MD, was standing by the window in a greatcoat over some singularly horrible blue and yellow striped pyjamas, dictating a memo about the Prince of Darkness into his rinky-dinky little tape-recorder.

"My dear fellow," he said, as Stephen came in. "How are you?"

"Fine. Fine," said Stephen untruthfully. "I forgot you were here."

"You are sick at heart," said Jock severely. "Panic, terror and loneliness, eh? Yearning tragically for your lost love, well of course you are. You must invent yourself a new one to love."

"What?" said Stephen. He was not really ready for metaphysics yet. Jock McCannon, who rarely slept at all, had the advantage of most people in the early mornings.

"It's all invention, Stephen," he said now, squeezing a few drops out of last night's bottle. "We live in illusion. Love is the great imaginative act. We need to love. So we invent the lovable person. We fuse the monstrous dream of our longing with the perishable clay of some poor wee lassie who happens along at the right time. Am I not right?"

"No," said Stephen, speaking from hope rather than experience. "It's not like that at all."

"Ah, well. It's been a while since the McCannon loins thundered out their imperious demands. Perhaps things are different now. Yes, my wisdom is spurned. When my usurper seeks enlightenment, he calls for some rinky-dinky little *shrink* to set his house in order."

"Look, Jock," said Stephen wearily. "You mustn't feel offended. I do value your judgement very highly."

"No matter, no matter."

Jock fixed Stephen with a piercing gaze from his celebrated clear-blue alcoholic eyes.

"D'ye feel a chill in the air, Stephen?"

"Not particularly."

"A psychic chill. This morning the Prince of Darkness

officially assumes his throne. Will you attend the inaugural address?"

"Yes, I thought I would."

"Well, naturally, as head of the practice," said Jock, with a trace of bitterness. "But be careful, Stephen. Jack Daniels is a fitting name for the Great Tempter. His taste is sweet, but when we drink, we die."

Dr Rose Marie was smiling faintly to herself as she brewed Blue Mountain coffee in her clinically neat kitchen. She put the cups on a tray and carried them through into the bedroom. Someone was lying in the bed, dark cropped head face down into the pillow. Rose smiled another of her smiles. This one had elements of triumph and of tenderness in it, and it was a smile that not many other people ever saw. The person in bed shuffled, turned, and blinked.

"Blimey," said Grete Grotowska.

"Good morning," said Rose softly, putting the tray down on the table and sitting on the side of the bed. "You slept very well."

Grete struggled up in bed and stretched. She was wearing a skimpy black cotton vest that made her skin look very white.

"Oh yes, I can do sleeping when I get the chance. What am I doing here?" She grinned. "Big mistake I think."

"I hope not, Grete," said Rose gently. "I'm *very* glad you stayed."

Grete drank some coffee, untidily. Some of it ran down her chin, and her pointed red tongue flicked out from the corner of her mouth to lick it off. Rose Marie found herself shivering slightly although it was warm in the room.

"Well, that's good," said Grete. "I don't like to disappoint." She smiled again. "My life. What a disaster."

"Tell me."

"No, not your worry," said Grete. "Only people, eh?"

"Grete," said Rose softly. "I ... I sense you've had some very bad times with men."

Grete nodded emphatically.

"You can say that twice. I tell you something else too. Men have had some very bad times with me."

45

"Forty quid for *hockey sticks*, though," said Bob Buzzard at the breakfast table. "It beggars belief, Daphne. And why *hockey sticks*? Hockey's a game for fat girls and chaps in turbans, isn't it? I'm seriously thinking of taking the boys away from that place, let them take their chance in Bash Street with the rest of them."

"If you do that my darling, I shall quite simply leave you," said Daphne Buzzard, who believed in nipping things in the bud.

"Right. Hockey sticks. Fine. Practice collapsing about me, old fart totally senile, dyke won't treat male patients, Dickie Dado wants to bring the shrinks in, that's the level of *his* thinking, well I'm sorry but I'm not carrying that shower any more. It's not my nature, Daphne, but I'm going to start looking out for number one!"

"Robert," said Daphne, in a tone that he had come to recognize as red alert territory.

"Yes, my darling?"

"You always said I was your number one, my darling."

"Well of course you are, my darling," said Bob, moving to her side like a trained retriever.

"We haven't had nookie since a week last Wednesday," said Daphne, wrinkling her nose in that way she had.

"Really? Long as that?" said Bob in an unnecessarily hearty way. "Right. Serious nookie on the agenda tonight. And Daphne."

"Yes my darling?"

Bob knew when to make the supreme sacrifice.

"You take the BMW today. I'll take the Fiat."

Bob had cause to regret his gallantry quite soon after that; the Fiat was seriously lacking in poke, and Bob spent half a minute or so staring death in the face, on the wrong side of the road, cursing the pathetic little rotbox, until he managed to squeeze in front of the lorry, slither across its bows into the Lowlands entrance, stave off two nuns in a battered Mini by a brilliant piece of defensive driving, and hurtle towards the only vacant car-parking space. Unfortunately an elderly and immaculate white Rover 3.5 was gently backing into the same space, and the rotbox hit it hard.

Bob leapt out of the Fiat, ready for violence.

"Brilliant!" he yelled. "You must be blind as a bat, buddy!"

A plump middle-aged man in a bow tie emerged rather more slowly from the Rover.

"You drove into my car!" he said in a trembling voice. "You maniac! It's Buzzard, isn't it?"

Then his face changed suddenly to something like panic, and he turned and ran away towards the central complex.

"I'll be in touch!" he shouted over his shoulder.

Good God, thought Bob, he's done a runner.

"It's no use, Platt!" he shouted after the fleeing figure. "I know you! You can run but you can't hide from Robert Buzzard!"

The Great Hall of Lowlands University was packed for the Vice-Chancellor's inaugural address. The stage was full of chaps in robes of bizarre splendour, the splendour in general being in inverse ratio to the prestige of the place of origin. Most of the flashy regalia emanated from such dim and suspect institutions as Lampeter, Sauchiehall, Rutland, Porterhouse and Lowlands itself, which under the Hemmingway regime had awarded Masters and above liberal trimmings of silk, fur, squirrel tails and the like; while places of solid achievement such as UCL and Imperial College decked out their graduates and doctors much more soberly. Stephen, dressed as a modest Birmingham MB, came somewhere in the middle for robemanship, nothing to sneeze at but quite overshadowed by Professor Piers Platt of Art History, who was glittering in some sort of medieval finery he had conned out of the University of Siena.

Jack Daniels, the new Vice-Chancellor, had chosen to dress for the occasion in a simple blue business suit, a bold and brilliant decision. As he neared the end of his oration, his blue eyes incandescent with eagerness and vision and sincerity, he seemed to many of his audience the very reincarnation of that other Jack whom he so much resembled.

"No man is an island, entire of itself," he said, in that

unmistakable harsh Boston accent. "Every one of us here today is part of the same endeavour, the same dream. All of you, I guess, will know by now that the University of Lowlands has been chosen to spearhead a massive research initiative, and that I have been honoured with the task of guiding that initiative. Centuries ago, our forefathers, yours and mine, crossed the ocean to make a new world founded on Europe's knowledge, Europe's initiative."

He paused to smile warmly at his many-hued audience, some of whose forefathers and foremothers had crossed the ocean rather against their wills and not altogether enthusiastic about the European initiative that was making a new world from their labour. But such was Jack's warmth and sincerity that many of them smiled back at him.

"Now, I like to think, we are bringing it all back home, where it belongs ... here is the New Frontier."

He paused.

"I hold knowledge, the discovery of knowledge, the creation of knowledge, to be an absolute good. Here at Lowlands, we can make it happen. The stuff we come up with is going to change the world."

Stephen, even though he could not see the Vice-Chancellor's face, was feeling strangely moved. There was power in the words, power in the body that vibrated with the words. Jack Daniels spoke with his strong back, his broad supple shoulders: he was putting his whole self in. One might have almost said his body thought.

"I guess we've heard a lot about the brain drain. Well, at Lowlands, we're reversing that drain ... we're gonna make the stream flow our way now."

Stephen was aware that Professor Piers Platt was beginning to fidget restlessly in the seat next to him. Odd. Surely he couldn't be bored. This was stirring, seminal stuff.

"We're gonna release and channel the well-springs of creation, and I'm not just talking about a trickle, I'm talking about a foaming torrent. I know it's there, just waiting to be released. Well ..." he paused and looked around his audience, smiling broadly ... "now we can let it flow."

With a muttered apology, Professor Platt pushed past Stephen and scurried for the side exit.

"A university should show us too," said Jack Daniels, "how life should be lived, when people get together and share the same endeavour, the same dream. The world, East and West, is going to look towards Lowlands. And they're going to say: 'Yeah. That's the way it should be.'"

He raised his eyes towards the back of the hall.

"I'm dedicating myself to that vision. It's a humbling task, and I approach it with humility. No man is an island."

He spread his arms wide.

"All I can say to you is ... here I am. Let's get together and do it, OK?"

The sound of the flush from the gentlemen's lavatory in the side corridor was quite drowned by the generous applause.

Dr Grete Grotowska was teaching her third-year group of Art History students. Well, to be precise, she was teaching Professor Platt's third-year group of Art History students. It came to the same thing. Grete had swiftly discovered that being the most junior lecturer in the department meant teaching Piss Platt's students as well as her own. Well, not much skin off her face. She was young, she was bright, she liked to put herself about a bit. Stir them up. Give them a bit of the stick.

She punched up a slide of Giorgione's "Concert Champêtre" and picked up a big book.

"Listen to this. I quote from Galliano in the standard work. 'The seated figure invites our inspection with the tactile lusciousness, the calm impersonal docility of a plump nectarine.' So. You hear what Galliano is saying?"

She peered at the students over her fierce round spectacles. No, they didn't hear what Galliano was saying, they were staring at her like frightened rabbits, all except the pretty boy with the rich daddy, who was looking bored and angry. So, she would tell them what Galliano was saying.

"He's saying women are like fruit, that's what he's saying, forget about the long words. Women: fruit. OK. Next pin-up."

The next pin-up was one of her favourites, Michelangelo's

"Dying Captive", which had figured prominently in her savage monograph on the iconography of the male nude.

"Does he look as if he's dying to you?"

Silence. Maybe the glasses were the trouble. She took them off and smiled.

"Come on. Don't be scared."

The pale one, the one who never took her eyes off Grete, Sarah, yes, that was her name, tried timidly.

"He looks as if he's ... just woken up."

Grete rewarded her with a big smile, just for her.

"Good, fine ... d'you think he knows we are looking at him?"

Carla, tall, South American, lovely skin, quite fanciable, started to get the point.

"I think he's pretending he doesn't know we're there, but really he does."

"Yeah, right," said Grete, and then, to encourage badness and boldness, went on: "He's having a nice little stretch ... pulling his vest up ... stroking his tit ... nice little dick, eh?"

The other boy, the chubbychopper, Marco was it, blushed like a red cabbage.

"Yes, I know," said Grete. "We're not allowed to talk like this about male nudes. Guess what Galliano says about this one."

"Slim and curvy like a green banana?" suggested Carla. Some of them laughed. Good. The first laugh.

"No, no. Men can't be like fruit. Listen. 'We feel the unmistakable presence of a divine power: in this masterpiece the soul triumphs over the corruptible flesh.' I should cocoa. But you see? Men have souls, women are fruit. That's what Galliano sees because his head gets in the way."

She looked at her watch.

"OK. For Thursday, just take these two images. Read up all you can about them. Note the way the experts talk about them, fruit, theology, all this. Then try to find some other ways of talking, ways that work for you, all right?"

"But Dr Grotowska." It was the Sarah girl again.

"Yes, Sarah."

"We haven't done anything like this before."

"Thinking for yourselves you mean? Don't be scared of it. It's what you're here for." They looked as if they didn't believe her. Well, bad cheese. She wasn't going to spoon with them.

"See you Thursday!" she said cheerfully, and strode off.

The pretty boy, Richard Everitt, caught Grete up in the quadrangle.

"Dr Grotowska."

"Hi."

She looked him up and down. Tall, nice body, one of those slanty fringes, good nose, probably gay and didn't know it, nice bit of stuffing if you weren't interested in brains.

"Could you explain the grade you've put on this?"

She took the essay from him to look, though she remembered well enough.

"Epsilon," she said. She counted on her fingers in case he didn't understand the notation. "Alpha, beta, gamma, delta, epsilon."

"But that's a fail!"

"Sorry," she said. "The work was not original."

"Are you accusing me of plagiarism?"

"Well," she said, "let's say it was a very long quotation and you forgot the quotation marks." She looked at his handsome stupid angry face. "Why copy out of books?" she asked, genuinely curious. "You don't find this boring?"

"I want this marked by someone else," he said. His voice was trembling.

"Someone who hasn't read Gombrich, right? Listen, Richard, *everyone*'s read *Gombrich*. Look, I don't want to be hard on you. Why not tear it up, write me a proper essay and we'll forget about this one. How that grab you?"

He took the essay from her.

"No thanks," he said. "Actually, I'd like the opinion of someone who understands the English language."

He strode away towards the Students' Union. Nice straight back, thought Grete. Nice muscly little bum. What a shame.

*

51

Professor Piers Platt was not enjoying his consultation with Dr Robert Buzzard. Dr Robert Buzzard, on the other hand, was having a whale of a time.

"Well, well. Bladder spasm, eh? No wonder you fled from the scene of the crime. How old are you? Fifty-five?"

"Fifty-two," said Platt, rather crossly.

"Well there you are," said Bob. "It's like the shock absorbers in the old Mark 1 Cortina, you see. Seventy thousand miles or so, leaking like a sponge. Well, it's back to the nappies and the plastic pants for you, Professor Platt. Proceed to Mothercare, do not pass Go."

Professor Platt was deeply shocked.

"Are you telling me there's nothing you can do?"

"Not much, buddy," said Bob cheerfully. "Not on the NHS, that is. Of course, if you were to consult me privately, I could prescribe you an excellent new Swiss urinary antispasmodic – it's not available for general release yet – that should sort you out in no time. As it is . . ."

"Dr Buzzard, I'm not a wealthy man."

"Fine," said Bob brutally. "Suit yourself."

"But in the circumstances . . ."

"A very wise decision," said Bob warmly. "I won't sting you, you know. I should think what you put away from last month's conference expenses should cover it. Don't worry about a thing, buddy." He put a hand on the poor old pisser's arm, and gave him the smile he reserved for private patients. "I'm looking after you now."

"Er, about the car . . ." said Platt. Damn it, he had come in here to complain, not to be patronized.

"Don't apologize," said Bob warmly. "Not your fault. Nigel Mansell himself couldn't cope with bladder spasm. I know a very reasonable body man, he'll give you a rock bottom price for cash. And the same of course applies to my fees. Cheap, convenient and entirely confidential. Your secret's safe with me. That's the beauty of private practice."

Julie Daniels wanted an art gallery. Her husband had brought her thousands and thousands of miles to this rural construction site. He was having a ball, hiring and firing, fund-raising, making his goddam inspirational speeches, and no doubt fooling around with chicks in his spare moments. The least he could do, she thought, was give her an art gallery. Julie liked art. Art calmed your nerves. It had calmed her Daddy's nerves to think of all the art he had in his bank vault in Fort Worth, and it had calmed Julie's nerves to go and look at the stuff. Matisse was her favourite but Braque was all right too. She didn't know a whole lot about it, but she sure as shit knew what she liked. British people smiled this funny sort of smile when Julie said that, but Julie didn't pay no heed. She didn't see any Braque or Matisse in *their* tacky little houses.

And now she was standing with Jack and Charlie Dusenberry in this neat little space, white walls, good light, just right for a little collection of Post-Impressionists, with a few little Rodin and Degas maquettes dotted about, and the bastards were stalling her.

"It's a nice space," Jack said, smiling uneasily.

"It's a beautiful space, Jack," said Charlie Dusenberry. "I guess Computer Studies deserve a space like this."

Julie looked at Charlie Dusenberry. Light-grey suit, light-grey eyes, sincere tie. He had been around Jack so long that Jack didn't know how to function without him. A lot of people thought Charlie was just a gofer, but Charlie was a fixer. Julie had heard about some of the stuff Charlie had facilitated in Central America, and she never underestimated Charlie. On the other hand, Charlie never underestimated her.

"Charlie," she said ominously.

"Mrs Daniels?"

"This is gonna be an *art gallery*. You think I came along to talk about a *comfort station* for *computers*?"

Charlie Dusenberry looked at Jack Daniels.

"Julie, honey," said Jack, in that soothing voice he used when he was getting around to suggesting a couple of weeks down on the health farm or up at the clinic. "You're gonna have your art gallery. But I guess we have to wait a little while, we don't have the funding right now."

"Seven million from the Furtelbaum Foundation?" said Julie. Shit, did they think she couldn't read or what?

53

"Mrs Daniels," said Charlie, "the Furtelbaum funding has a laser tag on it. We tried every which way to tap it, but I guess the juice just wouldn't run."

"That's right, Julie," said Jack. "It's real frustrating."

Julie didn't scream at him. Julie liked to be dignified.

"You bring me six thousand miles to a tacky, roach-infested pissant *swamp*, and now you're telling me I can't have an *art gallery*?"

"Julie, honey," said the Vice-Chancellor patiently, "there are no roaches, those are ladybugs. Lowlands was a great place once, and we're making it great again. Sure we'll raise the funding, but it might take a year or two."

"Jack," she said. "In Fort Worth, Texas, even the sewage disposal plant has its own art gallery. I want an art gallery, honey. I want it now. And I don't want anything tacky."

The medical team were starting to see a significant number of students from Art History. First of all, a beautiful and wealthy young woman from Peru called Carla Maravillas presented at Jock McCannon's morning surgery, with nothing at all wrong with her flawless olive-skinned body that Jock could see. When he imparted this piece of good news to her, she laughed, and said that all it was, she hadn't come to England to work, she had come to, what you say, doss about, but all of a sudden there was all this thinking and writing to do. She needed a little holiday, two weeks on a beach at Copacabana would do, and she didn't want to hurt anybody's feelings, so she thought maybe she would get a medical certificate.

Jock McCannon was slightly shocked by this flagrant piece of honesty, but after a few moments' reflection he said: "My dear young lady. What an eminently sensible plan."

He reached for a form and started to write on it.

"Eh . . . nervous debility should cover it. I wish I could afford to join you, my dear."

Carla Maravillas smiled mischievously.

"Personal physician and chaperon?" she tempted. "My father would be happy to pay your expenses."

"Eh . . . *no*, my dear," said Jock regretfully. "I'm deeply touched, but I fear my duty is to stay and be spurned, stay and be humiliated, stay and bear witness. I hope you have a lovely time, Miss Maravillas."

The next day, Stephen saw a small chubby pink-cheeked boy called Mark Stibbs, also from Art History, also with nothing organically wrong with him.

"It's not AIDS, is it?" said the boy, struggling with his trousers. "I mean if it is I want to know. I can take it. I think."

"We'll get some bloods done if you like, Mark, just to set your mind at rest, but I don't see how you could possibly have AIDS. One steady girl friend, both virgins when you started." He was trying not to smile. "Mark: you just haven't got the track record for it."

"You think I'm just wasting your time," said the boy, who seemed quite close to tears. "I'm just a fat fool who's no use to anyone."

"You're not wasting my time at all," said Stephen. "You've got a cluster of stress symptoms. I know what that feels like." (Indeed Stephen knew what that was like; he had several of them himself.) "I'd guess you're in a panic about something. You're in your final year, aren't you?"

That did the trick. What Mark Stibbs needed was a really good blurt.

"Yes you're right. I am in a panic, it's really ... I mean Art History's supposed to be a doddle, and it *was* a doddle for two years, I was getting As for everything, and now we've got this new tutor and I'm getting Cs, it's like I've got to get my brain into a new gear and I can't do it, I wake up sweating in the night and I can't keep my food down and Liz is fed up with me .... I mean I'm not like most of them, it's just like finishing school for them, but I've got to get a really good degree. I've got to get a *job* out of this, and the way things are going I haven't got a snowball's chance in hell, oh shut up Mark, boring boring ... you think that's where the pain's coming from?"

"Don't you?"

The boy's eyes were wide with panic.

"What am I going to do about it?"

"Couldn't you try talking to your tutor about it? Or your personal tutor?"

"Same person," said Mark gloomily. "Yes. You're right. That's what I've got to do."

He raised his eyes imploringly to Stephen's.

"She's ever so fierce, though."

The day after that, a third-year Art History student named Sarah Matchett came to see Dr Rose Marie to say that she had fallen in love with one of the lecturers, and to ask Rose's advice about it.

"Why me in particular, Sarah?"

"Well," said the girl, shifting about in the seat, "everyone says you're gay."

"Do they? And on that basis, you thought I'd advise you about the way to seduce a member of staff?"

Sarah Matchett began to think that she had made a mistake in consulting Rose Marie.

"I just wanted to talk about it," she said. "I thought you'd understand. Made a mistake. Sorry."

"I do understand," said Rose, "and I will talk about it, but I don't think you'll like what I'm going to say. Most staff–student affairs, as you know, involve male staff abusing their power over women students. But *any* sexual relationship between a lecturer and a student means that a professional and power relationship is being abused. Especially so when it's someone who's teaching you and grading your work. You do see that, don't you, Sarah?"

"Yes," said the girl. "Suppose so. Oh, it's not fair. I mean it's *because* she's teaching me I . . . she makes the whole thing come alive, I've never met anyone like that before, it's as if I've just been pissing about till now."

She was a nice, sensitive, thoughtful, confused girl, Sarah Matchett, and Dr Rose Marie handled her in a very sisterly way. She pointed out that exciting teachers were very few and far between, especially, perhaps, at Lowlands. It was easy for a sensitive student to be thrown off balance. And Sarah was clearly a good student who responded positively: naturally Dr Grotowska would like such a student. It was good that a warm relationship should exist between an inspiring teacher and an able student: a warm and rewarding *working* relationship. Anything else was strictly off limits and would inevitably cause pain. It was excellent advice, impeccable advice; but it was not entirely disinterested.

Minutes of a Group Meeting held on 17 October
Present: Dr Daker (Chair), Dr Buzzard, Dr McCannon, Dr Rose Marie, Nurse Gahagan

Dr Buzzard enquired when the shrink was coming. Dr Daker said that he had tentatively arranged it for a week next Thursday after evening surgery. Dr Rose Marie enquired whether the psychiatrist would be a male psychiatrist. Dr Daker confirmed that that was so. Dr McCannon wondered whether Dr Daker was thinking of Mervyn Lillicrap from the Crisis Centre. Dr Daker confirmed that he was. Dr McCannon said that in that case there would be tears before bedtime.

Nurse Gahagan wanted to know what was the matter with the Art History Department. Dr Buzzard informed her that they were a total waste of space, simple as that. Nurse Gahagan pointed out to the meeting that though Art History was only a little department, more than a dozen of them had presented within the last two weeks. They were falling apart at the seams. Dr Daker thanked Nurse Gahagan, and promised to look at the cases to see whether there was a pattern. Dr Buzzard said there was no need for that. It was obvious that they were due for the chop. The Art Historians would be down the Job Centre with the philosophers, and not before time either. In Dr Buzzard's opinion, this was a very sound move. In Dr Buzzard's opinion, Jack Daniels might be a bit of a barbarian, but he could certainly sort out the no-nos.

Dr Buzzard was, for once, there or thereabouts. The Vice-Chancellor and the Finance Assistant were at that very moment taking a careful look at Art History.

"How does it look, Charlie?" said Jack.

"Euthanasia territory," said Charles Dusenberry, flipping the file open. "Sure, he's trying. Foreign students on full fees. British students mostly from wealthy families, not too bright, most of them, so he gets the odd little endowment, but the academic standard's lousy. We don't show in the top forty."

"What's the research profile?" said Jack. "I thought the guy was supposed to be a distinguished scholar?"

"Well, yeah, I guess he was. Hasn't done much in the last ten years, though. He has himself a nice time, gets all his teaching done by junior staff and part-timers, so he can go swanning off round palazzos in Florence and Siena. I guess we're in Asshole County here, Jack."

The Vice-Chancellor sighed.

"Yeah," he said, pressing the intercom button. "OK, Elaine, have him come in. You know, Charlie, I'd really like to put a piece of culture up front." He paused. "But maybe not this one, right?"

The door opened and Professor Piers Platt came in. Bow tie with spots on. Pink cheeks. Plump gut. The suit must have set him back a few hundred bucks. Yeah, he looked like a guy who had been having himself a nice time.

"Professor Platt," said Jack Daniels with great warmth, rising and offering his hand, "it's really good of you to drop by ... it's Percy, right?"

"Piers, Vice-Chancellor," said Platt rather stiffly.

"Yeah? I guess you won't have met Charles Dusenberry, helps out with finance? OK, Perce, let's talk."

Jack led the way to an area of deep soft seating, and sank the Professor of Art History into the deepest and softest chair.

"Perce, I wanna tell you how much I personally appreciate the fine work you've done in your years at Lowlands."

"Thank you, Vice-Chancellor," said Platt warily.

"Now Charlie and I have been talking about the way the overall structure's going to pan out over the next five years."

"I see," said Platt. The man called Dusenberry was smiling at him. It was a worrying sort of smile. But Piers Platt had an ace up his sleeve. Charles Dusenberry was not going to worry him.

58

Jack Daniels let a little pause develop as he looked pleasantly, almost affectionately, at the little man in the bow tie.

"I guess a place like this has done well to keep a distinguished scholar like you all these years, Perce," he said.

"You must have turned down some real tempting offers," said the man called Dusenberry.

"But you know how it is," said the Vice-Chancellor. "A little department in the sticks isn't going to satisfy a guy like Perce. He wants expansion, we'd love to give it to him, but right now we just can't deliver." He turned to Platt. "So we don't have any hard feelings, Perce. If you tell us you have to go ... I guess we just have to let you."

"I'm very flattered, Vice-Chancellor," said Piers Platt, "but I have no plans to leave. I am quite content to stay and make my contribution here at Lowlands."

"Perce," said Jack gently. "We're trying to tell you we have a little problem here."

"What problem is that, Vice-Chancellor?"

"I guess you know the Prettiman Report suggested closing down the department," said Charlie, who was getting tired of all this pussyfooting around.

"I do," said Platt. "And such a decision would be very much to the university's detriment."

"Perce, believe me," said Jack Daniels sadly, "we all feel that way, but I think we're in a no-win situation here." He was already starting to move into his "end of painful meeting" body-language. Jack and Charlie had been known to can guys, start to finish, in less than two minutes, smiling all the way. But this one was strangely stubborn.

"Vice-Chancellor," he said. "I think you should listen to what I have to say."

"Well, sure, Perce," said Jack easily. "Take all the time you want."

Charlie Dusenberry sighed audibly.

"I shan't waste your time," said Platt briskly, "by pointing out the gross misconceptions underlying that report. But I do think you'd be interested to hear that I have just secured a very significant endowment for the university. Lord Everitt – perhaps you've heard of Everitt Construction Holdings? – is offering to Lowlands a small but very distinguished collection of nineteenth- and twentieth-century paintings and drawings, ah, conservatively valued at several million pounds, together with a very substantial sum to purchase further major works by major artists."

Only a dog, or perhaps another fourth-generation computer, would have been able to hear the sound of Jack Daniels's brain suddenly whirring into fast-forward.

"Lord Everitt's son," Platt went on, "happens to be a student of mine. Were the department to close down ... well, no doubt Richard would find a place in some other institution ... and so would the bequest."

"Perce," said Jack Daniels with tremendous warmth, "you don't know how happy this makes me. You know Charlie and I have been fighting to save Art History at Lowlands .... Hell, we may have projects here that are gonna ensure our civilization's survival. But we have to remind people what civilization is all about, too. You know what I'm saying?"

"Indeed I do, Vice-Chancellor," said Platt.

"Perce, I want you to go ahead fast on this one. The Lowlands collection. People are gonna come on pilgrimages to see it, Perce. OK. Now this is just off the top of my head ... we're talking serious money here, and I'd like Charlie along to hold your hand on the figures aspect, that OK?"

"Of course," said the Professor of Art History, nodding his head graciously at the figures man.

"And, ah ..." and here Jack Daniels seemed a shade embarrassed ... "I guess Julie'd like to come along for the ride."

The food in the Coffee Bar was just a little bit better, or a little less vile, than the food in the Refectory, and Stephen was having difficulty finding somewhere to sit. Then he saw a place, at a table for two; woman on her own.

"Excuse me," he said, balancing his tray precariously, "d'you mind if I ...?"

The woman looked up. It was Grete Grotowska.

"Oh. Hi," she said, not smiling.

"Look, I'll ..."

"Come on," she said. "Sit down. It's no big deal."

She looked pale, tired, even a bit depressed, perhaps. Stephen applied himself to his horrible rissole and chips, and she watched him for a while.

"Er ... how are things going?" he said.

"Oh, you know. Way my life goes. Terrible disasters."

Her face came alive when she spoke. She seemed to relish the disasters. That was a trick Stephen would have liked to master.

"I have landed myself in a crap department. My professor ... what a jerker! Professor Platt. Nothing going on in here at all!"

She pointed to the sides of her neat small head with both index fingers.

"And so *lazy*! I have to do all his teaching on top of my students! I think I'm ... what do you call the woman who does all the work? I think I'm the scrubber of the Art History Department!"

Stephen smiled.

"How d'you find the students?"

She made a face.

"Oh, nice people, I suppose. But they don't know anything. No one ever made them think before. They hate to think, you know!" She said it in an excited conspiratorial sort of way as if sharing a secret.

"We've, er ... been seeing quite a few of them at the Medical Centre lately."

She bristled up instantly.

"Oh? What are you saying here? I'm making them ill, is that it? Maybe I should be like Platt? Do nothing all year, then set the easy exam, leak the questions, leak the answers. Everyone happy. No work for the doctors. You think I should do that?"

"No, I don't think you should do that," said Stephen. "I don't think you *could* do that." It was odd; he couldn't seem to stop smiling. It was almost as if he *liked* her. She smiled back at him, a sudden big toothy little-girl smile.

"Right. Rude nasty girl, yes?"

Her sharp tongue came out to lick the last bit of yoghurt off her spoon. She banged down the carton.

"Is that all you have for lunch?" Stephen couldn't help asking.

"Hey. Listen." She was pointing the spoon at him. "Get this in your thick head. I'm not anorexic. Just don't like ketchit."

"What's ketchit?" asked Stephen, puzzled.

She pointed at his abandoned rissole.

"Like that."

"Oh. *Cat* shit. Right."

"Hey," she said, as if struck by a sudden brilliant idea. "You want to see me eat? You like to come round to my place? I'll cook you a meal, you watch me eat, we get nice and drunk together, I tell you stories. Yes?"

"Well, that's awfully kind of you," said Stephen warily, "but I'm not sure it'd be a good idea."

"*You* don't like to eat?"

"Yes, of course I do," he said awkwardly.

"You have to rush home every night to your wife and babies?"

"No. No wife, no babies."

"So?"

"Well," he said. "You're my patient, for one thing."

"Am I asking you to jump on my bed? You think I want your body?"

"*No!*" Oh, God. They were both shouting now. He was aware of people at neighbouring tables listening with some enjoyment.

"You think I'm a nasty person?"

"No! All right! I accept! Thank you very much!"

"Well don't do me any favours!" she yelled back at him.

Jock McCannon was surprised to receive a visit from Rose Marie, and even more surprised when she brought a bottle of Bells with her as a present. The bonnie wee lass was clearly up to something, and would no doubt get round to it in time. She was anxious, it seemed, about the impending visit of the psychiatrist. He might uncover emotional conflicts that none of the team could deal with, and Dr Rose Marie, she confessed, was feeling particularly vulnerable at the moment.

"That must be a novel sensation for you, my dear," said Jock. She was sitting very close to him, she smelt clean and sweet as a bank of heather, and despite what he knew of her serpentine wiles, he felt an old man's tenderness for her.

"Jock," she said, breathing deeply and steadily. "I ... I think I've fallen in love."

Jock looked at the whisky in wild surmise. Wonders would never cease. The wee lassie had flipped.

"Dr Rose Marie," he said, with old-world courtesy. "I am deeply honoured, of course. And deeply moved. But I'm sure you'd find it more rewarding to bestow the gift of your lovely self on someone who can still cut the mustard!"

He was rewarded with the rare sight of Dr Rose Marie blushing.

"Jock ... please ... I don't think you understand."

"No, no, my dear, not another word," he said firmly, steering her towards the door. "Believe me, this is an illusion, and it will pass. These are trying times, we are all vulnerable now. But we are professionals, my lovely girl, we must remember that."

When he had got the door shut behind her, he walked over to the cloudy mirror on the wall, and examined his reflection. Passing strange, he thought. And then: well, what of it? Jock McCannon is still a fine man, for those who have the wit to see it.

Paying one of his increasingly rare visits to the teaching rooms of the Art History Department, Piers Platt almost tripped over the feet of a pale uninteresting girl – third year, was it? Sarah something? No matter, there were more important things in life – who seemed to be sitting weeping on the floor outside Dr Grotowska's seminar room. Odd creatures, women. Dr Grotowska was an odd little thing herself. Polish, of course. Still, she seemed to have quite an appetite for work. Perhaps her appointment, which he had bitterly opposed, was not such a disaster after all.

He knocked on the door and went in. Dr Grotowska was lurking in a corner sorting out some slides, and Platt, who liked to appear to take an interest in the work of his underlings, examined some of the many postcards and prints tacked up over an entire wall. He found this rather disturbing. The Belvedere Apollo and Michelangelo's David were cheek by jowl with press photographs of weightlifters and male strippers; there was even a full frontal of a Gloucester Old Spot boar who had been the Best Pig of the Rare Breeds Show.

"You see anything you like?" she said. "For you I make a special price!"

He turned round. She was grinning at him. It really was a shame about her teeth. And her hair. And her clothes. Although he had come to manhood in the fifties, Piers Platt had never seen the point of that Left Bank Juliette Greco type of woman.

"Ah ... I was wondering if you could cope with my MA group on Thursday afternoon," he said.

"I cope with everything else. Why not? Let 'em all come."

There was really no need to be rude. She should be flattered that he was prepared to entrust his postgraduates to a tyro.

"I wouldn't ask, of course, but it's unavoidable." He found it impossible to conceal his pleasure. "I, ah, I have important business in London."

"For the new gallery?"

"Yes, as a matter of fact."

"Who are you seeing?"

"Ah, well," he said beaming. "That must be kept strictly confidential, I'm afraid." But he couldn't resist telling her. He couldn't resist rolling the names round his tongue. "Siebermann and Flett have come up with some exquisite Braques. Major work."

The woman was grinning at him again.

"You're buying Braque? From Siebermann? What does he say he's got?"

Well, she wasn't getting anything else if she was going to take *that* attitude.

"Strictly confidential, I'm afraid, Dr Grotowska. Ah, by the way, I took the liberty of raising the grade on Richard Everitt's essay. He, ah, came to see me about it."

She dropped the slide she was peering at and stared at him.

"You *raised* it? What to?"

"Beta minus, I believe."

"It was *plagiarized*. He copied it out of *Gombrich*."

Piers Platt, who had recognized something vaguely familiar about the style, felt his cheeks going a little pinker. This would never do.

"The work *was* somewhat derivative, but sound enough, I felt," he said firmly. "He's an interesting student. I think perhaps you should pass on all his work to me for moderating. He needs very delicate handling. Sensitive boy. His family have been very generous to the university, incidentally."

"Huh," she said. "Yes, I can see how that would be sensitive. Everywhere you look, sensitive students. You know in Warsaw there was one guy in my class, so sensitive, he had to get A for everything. His papa was district police chief. Well, that would make anyone sensitive, I suppose."

It was time to remind Dr Grotowska who was who and what was what.

"You are *happy* in the department, aren't you, er, Grete?"

"Oh, as a pig in shit, I promise you."

"I did rather 'go out on a limb' for you," he said, untruthfully, but how was she to know that?

"And there I was thinking I was over your dead body." She was grinning at him again. "Hey. Why don't I come down to London with you? I used to know Saul Siebermann in Paris. And you know, two heads are better than one, even when mine is so small and yours is so very large, eh?"

Strange how difficult these foreigners found it to get the English idioms right.

"It's very kind of you, Grete," he said, "but it's one of those tiresome matters of protocol, I'm afraid."

"No women, no foreigners, fine, OK. I'll stay here and be sensitive with the sensitive people."

*
65

Piers Platt would not have let Grete Grotowska within a mile of the sumptuous panelling and deep-pile carpets of Saul Siebermann's discreet but opulent Cork Street gallery. It had been bad enough coping with the Vice-Chancellor's appalling wife on the long journey up to town in the Mercedes. She had insisted on launching into a long aria on the incessant Lowlands rainstorms, followed on the free-association principle by a detailed description of Niagara Falls; and while Dr Buzzard's pills were gradually getting Professor Platt's little problem under control, he had experienced some anxious moments. And when the chauffeur had started to whistle some military ditty between his teeth, Piers Platt had been obliged to be quite sharp with him.

But things were better now. The back room was hushed. Siebermann was affable, generous with the cigars, and really quite gratifyingly deferential. And the Braques, the Braques ... they were all and more than all that Piers Platt had hoped for.

"Remarkable," he said, peering closely. There were three of them, all variations on the same theme: a still-life in the forground, an open window with a balcony outside, a magnificently understated suggestion of seascape and sky in the distance. "D'you know," he gambled, "I'm inclined to place them as late as ... forty-seven?"

"Excellent!" rumbled Siebermann, to Platt's delight. "These two, forty-seven, this one, forty-*eight*." He beamed mischievously and took the professor's arm. "You know, Carnovsky was in here yesterday, he guessed fifteen years wrong?"

"Easily done," said Platt comfortably, feeling more chuffed by the minute. He'd see a few people got to hear *that* little story. Carnovsky had been preferred to Platt for the crucial Cézanne entry in the new encyclopaedia.

"Ah, why have they never been catalogued?"

Saul Siebermann twinkled, taking his time, and brushed a fleck of cigar ash off his lapel. It really was time that Platt awarded himself a Savile Row suit. Perhaps there might be some little arrangement possible with the Braques: Saul Siebermann seemed a most understanding sort of fellow.

"You know the two late summers in Juan les Pins?" said Siebermann. "Well, it seems he had a friend. *Une petite amie?*"

"Ah," said Piers Platt. "*Bien entendu.*"

"The freshness of the *tache*, you see?"

"The vitality of a man in love, perhaps?" said Platt, rather roguishly, for him, and they chuckled together, two men of the world.

"She died last year, you know," Siebermann murmured. "I heard a whisper . . . I went over . . . I was lucky."

They bowed their heads briefly in reverence for Siebermann's luck.

"You'll see that Melonbaum has endorsed the provenance," said Siebermann, passing the documentation over.

Platt sat down to read through the paperwork, though his mind was already made up, and Julie Daniels wandered over for another look at the Braques.

"Please, madame," said Saul Siebermann. "Not so close with the cigarette."

Julie screwed her nose up.

"You don't think the colours look kinda bright?"

Siebermann patted her arm kindly.

"Yes, indeed they do, madame! You know, most of us encounter the great painters first in reproduction, so when we come face to face with the real thing . . . what a revelation! Sunlight after a stuffy room . . . isn't that so, Professor?"

Platt looked up briefly.

"*Da vero, da vero,*" he said, fluttering his fingers vaguely but elegantly. "The resonance of the *Ding an Sein* . . . sometimes quite startling."

"Well," said Julie Daniels sturdily, "my Daddy's got two Braques in a bank vault in Fort Worth, and they sure as shit don't look like these."

"You don't like the paintings, Mrs Daniels?" Saul Siebermann, all regretful concern.

"Oh, sure, I like 'em. They're real pretty. Don't pay no heed to me, boys."

Platt handed the documentation back to Siebermann. "I'm satisfied," he said. "Ah, Mr Dusenberry, if you'd be so kind?"

Charlie Dusenberry rose from the window seat where he had been waiting patiently.

"I think it's time for *your* area of expertise to come into play."

Stephen was having supper in Grete Grotowska's tiny flat, and he was surprising himself by having quite a nice time. She had produced some vodka, and shown him how to drink it and what to say when he drank it (this exercise had needed some repetition before he got it right, so that what with the wine that followed he was feeling pleasantly relaxed, well, mildly ratted, to be honest) and now he was eating his way through a powerful stew which was hitting the spot in a very satisfactory way. Grete, clearly intent on impressing upon him her unanorexic state, was mopping up the last of her gravy with a hunk of coarse bread.

"How about *that* for eating?" she said triumphantly.

"Very impressive. The cooking's very good too."

She shrugged her thin shoulders. Her dress slipped down over one of them.

"Basic Baltic. Better than ketchit."

She smiled at him. She was, he now realized, quite extraordinarily pretty when she smiled; not his type, of course (ah, Lyn, Lyn!) but really very fetching, if you favoured that sort of out-of-control Nastassia Kinski kind of girl, which of course he didn't. Of *course* he didn't. And she was, after all, a patient. Quite.

"Thank you," she said. "You're a nice man, I think." She looked at him thoughtfully for a moment or two, and Stephen felt suddenly much drunker than he thought he had been. Deceptive stuff, this Polish vodka. Better go very easy on the wine from now on.

"Anyway," she went on, resuming the life story she had started with the vodka a couple of hours ago, "so I'm eighteen, I'm married, I'm in Paris, I'm Madame Dupont just like the school book, but no *chien qui s'appelle* Toto, and the whole deal is all about the passport. *Then* what does the bastard do? He only falls in love with me!"

"Well, it's not inconceivable," said Stephen mildly.

"He was OK till then, Antoine. *Bon copain*, you know? In love, he's like a psychotic baby. Crying, fighting, always wanting sex . . . ." She paused. "I hate sex, don't you?"

"No, I don't actually," Stephen admitted.

"You *like* it? All that *body stuff*?" She sounded incredulous.

"I wouldn't say I've had an awful lot of luck with it," said Stephen apologetically, "but . . . yes, I have got a sort of sneaking nostalgia for it. And, um . . . well . . . being in love."

She was giving him the thoughtful look again. Surely he hadn't said anything particularly original or weird?

"Hey," she said, as if something had suddenly reminded her. "I forgot to tell you. You have to be out of here eleven thirty. This is all right for you?"

"Yes, of course," he said, puzzled.

This seemed to relax her.

"So, your lover, she went off and left you?"

"She was offered this . . . yes, she did," said Stephen.

"Best thing for her, best thing for you," said Grete emphatically.

"Yes, well," he said, "I suppose I might feel like that in about twenty years." It was nice talking to Grete, like talking to a sister, not that he'd ever had a sister, but somehow with Grete it was easier to tell the truth than keep a stiff upper lip.

"You had good sex with her?" It was an extraordinary question, but he found himself quite unembarrassed by it.

"Yes, very good," he said.

She shook her head.

"I don't see it. I always think people pretend, you know? All the mess, all the stains, all the confusion, all the clinics, blimey who needs it? Well, you're a doctor, you should know."

Before he could respond, she was back with the life story again.

"Anyway, then I'm falling in love with this other guy in Paris. He was really nice, but we couldn't make it together; I used to go into spasm, so *embarrassing*, I don't know why, maybe because my husband used to rape me, you think?"

"Rape you?" said Stephen, shaken.

"Listen, I'm sorry," she said considerately. "Is this a bit heavy for the dinner conversation?"

"Er, no. It's fine. Just not quite what I'm used to, that's all."

"I just wanted you to know some stuff," she said, her eyes wide and serious. "I don't sleep with anybody now. Well, sometimes I do sleep with people, but I don't have sex with anybody."

"Yes, I see."

"I just thought you should know, that's what I'm like. You want to take me on, you have to put up with it."

"I didn't say I wanted to take you on," said Stephen.

"No, but you do." She was grinning at his startled face. "OK. Now you have to eat some pudding."

Some time later, after the pudding, after the coffee, he was sitting on her sofa with his feet up, and she was sitting on the floor with her legs crossed. She had a big glass of red wine. Stephen didn't feel any need to drink. He felt more calm and cheerful than he'd felt for a long while. He didn't feel any need to talk, either. Neither did she, apparently. Neither of them had said anything for some minutes. That was all right. Whatever this was, it was fine.

"It's funny," she said finally. "Mostly I don't like fair-headed men, you know. They are cold and boring. But you ... well, maybe a little bit boring, but not cold."

"Well. Thanks very much," he said.

"You're welcome." Such a nice smile.

"Grete," he said. "Why did you ask me round tonight?"

"You haven't enjoyed yourself?"

"Well ... yes, I have. Didn't really expect to."

"Good," she said. She looked at her watch. "OK. That's it. Half past eleven."

She scrambled up.

"Oh, Lord, so it is," said Stephen, surprised.

"Up you get. Where's your coat?"

She was actually starting to bundle him out. He felt confused and aggrieved.

"Look, are you fed up with me or what?" he said.

They were in the little hallway now.

"I *told* you half past eleven, you said all right, and now it's half past eleven, OK?"

"I suppose I just didn't realize you meant it so precisely," he said angrily.

"Listen, person," she said softly. "I'm sorry I push you out. We arrange it better next time, yes?"

Then she was kissing him, once on each cheek lightly, Polish fashion, and then suddenly her wide soft mouth was on his, her arms round his neck. He felt a little flutter of tongue, and then she pushed him through the front door and he was standing alone on a cold bleak concrete balcony.

He didn't see Rose Marie's car come round the corner and park under the street lamp.

When he got back to his bedroom in Kennedy Hall he found a large huddled shape in his bed.

"Oh, God," he said.

"I'm afraid Dr Daker is unavailable at present," said the shape woozily. "Perhaps I can help you."

"I *am* Dr Daker, Jock. You're in my bed."

"Good Lord, so I am," said Jock. "My dear fellow, I'm frightfully sorry. These Kennedy Hall chaps ... full of fascinating problems. So much *Angst* and *Weltschmertz*. And they all drink *far* too much whisky. A young man called, eh, Everitt, I believe, was kind enough to assist me to my pit."

"*My* pit."

"I, eh, thought you might not be back tonight. I thought you might have had a *bit of luck*. My dear chap, I'll turn out immediately."

It did not look very likely that he would manage it.

"It's all right," said Stephen wearily. "Stay there for now."

"You're a kind man, Stephen," said Jock, giving up the struggle.

"But really, Jock. This really is the last time. I've got enough on my plate without running a dosshouse."

Jock snored.

Bob Buzzard was putting Piers Platt through a battery of tests in the Body Lab. Headaches and dizziness, well, he could have told the old pisser to go easy on the Côtes du Rhône, but nothing was too much trouble for his favourite patient. He punched up another slide from the Isseyhaka vision tests.

"Come on, then, what's this one?" he said.

"Well, it's an extremely boring pointillist pastiche," said Platt testily. "A very long way after Bridget Riley."

"That's all? I mean don't hold anything back. You don't see any sort of shapes there?"

"Of course not."

Bob switched the light off and stared at him.

"Well, blow me down," he said. "How long have you been colour-blind, buddy?"

The poor old pisser went quite pale.

"It's all right, you know," said Bob, patting him on the shoulder. "You've got nothing to worry about, your secret's safe with me. That's the beauty of private practice."

Mark Stibbs went to see his personal tutor, found her surprisingly understanding, and got his head sorted out. Sarah Matchett, who was at bottom a sensible young woman, resigned herself to good grades and the occasional smile. Carla Maravillas came back from her two weeks on Copacabana beach and settled down to work for her third in Art History. Richard Everitt decided that it might be interesting to have another go at that essay. And Dr Rose Marie paid a private visit to Dr Stephen Daker.

"Were you thinking of going to the gallery opening?" she said.

"Yes, I thought I would. Are you?"

Rose took her spectacles off, the better to look deep into Stephen's eyes. She did this for so long that Stephen began to wonder whether she was adding deep hypnosis to her therapeutic repertoire. Then she said: "Stephen. Please don't be offended. I'm speaking as a friend. But ... don't you think it would be better for everyone if you stopped pursuing her?"

"What? Who?" said Stephen, genuinely puzzled.

"Oh, Stephen. Deviousness doesn't suit you. I'm talking about Grete Grotowska. She's very young, very vulnerable, she's had some very bad times with men. Of *course* you need to reassure yourself that you can still function in the sexual arena, but to force yourself on someone so fragile ... I just didn't think you were that kind of man."

"Rose," said Stephen. "This is crazy. That business with the medical was a misunderstanding. It's all over and done with."

"So why are you pursuing her?"

"I'm *not!*"

"I'm glad to hear you say that, Stephen," she said softly. "I hope I can believe it. Perhaps I shall be able to help her, after all."

"Help her in what way?"

Her eyes widened. "To find her sexual identity, of course. Isn't that what all of us want?"

The new Art Gallery, housing the Lowlands Collection, was clearly going to be a brilliant success. Amongst the younger universities, only East Anglia and Salford (if you rated Lowry) could match it. The three Braques enjoyed the most prominent position, displayed rather preciously on three free-standing easels (Professor Platt's idea). Platt himself was in his element, chatting up someone who would have to be Lord Everitt himself. Julie Daniels was doing a fine job on the champagne, talking at random to whoever came within range. Besides the expected academic luminaries, there were quite a few faces from industry and the City, and a very gratifying sprinkling of guests from the international art world, all gossiping and bitching away like there was no tomorrow. Everyone was having a lovely time, in fact, except for Stephen Daker, who was trying unsuccessfully to convince himself that he didn't mind Grete Grotowska so clearly being here with Rose Marie, and that he didn't mind the tender proprietorial style that Rose adopted towards her new friend. Grete had not spoken a word to him since the evening at her flat. Once tonight she had caught his eye and winked at him. What did that mean? What was the matter with him? Why couldn't he just have a drink and enjoy the paintings like everyone else?

Jack Daniels detached himself from a group of bigwigs and came up to Stephen smiling warmly.

"Like it, Steve?"

"It's beautiful. You must be very pleased with it," said Stephen.

"Yeah. I guess we made a statement here. This is what we're putting up front. This is the heart of it, Steve. This is the real thing."

Across the room Julie Daniels dropped a glass and said: "Oh, *shit*!" in her clear harsh Texan voice.

Bob Buzzard arrived late and headed straight for Piers Platt, ignoring the fact that Platt was explaining the *tache* and the *Ding an Sein* to an admiring group of listeners.

"Evening, buddy. Buzzard's the name. Saw the guide dog in the lobby, thought hello, Platt's here."

"Look, Buzzard," said Platt, drawing him away, "I don't find this very amusing."

"Just trying to cheer you up a bit," said Bob. "Bad news from the Fiat garage I'm afraid. They've diagnosed severe internal injuries. Massive trauma. Three hundred and fifty plus VAT, it's a scandal, isn't it?"

"Yeah, it's just what you would expect," said Grete Grotowska to Rose Marie, as they worked their way round towards the Braques. "Nice safe taste, nothing to make you pop your socks ... blimey. These are something else."

"They're ... beautiful, aren't they?" said Rose, breathing deeply, as if to inhale the genius. She was clearly responding to the Braques. As a woman.

"Yeah, very pretty," said Grete, smiling.

"I *love* Braque, don't you, Grete?"

Grete had her face very close to the middle painting.

"You don't think the colours are maybe a little bit bright?"

Julie Daniels, wandering past, heard this.

"Hey, yeah, you know that's just what I said. But you and me, honey, we don't know diddleysquat. It's all to do with the, what was it, the throbbing power of the dingaling or something. Ask the jerk in the polka-dot tie, he'll tell you."

She went off, somewhat unsteadily.

"Everything OK? You happy, Charlie?" said Jack Daniels to Charles Dusenberry.

"Yeah, I guess. Everyone else is."

"I like to see Julie happy," said Jack comfortably. "Hell, I like to see everybody happy."

"How about friend Perce?"

They turned and looked at friend Perce, who was explaining the *tache* and the *petite amie* to the head of security.

"Well, he's got us an art collection, Charlie. I'd say he's given us his best shot. Maybe there isn't a lot left for him to do at Lowlands."

"I figured that," said Charlie. "Yeah. Wait till the rich kid graduates. Then let the asshole go."

"Seems kind of a shame, you know? Still . . . I guess that's what civilization's all about," said the Vice-Chancellor.

Stephen was thinking about cutting his losses and going home to his lonely bed at Kennedy Hall, when Grete Grotowska came up to him, excited and breathless, her bright-red glass earrings catching the light.

"So. Having fun?"

"Well, no," he said. "Not really."

"You think I'm giving you the hard shoulder? Hey, come here. I've *got* to tell this to someone."

She looked around, then pointed to the Braques, and whispered in his ear.

"I *know* the guy who did those!"

"Braque?" said Stephen, baffled. "I thought he'd been dead for years."

"No, Tadeucz *Slawek*. He works in Paris, I know him, he had a fight with my husband once. Braque is his very best thing!"

She seemed delighted about it. Stephen was shocked.

"You're saying they're *fakes*?"

"I've even seen one of them before. Tadeucz did them for a guy called Siebermann three years ago. The clever bastard! I must phone him up and tell him. He loves to be in permanent collection!"

"Look, though," said Stephen. "I mean what are you going to do about it?"

"What do you mean?"

"Well . . . shouldn't you tell Professor Platt, or the VC?"

"You think they'd believe me? I'm just a rude nasty girl from Poland. Anyway, Stephen. Just look at them all. All those people. Everyone so happy. They want to see Braque. So they see Braque."

"But they're *not* seeing Braque."

Something was going wrong; they were starting to quarrel again; he was too stubborn, or pompous, or stupid, or prim, or honest, or something, to be able to share her amoral delight. And they seemed to be talking about something else besides Braque.

"*How* can you say what they see?" she hissed fiercely. "*You* saw Braque till two minutes ago. You think you *know* what is genuine? You see what you want to see like everyone else!"

"But I don't know anything about art," he said stupidly.

"Art. People. Whatever. You think you know *me*?"

"I don't know. I'd . . . like to."

"Well, not tonight, if that's what you're thinking."

He was aware of Rose Marie standing in the background, waiting, smiling.

"People, eh? Problems," said Grete, more gently, or at least less contemptuously. She turned to Rose. "OK, I'm coming."

Then she gave Stephen a really nice sweet sad smile that almost, but not quite, made up for the sight of her a few seconds later going out through the door arm in arm with Rose.

76

He took a last look round the gallery before leaving himself. Everyone was happy. Everyone was seeing Braque.

Jock McCannon was sitting with his carrier bags on the carpeted floor in a quiet corridor outside Rose Marie's flat, and he was full of inner certainty. Of course. How had he not seen it before? The wee lassie was offering him love, but not carnal love. It was a daughter's love. It was Cordelia's love for Lear. Dear daughter, I confess that I am old ... age is unnecessary ... he pulled himself together as he heard the lift door and the soft footsteps along the corridor. Two people's footsteps. Cordelia had brought a young friend.

"Jock?" said Rose Marie. "Are you all right? What's the matter?"

"Nothing at all, wee lass. Jock has heard your inner cry. I have come to stay with you, Rose."

"Jock, it's not convenient."

"Who is this?" said Grete Grotowska. "Your *father*?"

"My dear, you speak better than you know," rumbled Jock, staggering to his feet. "I'm sure we shall all muck in together famously. I've not come empty-handed."

He produced a huge take-away container and held it up triumphantly.

"Mutton biriani!"

It had been a difficult evening for Mervyn Lillicrap, and it was by no means over yet. But a boyhood in the back streets of Tonypandy and five years at the Crisis Centre had made Mervyn Lillicrap a connoisseur of human conflict. Time to start a little opening up.

"Right ... well, let me share with you a few of the reverberations I've been picking up," he said, smiling round at the little group. "I won't take up too much of the space. Then I'd welcome your comments, and we'll see how we go from there."

They were all glaring at him except for the nice one, the one who'd invited him, who said: "Yes, that sounds fine."

Mervyn cleared his throat. "Well, there's clearly a classic Oedipal situation ..."

"Oh, brilliant," snarled Bob Buzzard.

". . . with the, er, the displacement of the father figure . . . dead but he won't lie down, if I can put it colloquially . . ."

Mervyn tried a little chuckle at this point, but nobody joined in, and the father figure growled threateningly. Mervyn hurried on.

". . . the almost pathological unease I sense from Stephen here in the leadership role, well that's something I can identify with. What's more problematical is the sado-masochistic fantasy hovering around Bob's relationship with both patients and colleagues . . ."

"*Robert*, you little bastard!" said Bob in a savage undertone.

". . . particularly the erotic tension inherent in his interaction with Nurse Gahagan."

"You dirty-minded little get," said Maureen.

"Maureen, he's just using a metaphor," said Stephen.

"Well he can keep his metaphors to himself."

Mervyn was determined to get through it.

"And then there's the overpoweringly mingled, ah, controlled hostility and sexual attraction which I'm picking up from Dr Rose Marie." He paused. "Well . . . perhaps I'll stop there for a moment and open up a space. Er . . . these things work best if we allow ourselves to be quite free and uncensored." Dew Mawr. Why had he said that? These people were quite uncensored enough without any encouragement from him.

"Thank you. Mervyn," said Stephen. "Er . . . anyone?"

"How would you like a punch in the snout, Mervyn?" asked Bob Buzzard.

Mervyn yelped.

"No, actually, that's not *quite* what I want to do with you. If I can free associate a minute, don't want to take up anybody's *space*, but Mervyn here reminds me of a snivelling little shit we had in junior dorm, *Jenkins* his name was, and what we used to do with *Jenkins* was hold him head down in the bogs and pull the chain. All right, Dr Lillicrap? Fancy that, do you?"

"You realize you're confirming my tentative hypothesis?" said Mervyn in a rather squeaky voice.

"Yes, that's just what *Jenkins* said before the waters closed over his greasy little head," said Bob. "Well, I don't want to hog the discussion. Rose?"

Rose smiled sweetly.

"I'd have found Mervyn's analysis much more convincing," she said, "if he hadn't spent the last half hour trying to look up my skirt."

"I never!" gasped Mervyn, suddenly right back in the girls' playground at Tonypandy Junior.

"Yes, you were," said Maureen. "I saw you. You're just like a dirty-minded little boy, you are. With your nasty piggy little eyes."

"Maureen!" said Stephen.

Mervyn raised a trembling hand. "No, no, Stephen. Free intercourse – interchange – is of the essence. It's just that I . . . I'm not quite used to . . . Down the Crisis Centre they're not so . . . forgive me a moment . . . nasty *and* piggy?"

"I have to speak as I find, Dr Lillicrap," said Maureen.

"Yes. Yes. Of course."

Jock McCannon, who had been austerely silent till now, entered the discussion with a voice that rumbled like thunder.

"Dr Lillicrap."

"Yes?"

"We all need help. We are all poor forked creatures. Even psychiatrists."

"A lot of people don't realize that," gabbled Mervyn.

"Yes, yes. There's a lot of pain, isn't there. Tell me, Mervyn. How does it feel?" Jock's compassion was quite excruciating.

"Well I can't pretend it's not a strain, Dr McCannon."

"No. No. Tell me, Mervyn. How does it *really* feel, *right now*?"

"T-terrible." He could hardly choke the word out. But Jock was still not satisfied.

"How does it *really* feel . . . *deep down inside*?"

"I . . . I . . ."

And then the sobs came, would not be denied, lovely terrible hot choking sobs that shook Mervyn Lillicrap's skinny little body, rocked him to and fro. He was falling apart and there was nothing he could do about it.

"Poor wee man," said Jock.

"We're here, Mervyn," said Rose Marie softly. "We're here to help you."

"I'm sorry I looked up your skirt," he sobbed.

"All right, Mervyn," she said gently.

"Just don't do it again, that's all," said Maureen.

"Mervyn," said Jock, and it was like the voice of God piercing through the storm. "Would you like someone to hug you, Mervyn?"

Mervyn could not speak, but he could nod.

"Who would you like to hug you?"

Wordlessly, Mervyn pointed a trembling finger at Bob Buzzard.

"Oh, Lord," said Bob, outraged. "Look here, have I got to?"

"I think perhaps you should, Bob," said Stephen.

"Oh, Lord. Come on then," said Bob. He gritted his teeth, spread his arms wide and turned his eyes up to the ceiling as Mervyn Lillicrap crawled into his embrace.

"Look here," said Bob, patting Lillicrap awkwardly on the back, as if to bring up wind, "if one word of this gets back to Daphne there'll be hell to pay."

"You see, Stephen?" said Jock benignly. "In a crisis, we work very *well* together as a team."

RUST'S BLOCK

Rust is back at Lowlands, and he is blocked. All right, we know: boring, boring, heard it, writer's block, just another word for bloody idleness, ought to try working at a proper job, why is it always *writer's* block, when are we going to hear about *milkman's* block, who is going to pen the agonies of *estate agent's* block? (Actually, Rust has come across quite a few estate agents with estate agent's block, and pretty nearly every solicitor he has ever dealt with has had terminal solicitor's block.) Anyway, Rust doesn't give a fart about milkman's block, to be frank, because Rust is a writer and writer's block is what he has, and he feels bloody terrible.

Funny how it's always writer's block, not Author's block. When Authors are blocked, they call it writer's block. Rust did himself, when he was an Author. The fact is, writer's block is neither here nor there to an Author. It's nobody's business but your own. Look at Joseph Heller, thinks Rust. Ten years to write a novel, nobody minds, maybe not even Joseph Heller. Take your time, Joe, they say, and when he finally manages to squeeze one out, everyone's grateful. Even Rust is. But Heller's an Author. Rust is a writer, and he has to get himself together in seven days minimum, or he is up shit creek without a paddle. Riddington is getting jumpy already. Powell has been ominously silent. They are probably weighing up the pros and cons of junking Rust and getting in another writer, Dirk Dynorod or someone like that, one of those fast loose writers, and that'll be that, no second series, no thirty-five grand, no dog kennel in Hornsey, no bloody fun, no bloody games . . . .

Writer's block is like terminal constipation. The whole business of writing is like excretion, Rust often thinks. Everybody understands that. You can tell that from the way everyone always asks writers what they have in the pipeline. When people ask Rust that, he usually replies with his celebrated rapier wit that what he has in the pipeline is a large mutton biriani and a few beers and Scotches. Actually it's worse than that. What Rust has in the pipeline at the moment, besides the aforesaid, is a solid painful unbudgeable rock-like mass consisting of five whole turgid unwritten episodes.

So far he has managed to unload himself of two, with a great deal of straining at the word-processor. Now they lie lifeless, dark, reproachful in Riddington's office in Threshold House. Ken was quite decent about them, considering. "They're ... they're ... all right, Ron," he said, gloomily. "Just ... well, just not quite what we were hoping for, that's all." Rust asked him if he could be a bit more specific, give him a few pointers he could go away and work at, and Ken sighed and groaned a bit, then said, "Well, it's just that we feel they could be a bit more *interesting*, that's all, and ..." his brilliant critical brain searching for the perfect encapsulation of the creative problematic ... "and a bit, well, *funnier*." Thanks a lot, Ken. Just what a chap needs to get him going. More interesting, and funnier. OK. Fine.

This is even more of a problem than it sounds, because Rust does not know how to be funny. Rust is never deliberately funny. When he's not blocked, he pours out the bitter realities of life as he has experienced it, all the cruel ironies, the humiliations, the embarrassing little infections, rejections, ejections (Rust has been ejected from places you and I would never even be invited to, or wish to enter) and people fall about laughing. Even Riddington laughs, once Tucker has explained the humour to him. Rust never laughs. Rust has no sense of humour at all. He doesn't mind. He doesn't mind them laughing at him, so long as they pay him, and he can continue to squeeze out the episodes. He is the William McGonagall of BBC2.

So what's to be done about this block? He has tried all the usual things. Bells whisky. Mutton biriani. Sneaking up on the word-processor at four in the morning. Making his mind blank and forgetting all about his problems (sometimes he can maintain this state for five or six seconds at a time). Reading people like Heller and Lurie with a view to stealing good ideas undetected. More Bells whisky. Planning suicide (not constructive, but an enjoyable alternative to thinking about the serial). More Bells whisky. Solitary walks. More Bells whisky. Nothing.

Suddenly he thinks that what he would really like is a nice massage, but he doesn't know anyone who would give him one. Rust himself is not bad at massage. In his encounter group days he was into the lot: deep-tissue, Rolf-Reichian, casual Californian, you name it. He learnt most of these from a bloke called Hans Lobstein. Hans Lobstein never seemed short of someone to give him a massage. That was probably why he always looked in such good nick for his age, with a tall, sinewy, well-cared-for-looking body. Rust's own body, as we know, is short and ill-cared-for. Yes, what he would like is a perfectly ordinary Swedish relaxation massage, which, belying its name, has always left Rust feeling definitely perky. Anyway, no chance of that at Lowlands. No one massages anyone at Lowlands. No one touches anyone else at Lowlands. They just walk around giving each other hardeye.

All this thinking about massage is just a diversion. He is trying to avoid thinking about deep psychic pain. That's what it always comes down to in the end: pain and fear. Rust is going to have to engage with it. But he can't do it in this foul little cell. He'll go out and engage with it in his Mercedes. His Mercedes hasn't moved since its traumatic trip to London. It doesn't seem to want to be driven any more. That's all right with Rust. He has nowhere to go. He'll be quite happy to sit in its peaceful dark-blue velvety embrace, playing with the buttons.

There seem to be an amazing number of security men about this year. Can *they* be anything to do with Rust's block? Rust doesn't see how they can be. He likes security. A lot of men in dark-blue suits too, some of them with walkie-talkies. Some people think the men in blue suits are secret policemen. Rust doesn't care if they are. Rust has no secrets. Rust is a blurter.

Rust arrives at the car park and unlocks his frail elderly Mercedes coupé. Ah, it's so beautiful. Rust loves it so much. He'll never be unfaithful to it. What does he care if it isn't a goer? Love is a spiritual thing. It's about feelings, not physical geography. He gets in, sinks into the blue velvet, hears the door clunk shut, and knows immediately what it is. It's the Polish girl. He doesn't want to write about the Polish girl. Eh? That one really came up from the floor. *Why* doesn't he want to write about the Polish girl? He's *crazy* about the Polish girl. Take your time, Ron. It'll come. Yes, now it's coming.

It's a new version of the old thing, but worse than ever before. Many times in the past, Rust has created a perfect person from the best bits of women he has known, seen her cast, dressed, rehearsed in the lines that he has always wanted to hear women speak to him (in real life women speak their own lines, and bloody unpleasant most of them are too) . . . but when it comes to the show, it's always someone *else* that gets all the fun. Some *actor* who probably doesn't even *fancy* out-of-control Polish girls with wonderful wide mouths always moving . . . stop it, Rust. You'll drive yourself crazy.

So now he has it. And now he has it, he knows what he's going to do about it. If he, Rust, can't have her, he's sure as shit not going to let that bloody doctor have her. It was bad enough last time, with that one based on the best bits of Carol. Rust swears a solemn oath to himself not to let the doctor have the Polish girl. What's more – and now he's beginning to enjoy himself – she's going to give him a really bad time. And, and – he's really cracking away now – why shouldn't she have a bad time herself? She deserves a bad time, after all. She gave Rust a terrible time in Poland. Right. Right. Got it. Right.

Rust leaps unblocked from the frail Mercedes and runs back to his noxious cell and his silent word-processor, desperate to relieve himself of Episode Three before the feeling goes away, or worse, before the episode catches him short.

3

"MAY THE FORCE BE WITH YOU"

A misty autumn dawn was reluctantly breaking over the University of Lowlands. It was very quiet. A small package tour of eider ducks who had made an overnight stop at the lake were grumbling querulously about the poor quality of the waterweed, and looking forward to some decent Scotch crabs. High on the bleak concrete roofs, the surveillance cameras turned their slender necks this way and that, blinking silently like owls in the first faint rays of sunshine, recording their foreshortened fuzzy black and white images of the security men who lounged in pairs outside Cybernetics, Experimental Psychology, Microbiology, Electroacoustics and the other squat sensitive buildings. Everything quiet. Everything under control. Not even a nun to be seen. Just one figure moving, a tall stooped figure in a huge caped greatcoat, wandering through the silent campus muttering into a tape-recorder.

Mr Sweet had it all taped. Mr Sweet was the head of security. Fourteen little black and white TV monitors afforded Mr Sweet a view of every corner of the university he had a whim to inspect. And for Mr Sweet, the dawn campus was far from silent, it was alive and twittering with static, buzz, electricity, noise and signal as he administered his daily dawn ritual of signing off the night watch.

"Microbiology signing off, Mr Sweet, nothing to report, over."

Bleep, barp.

"Thank you Alistair." Splat twitter whoosh. "Come in Number Five." Bleep barp.

"Yes this is Patrick from Laser Engineering, all very quiet and cosy, the old feller's still about and will I bring the kippers up now?"

"Not before seven hundred hours Patrick, and let the old feller mooch, we are keeping a dossier on the old feller, over and out."

Mr Sweet laid down his glossy magazine open at a double-spread pin-up of the new Belgian sniper's rifle, and breathed on his ballpoint to make an entry in his log book. Directly above his head one of the little screens showed Number Seven, the only guard who had not yet called in. He was standing in the ankle-deep wet grass staring at the student residential block opposite.

"Come on. Come on. Please. Make it today," whispered Peter Wagstaff to himself. The curtains opened, and she was there. A tall dark-haired girl in a white nightie, stretching her arms above her head.

"Now. Now. Please. Now. Please."

Fifty yards away, she crossed her arms, lifted the hem of the short nightie, and started to draw it up over her wonderful secret only-for-Peter-Wagstaff body. Then something sharp and hot hit him on the left ear.

"Ow! Shit!" he said, swinging round. Twenty yards away, two nuns were walking sedately past. They nodded to him benignly and he gave them an awkward salute. Then he turned back to the window. She had gone.

"Number Seven to Control. Nothing to report. Over and out."

"Seven hundred hours, gentlemen," said Mr Sweet from his eyrie in the Poulson Tower. "The night watch is over. Congratulations, lads. We've kept the bastards at bay. Mr Sweet at the controls, over and out."

Mr Sweet decided that he deserved a little treat. He unlocked the middle drawer in his desk, and reverently slid out a bulky gleaming leather holster. His stubby fingers caressed the zip. The cold gleaming weight of the Magnum flopped into his hand. He lifted it with both hands to his face, and sniffed luxuriously.

On the steps of Kennedy Hall, a tall strongly built student in a boiler-suit was beating up a small wiry student in motorcycle gear, who was doing his best to cover up, but making no attempt to fight back.

"Look, I know you're cross with me, Allie," said Sammy Limb, clasping both hands over his genitals.

"Brilliant!" she said, punching him in the stomach and following up with a slap across the head.

"I don't deserve this. Ow!"

"Yes you do," she said, pulling him up from where he had fallen. "I know what you were doing in Manchester. You just ... spoil ... *everything*, don't you?"

Sammy fell down again.

"Think we ought to talk about our relationship."

She kicked him a couple of times, not very hard.

"It's got *nothing* to do with our *relationship*!"

"Right. Got that, Allie."

"Good," she said. "I'll see you tonight then."

She strode off towards Thatcher Hall, and after a few minutes Sammy Limb got up, found his motorcycle helmet, and tottered into Kennedy to recuperate.

Stephen had started jogging again. It wasn't the same without Lyn, but it was something. An act of faith in the body. And he was finding that he could actually still do it. There was a bit of a bonfire smouldering in his lungs, but the legs were not too bad at all. He was almost beginning to enjoy it. As he came out of the trees and on to the path by the lake, a small flock of eider ducks took off, flurrying the water. Nice. Nice to be a duck. Did ducks have problems? Did the head duck ever worry about his leadership role, did the other ducks give him a bad time, did he have trouble with female ducks, did they flap off to Hong Kong or turn out to be lesbian ducks? Shut up. Think about the jog.

Fifty yards ahead of him a woman in a black mac was walking along the path, head down, hands deep in pockets. When he was ten yards away, she stopped and turned to face him, and something made Stephen stop too. It was Grete Grotowska. Her shoulders were tense and her face looked angry and frightened. She did not look pleased to see him at all.

"Hello," he said.

"What do you want?"

"Nothing. I'm just ... I didn't realize it was you."

"No?"

"Look, I'm ... just out for a jog, I didn't mean to ... look, why don't I just jog off?"

Her face relaxed a little, but she still looked very sad, or worried, or whatever it was. Neither of them had moved. It felt very strange to Stephen.

"It's all right," she said. "It's not your fault. I thought you might be someone else."

"Oh," he said. "Er ... who?"

"Not your problem." She was biting her lip.

"Look, are you all right?"

"So-so." She was trying to do one of her grins for him but it wasn't coming out right. He wished he could soothe her, or comfort her, or do something that would give her her grin back.

"You look so pretty," he said. "Oh, Lord. Sorry. I don't know what made me say that."

"You didn't mean it? You've changed your mind now, or what?"

Oh, Lord. Now she was looking upset again.

"No, look," he said hopelessly. "I didn't mean ... it's just, well, here you are, obviously trying to have a walk on your own, and you look ... worried, or upset, and I come barging up and ... you see what it is, I find I keep thinking about you, and I've no idea where I stand with you, or even where I want to stand with you ... so just barging up and saying something like that doesn't seem particularly helpful, in fact bloody crass and intrusive .... I think I really should just jog off now."

She was silent for a few moments, perhaps weighing up in her mind whether she had ever heard such an imbecilic utterance before. Then, without smiling, rather as if she had finally decided to go in and have it out with the bank manager, she said: "You want to come out for a drink this evening?"

"Well, yes," he said, stunned. "That would be nice. I mean, that's if you ..."

"OK."

They stood there, ten yards apart, without speaking, for quite a long while; and then Stephen jogged off.

Minutes of Group Meeting No. 5, Autumn Term
Present: Dr Daker (Chair), Dr McCannon, Dr Rose Marie, Dr Buzzard

Following a complaint by Dr Buzzard that Nurse Gahagan's minutes of previous meetings made him look a bloody fool, Nurse Gahagan said that she would not attend Meeting No. 5, and they could jolly well see how they managed to get along without her. Dr McCannon offered the services of his rinky-dinky cassette recorder, and that is why these minutes are presented as edited extracts from the transcript prepared by Mrs Kramer.

Dr Daker: I've er had a memo from the VC. He's invited me to sit on Senate as a co-opted member.

Dr McCannon: So the Prince of Darkness has bought your complicity has he?

Dr Rose Marie: Stephen, I'm very happy for you; I'm sure you'll be able to do a lot of good.

Dr Buzzard: Absolutely, half of Senate are tottering about with senile dementia, Stephen can certify them brain dead, then it's off with them in the minibus to the geriatric ward.

Dr McCannon: You are all very naive. Daniels has darker purposes than that. Lowlands has become a place of dark secrets, guarded by meat-faced thugs with walkie-talkies. And why does Lowlands prosper when all around are going to the wall? What are the sources of our new-found wealth? To what fell purpose is the money put? What do they guard, the meat-faced men? Microbiology, Laser Engineering, Electroacoustics, Experimental Psychology. Dark secrets. Dark secrets.

Dr Buzzard: He's flipped. One more for the minibus.

Dr Daker: Could we move on? The VC was interested in how we are developing the practice.

Dr Buzzard: Now you're talking, buddy. Shit! Look at that! Coffee all over it! Oh, *bloody* hell. Look, I'm absolutely sick of ... *shit*! .... Stress Clinic. Using all the Body Lab facilities we can monitor 47 significant factors then individualize preventive programmes as well as exercise and treatment programmes. What I'd like to do is compare stress levels of the senior bods here with their counterparts in business and industry. Forge some useful links. Say goodbye to coronaries and burnout. Charlie Dusenberry in Finance is going to grease the slipway with a bit of cash from the Slush Fund. Overtime for young Maureen and the old bat and a few other bits and bobs, oh God, look at those trousers, just back from the cleaners too.

Dr Daker: Well that sounds excellent Bob.

Dr Buzzard: Robert?

Dr Daker: Robert. Er Rose? The Male Sexuality Workshop?

Dr Rose Marie: Thank you, Stephen. I've established a pilot group, and I'm also going to work on an individual basis. I'm very grateful for this opportunity, Stephen. A brilliant insight. I think I've been underestimating the plight of men, in this fearful and beleaguered sexual climate. You're confused, guilty, trapped like wounded animals in a sexual labyrinth of your own making. I feel that I can help.

Dr Buzzard: Well don't look at me. I'm a happily married man. For a healthy life, stick to the wife. Simple as that. And as a matter of fact I happen to think that sex is very much overrated. And so does Daphne. I think. Well it's not the sort of thing you discuss is it? Why are we discussing it now? By God it's stuffy in here. What's the matter with the air conditioning? What are you all staring at?

Dr Daker: Thank you, Bob. Robert. Very er useful contribution. Er Jock?

Dr McCannon: The task I have set myself is nothing less than to probe the psychic health of Lowlands University. To bring the Dark Secrets into the light of day. My investigations will take the form of Action Research. That is all I choose to say at present.

Dr Buzzard: Gaga. Absolutely gaga.

Dr Daker: Well thank you all very much. I think we're really moving forward now, don't you?

Dr Rose Marie: How do you see *your* role, Stephen?

Dr Daker: Oh, I'm head of the practice, Rose. My job is to co-ordinate the team.

Dr Buzzard: Idle bastard. Oh *shit*! Look at that! All over the . . . look, quick, one of you, it's all going into the . . . *shit*!

(recording terminates)

"Well, Mr Sweet," said Stephen. "What seems to be the trouble?"

The patient, a bulky man in his late forties, dressed in a tight and bulging dark-blue uniform and carrying a peaked cap in his hand, did not immediately reply. He was on his hands and knees completing a thorough examination of the consulting room by running his hands over the underside of the couch. Then he grunted, looked sharply at Stephen, and sat down in a chair.

"Heartburn. Feeling of constriction. Occasional pains across the chest and under the arm. Occasional difficulty in breathing."

"I see," said Stephen. "Just slip off your top thing, would you, and come over to the couch."

Mr Sweet glared at Dr Daker in a very suspicious way.

"Is this necessary?"

"Yes, it is, Mr Sweet. It's absolutely essential if you want me to examine you properly."

"All right, Dr Daker," said the head of security, standing up ponderously, and walking to the couch. "You've got your job to do I daresay. Just as I have mine."

He unbuttoned his tunic, revealing a flannel vest over

which was a tight leather harness supporting an enormous leather holster.

"Good Lord," said Stephen, trying without much success to find a space to insert his stethoscope. "Er ... what *is* all this?"

"Special equipment, Doctor."

"What's it for?"

"Emergencies."

"What sort of emergencies?"

"Use your loaf, Doctor," said Sweet, tapping his nose.

"Yes, I'm trying to do that," said Stephen. "Look, I wonder if this, er, harness thing might be the source of your discomfort? It's ... I mean do you have to wear it so tight?"

"Yes," said Sweet.

Sexual deviations were always difficult to handle, and Stephen's experience with this one was not extensive.

"Do you mind if I ask why?" he said gently.

"Because the bloody mail order firm sent the wrong bloody size, that's why!" snapped Mr Sweet. "Can't rely on anyone outside the Force these days. D'you know I had to purchase this gear out of my own pocket? D'you know how much this sort of stuff costs? No, you don't know, and you don't care. Don't suppose for a moment you've considered going armed yourself."

"No, I haven't," said Stephen, intrigued. "Do you think I should?"

"Why bother? You've got me to look after you." He buttoned up his tunic. "You've no idea what goes on in this place. Ha! I could write a book, Dr Daker. I could write a book!"

"Er ... what kind of book could you write?"

"My part in the unrelenting struggle to protect society from those determined to destroy it, Dr Daker!"

"I see," said Stephen. "Mr Sweet ... do you ever get the feeling that you're ... overworking? Letting things get on top of you?"

The head of security leaned forward urgently, his knuckles white as he grasped the edge of the desk.

"Who have you been talking to? Who's been putting that about?"

"No one. Really. I was just hazarding a guess."

"Forget it, Dr Daker," said Sweet. "I'm on top of things all right. You can sleep sound in your bed at night. I've got it all under control."

Peter Wagstaff, Security Guard No. 7, had not felt so cosseted and cared for since the days when Auntie Beryl had played submarines with him at bathtime. The nice lady doctor not only seemed concerned about his ear, she actually treated him like a person as well, which is a rare event for security guards.

"Ears are such delicate things," she said softly, as she applied a soothing lotion. He closed his eyes. Her scent was wonderful. It was as if he was back there in the lovely steamy bathroom, with Auntie Beryl squeezing out the sponge and ... no. He was a man now.

"Still tender?"

"A bit," he said, gulping.

"Oh, Mr Wagstaff. Did I hurt you? I'm *so* sorry."

Oh, Christ. Any more of this and he was going to ...

"Big boys don't cry, do they?" she said. "Forget about that, Mr Wagstaff. The really brave thing is to let the feelings out. What's it all about, Mr Wagstaff?"

She was stroking his brow gently with her cool hand. This is what it must be like in heaven, he thought.

"I'm just so lonely, doctor," he whispered. "All the blokes ... you know it's all how's it going Pete, getting much lately, and I know they're laughing at me, they don't really like me, and I'm *not* getting much. I'm not getting anything, doctor."

"What would you *like* to be getting, Mr Wagstaff?"

He couldn't possibly tell her what he'd like to do to the tall girl in the white nightie. He could hardly articulate the thought to himself.

"I don't deserve anything. I'm not lovable. I'm disgusting," he said.

"Mr Wagstaff," said Rose softly. "To be lovable, first we have to learn to love ourselves. And there's a little group you can join ... I run it myself ... where you can learn to do just that. In a very real sense."

Bob Buzzard wasted no time in organizing the ancillary staff for the new Stress Clinics. He explained to Mrs Kramer that the clients would not be the usual riffraff, and admirable though her abrasive style was for students and the like, the punters at the Stress Clinic would need more of a tender touch. Mrs Kramer said that she would do what she could.

Now it was young Maureen's turn. He had discovered that she was fully qualified in massage, and he was giving her a quick audition, lying on the couch in his consulting room with his shoes off and one trouser leg rolled up to the knee.

"This is ridiculous," said Maureen. "I mean you should have all your clothes off for a start. Come on, strip off, why don't you?"

"Never mind about that," said Bob, blushing scarlet. "This is just a limited experiment. Come on, we haven't got all day."

"Wait till the *Nursing Times* hears about this," said Maureen grimly, taking hold of his foot. "Right, relax, will you?"

"Ow! Dear God!" yelled Bob. What was the mad tottie doing, trying to pull it clean off?

"Plenty of strength in those thumbs, eh?"

"Stop! Stop!"

She paused, and Bob got his breathing back to normal.

"Maureen," he said. "I'm a *company chairman* with *hypertension*. I want a *relaxation* massage."

"Oh, one of them. Waste of time, them. No good unless it hurts."

"Just try, would you," said Bob, resisting a strong impulse to boot her in the backside. "I would be extremely grateful. Think about Bruce Springsteen or whoever he is, that fellow you fancy."

"It's not easy in the circumstances," said Maureen, but she managed to moderate the pressure by about seventy per cent or so until it was quite tolerable. If it weren't for the face she might just about do.

"Yes, that's more like it," said Bob encouragingly. "Yes, not bad at all if you like that sort of thing. Yes. Er, d'you think you could smile a bit?"

"You're asking too much," said Maureen.

"No, you're quite right. You just haven't got the ... thank you, Maureen."

He sat up and reached for his socks.

"I'll let you know if we get any masochists."

Maureen walked out of the consulting room.

"Right," said Bob to himself. "Plan B."

"We'll get Maureen to give you some anti-inflammatories to stop the pain," said Jock McCannon to Sammy Limb. "And what, after all, is a cracked rib to a man in love?"

"Well, I dunno," said Sammy. "Think she might just be using me."

"As a kind of exercise machine?"

"No, cos I can get into places. I let her down last night, see. They was all counting on me, but I was stuck in Manchester."

"Eh, who was counting on you, Sammy?"

Sammy looked a bit shifty. "Don't know if I should tell you."

"I am your doctor, my dear fellow," rumbled Jock expansively. "You can tell me anything and be assured of total confidentiality."

"Well," said Sammy. "It's sort of a pet lovers' group."

"Ah," said Jock, who was quicker on the uptake than many people gave him credit for. "A kind of informal branch of the RSPCA, I dare say? Out of the goodness of your hearts, you devote your leisure time to monitoring the welfare of our furry friends?"

"Yeah, well, sort of. I'm only in it because of Allie."

"And have you considered the broader implications of your welfare work? Where would medical science be without animal experiments?"

"I don't think we're talking about medical science, Dr McCannon."

"No," said Jock. "I tend to agree with you. The MRC withdrew its puny grant five long years ago. Darker purposes are afoot, Sammy. I think we may have *interests in common*. Yes."

Jock paused, as if in his discourse he had forgotten some essential point which needed urgent attention. His brow furrowed, and then cleared.

"But my dear chap, what are we thinking of? You're under the weather, you need a tonic!"

He reached into a carrier bag which lay on the floor and produced a bottle of Bells and two glasses.

Bob Buzzard was working on Plan B. A magazine lay open on the desk of his consulting room, open at a double-page of advertisements, most of them featuring photographs of young women, and Bob was talking on the telephone.

"Hello. Would I be speaking to Natalie? Well, er, Natalie, I refer to your advertisement in 'Flexible Friends'. Excellent photo, I've got it in front of me now. What I want you to do, Natalie, is describe your massage services to me in detail."

He listened with some astonishment to Natalie's reply.

"*No*," he said. "I am *not* some wally trying to get his rocks off for fourpence. This is a serious enquiry from a University Research Project . . . hello? Hello?"

The line had gone dead.

"Extraordinary," said Bob aloud, and dialled another number. "Hello? Suzanne, please."

Stephen was making his debut on Senate, and doing his level best to understand the language and the power structures. It was clearly an honour to be on Senate. Stephen recognized most of the celebrated heavy operators in the university; not just any old professor got on to Senate. Senate was overwhelmingly male, and predominantly middle-aged; and interestingly enough, most of the heavy operators were heavily built men, too, with big shoulders and thick necks, men who carried their fat and their power well. There was also a sprinkling of much younger men from the newer departments at the cutting edge: Microbiology, Cybernetics, Electroacoustics. Some of these looked quite absurdly young to be professors, till you noticed the calm assured contemptuous self-satisfaction in their intelligent faces. The young whiz-kids. Doing fine.

Jack Daniels was in the chair, with Charles Dusenberry of Finance by his side, and he was talking, so far as Stephen could make out, about recruitment.

"Well, I guess we'd like to congratulate the Overseas Development Board for its tireless work ... what are we looking at, two thousand full-time-equivalent from the Far East by 1991, Professor Eugenides?"

Professor Eugenides, plump, glossy and tanned in his grey silk suit and dark glasses, beamed at his Vice-Chancellor.

"At full overseas rates we predict substantial capital gain; Mr Dusenberry has prepared the detailed financial forecast, Appendix 88.3.74a. The switch out of Malaysia and into Korea and Central and South America should put us well ahead of the field for the next five years."

There was an appreciative murmuring, and then a loud harrumph from the corner, as Professor George Bunn of English Studies entered the field. He was a stout, rumpled sort of man in his late fifties, who always looked as if he had been dressed by someone else, in a hurry.

"Don't suppose any of these chaps speak English, Eugenides? Read books, hold a pen, any of that sort of stuff?"

"Looks like a growth area for English, Professor Bunn," said Eugenides silkily.

"I didn't take the chair in English to run a bloody Berlitz school!" shouted Bunn.

"I guess we all have to move with the times, Professor Bunn," said Charlie Dusenberry diffidently. "Professor Eugenides used to run the Classics Department."

"In the days when we still had a proper university here," said Bunn.

Jack Daniels flexed his heavily muscled shoulders and smiled warmly round, exuding respect and love for all his professors, great and small.

"The way I see it, and I guess everyone here sees it, is *whatever* we're doing, the bottom line is excellence, right? You stand for quality, George, you deliver a quality product, and we need a quality product to compete in the world market. We're all together on this one. Right?"

George Bunn snorted, mildly and temporarily mollified.

"OK," said the Vice-Chancellor. "Lowlands University Business Services Ltd. Charlie?"

"We're going for a twenty per cent per annum growth on a five-year plan marketing the university's skills and resources to business and industry nationally and internationally. Cybernetics and Electroacoustics are the star performers here, eighteen major research and consultancy contracts."

Professor Fuseli of Cybernetics and Professor Middling of Electroacoustics, neither of whom looked much over eighteen years old to Stephen, smiled their smug acknowledgement of superiority.

"I guess we'd like to see that kind of thinking on a university-wide basis," said Jack Daniels.

"Shakespearean sonnets for the boardroom bog paper, that sort of thinking?" said Bunn.

Jack Daniels decided to let that one go, and then, to Stephen's considerable alarm, said: "We have Steve Daker here from the University Health Centre, and I guess we could all learn from the new initiatives that Steve is pioneering. Steve?"

Stephen had been following the exchanges rather like a Martian at a tennis match. Now, suddenly, all the eyes were on him. It felt extremely daunting.

"Well, er," he began, in characteristically masterful fashion, "these are still in very early stages, but Dr Buzzard is initiating a stress clinic which he thinks might involve businessmen as well as academics, and, er, Dr Rose Marie has started a sort of counselling group for men to complement her Well Woman Group ... but really I think I should say that we haven't really envisaged these as, well, business ventures. Our real priority remains, the, well, the health of the students and the staff here."

He sank back in his seat. He was trembling violently. Still. He had said something, and it hadn't been total rubbish, had it?

"Good for you, Daker!" said George Bunn.

"I guess Steve's a little modest here," said Charlie Dusenberry. "I've had good meeting with Bobby Buzzard, and I think we have a real growth area here. We can market stress. No question about it. And if you guys can package men the way they packaged women in the seventies, hell, the sky's the limit."

That evening, Dr Rose Marie was nearing the end of her first meeting with the Male Sexuality Workshop. The pilot group comprised eight in all. Most of them were between eighteen and twenty-five, and most of them were undergraduates, but there were one or two exceptions, like Gregory Wing, Reader in Anxiety in the Psychology Department, and Peter Wagstaff, Security Guard No. 7.

"Well, let's sum up so far," said Rose, smiling encouragingly. "James has shared his feelings about his 'willy' in a *very* open way."

And James, a pink-cheeked English student, was awarded a special smile of his own.

"And we've also heard from Albert's *dick*, and Gregory's *little man* ... *very* rich associations there, Gregory ... Peter's ... cockle, was it Peter?"

"Winkle," said Peter Wagstaff.

"Yes, of course. I'm so sorry, Peter, *winkle*, of *course*, curled up and cosy in its little shell, vulnerable and shy, safe and hidden ..."

"Except when someone hooks it out with a *pin* and *chews it up*," said Gregory rather savagely.

"I *knew* someone was going to say that," said the security guard, writhing in distress.

"Nobody's going to do that to you here, Peter," said Rose soothingly.

"Not in a literal sense, perhaps," said Gregory.

It was time to give Gregory a little hardeye.

"Yes, I know, Gregory. It's a very frightening feeling to be a man just now. I'd like you to try and stay with that feeling, Gregory. All right? Now, David, you talked about your diddle, didn't you? And then there was Deng's ... fat poy?"

Deng, a slim Malaysian boy, nodded and smiled.

"Ian's Jimmy Riddle ... and Winston's teapot."

She smiled round again.

"Now these very poignant memories and associations from early childhood are absolutely crucial if we're going to work towards a real understanding of our sexual selves. I think what's emerging – and I find this very moving – is a shared group perception of male sexuality as something terribly fragile and delicate, fraught with fears and anxieties ... and we might well be feeling that it's perhaps too fragile to be put to the test in an interpersonal interaction. Yes?"

One or two of the group were nodding. Rose was really getting through to them. James even had his thumb in his mouth.

"Well, these feelings are nothing to be ashamed of," said Rose soothingly. "It's quite rational and sensible to be terrified of AIDS. And it's certainly rational to experience performance anxiety."

"I never had performance anxiety," said Winston sturdily. Winston was quite a difficult case. He came from Handsworth, was a prolific scorer in the basketball league and the disco, and had been gazing at Rose Marie's breasts with a beatific smile throughout the session. If she could succeed with Winston, she could succeed with every phallocrat in Lowlands.

"Winston," she said sweetly. "I'm afraid I have to tell you that women today are finding that men *don't* measure up as sexual partners, they are discovering that men are simply not physically or emotionally equipped to satisfy women. It's partly a question of subtlety and insight, partly, I'm afraid, simple physiological endurance. When you've done a bit more reading and thinking, Winston, I'm *sure* you'll experience performance anxiety."

She made performance anxiety sound like a really rewarding experience.

"Impotence is easy when you get the hang of it," said the Reader in Anxiety.

"Oh, triffic," said Winston.

"I'd like us all to feel very positive about this," said Rose Marie. "We are ... you and I ... pioneering new insights. Orgasmic dysfunction used to be seen as a pathological

100

condition, something to be treated, something to be cured, something wrong with you. As we move into the nineties, more and more men are going to *achieve* impotence, *learn* to keep themselves to themselves, enjoy and openly celebrate sexual abstinence."

"Blimey," said Winston. "I felt fine when I came in tonight, you know? Now, I dunno, it's like I can hardly raise a smile."

"You've worked *very* well, Winston," said Rose generously. "You all have."

She looked at her watch.

"Right, I think that's about as far as we can go this evening. Next week, we'll talk about things we don't like about our bodies, and watch some videos about cervical cancer."

Stephen had had a very tiring day, he realized. He hadn't exactly flogged his guts out at Senate, but the sheer effort of staying alert and trying to understand things had exhausted him. So he had anticipated his drink, or drinks, as they turned out to be, with Grete Grotowska, with very mixed feelings. However, here he was in the bar with her, and so far things seemed to be going quite well. She didn't seem to hate him, she didn't seem to be frightened of him, and while she still seemed very tense, and looked up sharply at the door every time it swung open, and had smoked seven cigarettes, or parts of them, in an hour, she seemed to be more or less content in his company. She had drunk two glasses of white wine, he had drunk two halves of bitter, and he hadn't the faintest idea of what was going on, but it seemed on the whole all right. Most of the time they had talked about other people in the bar. She had been brilliant, witty, and rather cruel about them; he had been kind, informative, and probably very boring about them. And now here they were. In a silence. Looking at each other. And, for the first time, she had got her grin working.

"You think I smoke too much?" she said, stubbing out rather more than half of cigarette number eight. "Disgusting person, eh?"

"Well what d'you expect a doctor to say? Actually though, I don't find it disgusting."

"Big relief," she said, and actually looked as if she meant it. Stephen, for no reason that he could think of, remembered a girl he had gone out with in the sixth form who had smoked a lot and who had been, or seemed, quite wonderful. He hadn't thought about her for ten years, but now he did. Jill Jump, that was her name. He started to tell Grete about her, then stopped, embarrassed.

"More," said Grete. She was smiling. Stephen felt very strange, as if he was getting dragged backwards into some kind of falling in love that he ought to stay away from, some kind of out-of-control feeling that had to do with people who smoked a lot and made him suffer, people like Jill Jump and Grete Grotowska.

"She only went out with me a few times," he said. "I think it was just to annoy her real boyfriend. She was a bit out of my class. Well, we'd go to the pictures, and sit in the back and she'd smoke, and then she'd lean over and kiss me. And I'd breathe in her smoke, and her scent ... and, *her*, I suppose. She tasted so ... amazingly grown up."

Grete leaned over the table and kissed him briefly on the mouth.

"You. Person," she said.

"I just don't know what you want from me," said Stephen.

"I don't know that either," she said. She was looking at him very seriously. "People, eh? Listen. I like you and you make me feel safe. You're too straight, I'm afraid I'm going to get bored with you and hurt you. But I think you're a good person, will that do for now?"

Someone came through the swing doors and she turned her head sharply, then relaxed.

"Look, there *is* something the matter, isn't there?" said Stephen.

She smiled. "Not your problem."

It was No. 6's turn to do the early check on the bar that evening, always a popular duty. Never any trouble in the early evening, just a chance for a quick half and a chat with the barman. No. 6 noted the women's karate group quietly supping their orange juices and pints of milk, the members of the professorial poker school limbering up over a few malt whiskies, and the doctor talking to the Pole again, well that was one for the boys with the dark-blue suits, nothing to do with No. 6. He put down his glass, nodded to the barman, and went out into the pleasantly chilly air. Light still on in the VC's office. Buggers for work, these Yanks.

"I'm ... very flattered that you take an interest in the work, Vice-Chancellor," said Rose Marie.

"Hey," said the Vice-Chancellor. "*Jack*. OK?"

Jack Daniels looked more like Jack tonight than the Vice-Chancellor. He had taken time out at six to swim forty lengths of the pool, and had changed into sweatshirt, slacks and sneakers. Rose had slipped home to change into something black, loose and practical from Warehouse, she didn't quite know why: Rose had an instinct, and she liked to follow it, and it seemed that tonight her intuition, as usual, had been the right one. There was a certain piquancy in the air.

"I guess what it is, Rose," said Jack, brushing back that boyish lock of hair, "I guess everybody's valuable but some people are special. I'd like to help you develop your role in the university, Rose." And now his bright-blue eyes were looking directly into hers. "And I'd like to get to know you better."

Dr Rose Marie lowered her eyes modestly, then looked up again.

"Don't you think there might be ... certain problems there?"

"Every problem's an opportunity in disguise," said the Vice-Chancellor.

"I shouldn't really be here now," she said.

"No? Where should you be now?"

"With the Women's Group," she said. "Reclaiming the night. Women don't find this university a very reassuring place at night, Jack, despite your security force. If they could see me now, they'd think I was ... flirting with the enemy."

103

Jack smiled.

"Yeah?"

"It's strange how ... *shy* I feel in this office," she said softly. "You have ... such a big desk, Jack."

"It is kinda big," said Jack modestly.

"I was wondering ... I know you're awfully busy, but I thought you might come round to my flat one evening. I know you'll think I'm silly, but I'd find it much less ... daunting there. We could have a proper talk. Oh dear, I'm being presumptuous, aren't I? You couldn't spare a whole evening just to talk to me."

"I guess I might find a window in my diary, Rose," said the Vice-Chancellor.

By ten o'clock, the university bar was packed. The rugger types were two-deep at the bar. One big table was dominated by the Women's Group, all ready with the banners and hockey sticks to reclaim the night at closing time. At another table, Dr J. G. McCannon was engaged in serious conversation with another, smaller group of activists, who included Sammy Limb and his fierce girlfriend Allie. And, rather to his surprise, Stephen was still sitting at the little corner table with his puzzling Polish friend. Perhaps because of the noise, they had moved closer together, his head only a few inches from her small dark neat head. He could inhale her smoke, her scent, well ... *her*, he supposed. And he was actually feeling something rather like happy.

"It's all right, this, though, isn't it?" he said. "People still manage to have a nice time. I'm having a nice time. Are you having a nice time?"

"Not bad," she said.

"Old Jock McCannon thinks Lowlands is a little police state, full of evil conspiracies. Good Lord, there he is now. Looks happy enough. And here we are. Safe and warm. Two friends having a quiet drink."

She looked at him seriously.

"You're really my friend?"

"Well, of course I am. Look, what is it, Grete?"

"He's found out where I am," she said. She was biting her lip again.

104

"Who?"

"My husband. Antoine."

"But ... he's in France, isn't he?"

"He says he's coming over to see me. I don't want to see him."

"Oh," said Stephen. "Well, can't you just tell him to get lost? That's what women do with me. Seems quite easy."

He realized as he was speaking that he had had quite a few drinks.

"I think he wants to kill me, Stephen."

"Oh, look," he said. "Surely not. You're exaggerating, surely. Aren't you?"

Suddenly her face was closed against him. "Yeah. Hysterical Polish person. It's all right. Forget about it. I have to go now. Thank you for the drinks. I had a nice time, don't worry."

She stood up and started to pull on her black mac.

"But look," he said, "where are you going? You ... I mean you can't just tell me something like that and then disappear."

"You think?" she said. "Watch this."

She turned and walked towards the door. When she had got halfway there, she turned, and came back to the table.

"Smoky kiss," she said, and for a brief moment her mouth was on his again. "Nasty, eh?"

She turned and walked out of the bar.

Bob Buzzard was bright and early next morning. He strode cheerfully through the waiting room, already full of malcontents and malingerers. Never mind. If things went well tonight, he'd be into a different class of client altogether. Right, let's check out the Body Lab; he wanted everything absolutely squeaky clean for the big night.

He opened the door and went in. Oh, Lord, they were all in his Body Lab mucking things up, the whole useless shower. Dickie Dado and the dyke were fiddling about with his glossy brochures and the mad old fart was giving himself a coronary on an exercise bike.

"Oh, my God," said Bob. "Off there, please, Jock, we

105

don't know where you've been. This is sensitive equipment, I really must insist my lab be out of bounds to casual loiterers."

"Have a care there, my dear fellow," wheezed Jock, as Bob lugged at his collar.

"It is your personal private laboratory now, is it Bob?" said Stephen.

"Oh, sorry, Stephen. Didn't see you there," said Bob, wiping the saddle free of any lingering traces of McCannon. "Well. You know. Bit on edge. Big night tonight."

Oh, God. Now the old fart was mucking about with the brand new spotless white towelling wraps.

"What rinky-dinky little dressing gowns," said Jock, holding up one of them against his horrible old body. "Tell me, Bob, will *you* be wearing one of these? May I come and take some candid snaps with my little Polaroid?"

"I'd be extremely obliged, Jock," said Bob, taking the robe from him and throwing it in the linen basket, "if you'd keep well away tonight. You could give a stressed executive a very nasty turn."

"Have no fear," said the old fart. "I have a prior engagement."

"That's a relief," said Bob.

The uppity dyke picked up one of the brochures and started to read aloud from it.

"Lowlands University Stress Management Services. A *Robert Buzzard Clinic*?"

"Thank you, Rose," he said, taking it from her. "Er, look, Rose . . . ."

"It's all right, Robert," she said sweetly. "I too have another engagement."

"Fine, excellent."

"I'm free this evening, Bob," said Stephen.

"Ah. Did actually want a private word with you, Stephen."

"Come on through," said Stephen.

"The thing is, buddy," said Bob, pacing up and down, "I've put a lot of personal investment into this thing tonight."

"Financial investment?" said Stephen, startled.

"Good Lord, no, never use your own money. But some things are more important than money. Time, talent, aspirations, dreams. Got some of the top business talent in the region coming in to sample the facilities. Look, old buddy. I . . . well, I'd like this to be my show. You do understand?"

"Bob, of course I do."

"Robert?"

"Robert."

"Take it as a personal favour if you could show up at the start, five minutes hello and welcome as head of the practice, then over to Buzzard, Daker off home for an early night."

"I'd be delighted, Bo – er, Robert. And I do wish you the very best of luck," said Stephen.

Night was falling, and the air was twittering and crackling with the benisons of safety and security as Mr Sweet monitored the start of the night watch from his little office high in the Poulson Tower.

"Control to all personnel. Special alert on Experimental Psychology tonight, Five and Seven to be permanently on hand with the woofers, regular hourly back-up checks by Seventeen through Twenty-five. Late call requested by the Health Centre, that'll be you, Alistair. And best be on your toes gentlemen, because tonight Mr Sweet will be going walkabout in person, over and out."

A lorry stopped on the perimeter road to drop off a hitch-hiker. The hitch-hiker was about twenty-five years old. He was dark, unshaven, not very clean, and strikingly handsome. He watched the lorry's lights recede into the distance, and took a flat bottle from an inside pocket in his battered leather jacket and drank from it. Then he pushed his way through a low hedge and walked towards the dark bulk of the central complex.

"That's the number, Charlie," said Jack Daniels, handing him a little card. "Don't give it to anyone else."

"OK, Jack," said Charlie Dusenberry. "Have good meeting." His face was quite expressionless.

"It's my very pleasant duty as Director of the Health Centre," said Stephen, "to welcome you to this inaugural session of the Lowlands Stress Management Clinic."

He was speaking in the reception area of the Health Centre, largely for the benefit of the clients, who were tidily disposed about the pastel-covered space-capsule seating units. Professors Bunn, Eugenides and Skinnard (of Experimental Psychology) represented academia, and opposite them sat three well-fed and not particularly stressed-looking company directors. Mrs Kramer and Maureen Gahagan were in brand new uniforms for the occasion, and standing behind them were the three freelances Bob had brought in to help out. Their names were Suzanne, Glenys and Linda, and their white overalls were cut slightly short. Bob himself was wearing a strikingly smart new suit. It was a shame that he had cut himself shaving. But all in all, things looked very promising for Stress Management.

"This is one of the ways," Stephen went on, "in which we're developing and extending concepts of health care within the university, and also reaching out into the community at large. We're very grateful for your participation; you'll be making a real contribution to health research. And also, I'm quite sure, benefiting personally from the individualized and – he assures me – quite painless diagnostic and treatment modules that Dr Buzzard is pioneering. And now I'll hand you over to Bo – er, Dr Buzzard and his team."

"Thank you, Stephen," said Bob, smiling in a rather savage way. "I'll just introduce the *ladies*: Carmen, our administrator, Maureen our senior nurse, and last but not least: Glenys, Suzanne and Linda."

"Hi," said Suzanne, rather brazenly. Linda, who was tiny, Oriental and exquisite, giggled. Professor Bunn stared at her in some bemusement, but Salop, one of the company directors, started to perk up considerably.

"We're going to look after you," said Bob. "And I think we can promise you a night to remember."

108

Outside on the dark campus, security men waited patiently with their patient Alsatians, the Women's Group patrolled the perimeter paths with their banners and hockey sticks, and two nuns rustled and fluttered like great crows in the dark shadowy chasms between the hushed teaching blocks. And outside the Art History building, a young woman in a black mac was quarrelling fiercely with a young man in a battered leather jacket. He was shouting in French and she was shouting in English and Polish; he complained that she treated him like a piece of shit, she said she didn't want to treat him like anything, she didn't want to see him, she didn't want to hear from him, she didn't love him any more. He took hold of her arm and yelled at her to speak French when she spoke to him; she said she didn't know any French, she had forgotten French, she had forgotten him.

"*Biche*!" yelled Antoine, and hit Grete hard in the face with his free hand. She cried out with pain and kicked him very hard in the knee. He gasped and let go of her arm for a moment, and she ran away into the darkness.

"Grete!" he shouted after her. "I kill you for this! I love you!"

As Grete ran past the Women's Vigilante Group, they were already moving at a disciplined trot towards Antoine. He tried to run through the group to get to Grete and kill her, or love her, but he didn't get past the first woman, who caught him just under the nose with the heel of her hand and knocked him flat on his back. He sat up gingerly and felt his face. His nose was bleeding. He looked at the Women's Vigilante Group. The leader, who had knocked him down, was a good six inches taller and two stone heavier than him, and one or two of the others were even bigger.

"Come on," said one of them. "Let's get the bastard."

"*Merde*," said Antoine, severely alarmed. He scrambled up, turned, and fled towards the dark shape of the Engineering building.

It was very quiet and peaceful in Rose Marie's tasteful flat. Jack Daniels sat on the sofa, his jacket off, his tie loosened, having good meeting.

"Great to unwind, Rose," he said as she handed him a cut-crystal tumbler with whisky and ice in it.

He sipped.

"Hey," he said, impressed.

"Wild Turkey," she said softly. "Did I guess right?"

"You can get it here?"

"It wasn't easy," she admitted.

"Just for me?"

She did something with her shoulders and her mouth that was halfway between a shrug and a promise. Then she came and sat down by him on the sofa. Their knees were almost but not quite touching.

"Jack," she said. "When you talked about developing my role, what kind of thing did you have in mind?"

"I guess it depends a lot on you, Rose. Which way you feel you'd like to go."

"Really," she said.

"We're thinking of creating one or two new posts," he said casually. "We don't have a Dean of Women at this moment in time ... but I don't know, Rose ... maybe you're more into working with men right now?"

"I am, Jack," she said, her whole body expressing a deep inner conviction about working with men in ways that Jack could scarcely imagine, though he felt he had one or two initial clues. "But there's really no conflict. It's *because* I'm a woman that I find working with men so ... rewarding. They need so much help just now."

In her enthusiasm, she had moved much closer to him, and without being aware of it (of *course* she wasn't aware of it) she had put her hand on his knee.

"It's terribly important for men to adjust, Jack. Now that the days of the casual screw have gone for ever."

"Right. Yeah," said Jack. His tone was perhaps a shade less enthusiastic than hers.

"I knew you'd understand," she said.

"It's ... kinda sad, though, in a way," said the Vice-Chancellor. "Hell, I'm not thinking about our generation, but all those kids, just starting out on their sexual lives."

The hand she was so unaware of was stroking his knee now.

110

"What I'm trying to show them, Jack, is that there are all sorts of rewarding alternatives they may not have considered. What's that phrase of yours? Every problem is an opportunity in disguise?"

"I like your thinking, Rose," he said.

The telephone rang in the bedroom, and she went to answer it. He could see her through the doorway as she spoke, and she could see him, and their eyes were on each other throughout the brief conversation.

"Oh, *Grete*," said Rose. "I'm *awfully* sorry. I'm completely tied up this evening ... it wasn't anything urgent, was it?"

She listened for a few moments, smiling at Jack through the open door, and said: "Let's have coffee tomorrow – eleven in the coffee bar? ... Lovely. Bye, Grete."

Then she put the phone down.

"Well," she said to Jack Daniels.

Grete hung the phone up in the dank smelly little callbox outside the Students' Union, and started to cry again. She was bleeding from the cut over her eye where Antoine's signet ring had caught her, she was very frightened, and she could think of nowhere to go. Faintly, in the distance, she could hear him still shouting her name. But she could not be sure of the direction.

Peter Wagstaff and Patrick Donnelan were standing outside the Experimental Psychology building, warming their legs against two big furry Alsatians, and listening to the distant chanting of the Women's Vigilante Group.

"Students," said Patrick. "I tell you something, Peter. This dog here has more brains in his head than the lot of them put together."

"What time is it?" said Peter Wagstaff. "I'm ever so hungry."

"He also has a very strong sex drive," said Patrick. "But it's been trained out of him."

Peter Wagstaff sighed.

Less than a hundred yards away, in the shadow of the Engineering block, Jock McCannon, Allie Simpson and Sammy Limb were watching them.

111

"Am I to fight with wolves, then, in the evening of my days?"

"Oh, God," said Allie. "Why did we let him in on this? The whole *point* is opposing violence to animals."

"They mostly sneak off about ten, Doc, have a crafty nosh round the back of the canteen. That's when we go in." Sammy shivered.

"Ah. And what if they are unmoved by pangs of hunger?"

Sammy held up a bag.

"We've got some aniseed. Might work."

"I should be happy to assist you there, Sammy. Laying false trails is more my style these days than breaking and entering," said Jock.

In the distance, someone was howling: "Grete! Grete!"

Diagnosis and testing were nearly completed in the Lowlands Stress Laboratory. Salop was still on the treadmill, fine round belly hanging down over boxer shorts, and various parts of him wired up to machines, and Bunn was still stepping wearily on and off a bench. But the rest of the clients were relaxing in their fluffy white dressing gowns, waiting for the treatment stage, half hypnotized by the jolly flashing lights and machines chattering out printout.

"Excellent, Mr Salop," boomed Bob, "you're in fantastic shape, we'll have the full analysis soon." God, he thought, I've seen some horrible sights in my life. "Linda! Where's little Linda?"

"Here I am, Dr Buzzard."

Bob spoke to her slowly and clearly; he was always considerate about foreigners and their problems. He took her by her delicate little Oriental hand and pointed to Eugenides.

"Linda, would you take that gentleman over there, no hair on head, see? To the *relaxation lounge*. Big big room. Many sofas."

"What a wally, eh?" said Linda as she passed Maureen. She took Professor Eugenides by the hand, giggling prettily, and led him out.

Maureen went over to Suzanne, who was measuring drops

of pink liquid from a glass dropper into glasses of a clear fluid.

"Everything OK Suzanne?"

"Just wondering when we start work," said Suzanne, rather puzzlingly.

"You're an agency nurse, right? Is the money good?"

Suzanne shrugged.

"Six hundred in a good week."

"No! Where d'you train?"

"Just sort of picked it up as I went along," said Suzanne, taking the tray out to the relaxation lounge.

"Mr Sweet to all personnel. There is something on the go tonight. I do not like the smell of things. Alex to take over at Control. I am coming down."

He slid open his drawer, and took out the holster with the Magnum in it.

Grete was running across the open campus.

"Grete! Grete!"

She stumbled, fell, scrambled up, ran on.

"Grete!"

There was only one place she could think of now.

Stephen had decided to take Bob Buzzard's advice. An early night seemed like a good idea. He was in the middle of cleaning his teeth when the doorbell rang. Cursing mildly, he went to open it, and Grete fell into his arms, breathless, weeping, her face streaked with blood and dirt.

"He's here, he knows where I live, he's seen me, I couldn't think of anywhere else to go!"

"You've hurt yourself," he said. She felt so thin, and she was shaking. "Come on, let me have a look."

He led her into the bathroom and sat her on the stool. She submitted docilely to having her head bathed, clinging tightly to his free hand.

"It's just a graze," he said, "but you're going to have a nasty bruise. How did you get this?"

"Antoine," she said.

"He hit you?"

"So amazing? You don't ever hit women?"

"No, I don't."

She started to tremble again.

"Hey," he said. "You're all right now. You're safe."

She leant her head into him and he put his arms round her.

"Can I stay here tonight please?" she said indistinctly.

"Yes, of course you can."

"I won't come in your bed."

"No, of course not. You didn't think I was expecting that?"

"People sometimes do, it's not so very strange. You're a nice man, I think." She was pushing her head against his shoulder, rubbing against him.

"Look, um ... shouldn't we phone the police or something?" he said after a little while.

"No, I don't want them," she said. "Can we please stay here like this for a little while?"

"Yes. Yes, of course," he said. Yes. That'd be fine.

The Stress Management clients found the pink muscle relaxant surprisingly pleasant: Professor Bunn pronounced it not altogether unlike a pink gin, and called for another round. Then Dr Buzzard explained the next phase of the treatment.

"We now move on to in-depth individual work," he said. "Research-based massage. I hope to demonstrate to you this evening, with the help of my expert team, how we can reduce stress and tension levels to an unprecedented low. Now you can't get this on the National Health, obviously, but I would draw to your attention that the Lowlands team are available at attractive rates on company and private individual health plans. Pukka medical expenses, no queries on the credit card, no problems with the little woman. And totally *safe*. Those of you with large export interests, and this'll be of interest to you as well, Professor Eugenides ... I can arrange reciprocal facilities in the States, throughout Europe and in the Far East. No more need to wonder what the overseas reps are up to. Well, that's enough from me. Any of you who feel you need a little more muscle relaxant, by all means avail yourselves. And now it's over to Glenys, Suzanne and Linda."

"OK boys," said Suzanne, smiling invitingly. "Who's going to be first?"

Antoine Dupont was having a terrible time at Lowlands University. Drunk, deranged, in fear of his life from the *femmes sauvages*, exhausted, lost and lonely, he wandered alone on the dark campus, calling for Grete. He loved her so much. He hated her so much. She didn't love him any more. Life was *merde*. He would find her, and kill her, he thought. Then no other *salaud* would be able to have her. His bottle was almost empty. He tilted it and let the last drops gurgle down his throat.

"Snap!"

He cried out. It was an apparition, a ghostly *vieillard* in a huge cape, grinning at him with horrible yellow teeth, and raising a bottle to his lips in mocking salute. Was it Death?

"*Fous le con, vieillard*!" He put his arm across his face. He was too tired to run any more.

"Ah," said Jock. "You must be one of our overseas students. You seem distressed, my dear fellow."

"I have lost my woman," said Antoine. "People try to kill me. I think I kill myself. But first, I kill someone else. Perhaps I kill you, old man."

"Yes, yes, perhaps," said Jock, putting an arm round his shoulders. "Let's have a drink together and talk about it. I feel that what you lack is a sense of purpose, a mission in life ... as for women, there are many women in this very university ... a fine young fellow like yourself should have no problem ... look, here are some women now!"

It was the *femmes sauvages*, closing on him at a steady trot.

"There he is! Get the bastard!"

"*Merde*!" gasped Antoine, and found he had the strength to run after all.

"Not that way, my dear fellow!" shouted Jock.

*

Suddenly Prince was growling and tugging on the lead, hackles up, teeth bared.

"Bugger me!" said Patrick.

Some sod in a leather jacket was trying to get into Experimental Psychology.

"Oy! You!"

Antoine, flinging himself desperately against the reinforced glass doors, saw them, turned, and ran round the side of the building. The dogs were close behind.

"Now!" hissed Allie. "Go go go!"

"I want to go to the lav!" said Sammy.

She hit him across the side of the head. "*Go!*"

They ran round to the side door, Sammy did the business, and they were in.

Bloody good job I decided to go walkabout, thought Sweet to himself. Everything's gone to pot here. He spoke into his walkie-talkie.

"Number One to control. Experimental Psychology appears to be unmanned. Proceeding to investigate."

And then he saw him. The old feller. It had been the old feller at the bottom of it the whole time. It was down to Sweet, that was. He should have moved sooner. Well, he'd get the old bastard now.

"Hey! You! What have you got in that bag?"

Jock lurched into a lumbering trot, away into the darkness.

"Stop! Armed Security Guard!" He struggled with his harness. *Bugger* that bloody mail order firm.

And then suddenly the entrance of Experimental Psychology was ablaze with lights, all the alarms were jangling like buggery, and oh no, there they were, *beagles*, looked like a whole pack of them, running out of the front door and scattering in all directions.

"Halt! Halt!" yelled No. 1 to the beagles.

Oh, my God.

She stood in the doorway of the bedroom, peering into the

darkness, in her black vest and pants, with the quilt draped over her shoulders. He was sound asleep. Quietly she walked over to the bed, pulled back the cover, and got in with him, snuggling up tight.

"What?" he said.

"Ssh," she whispered. "Go to sleep."

He turned and flung his arm round her. Hello, Lyn. No, Grete. Funny. Work it out logically. No. Too sleepy.

"You smell nice," he said. "Hey. Not supposed to be in here you know."

"Ssh. So much noise out there. I couldn't sleep. I just come in your bed for a sleep. OK?"

"Mm," he said.

"No funny business."

"No."

"You don't mind?"

"No."

"OK. Now you and me have a good sleep."

She cuddled into him, purring.

"Grete."

"Sleep."

"Yes. All right."

Out in the night campus, all was noise and confusion. Searchlights and torchlights sliced through the darkness, picking up bizarre stroboscopic flashes of the bright brown and white beagles bunching and wheeling, drunk on fresh air; a desperate scarecrow figure in a battered leather jacket stumbling away from a grim squad with hockey sticks and banners; a frail figure in motorcycle gear running for his distant abandoned bike; two men in uniform being dragged across the grass by two powerful German Shepherds. The security cameras on the corners of the dark buildings swivelled their long necks wildly this way and that, deranged and disorientated.

Jock McCannon, his greatcoat flapping, was loping away from the lights towards the sanctuary of the Health Centre, carrying a plastic shopping bag from which something was leaking. Behind him the sharp yelps and shouts of the

117

beagles changed to a strange, semi-musical sound, an extravagant baroque keening, as if they had burst fresh from a weekend workshop at the Alternative Music Centre. They had picked up the aniseed trail.

Jock turned and saw them coming.

"Pour on! Pour on! I will endure!" he boomed hoarsely to the cold inimical moon.

Then he thought better of it, and took to his heels again.

As the searchlight swung round, the head of security caught a glimpse of the flapping greatcoat and the buoyant boisterous white sterns of the beagles.

"That's him! That's him! After him, lads!"

No one responded.

"Number One to Control. Number One to Control. Come in Alex!"

Nothing. Bloody cut-price Taiwan technology. He stared round. No support. Only a couple of nuns standing quietly, twenty yards away, regarding him with benign interest.

"Oh, my God," said Sweet to the nuns. "I've got to take the bastard out myself."

It was very peaceful in the Relaxation Lounge of the Stress Clinic. The managing director of Eastern Universal Nipples was relaxing in his fluffy robe on one couch, Professor Bunn of English Literature was snoring peacefully on another. Mrs Kramer was watching over them from behind the counter, and calculating her overtime, which looked very satisfactory indeed, when the door burst open and Dr McCannon staggered in, surrounded by a lot of noisy brown and white dogs. *Such* a character, Dr McCannon, *such* an eccentric; one had to remind oneself how distinguished he was.

"*Do* go through, Dr McCannon, I'm sure Dr Buzzard would be delighted to see you, but perhaps your, er pets should wait outside ...? Oh, I see, well I'm sure you know best."

With a hoarse cry, Jock stumbled through the connecting door and vanished into the Body Lab corridor. The dogs went with him.

"That's Dr McCannon himself, you know," she explained to the gaping nipple manufacturer. "We *are* in luck tonight!"

The main door opened again. Nothing happened for a second or two, and then Mrs Kramer found herself staring down the barrel of a .45 Magnum, held in both hands by the sweating, trembling, wild-eyed head of security.

"I'm *so* sorry, Mr Sweet," she said. "It's a private clinic tonight. Perhaps you'd like to make an appointment?"

Sweet advanced on her, gibbering and slavering. Mrs Kramer made an executive decision.

"Well, in the circumstances, perhaps you'd better go through."

She pressed the buzzer, and the door opened.

Bob Buzzard had supervised the start of the research-based massage, but after a while he'd judged it best to leave it to Suzanne and the other totties; they seemed to know what they were doing all right. He went back to the Body Lab and poured himself a stiff muscle relaxant. Best to stick with what you know.

"I find it all rather sad, Maureen," he said in what he hoped was a worldly way. "But then I'm in love with my wife. We all have to be broad-minded these days."

The door opened and the head of security came in with a gun in both hands.

"Freeze!" yelled the head of security.

Maureen froze. Bob Buzzard collapsed smoothly on to the carpet in a dead faint. And Mr Sweet went through into the massage room.

The massage room had low lights, soft music, a scented atmosphere. Suzanne and Linda were working with dedicated ingenuity on Mr Salop of Eurochips (UK) and Professor Eugenides of the Overseas Development Board, creating a soothing symphony of sound blended from Linda's musical giggle, Eugenides' appreciative grunts, and the slap and slither of soft hands on oiled flesh.

"Turn over now, Professor," said Suzanne softly. "That's it. Oh, *what* a big boy!"

119

The door opened.

"Down on the floor, the lot of you!" yelled Sweet.

Linda and Suzanne screamed and backed away. Salop raised a trembling hand. And Professor Eugenides reared up, clutched his throat, and tumbled off the massage table with a horrible gurgling sound.

Sweet stared appalled. Who were these people? What had he done? Where was the master-criminal, the old feller? Something had gone horribly wrong.

Maureen Gahagan marched in and surveyed the scene, hands on hips.

"Now look what you've done!" she said crossly. "You've only killed Professor Eugenides!"

Sweet felt his knees buckling. There was nothing he could do about it. The gun slipped from his hands, and he slid slowly down the wall and sat on the floor.

"I didn't mean to, honest," he said.

The door opened and Jock came in, spruced up, dignified, master of the situation.

"Eh, what seems to be the problem, Nurse?"

"Heart, I think, Doctor," said Maureen, on the floor with the patient.

"Fine, fine," rumbled Jock. "Stand clear." He bunched his fists together and brought them down solidly into the patient's fat brown oily chest.

"Who – who are you?" gasped the head of security.

"J. G. McCannon, senior consultant physician. How fortunate I happened to drop by!"

In Dr Rose Marie's bedroom, the Vice-Chancellor and the Director of the Male Sexuality Workshop were exploring post-modernist alternative strategies and disguised opportunities. The session had proved both creative and rewarding; but it had involved some formidable conceptual leaps for the Vice-Chancellor, and he was experiencing a little residual culture lag. He tried to articulate this to Rose as he lay comfortably with his head pillowed in her lap.

"I guess I feel kinda strange ... maybe Europe's different from the States. Don't get me wrong, Rose, I'm having a swell time ...."

120

"I'm glad."

"But, ah, well ... I kinda thought we'd ... get it on, you know?"

"Oh, Jack," she whispered. "We *are* getting it on."

"We are?"

It was time, Rose judged, to move into another gear. After all, sex as a purely conceptual art was a difficult *Gestalt* to encompass in one go, even for a mind as agile as Jack Daniels's.

"Listen, Jack," she said softly, allowing her fingers to wander absent-mindedly, as it were, over some crucial areas of mutual interest. "I'm going to tell you a secret. Normally, I only respond emotionally to women. Does that shock you?"

"It ... surprises me a little, I guess."

"It takes a very unusual kind of man, Jack, to interest me. A very rare and special kind of man. Someone who has the ... formidable phallic power I sense in you, Jack."

"Really?" said the Vice-Chancellor.

"Well," she said, almost bashfully. "I *mean* ..."

And the evidence, indeed, was undeniable.

"Oh, *yes*," said Rose reverently.

The telephone rang, and she leaned over and picked it up.

"Hello? ... It's for you, Jack."

Jack took the phone.

"Shoot. Charlie, this is a bad time."

He listened to Charlie for a few moments.

"OK Charlie, I'll be right there."

He put the phone down.

"Ah, *shoot*."

"You have to leave now?"

"I guess."

"Oh, dear," said Rose Marie. "It seems such a shame to ... leave things up in the air."

The Arts Council Fellow in Creative Writing was going like the clappers, his stubby yellow-stained fingers flying over the keys. The beagles were everywhere, wonderful jolly mindless noisy gambollers, charging through the Medical

Centre, crashing through the Engineering block, disrupting and exploding the dead routines of the soulless swamp, swashbuckling symbols of the unconquerable power of the suppressed wish. He flung himself back in the chair, pressed the button, and lit a Camel as the printer chattered away. The door flew open, and a dozen beagles ran into Rust's little room, leaping on to his bed, knocking over his table and chair, engulfing him in a flurry of rich warm fur and scrabbling claws, and – his last glimpse as he disappeared beneath them – chewing up his episode.

Sammy managed to get to his bike and start it up. Then he saw the poor bastard in the leather jacket stumbling towards him pursued by six big women and a couple of Alsatians. Sammy had a kind heart.

"Here you are, mate, hop on!" he said.

Antoine hit him hard on the side of the head with an empty bottle, and Sammy fell off. Antoine got on the bike and roared off. Sammy sat up and tried to explain he hadn't meant it like that, but then he felt very poorly and fell back again.

Jack Daniels, gunning the big Mercedes fast along the perimeter road, saw the single headlight bump and swerve into his path. He braked and swerved. The motorbike clipped the offside wing of the car and went into the ditch. The Vice-Chancellor drove on. In the ditch, Antoine lay very still under the motorbike, the wheel still spinning.

It was dawn. The grass was littered with abandoned banners and bottles. Down by the lake, an Alsatian was playing happily with half a dozen beagles. Near the Psychology block, Sammy Limb sat up groggily and felt the lump on the side of his head. Two nuns were watching him with benign interest. In the ditch by the perimeter road, a man awoke to find himself lying pinned under a motorbike.

"*Merde*," said Antoine Dupont.

*

122

Stephen opened his eyes. He was lying in his own bed with Dr Grete Grotowska, and they had their arms round each other. How very extraordinary.

"Good morning," she said. "Did you have a good sleep?"

"Yes," he said. "I had a wonderful sleep."

He was remembering now. He reached up and touched the bruise on her eyebrow.

"How about you?"

"Best sleep for a long time."

"Well," he said. "Now what?"

The telephone rang and he reached for it.

"Yes, sure," he said. "In half an hour? Nothing to panic about, is there? Good. Right. See you then."

"Work?" she said.

"Yes, work," he said.

"Can I wait for you here?"

"Yes," he said. "Yes, of course you can."

On the perimeter road, a lorry slowed down and stopped to pick up a groggy, dishevelled looking hitch-hiker in a brown leather jacket. Antoine Dupont had had enough of Lowlands University.

Stephen strode into the Health Centre, whistling. To his surprise, they were all there waiting for him. Rose looked concerned and sisterly, Maureen and Mrs Kramer both looked dog tired for some reason, Bob was twitching, but old Jock for once looked on top of the world.

"Morning," said Stephen. "Lovely day, isn't it? How did it all go last night?"

Jock cleared his throat. "Well . . . ."

RUST'S PECULIAR FEELING

"It's very nice, Ron," says Ken Riddington.

"Really?"

"Very nice indeed. Lovely. We all love it. Jonathan loves it. David loves it."

"Has David seen it then?"

"Well, no, he hasn't actually seen it yet, but he's going to love it."

"Oh, good," says Rust. "What's the problem, then?"

"Well, you know what the problem is. We can't possibly *do* it, that's what the problem is. Far too expensive. That's why I can't show it to David. You know what he's like. If he sees it, he'll want to do it, just as it stands."

"Well, let him see it then."

"Come on, Ron. Be your age."

Rust doesn't like people telling him to be his age. It reminds him how old he is. He's not as old as Ken, but he's old for a series writer. Most series writers are dead at Rust's age. David Tucker, the director, is younger than Rust. (Well, most people are.) David Tucker likes crane shots and helicopter shots and crowd scenes and montages and wildly expensive dream sequences, and he sulks when Riddington won't let him do them, which is nearly always. Rust likes all these things too, and he likes Tucker, even when he's sulking. Tucker has artistic integrity, and he likes to spend money, too. Ken hates spending money, his own or the BBC's. That is why Rust is conducting his end of this script conference from a dank and smelly pay-phone in Kennedy Hall. Ken has realized that even at peak morning rates, it works out much cheaper than getting Rust up to town and probably getting stuck for a pizza in the Hat Shop or a pie in the Bush.

"What is it, Ken? Is it the beagles?"

"No, it's not specifically the beagles. I should think we could run to a few beagles, Ron," says Riddington generously.

Rust smiles to himself. Riddington is being more generous than he thinks. Clearly he does not know beagles. It's not that they're expensive to acquire, it's what they're like when you've got them. Rust used to own a beagle in his Wolverhampton days, the days of his very first marriage. On one memorable afternoon this beagle, whose name was Daniels, sexually assaulted his wife, the cat next door and a Habitat sag-bag; and ate a Christmas cake, a transistor radio and a Polaroid camera. Rust is looking forward to being on location when they film the beagles.

"So what is it then?"

"It's the whole thing, Ron," says Riddington helpfully. "All that night shooting, all those *people* ... you realize you've gone and written *lines* for half of them?"

Rust knows what he means. Every time a minor character opens his mouth it costs Ken a couple of hundred quid. Ken has really got to like the nuns, except that their stunts are so expensive. Being a producer is a terrible job. *Everything* costs money.

"Just have a look over it, Ron, before we let Tucker loose on it, eh? Just see if you can make it a bit, well ..."

"Cheaper?"

"That's it, Ron, knew you'd understand. Make it a lot cheaper."

"Anything else?"

"Well ... we did think it was getting a bit sexy. Thought you said no one was going to have it off in this series."

"No one *is* having it off, Ken."

"No, but ... they're not half getting into bed and talking about it, Ron. It's not me, you understand, God knows ... it's just that we want to responsibly reflect the post-AIDS climate."

"You mean you want one of the characters to get AIDS?" says Rust, knowing he's on safe ground. "Look, they can *all* get it if you like, serve 'em right for being doctors. Only thing is, they'd have to have it off first."

"God, no, I didn't mean that, Ron. We just want to be, well, you know, responsible."

"It's all right, Ken. I've got it covered."

"What d'you mean, you've got it covered?"

"Look, there's someone here wants to use the phone," says Rust untruthfully.

"All right, Ron. God bless. Lovely, lovely script. Love to do it just like that, but you know how it is."

Back in his noxious cell, Rust has a brood. He's not sulking. He knew he'd have to make it cheaper. It's the other stuff. Ken's right, in a way. Rust didn't want all that to happen. That Polish girl has let him down, for a start. What does she think she's up to? If Rust were her, he wouldn't trust that doctor farther than he could throw him. And there she goes, creeping into his bed in her little vest and pants; it was all Rust could do to put the mockers on the funny business. Very strange. He doesn't feel quite in control, somehow. It's not as bad as being one of those doctors, but it's starting to get that way. The beagles. Rust really doesn't want to confront that beagles business. For the time being, he is putting it down to the Bells. There are some very nice aspects about not feeling quite in control; a bloke can certainly storm away on the word-processor. But there's a nasty side to it as well. Once or twice lately, Rust has had the uncomfortable feeling that somebody might be writing *him*, the way he's writing the doctors. Some sod like God, someone with that sort of brutal irony.

No, that's not quite right. Rust does not believe in God, for a start. It's something to do with Lowlands University. Here Rust is, in Lowlands University, thinking he's been *writing* Lowlands University. But what if Lowlands University is writing *itself*? What if Lowlands University is writing *Rust*?

Odd, too, that Riddington brought up the AIDS business. For some time now, Rust has had the uncomfortable feeling that the University of Lowlands is developing AIDS. Not the people in it: the university itself. Despite all the busy construction work, all the little men in yellow helmets shoring up the bright façades, all the frantic relocation of departments, all the overseas investment pouring in, Rust has increasingly been aware of odd little cracks and lesions developing in the piazzas and along the walkways. The buildings sweat at night; some of them look feverish. Odd emanations of yellowish steam or smoke ooze at irregular intervals from the gratings. Some of the concrete façades have developed large dark spreading patches like Kaposi's sarcoma. And Rust is aware of strange vibrations everywhere, somewhere just below the normal human hearing threshold. Spine-jarring vibrations, homing in on him. Someone, or something, is after his bone-marrow, he is beginning to think.

Yes; the university must have acquired an immunity deficiency syndrome, and no one is aware of it but Rust. Doesn't this make him doubt his diagnosis? Yes, it does; but then again, it is the nature of the true artist to be super-sensitive to the dark secrets and the bad vibrations, to use the cleft stick of his talent to divine the heart of darkness under the designer cobblestones. Rust feels frightened, he feels inadequate, but he knows he must stay and bear witness.

Besides, the university is paying him and housing him. And a new deadline is looming on the horizon.

4

"BAD VIBRATIONS"

A short unmemorable man was sitting on a low wall with a notebook and pencil, watching two nuns. The nuns were standing over a grating near the parched fountain, as if trying to peer into the darkness below. Every so often, odd emanations of yellowish steam or smoke oozed from the grating. And there was a sound, too. Perhaps not exactly a sound. A low, discordant, spine-jarring vibration, as if some vast organism was out of harmony with itself. Gradually it became louder, more penetrating. It acquired a sort of rhythm: a hesitant, quirky, wrenching sort of rhythm with irregular intervals and frustrating pauses. The nuns began to sway gently to the strange rhythm. Then they were moving, their black boots scraping and stamping on the cobbles, their heads swivelling blindly this way and that. The nuns were dancing.

It was the third morning that Stephen had woken to find Grete Grotowska in his bed, sleeping soundly, her cropped dark head nestling into his shoulder. They had had three nights together, three decorous nights with Stephen in his rather endearing old-fashioned striped pyjamas and Grete in her scratty black vest and pants. Three brilliant sleeps, as Grete put it. But it had been four nights now since the Night of the Beagles when Antoine Dupont had come to Lowlands to kill her, and on the second night, Grete had not slept in Stephen's bed, or in his flat. Stephen couldn't stop thinking about the second night. He knew it would be a mistake to ask her about it. It was nobody's business but her own. She would be angry at the intrusion into her privacy, and if she told him the answer, he wouldn't like hearing it anyway. But he asked her. Though she was angry at the intrusion into her privacy, she told him the answer, and he didn't like hearing it at all. They lay quietly together for a while, and he made up his mind never to intrude into her privacy again. Then he said: "Um ... when you stay with Rose ... do you ... um ...?"

"Do I what?" She was up on one elbow now, her angry little cat face full of contempt. "Do I sleep in her bed, do we take off our clothes, do we make love, do we have it off, is this what's bothering you? Do you think this is any of your business?"

"No," he said. "You're quite right. I'm sorry. Forget it. Let's talk about something else."

"I sleep in her bed," she said. "I don't have any funny business with her. Now you know."

"Thank you," he said. Suddenly he felt fine again.

Grete got out of bed and stood over him, glaring down angrily.

"Look at you, so pleased because someone else isn't getting where you want to be. Listen, I don't *want* any of that stuff, I don't want people getting in my body and try to make me come and angry when I don't, and hit me, and cry, and go on to me, on to me, who did you see, where did you go, I don't *want* that, I *told* you that, I thought we were having nice peaceful time, but now I think you are lying there thinking how can I get in her body and give her a bad time!"

"No, I'm *not*!" He sat up, feeling aggrieved and insulted. "And don't you think it's a bit bloody arrogant, this assumption of yours that everyone fancies you, everyone's desperate to have it off with you, have you thought of that? Did *I* come creeping into *your* bed? No I didn't. Right. Well."

"You don't fancy me? You think I'm disgusting or something?"

"Yes of course I fancy you, that's not the point!" he shouted, vaguely aware that perhaps it *was* the point, in a

129

way. "The point is, if you could get it in your thick head, I am *not* trying to *seduce* you, all right?"

She was grinning down at him now.

"You know you have a bugger in your nose?"

"*Bogey*! The word is *bogey*!"

She started to laugh, and after a moment, so did he.

"Listen," she said, sitting down on the bed. "I tell you something. Antoine phoned me yesterday, he's back in Paris. For good, he says. Lowlands University scared him crapless, he says he was lucky to get out alive. Now he says he understands life is a precious gift, and he will enjoy it however shitty. And wish me good luck. Amazing, yes?"

"Yes," said Stephen. Then, after a moment, "Look . . . if he rang yesterday, you could have gone back to your flat last night."

"I know," she said. "But I wanted to stay here again. You see I am hooked on your beautiful pyjamas."

He reached out his hand and cupped the back of her head. She smiled at him. And then the window started to shake and rattle to a deafening spine-jarring vibration. Adie Shaw was at it again.

Adie Shaw was a third-year Electroacoustics student from Glasgow, with a pleasant boyish smile and an interesting hairstyle that looked as if he had balanced a large slab of cake on top of his otherwise shaven head. His room on the second floor was not hard to find; you just followed the spine-jarring vibrations. Adie Shaw seemed very pleased to welcome Stephen into his room, which looked like a pirate radio station, black boxes banked on top of each other to ceiling height. And after Stephen had reeled about gibbering and pointing for a while (Adie's sounds were genuinely painful to the ears) Adie got the message and switched off.

Stephen explained, with as much courtesy as he could muster, that he was making an official visit as warden of Kennedy Hall, since Adie Shaw had ignored two letters from the Hall committee. Now he was here to say that if Adie could not keep his noise down to acceptable levels, he would have to get out.

"Ah, look, man," said Adie Shaw. "How am I going to

shift all this gear? Oh that's real victimization, I'm surprised you're not blushing."

"Adie," said Stephen. "*You* are victimizing everyone *else* in Hall. People are trying to sleep. People are trying to work for finals."

"*I'm* working for finals. I'm working eighteen hours a *day* for finals, Dr Daker. This that you're interrupting now is a finals *project*."

"What in?" said Stephen, baffled.

Adie Shaw told Stephen all about electroacoustics, and what a terrible, terrible department it was: how Adie had arrived from Glasgow full of idealism, imagining that electroacoustics would be full of people like him, playing in noise bands dedicated to producing new strange sounds and getting the beauty right into people's bodies. And how he had found that electroacoustics at Lowlands was not like that at all: it was all about explosions, and sonic boom, and bugging, and sonar, and big fat sexy defence contracts. It was about bad vibrations, and only the maths was beautiful.

"You're a doctor, right?" he said earnestly. "You must be into making life better and richer and all that, not screwing people up? Well, you ought to *cherish* me."

"As the acceptable face of electroacoustics, you mean?" said Stephen. Despite himself, he found Adie Shaw rather an appealing personality.

"That's right," said Adie Shaw. "So you'll explain to this Hall committee thing that it's all about freedom against oppression, and beauty against terror and that, OK?"

"Ah ... no," said Stephen. "I did find all that very interesting, but as for the strange new sounds, well, this is your final warning from me as warden that either you find somewhere else to make them, or pack them in altogether. Sorry."

"That's all right, Dr Daker," said Adie Shaw. "No hard feelings. I understand your problematic role in the apparatus of oppression. And you really thought the sound was horrendous?"

"Yes, I did," said Stephen sincerely.

"That's very encouraging. John Peel said we wanted to be a bit louder."

"I ... hoped I might be going to see you last night, Grete," said Rose Marie.

"Yes. Well. People. You know," said Grete.

The two women were sitting in the half-empty coffee bar. It was only ten o'clock. A small unshaven man with a black coffee and a hangover was staring at them glumly from a table in the corner, and two nuns were having a good giggle over the Rag magazine.

"I phoned actually," said Rose after a moment. "You weren't at home."

"No. I went to stay with someone."

"Grete," said Rose. "I know I have no right to ask who."

"Stephen Daker."

"Oh."

"Yes, I went in his bed, no we didn't have sex, OK can I go now?"

"Grete ... please don't be angry with me. I ... oh dear. I don't think I've felt like this about anyone since I was in school."

"And how is that?"

"Helpless," said Rose. "It's ... quite embarrassing, Grete. Finding myself thinking about you all the time. Wanting to see you. Wanting to be with you. I ... I just don't know what to do with myself."

"You could have a little wank," said Grete, grinning.

"*Grete. Please.*" Rose couldn't help looking round to see if anyone had heard. The unsavoury-looking little man at the corner table had taken out a notebook and was writing something in it.

Bob Buzzard was feeling bloody odd. It had started this morning in bed. He hadn't wanted to get out of it. Four days since the Stress Clinic fiasco, and now the reaction had set in. Lost the will to live. Simple as that. Happen to anyone. Up shit creek. Finish. Well, of course, Daphne had got him going, by threatening to burn the house down, tower of strength, that woman. Must remember about nookie. Bob hadn't felt much like nookie lately, one way and another, but a chap neglected nookie at his peril. And, oh, Christ,

132

another bloody Group Meeting to face with the old fart and the uppity dyke and Dickie Dado all smirking at him, and oh *Jesus* Christ, Freddy *Frith* was coming to stay. How was he going to face Freddy Frith? How could he tell Freddy the boys were at Spratts instead of Winchester? Freddy was with Schlemmer-Klee, where even the reps drove brand new Audi Quattros. Oh, Lord, *why* was he feeling so dreadful? Was he having a mid-life crisis? Why couldn't he get *on* with his life?

Minutes of a Group Meeting
Present: Dr Daker (Chair), Dr Buzzard, Dr McCannon, Nurse Gahagan

Following a complaint from Dr Buzzard to the effect that some silly sod had edited the tapes of the previous meeting so that he came out looking like a bloody idiot, it was agreed to revert to the customary form, if Nurse Gahagan was agreeable. Nurse Gahagan said that she was.

Dr Daker began the meeting with an update on the events at the Stress Clinic. He regretted to report that the former head of security was in the secure ward and likely to be there for some time. Professor Eugenides however was making a good recovery from his coronary and hoped to make it for the Hawaii recruitment drive next month. Nurse Gahagan commented that it would take a lot more than a coronary to keep that dirty old swine down, and asked the meeting if members were aware of what Professor Eugenides had asked that Linda to do for him. Dr McCannon remarked that one had to expect things like that when one organized a bordello in a health centre. Dr Buzzard told Dr McCannon that he was an evil old sod who had deliberately sabotaged the Stress Clinic by letting a pack of beagles loose in it. Dr Daker proposed, and Dr Buzzard agreed, that the Stress Clinic project be put on the back burner for the foreseeable future.

Dr Rose Marie apologized for her late arrival, saying that she had had personal business to attend to. She did not say who it was with but we all knew anyway, and Dr Daker did not look too pleased about it to say the least. Dr Daker invited Dr Rose Marie to give an update on the Male Sexuality Workshops. Dr Rose Marie said that ninety per cent of the original intake were now anorgasmic, celibate, alternative-strategic, or post-interactionally-autonomous. Dr Daker asked what that meant. Nurse Gahagan said it meant they didn't come, or they didn't penetrate, or they did it by themselves, or they'd given it up as a bad job. Dr Rose Marie said she would feel even happier about it if her male colleagues were able to demonstrate similar responsibility in their own conduct. (Getting another one in at Dr Daker of course; there is no love lost between those two since that Polish girl came on the scene.) Dr Buzzard said at least he, Dr Buzzard, had a clean sheet there. No problems on the Buzzard front, he assured the meeting. Dr Rose Marie said that she was not thinking about the Buzzard front. Nurse Gahagan said that the Buzzard front did not bear thinking about. (Ha ha.)

Nurse Gahagan (who was just about the only person in the meeting with any sense about her at all) pointed out that there were a lot of very groggy-looking patients in the waiting room. Dr Daker expressed surprise, finals still being some way off, and asked for the views of his colleagues.

Dr McCannon got up and started to rave on about how the Prince of Darkness had insinuated his cold finger into the deepest tissues of the campus. He said that well might we scamper this way and that, seeking to massage away our stress and sanitize our sexuality, but that death had many forms. The beagles might run free, the black-booted beetles of repression might be temporarily thwarted, but that deeper still, in the very bowels of the campus, the dark vibrations of unimaginable evil were rumbling through the bones and nerves of every living soul at Lowlands. Murder would out.

Dr Daker thanked Dr McCannon for his input, and said that he would certainly bear all that in mind. There being no other business, the meeting concluded at 10.45 a.m.

There were indeed a number of groggy-looking students in the waiting room, and a significant number of them were students of electroacoustics. They tended to have nervous tics, and poor co-ordination, and some of them were shaking their heads in a baffled way, as if they had something in their ears. One in particular was unable to sit upright on the seat, and rolled off twice, lying on his back and waving his legs like a stranded beetle.

Subsequently, Dr Rose Marie saw Karen Cartwright, who was worried about Professor Middling's Pyramid Failing Policy, and suffering from temporary threshold shift (acute deafness) which she attributed to having overdone participation in Professor Middling's low-frequency vibration experiments, which were hard to resist because he paid volunteers ten pounds an hour.

Dr Robert Buzzard saw an RAF-sponsored student named Roddy, who was complaining about headaches and panic about the difficulty of the maths, and confessed to suicidal thoughts. Dr Buzzard told him that he was a waste of space, of course the maths was going to be difficult for a chap who didn't have much on top, and everyone got headaches, in fact he, the patient, had just given him, Dr Buzzard, a headache. As far as Dr Buzzard was concerned, it wouldn't bother him if the patient walked off and topped himself. Roddy asked Dr Buzzard if he would mind repeating all that, because he had a temporary threshold shift. Dr Buzzard told him to go and jump in the lake.

Dr McCannon saw a Mr O'Shea, who entered his surgery on hands and knees, being quite unable to balance on his feet. Dr McCannon said that he was familiar with that condition and advised the patient to ease up a little on the Scotch. Mr O'Shea said he never touched it, and Dr McCannon was at a loss how to proceed.

All these students were in the Department of Electroacoustics.

Stephen Daker would have been interested to know that, because he was hearing quite a lot about electroacoustics himself in the Senate meeting. Jack Daniels announced a new and very substantial research grant for the Vibration Research Institute, following Professor Middling's recent theoretical breakthrough in the field.

"It's kinda mean of me to say so," said the Vice-Chancellor, "but I guess Southampton and Salford must be feeling a little sick right now: this one puts Lowlands out in front."

"It also makes Electroacoustics the number three UK department *in any subject*, taking outside funding as our criterion," added Charlie Dusenberry.

"And naturally no other criterion comes to mind," rumbled George Bunn. "May one enquire the source of this largesse?"

"Sure, George," said Jack Daniels. "The Thomas Jefferson North Atlantic Trust."

An appreciative murmur went round the room, especially where the research scientists were bunched. Getting Jefferson money meant you were really entering the big league. Bunn cleared his throat noisily.

"Yes, George?"

"One speaks as an ignorant layman, of course, but aren't those the chaps who give chaps money to find new ways of killing other chaps?"

"Professor Bunn, forgive me for saying this," said Charlie Dusenberry coldly, "but that is an ill-informed view. Jefferson funds across a whole range of projects, and Middling's work in any case is purely theoretical."

"I guess we won't be wasting anyone at Lowlands just yet a while, George," said Jack Daniels. The scientists chuckled at the Vice-Chancellor's homespun humour, but Professor Bunn pursued his point.

"So what is the precise nature of the research?"

Farris of Microbiology, another young whiz-kid and money-earner for the university, groaned audibly.

"Professor Middling isn't here right now, George, maybe you could ask him yourself?" said Jack.

"Surely someone knows, in general terms, what the man is up to?" Bunn wouldn't let go.

"Vice-Chancellor, aren't we wasting Senate's time here?" This was Farris again, in his contemptuous drawl.

Suddenly Stephen heard himself bravely saying: "Er . . . I'd be very interested to know as well."

All the scientists looked at him in astonishment, as if the family dog had suddenly asked the time.

"I've, er ... recently developed a bit of an interest in the subject."

Farris got in first.

"Oh, really, Daker, this is Senate, not an elementary school. When there's a Ladybird book on the subject we'll get it in the library, till then you wouldn't have the remotest chance of understanding it. In any case I believe the project's classified."

"Aha!" roared Bunn. "I am grateful to you, Farris, for *that* information. Do please proceed, Vice-Chancellor. I must return to preside over the disintegration of the English Department, which, I would remind Senate, has at least as distinguished a reputation as Electroacoustics. And, no doubt when we have perfected a way of killing Russians by dropping Pope and Dryden on their heads, we shall enjoy equal research funding!"

On his return to the Health Centre, Stephen was approached by his colleagues, and was interested to hear that Electroacoustics appeared to be presenting as a department with problems. He agreed to make an informal approach to Professor Middling, and asked Jock McCannon whether in his view the best course would be to seek out the deep sexual anxiety.

"No, Stephen," said Jock bleakly. "Thanks to Dr Rose Marie's pioneering work, sex is practically a thing of the past at Lowlands. This university has fallen in love with death. That is where your answer will lie."

On his way over to Electroacoustics, Stephen passed the lake, where a well-built young man in RAF blue trunks was swimming doggedly back and forth across the leaden water under a cloudy sky.

The room was furnished rather like Adie Shaw's bedroom, except that it was about six times as large, with a large desk in the middle of it. There were four telephones on the desk, and a greasy-haired adolescent with a schoolboy's suit and a

137

head that looked too big for his body was talking into one of the telephones.

"I'm so sorry," said Stephen. "I was looking for Professor Middling."

"I'm Middling," said the adolescent. "Won't be a sec." He pointed to a chair, and continued to talk into the phone. He had a boyish voice, too, that squeaked now and then as though it hadn't quite finished breaking. "Yes, well we *can* help you on a consultancy basis, I'm afraid we're awfully expensive, does that matter? ... Oh, fine, Mr Dusenberry in Finance will sort out the contract for us, I'm quite hopeless about money. But I'll put a couple of bright boys on this one, it sounds like great fun. Bye for now then."

He put the phone down and smiled shyly at Stephen.

"That was a chap in Colorado, they just go on and on, those Colorado chaps. I hate to think what their phone bill must be. Are you Dr Daker?"

"Yes," said Stephen. On closer inspection Middling might just possibly be a very immature twenty-seven rather than seventeen. "I don't want to take up too much of your time, but I do think this might be important."

"Oh, that's all right," said Middling cheerfully. "Let's go out to lunch. My treat. I've found this place that does super ice-creams. Have you got time?"

"Well, yes. Thanks," said Stephen.

"Oh, good." Middling's round face lit up. "I've been looking forward to it all morning."

The restaurant was a really quite pleasant one, an old water-mill by the river which had been converted into a superior steak and hamburger place. They had driven there in Professor Middling's brand new Porsche 928, in a series of erratic lurches. The car, Middling said, had been recommended to him as a jolly good sort of car, so he had gone and bought one, but he found it hard to drive, like all cars, which was quite a paradox, cars being such tediously simple machines. Still he'd managed to spend some of his money at last. He asked Stephen whether he, too, found it a problem knowing how to spend all the money they gave him. Stephen said that though he had quite a few problems, that was not one of them. He suspected that he and Middling might be on quite different scales of remuneration.

Now they were in mid-meal, having consumed a steak and salad in Stephen's case, and a Monster Wally with French fries and all the sauces in Middling's, and Stephen had gently voiced some of his concerns about the pyramid failing policy and the use of students as guinea pigs in the low vibration project.

"Yes, well, of course I'll think about that," said Middling, polishing off his second bottle of Coke. "The thing is, it's so convenient to use our own students, you get much faster and easier feedback than you do with animals. And you know what they say, students are thicker on the ground than rats or rabbits, and you don't get so attached to them."

"*What*?" said Stephen.

"That's just a joke," Middling confessed. "Quite good, though, isn't it?"

"Look," said Stephen. "You must realize that repeated threshold shift results in eventual permanent and irreversible hearing loss. I do know they're all volunteers, and I accept that these are very low-level dosages, but in the face of the evidence you really can't continue, can you?"

"S'pose not really," said Middling. "This is very irritating." He looked quite cast down, as if the head beak had told him he couldn't keep a pet mouse in his desk any more. Then his face brightened.

"I say!" he called to the waiter, who came over smiling indulgently. "Bet you know what I'm going to ask for now?"

"Banana split, sir?"

"Right! Chocolate *and* raspberry sauce. And another Coke. Same for you, Daker?"

"No, I'll just have a black coffee, thanks," said Stephen.

"You've got very sophisticated tastes," said the Professor of Electroacoustics respectfully.

"Um . . . the other thing I wanted to discuss was the very high level of stress that's showing up among the electro-acoustics students," said Stephen when the waiter had gone.

"Really? Oh, I'm sorry about that. The thing is, Daker, some people find electroacoustics a bit difficult, they have trouble with the sums you see, and I suppose that gets them down a bit. Can't be helped, really," he ended cheerfully.

"You have a very high failure rate in the first and second years, don't you?"

"Oh, yes, we do kick a lot of them out. Most of them actually," said Middling, apparently with pride.

"But you get a very high calibre of student at entry?"

"Well, suppose so. Three As at 'A' level is the standard, but 'A' level is just baby stuff, you can't predict from it ... and actually, you see ..." here he leaned forward with a gleeful mischievous grin ... "I don't *need* more than half a dozen bright boys by the end of the third year, the rest of them just clutter up the place. So I evolved this pyramid failing policy, weeding out the dozy ones as we go along, it's very cost-effective. I'm hoping to get the VC to adopt it as university policy for every faculty ... ah, *here* we are!"

The banana split had arrived. It was enormous.

"Two parasols *and* a sparkler, you *are* spoiling me!" said Middling, falling to. Stephen took a sip of his coffee.

"Um ... the dozy ones, as you call them ... they're not really dozy are they? They'd get degrees in other places?"

"Oh, yes, 'spect so," said Middling with his mouth full. "They'd get firsts and upper seconds in *some* universities I could name."

"So ... forgive me if this seems rude ... don't you think your policy's a bit inhumane? Don't you worry about damaging people?"

Middling put his spoon down to think about that one. It seemed to be a new concept to him.

"Well," he said modestly. "Bit outside my field, that sort of thing. I should ask a philosopher." He leaned forward earnestly, his eyes round as saucers. "I'd hate to be a philosopher, wouldn't you? All that woolly thinking, and not a hope in hell of standardizing the data!"

"You just don't understand at all, do you?" said Stephen, who was feeling increasingly frustrated. This man Middling was just an overgrown schoolboy.

"Oh gosh," said Middling. "My turn to be rude I'm afraid. You see, um, I 'spect it's fine to be a medical man and not be very bright, but you've got to be rather clever to be a theoretical scientist."

"And you're rather clever?"

"I'm *very* clever," said Middling impatiently. Stephen suddenly realized that this absurd little man was probably feeling just as puzzled and frustrated as he was; that from Middling's point of view, too, this conversation was like talking to a child. "And, well, I sort of think if you're not capable of significant original research you shouldn't be in a university at all. Everyone else just clutters up the place; of course you need cleaners and porters and things, and doctors, I suppose, in case you get ill ... but all those are just support services, aren't they?"

"And what about the students?" said Stephen. "You don't care about them at all?"

"Well," said Middling reasonably, "most of them are just wasting their time and ours, it's hard to get interested, isn't it?"

It made sense as a world view. Professor Middling wasn't being deliberately brutal or inhumane. It was simply that, from his point of view, anyone with an IQ of under 175 or so was just not interesting enough to bother with. This was probably why he hardly ever bothered to turn up at Senate. Farris and Brahmachari were the only people clever enough to have a conversation with, and he could do that in the lab or on the phone or over a banana split. The university needed Professor Middling much more than Professor Middling needed the university. He could take his brain anywhere in the world, and the money would follow him. Professor Middling could do what he bloody well liked; he knew it and the university knew it. Stephen decided to give up. He'd made his point about the threshold losses. There was nothing he could do about the failing policy. He had the sudden chilling thought that he was looking at the future sitting across the table licking up the last of the chocolate sauce.

"Adie Shaw is one of yours, isn't he?" he said. Silly, really; Middling probably had no idea who Adie Shaw was. But to his surprise, Middling looked interested.

"D'you know him? Funny chap, isn't he? Actually, he *is* quite bright, but he's interested in all the wrong sorts of things. *Musical* vibrations ... well that's been a dead end for fifteen years, theoretically speaking. Waste of talent does make me rather cross I'm afraid."

One last try.

"But look – can't you see your whole departmental policy is a systematic waste of talent?"

Oh, God. He realized he was almost shouting. But Middling smiled back mildly.

"No need to get ratty with me, Dr Daker, I've really enjoyed our lunch."

The Vice-Chancellor was talking on the telephone.

"No, it isn't an earth tremor, Julie, it can't be, honey, we're not on a fault line .... Well I guess you could try to enjoy it, Julie. No, honey, I can't right now, I'm all tied up in a working lunch. No, Charlie can't come to the phone right now. He says to say hi for him. Honey, I have to go now. I have to go now, honey. Listen, why don't you and Consuela hose down the Rottweilers, you know you like that .... Well, it was just a thought. Sure I love you. Julie, I have to hang up now."

He put the phone down.

"Rose, I'm real sorry," he said. "She gets kinda jumpy if I don't call."

"You're a very caring man, Jack," said Rose Marie, her fingers moving lightly on his smooth brown muscular back.

The Vice-Chancellor of Lowlands and the Director of the Male Sexuality Workshop were having their working lunch in the Director's flat, the better to explore new insights and alternative interactional strategies.

"You see, honey," said Jack Daniels, returning to the topic they had been discussing before his duty call, "Electroacoustics is kinda special territory. The work they're doing there ... well I guess it's worth making a few sacrifices for."

"No, don't turn over," said Rose. "You'll find it more rewarding this way, believe me .... Professor Middling's research project must be *very* special. What is he working on, exactly?"

"Well, it's kinda secret, I guess, and kinda technical. But if it pans out, and all the signs are good ... I believe we're talking about saving Western civilization. Oh, yeah. Oh, that's good."

His last two remarks referred not to saving Western civilization, but to that small area of Western civilization comprising Rose Marie's knowledgeable fingers and his own powerful thighs.

"Saving Western civilization," sighed Rose softly. "You know, Jack, I find it so ... thrilling, I suppose is the only word ... being so close to the centre of power."

"Maybe if I turned over, you might feel even closer," he said.

"Oh, Jack ... ."

Bob Buzzard had gone on feeling bloody odd. He had felt bloody odd all day. Been a bit sharp with one or two of the patients. He hadn't *really* told that RAF idiot to go and jump in the lake, had he? Surely not. And what the hell if he had, eh? Just another bloody idiot. Patients. He never wanted to see another patient again. What *did* he want? He didn't know. What did Daphne want? Wanted him to get on with his life. Wanted nookie, probably. Why did nookie seem so daunting all of a sudden? There was something else he had to remember, but he couldn't think what it was. He *did* feel a bit under the weather.

Without any prior decision, he found himself blurting out all of this, or some of it, to the old fart after evening surgery, and the old fart had been frightfully sympathetic. In fact, here he was, lying on the old fart's horsehair couch, the old fart himself crouched out of sight with a monster shot of Scotch and a little black notebook, taking down the details of one of Bob's hairier recent dreams. Without quite knowing how it had come about, Bob Buzzard was in analysis.

"Right. Fine," he said. "If you insist. I'm alone in a dark and steamy jungle. Gym togs. Plimsolls. Lost the rest of the chaps. Got my elephant gun though. Not going too fast for you am I?"

"No, no, my dear fellow," said Jock. "I'm all ears."

"Right," said Bob. "Jungle floor starts to vibrate. I come to a clearing, and there on the other side is a huge wounded angry elephant."

"A bull or a cow?"

"An *elephant*! Do pay attention, Jock. Oh, I see. Yes. Female elephant. Anyway, the point is, I raise my elephant gun to my shoulder, sight along the barrel, start to squeeze the trigger ... and then the barrel slowly droops away ... amazing, eh? Then I wake up. That's it. Bet you've never heard anything like that one before."

"Robert," said Jock McCannon weightily, "in all my years exploring the dark recesses of the psyche, I have seldom encountered such a classically banal manifestation of the unconscious mind. Admit it. You made it up to please me, didn't you?"

"No I did not!" said Bob, affronted. "I don't mind telling you, Jock, it cost me something to ask for help, and if a single word of this gets back to Daphne .... "

"My dear chap," said Jock. "I am touched and honoured by your confidence."

"All right. Get on with the analysis."

"Eh ... tell me, Bob, what comes into your mind when I say the word ... *gun*? Just let your thoughts rove freely."

"Oh, Lord, do I have to? Right, er ... *gun*. Lock, stock and barrel. Chest. Chest of drawers. Lady with large chest for sale. Sail away. Up shit creek. Haven't got a paddle. Got a gun though. Big strong gun. Where's the trigger? Trigger ... trigger. Roy Rogers. Rogers ... rogers ... Roy rogers Trigger! What am I talking about? Get back to the gun. Gun. Bang. Fire. If I don't get my act together Daphne's going to burn the house down. Got to get my act together. Oh my God! Freddy Frith!"

He salt bolt upright on the couch, staring at Jock in horror.

"Freddy Frith, yes," said Jock, a therapeutic light dawning in his alcoholic old eyes. "Yes, now I think I understand. You feel a Freudian frisson. We are nearing the heart of the matter. The jungle floor is beginning to vibrate with a vengeance!"

"No! No! You stupid old sod!" yelled Bob, jumping off the couch. "Freddy *Frith*! I should have been home an hour ago! Daphne's going to kill me!"

"Lie down, Bob."

"No time! No time! I can't keep Freddy waiting!"

He rushed from the room.

"Extraordinary," said Jock, flicking on his little cassette recorder. "Eh ... *Daphne*, goddess of the dark forest, the lady with the large chest, *triggers* the vibrations that shake the forest floor, summoning from beneath the earth's crust the fire-god, the destroyer, Freddo Freothar ... Freddy Frith. Aye ... it all leads back to electroacoustics. Well done, Jock."

Stephen was in the bar with Grete, he with a glass of bitter, she with a glass of wine and a cigarette. It was becoming a little routine, a nice one, he was coming to look forward to it, though he told himself not to. Grete was not into routines, she made that quite clear. As an art historian, she worked long and regular hours; her students could set their watches by her. Her personal life she preferred to conduct entirely on impulse, it seemed. It was just that she had impulsively fancied a drink with Stephen on three successive evenings. He mustn't start counting on it.

"I just couldn't seem to get anywhere with him," he said. "It was as if ... part of his brain was missing. He didn't seem to see people as people at all. Like a mad little boy."

"So?" she said. "Many men are like this, I think. It's normal. This Middling, tell me, does he have big head, little boy shoulders, squeaky voice, tiny genitalia?"

"Yes, exactly!" said Stephen. "Well, I don't know about the genitalia."

"I thought you doctors always looked in people's pants." She was grinning.

"Anyway," he said. "How do you know about Middling?"

"I don't," she said. "It's a type. You forget my special

subject: iconography of male nude. Many scientists have this physical configuration."

"I wish I knew what he was really up to," said Stephen.

"He wouldn't tell you?"

"He said it was a *secret*. He sounded like a little kid. I don't know. Doctors are supposed to be perceptive, but sometimes I don't think I know what *anyone's* up to. Middling. Jack Daniels. Jock. Rose Marie. You."

"People, eh?" she said, smiling. "Listen, person. I want to come off your list. I don't want to be your patient any more."

"Oh?" he said, a bit hurt, momentarily. Then he saw another interpretation. "*Oh*."

"Just don't get too excited about it, OK?" she said.

Stephen was wondering just how he could explore the implications of all this, when Adie Shaw suddenly plonked himself down uninvited on an empty chair.

"I've cracked it, Dr Daker! Oh. Am I interrupting anything?"

"Grete Grotowska, Adie Shaw," said Stephen. "The man with the horrendous sounds."

"Hello," said Adie. "Well, I've cracked it. I'm presenting my final year project as a live performance. Thought you'd like to come along and hear it. And what about you, Grete? Do you like music at all?"

"Yes, I like music," she said. "You call that music, the noise you make?"

"I think it's beautiful," said Adie simply.

"Listen," she said. "You make sounds like that where I come from, they give you twenty years' hard labour."

"Really?" he said, sounding very pleased to hear that. "Hey, can we use that quote in our publicity?"

"Sure," she said, grinning. "And I come to your performance. And I bring this man here."

"Friday night," said Adie. "In the Union. Just got to check it out with my professor."

"Listen, I have to go now," said Grete.

"But I thought we were having a drink," said Stephen. She shrugged.

"So we had one. Thank you for the nice drink."

Stephen looked up and saw Rose Marie standing in the doorway.

"I see you on Friday," said Grete to Adie. "I see you soon, eh?" she said, squeezing Stephen's hand. Then she walked away. Adie watched Stephen watching her go.

"Bad vibrations, eh?" he said.

Freddy Frith was a chap of about Bob's age, and he was wearing a very smart suit indeed. People often thought of Freddy Frith as doggish, but at the moment he was looking somewhat hangdoggish. He was sitting at the kitchen table of the Buzzard home with Daphne Buzzard, and the atmosphere was a trifle tense. They had both been silent for some time, waiting for Buzzard. They both started slightly as they heard the BMW squeal round the corner and growl on to the gravel.

"Er ... look," said Freddy Frith.

Daphne Buzzard looked. She gave him one of her looks, in fact, and he subsided into uneasy silence. Then the door opened and Bob charged in, bonhomie covering terror.

"Freddy! Old Buddy! How *are* you?"

"Er, fine, Bob. Just fine," said Freddy hollowly, clearing his throat.

Oh, Lord, thought Bob. Poor bastard looks as if he's had an hour or two of the rough edge of Daphne's tongue.

"Sorry I'm late, had to sort something out with the old fart, what it is for us workaholics. Well, well. Hope Daphne's been looking after you all right."

"Oh, yes. Er, fine."

Chap didn't even have a drink. Freddy didn't look right without a drink. You'd think old Daphne would at least have given him a drink. What *had* they been doing, swapping recipes or what?

"Freddy and I have been to bed, Robert," said Daphne, in a conversational tone.

"Oh, good," said Bob. "*What? Really?* Oh, I see, you're joking. Ha ha ha! Nearly got me there. Well, well."

They just sat there staring at him.

"You *are* joking, aren't you? She's joking, isn't she?"

"Robert, my darling," said Daphne. "*Since* you can't be bothered to come home, and the soufflé was *completely* ruined, and Freddy is so remarkably short of intelligent conversation, but rather a *dish* in his way, with quite a little reputation in the *nookie* field, well, what with one thing and another, suddenly it seemed like a good idea to see what I've been missing out on all these years, my darling."

Good God. Bob's ears were buzzing. His heart was pounding away like the tappets on a sick Fiat.

"This true, buddy?"

"Er, 'fraid so," said Freddy Frith, wincing.

Chap didn't know what to say. Chap didn't know what to do. Chap's whole life, or selected highlights of it, was flashing past a chap's eyes. Was he going to faint? Was he going to puke? Then, suddenly words came to him.

"Right, buddy. On your feet. Outside. You and me. To the death."

"Look, Bob," said Freddy nervously, "... couldn't we talk it over like mature people?"

"Certainly not!" said Bob, dragging him up by the lapels of his four hundred quid suit. "Out, you!" And turning back to Daphne, he said: "And I'll attend to you later, my darling."

"Oh, Robert," she said, deeply stirred.

Adie Shaw, in return for two pints of lager, was quite happy to give Stephen the Ladybird version of what went on in Electroacoustics. It went like this: what we call sound is really just vibration. Professor Middling was interested in something called critical resonance. The opera singer who shatters a wine glass has produced a note which vibrates at a frequency which matches the critical resonance of the glass. Everything has a critical resonance: cars, aircraft, buildings. What we call metal fatigue is a matter of vibration frequency and critical resonance. All this has been well known for some time. A few years ago the Russians were working on the practical possibilities of vibrating buildings to pieces. Adie himself was interested in the musical applications of critical resonance. Middling's crucial contribution had been to work out the fundamental mathematics of critical resonance. Now this had been done, it was theoretically possible to vibrate anything to pieces.

"Yes, I think I see," said Stephen. "I sometimes feel as if I'm getting near *my*, what was it, critical resonance."

"Well, yeah," said Adie. "Middling's sums would work for people too. You'd get different resonances for different parts of the body, you know, spine, heart, liver, skull . . . and select the bit you wanted to shake to pieces. No problem, in theory, now Middling's done the sums."

"You're not serious?" said Stephen, deeply shocked.

"Why not? Ah, you should see the proof, you know. The mathematics of it is really stunningly beautiful."

In another bar, the University Athletics Club bar, to be precise, Bob Buzzard and Freddy Frith were having a serious man-to-man conversation about the mystery of life. They had murdered three quick pints without coming to any viable conclusions.

"Women, eh?" said Bob, summing up the conversation so far. "Who knows what goes on in their heads?"

"Well," said Freddy supportively, "at least it didn't put you off your squash game. Five nil to Buzzard. You were like a mad bull in there."

"Thanks, Freddy. Mind you, it's a shattering blow. What can a chap believe in any more?"

"I feel absolutely frightful about this, Bob. It sort of caught me on the hop, if you see what I mean." He leaned forward earnestly. "Of course you know I've always had a soft spot for Daphne, but I never really saw her as a goer."

"Nor did I, Freddy," said Bob gloomily. "Nor did I."

There was a question a chap had to ask. Perhaps a chap should postpone it for another pint or two. No. Bob Buzzard had never funked a tackle.

"Look here, Freddy. You did, um . . . take precautions?"

"Oh, absolutely. Well, you know. Company man through thick and thin."

"Sorry?" said Bob.

"Schlemmer-Klee. We're market leaders in Western Europe now."

"Sorry, I don't quite ..."

"Rubber johnnies," said Freddy. "This AIDS business has been a real shot in the arm for chaps like us. It's a funny old world."

"Quite," said Bob. "Bloody hilarious."

"Actually," said Freddy, "if this, er, other business hadn't come up, I was going to sound you out about a possible opening. Schlemmer-Klee are looking for a good man to look after the South-West."

"Really," said Bob. "Robert Buzzard, rubber johnnie rep. Not exactly what I dreamed about at Shrewsbury."

There was a bit of a silence then, during which Bob had a bit of a think.

"Look here, Freddy," he said eventually. "You and I go back a long time. Known you longer than I've known Daphne, even."

"Absolutely," said Freddy.

"I think Daphne's setting me a bit of a challenge. That's the way I see it."

"Don't quite follow you, buddy."

"Women are changing, you know," said Bob. "See a lot of them at work, know what I'm talking about. Daphne wants to see if I can rise to the challenge and be a sort of New Man about this. And I'm not going to let her down."

"That's the spirit," said Freddy supportively, without quite knowing what he was endorsing.

"What we're going to do, buddy, we're going to motor on back to Buzzard Mansions, and just be very mature about the whole thing. All good friends together. Daphne will be tremendously impressed."

Freddy looked a bit doubtful.

"You don't think it might be better if I sort of slope off, and you go back and say you've given me a fearful hiding, then sweep her off to the nuptial couch, sort of thing?"

"No, no," said Bob firmly. "That's what the Old Man would do. We're going to be New Men."

"Well. You know her better than I do, Bob."

"Right, buddy," said Bob, standing up. "Off we go."

"It's there in black and white, Professor Middling," said Adie Shaw the following morning, pointing out the paragraph in the university handbook. "Final year students may present their project as a live performance."

"Oh, really, Shaw. Those regulations date from the days when Acoustics was a Micky Mouse department full of musicians and architects and people like that."

"Shame you never got around to altering them then," said Adie, smiling winningly.

"This is really very silly of you, Shaw," said Middling crossly. "You know you're putting your degree class at risk. I used to see you as a very promising student."

"Oh, don't give up on me yet, Professor Middling. I think you'll find my project very interesting."

Later the same morning, Stephen had a rather puzzling visit from Charles Dusenberry of Finance, who was accompanied by a tall, silent, smiling man in a dark-blue suit. After a few phatic banalities, Dusenberry said: "Jack wants you to know he really appreciates the quality of your caring for the students in Electroacoustics, Steve."

"Oh, thanks very much," said Stephen. "Actually we're still rather concerned . . . ."

"Jack wants you to know it's all been taken care of."

"In what way?" said Stephen.

"You don't need to worry about it any more, Steve. Jack wants you to know that."

"Yes, but . . ."

"Eric Middling's kind of a special guy, Steve. These, what do you call them here, boffins, right? It's easy to upset them without meaning to, you know? Jack feels he'll be happier if he can get on with his work without interruptions."

"Well, I daresay we'd all like that," said Stephen.

"Jack'll be glad to know we all feel the same way, Steve," said Charlie Dusenberry. He looked at Stephen silently for a few moments, apparently with friendly interest.

"Your friend Dr Grotowska . . . she's Polish, is that right?"

"Yes," said Stephen, baffled. Something made him glance across at the tall man in the blue suit sitting quietly in the corner. The man smiled pleasantly back at him.

"Well, I guess that's fine," said Charlie Dusenberry. He rose and held his hand out. "Nice talking with you, Steve. You give good meeting."

Bob Buzzard sat at his desk staring into space, his face a tragic mask. Someone knocked at the door. He did not speak. The door opened and Rose Marie came in.

"May I?" she said. "I was just wondering if you had the printout for the anxiety and stress count ...?"

He did not reply. It was if he hadn't heard her, hadn't even noticed she was there.

"Bob? Are you all right?"

"She's left me," he said. "She's left me, Rose. Daphne's left me. She's packed her bags and gone back to mother. What am I going to do?"

"Oh, Bob," she said, sitting down opposite him. "I'm so sorry."

"You're a woman, Rose. You understand these things. She says she's lost all respect for me. D'you think she's gone off her trolley?"

"Well," said Rose, choosing her words carefully, "that is a possibility, of course. But there *are* other explanations that might be more likely."

"Really? Been racking my brains but I can't think of any."

"It can't always be easy for her, Bob. Living with a man who's so full of that ... restless, vibrant energy. Perhaps she just needs ... breathing space. Perhaps you both do. A crisis in a marriage can often be very creative. An opportunity for learning, an opportunity for growth."

Hope dawned on Bob's baffled doggy frowning face.

"Yes," he said. "Right. Yes. See your point. Breathing space. Yes." He leaned across the desk and confided: "As a matter of fact, Rose, we *have* been going through a bit of a hairy phase."

"A ... hairy phase, Bob?"

"Well. You know. Haven't been feeling quite the thing

152

myself lately. Bit jumpy. Rumbling guts. Dreams about elephants. Trouble on the nookie front. She's a fine woman, Rose, but she can be a bit of a strain to live with. Breathing space. That's it. That's what we both need. You're a brilliant woman, Rose."

Her smile was almost tender.

"I'm ... so glad to be of any help, Bob."

"Look here," he said. "Are you doing anything on Friday night?"

On Friday night a wind blew up, ruffling the sullen surface of the lake, tossing dirty sheets of paper and cardboard round and round the bleak piazza, driving dark clouds across the opaque and brownish sky. It made people restless. People who had promised themselves an early night found themselves going out on to the walkways, and drifting aimlessly towards the Union building to join the vast numbers who had heard that something weird involving Adie Shaw was going to happen there. The air was full of sounds; awkward, wrenching, spine-jarring sounds, as if the very foundations of the central complex were shifting and moaning.

Inside the Union building the scrawny armies of the dispossessed swarmed about from bar to terrace to balcony to walkway, drinking like fish and smoking like beagles, waiting for something to happen. Brain-numbing recorded rock drowned conversation. Down on the stage Adie Shaw's band were setting up their instruments, making final adjustments to their terrifying wall of black boxes, and generally hyping themselves up to sound horrible. They had been guaranteed four dozen veggie-burgers, six cases of Crucial Brew, and two bottles of vodka to sustain them through the evening. Knowledgeable aficionados in the audience went quiet and respectful when they saw the ear defenders coming out. When Adie Shaw's band brought out the ear defenders, things were getting critical. Serious noise was being contemplated. They were going to play with extreme prejudice.

Up in the balcony, Stephen and Grete found themselves

borne by the tide towards the Winnie Mandela bar, where Stephen joined the howling mobs trying to get served. He was happy. Grete had announced that she was going to get nice and drunk tonight because she wasn't driving, and she wasn't driving because she wanted another night with the brilliant pyjamas.

"Evening buddy!"

Stephen managed to turn his head – any further movement was impossible – and to his surprise saw Bob Buzzard, sweaty and mad-eyed in a cricket sweater, arm in arm with Rose Marie.

"What on earth are you doing here?" Stephen said, or rather shouted.

"Breathing space! Breathing space!" yelled Bob wildly. "Actually there isn't any breathing space! Look at them! Bloody students! They're all as drunk as skunks, buddy! No wonder they all get so ill! Alcoholic poisoning! Go home and do some work! Come on, let the dog see the rabbit! Man here wants a drink!"

He hurled himself into the crowd of backs three deep at the bar, some of whose owners looked inclined to violence, but Buzzard battled through and made it to the front, where he set about securing the attention of the student barmaid.

"Now here's a fine-looking girl!" he yelled. "Bet you can't guess what I do for a living! I'm a rubber johnny rep!"

"Is he all right?" said Stephen to Rose.

"No, he isn't, Stephen. He turned up at my flat in a highly excited state and I thought it wisest to get him somewhere where there were other people about. But it seems to have gone to his head rather."

Stephen could see what she meant. Bob was now telling a huge neckless twenty-stone rugger type that it was no use poking him, he was here first, and if he wanted a punch on the snout he was going the right way to get it.

"This Daphne business has hit him very hard," said Stephen.

"Yes, I think he might be heading for a crisis. I'm glad you're here, Stephen. I think he might be more than I can cope with on my own."

"Over here! Over here! The drinks are on Buzzard! I say, you look like an opportunity for growth and learning, what are you doing after the show?"

Professor Middling was not enjoying himself at all! He had never seen so many people in one place before. Quite clearly there were far too many students in Lowlands; the sooner his pyramid failing policy was universalized the better. And why did all these student things have to start so *late*? Eric Middling liked to be tucked up in bed with a chocolate milk and a sheaf of printout by ten o'clock. It was ten past ten now, and the beastly thing still hadn't even started. Oh, Christmas. Here was that awful man Bunn from Eng. Lit. and that old doctor that looked like Worzel Gummidge with him, and you could see they had both been drinking alcohol.

"Evening, Middling! We've come to see your little performance!"

"It's *not* my performance, Bunn. It gives me no pleasure to be here at all."

"Oh dear, oh dear, oh dear, never mind. What are you drinking?"

"Coca-cola."

Jock McCannon's cadaverous face loomed closer.

"When Freddo Freothar breaks the earth's crust, we shall all drink *fire*, is that not so, Professor Middling?"

"What?" said Middling, alarmed. He had heard that McCannon was deranged; clearly it was true. "What are you talking about?"

"*Bad vibrations*," said Jock, with dreadful intensity.

Middling fled.

And found himself face to face with a thin dark young woman he'd seen earlier with that chap Daker. She was smiling at him. Oh, Christmas.

"Hello," she said.

"Hello. Er, I'm sorry. Do I know you?"

"Grete Grotowska," she said. "And you are Professor Middling, yes?"

"Yes, I am. How did you know me?"

"Someone described to me your wulnerable little body,"

she said, smiling. "I'm sorry, this embarrasses you? I embarrass many men. I am Polish, you know."

"Oh, yes, I see," he said.

He had never felt particularly pleased to see Adie Shaw, but he was extremely relieved when his student came up grinning and said: "We're all set, Professor Middling. Ready when you are."

"This really is a tedious waste of time, Shaw."

"Oh," said Adie Shaw, "you're going to love it."

He ran back to the stage, and the recorded rock faded to silence.

"OK, folks, this is it. Adie Shaw and 'Earthworks'."

"Roadworks" might have been a more appropriate title, thought Stephen, but still inadequate to convey the totality of the experience. The bass and drums certainly sounded rather like a road crew improvising with a couple of pneumatic drills, some air brakes and a pile-driver, but there were other sounds as well, a sort of subterranean earthquake syndrome, and an increasingly worrying angry buzzing sound, as of some vast furious insect running amok with a chainsaw. This sound seemed to be achieved partly by the lead guitarist, who was attacking the strings with a hairdryer, partly by Adie Shaw himself, who was rushing furiously from one black box to another twiddling knobs.

Stephen realized that he had involuntarily moved at least ten yards further away from the band, but most of the audience had gone the other way, flooding towards the stage, and leaping about in a wild unco-ordinated way. He could see Bob Buzzard, his eyes shut and his fists clenched, bouncing up and down on the spot. He turned to Grete to point Bob out, and realized that she had left his side and was down among the dancers herself. My God, and so were Jock McCannon and George Bunn. Had they all gone mad? Two nuns were there too, weaving a sinister pattern through and around the other dancers. Stephen realized that he was standing next to Professor Middling, who was wincing and blinking in an irritated way.

"Awful, isn't it?" shouted Stephen.

"I don't know anything about music!" squeaked Middling.

"I'm an acoustician. And in terms of acoustics, this is totally devoid of interest. Silly fellow's barking up quite the wrong tree!"

A few seconds later, the sounds became more damaging: a new grinding element had entered, suggesting an enormously amplified recording of the jagged pieces of a broken bone rubbing on each other. Adie Shaw, grinning up into the darkness where his professor was standing, moved over to a stack of black boxes he had not touched before, and turned some more knobs. The effect was immediate. The bass beat, even from thirty yards, was like being kicked in the base of the spine. The dancers began to reel away from the stage, some clutching their faces.

"Wait a minute," said Middling. "This is really quite interesting." He started to walk forward down the steps into the emptying space. Bob Buzzard staggered backwards past him.

"Daphne! Daphne! Come back! I'm a new man!" he muttered. Then he slumped into the bar counter and slid slowly down it to the floor.

Middling stepped into the empty space immediately in front of the band, his eyes wide and his mouth open, as if he had been vouchsafed some visionary insight. He was alone in the circle of light. Adie Shaw saw him, and smiled as if acknowledging some kind of kinship. Then he turned the last knob. Middling jerked twice, sharply, as if he had been kicked in the back of the knees and then hit on the back of the neck. His fingers opened, and the glass of Coca-cola fell and shattered on the floor. Then Middling himself pitched forward on his face and lay still. With a final sledgehammer chord, the music stopped.

"We call that one 'Bad Vibrations'," said Adie Shaw.

Professor Middling was not killed outright by "Bad Vibrations". After the third day in sick bay (Charles Dusenberry had refused to allow him into the City infirmary, and had brought in two very distinguished doctors from the Sweetwater USAF base to assist the medical team) it was apparent that he was recovering, though he had severe temporary threshold loss, which might well develop into a permanent hearing impairment. When he was well enough to be talked to, Stephen congratulated him on his progress, and suggested gently that perhaps he shouldn't be too hard on Adie Shaw, who had no doubt been carried away by enthusiasm.

"Oh, I'm not cross with Shaw at all," said Middling. "His study is first-class original work. And he's, um ... well he's actually stumbled on one of the short cuts we were looking for."

"Oh, good," said Stephen, not quite understanding.

Middling glanced furtively across at the tall man in the blue suit who had sat quietly reading in the corner for the past three days.

"Um, keep this under your hat," he whispered, "but those chaps in Omsk are going to have to pull their socks up now. Anyway, as soon as I get out of here I'm going to treat him to a great big banana split!"

A week after that, Stephen and Grete saw Adie Shaw outside Kennedy Hall. He was getting into a new white BMW convertible.

"Adie!" said Stephen. "What's all this? You must have landed a major record contract!"

Adie looked rather embarrassed.

"No, it's not a record contract. The band would never sell out. No, it's more of a consultancy contract, like."

"Oh," said Stephen.

"Yeah. Some people in Colorado. It's surprisingly easy work, you know. But the mathematics of it is beautiful."

RUST GETS EXCITED

Rust is excited. Rust is so excited that he can hardly bear to keep still. Riddington and Tucker are seriously considering tying Rust to his chair, or sedating him with Valium. They have never seen Rust in such a state. So what's going on? Has Riddington abandoned the habits of a lifetime and invited Rust to a blow-out at the Connaught? No, he hasn't. In fact the three of them are sitting in a small conference room in Threshold House, a really horrible depressing room with too many sick-looking yellowish tables stained with the blood and tears of many an abortive meeting. There are too many yellowish sick-looking chairs with hard green seats, darkened with the sweat and shameful secretions of a thousand rejected actors, worn-out writers, pensioned-off producers. It's a dank, steamy, ill-ventilated room. They have tried opening the windows, but the crazed roaring Shepherds Bush traffic makes conversation impossible. Riddington and Rust are smoking like beagles and Tucker is trying not to smoke. All three of them are drinking BBC tea from misshapen plastic beakers that leak on to their laps. And Ron Rust is euphoric.

They have decided they'd like to involve him in casting. And not just any old casting: they want him to help them cast the Polish girl. For two days they have been sitting in this room while a succession of talented and beautiful and desperately anxious actresses have come through the door and sat in the hot seat and talked and laughed nervously and fidgeted and read scenes, and generally tried to embody Rust's wish-fulfilment fantasies. Rust thinks they are all wonderful. He would like to cast all of them, even though most of them are nothing like the Polish girl that burns in his head. He is having such a good time that he is thoroughly ashamed of himself. Rust is a coarse-grained man, as writers go, but even he has a certain minimal empathy: he feels the embarrassment, the humiliation of these women, most of whom are so far out of his class as human beings that in normal circumstances they would not consider even looking at him much less talking to him. That so much should depend for them on making a favourable impression on three slobs like Tucker, Riddington and Rust.

Most of them have played it brave and insouciant, as if they just fancied dropping in for a chat, and didn't care whether they got an offer or not, and it's just sheer chance that they are wearing black today, have either scruffed up their hair or hidden it, and happen to have seen *Sophie's Choice* six times in the last three days. Rust has now heard eight imitations of Meryl Streep's imitation of a Polish accent. He doesn't mind. He loves them all. He has been bowled over by a jet-lagged tearful French actress who kept falling out of her dress; he has been totally smitten by a tall, broad-shouldered American actress with calm steady blue eyes, who brought to the part a wonderful compassionate composure that was quite inappropriate but at the same time absolutely perfect.

The actual reading is the most grotesque bit. The actresses, of course, read the Polish girl. Tucker, Riddington and Rust take turns reading the other parts. Tucker is rather a good reader, and he particularly enjoys doing women. He plays women very perkily, sometimes with a little wriggle, very disconcerting in a chap as straight as Tucker is. At least, it disconcerts Rust, and some of the actresses are hard put to it not to fall off their chairs. Riddington, it has to be said, has trouble with the long words. Rust reads fluently but hammily. The main trouble with Rust, of course, is the way he looks. Most of the actresses keep their heads down when they read a scene with Rust.

Rust has been excited for two days. He didn't think he could get any more excited. But he is. He is beside himself. Sitting opposite him now is a real Polish actress, and she has a face like a fierce little cat. She looks like big trouble. She is thin. She is quite small, not more than a couple of inches taller than Rust, and she is so nervous she can't keep still. She is smoking one of Rust's cigarettes in a wild sort of way, scattering ash all over old Ken, she has dropped her script on the floor twice (the second time Rust and Tucker cracked their heads together picking it up for her) and she is bloody wonderful. Her hair is a bit on the fair side and a bit long, but who gives a fuck about that? This is the one. This is the Polish girl.

The clincher for Rust, if he needed one, comes in the reading. They are doing a bit out of the second episode and it's going really well. Rust is doing the doctor. She has invited him round for a meal and he is being a dickhead about it.

"You have to rush home every night to your wife and *babies*?" she says. No one else has made the babies sound funny. Tucker is making funny high-squeaking sounds; that's the way Tucker laughs.

"No. No wife, no babies," says Rust, suddenly invaded by self-pity.

"So?" She is looking at him challengingly, her head on one side. She has actually brought herself to look Rust right in the eyes. He feels very strange. He wonders if he is dreaming.

"Well," he says. "You're my patient, for one thing."

She doesn't even bother to look down at the script. She must have actually learnt this scene.

"Am I asking you to jump on my *bed*?" she says. "You think I want your *body*?" She invests this last sentence with such incredulity and contempt that Rust experiences the true horror of his short unsavoury body, the true irony of his life as a writer, as if for the first time. To think that he ever felt bad before. To think that he ever thought *that* felt bad. He can't go on with the scene. He can't move. He can't speak. He'd like someone to come and pick him up like a sack of rubbish and toss him out of the window. After a few moments he manages to look at Tucker and Riddington. Tucker is hugging himself with delight. Even Riddington is sort of smiling. It's all over. They've cast the Polish girl.

Going back to Lowlands in the train, three silly little miniatures of Bells lined up in front of him, Rust thinks about bodies. Not women's bodies. It makes him too sad to think about women's bodies. He's thinking about men's bodies.

161

5

"VULNERABLE HUMAN BODIES"

George Bunn, Professor of English at Lowlands University, devoted very little time to thinking about his body, or indeed anyone else's. If interrogated on the subject, he would have said that his body seemed about right for the sort of man he was. The only other body he had anything to do with belonged to his wife Joan; and her body seemed about right for the sort of man he was too. George Bunn was tall and fat, and Joan Bunn was tall and thin. They slept together like two spoons, her thin front to his fat back, and she still sometimes liked, when not sleepy, to lie with her head resting on the warm pillow of his belly. They still copulated from time to time, in a leisurely absent-minded sort of way, often breaking off in the middle for a lively interchange of views about Pope, or eighteenth-century wooden legs, or pubs in the Lake District; sometimes on these occasions quite forgetting to complete the carnal act.

All this seemed about right to George Bunn, as did everything else about his body. He ate a lot of his wife's excellent food, he drank a good deal of claret, his bowels moved obediently and satisfyingly at ten past eight every morning, and he always felt well. (Oh God, you will no doubt be thinking by now, poor old Bunn is being set up for some gruesome terminal illness. Take heart. Altered Priorities at Lowlands.)

All of us have vulnerable human bodies, as G. Grotowska stresses in her pioneering work "The Iconography of the Male Nude", but George Bunn's seemed a good deal less vulnerable than most. There is, however, one interesting fact about George Bunn's body that we should know: he preferred not to wear any clothes on it. He had made this discovery as a National Service officer in Singapore in the fifties. The tropical kit had failed to materialize, and rather than swelter and suffer under the rough male kiss of standard-issue khaki, Bunn and some of his less hidebound fellow officers had chosen to go about naked on all but the most formal of military occasions. Absence of sartorial impedimenta, he found, raised the spirits and sharpened the wits. The habit persisted, and now most evenings would find Professor Bunn in his study, massive, pink and naked, tapping away at his typewriter before a roaring fire.

He was a happy man, George Bunn, and he liked most things about his life, except what Jack Daniels was doing to Lowlands University.

Stephen Daker, as a doctor, was constantly reminded of the vulnerability of the human body. He had also never felt tremendously at home in, or confident about, his own; until Lyn Turtle had taken it over, coaxed and cajoled it into tolerable fitness, and helped him to discover what an inexhaustible source of pleasure it could be. Now he was discovering shyness and self-consciousness all over again. His relationship with Grete had reached an interesting stage. She slept with him often, she kissed him and cuddled him, but she still kept her skimpy black vest and pants on when she went to bed with him; he had not seen her completely unclothed since the first day he had met her. Grete, on the other hand, had seen a good deal of Stephen. She liked to dry him after his morning shower, and when she had done that she would lie beside him or crouch over him, her thin fingers moving thoughtfully over his body. Sometimes she would talk to him while she did this, making both theoretical and personal comments; sometimes she would sing softly to him in Polish words that he didn't understand and she refused to translate. Her fingers would wander all over him, including his penis, but she always desisted when it showed signs of becoming, as she put it, red and angry. She found it, she said, much more pretty when small and sleepy. Stephen found this extremely pleasant and intensely disconcerting and painful, both in a general and a highly specific local sense. In the general sphere, there were clusters of incompatible emotions which included lust, tenderness, insecurity, resentment and guilt (for what was all this doing to his tender memories and hopeless yearnings for Lyn?). In the local sphere, he was suffering from bachelor's balls. Still: he was a patient man, and as a doctor he was well aware that as forms of suffering go, the sort he was experiencing was not the worst sort in the world.

Bob Buzzard was not the sort of chap to let his body go to pot, even if his marriage had blown up in his face. He had stepped up the squash and the swimming, and also initiated a few labour-saving efficiency devices at Buzzard Mansions. Simple commonsense stuff that a woman would never think of. If you left the lights on all the time it would save turning them on and off. And he'd organized the cooking too. One big pot of stew would last the week: saved shopping, saved thinking. Brilliant. Washing up once a week, too, early Friday night before he went out to unwind with a few jars at the Rugger Club bar. Odd thing was, when Friday nights came round he didn't much feel like washing up. Well, so what? He could hang loose: he was his own master now. Maybe he could shave once a week too, that would streamline the operation no end. Bob had the odd panicky moment when it seemed to him that perhaps the house was looking like a bit of a dog's breakfast, and that maybe he was starting to look not quite the thing himself. And he had had one funny turn in one of Dolly Daker's pathetic Group Meetings. They'd all been wittering on about sexual harassment, Dickie Dado calling for a positive initiative, uppity dyke rubbishing the rugger fraternity (only decent bunch of chaps in the whole place in Bob's opinion) and the old fart had launched into some loony diatribe about sensitive men being pursued by rapacious women, lecturers seduced by their students, and patients harassing their doctors. Bob had felt constrained to point out that that sort

164

of thing was no bother to a chap who knew what was what. When the odd tottie rolled her eyes at him, he simply remembered that he was in love with his wife. Then he remembered that he didn't have a wife any more, Daphne had left him, three weeks and not a bloody dicky-bird, and he'd found himself blubbing right there in front of his dreadful colleagues. Well. One little lapse didn't mean a thing. Bob wasn't going to weaken. Daphne would soon learn her lesson and come back. In the meantime, here was an opportunity to get on with his life, catch the thingy by the whatsits. And the way Jack Daniels was forging ahead, it looked as if there were going to be plenty of whatsits for a chap who knew a thingy when he saw one.

"You'll all doubtless have read in the press," said the Vice-Chancellor in Senate, "that the UK is moving towards a two-tier university system."

"Thought we already had one," growled the Professor of English Literature. "Oxbridge and the rest."

Jack Daniels looked round the room, identified the source of the growl, and smiled a little wearily.

"Hi, George," he said. "I guess that view is a little behind the times? The Government's thinking is in terms of ten to a dozen universities specializing in high-level research and postgraduate work. Centres of excellence, George. That's the name of the game. They'll draw in the very top people in the relevant fields, and reward them appropriately."

"What happens to the rest of the universities?" said Farris of Microbiology, looking as if he had a fairly shrewd idea.

"Don't need a Nobel Prize to figure that one," said Charles Dusenberry. "They'll lose funding, they won't get any research staff, in five years' time they'll be no-account diddleysquat cow colleges."

His words had a calm brutal conviction about them, and several members of Senate went rather pale. These did not include Farris, who was fire-proof and knew it; or George Bunn, who regarded Charlie Dusenberry rather as if he were a Martian in a space comic or a minor Laputian out of *Gulliver's Travels*.

"Hey, you guys," said Jack Daniels, his visionary smile warming the whole conference chamber. "We're *winning*. I guess we already have some of the special people right here at Lowlands. We're coming up with all the right stuff. We're leaders in five significant fields, including management strategy. What I'm saying – and this is confidential to members of Senate at present – we're right in line for the top league." The boyish smile, the brushed back lock of hair. "And, well, I'm just so proud and happy to be part of it all. I guess you are too."

Was he? Stephen wasn't sure. In some ways the new Lowlands was a paradise compared to the Hemmingway regime with its constant crises and desperate lunges for money on any terms. It did feel nice to be part of a success story. But when he looked around at the confident, untroubled, somehow value-free faces of the new power group at Lowlands – Farris, Middling, Brahmachari, de Souza – he felt uneasy. There seemed to be two tiers at Lowlands too, and he didn't feel as if the Medical Centre was in the top tier. He was quite sure that the undergraduates weren't. Professor Bunn clearly had his doubts too.

"I'd like to check my translations from the American, if I may, Vice-Chancellor," he said. "By 'relevant fields of study' and 'the right stuff' I take it you mean the stuff that's right for the arms industry, the drugs industry and the international money market? And did I hear something about appropriate rewards for the special people? I take it that means you'll be paying the Professor of Microbiology twice as much as the Professor of Philosophy – oh, forgive me! I forgot. We have no philosophers now. So convenient. They asked such awkward questions: what is justice, how should we live, all that sort of nonsense. Vice-Chancellor, is the pursuit of knowledge only worthwhile when it attracts the filthy lucre of ignorant and destructive men?"

He sat down heavily. Farris of Microbiology sighed aloud. Bunn had always been an anachronism, in his view. Now he was becoming a tedious nuisance. Moreover, he clearly didn't realize that the Professor of Microbiology already earned six times as much as the Professor of English, through his many consultancy contracts.

"Is this a school debating society, Vice-Chancellor?" he said, looking at his watch. "Some of us have important work to do."

"I guess George Bunn has as much right to be heard as anyone," said Jack Daniels, smiling warmly. "We're all aware of his towering international reputation as a literary scholar. George: I believe in the Western way of life, just as you do. And I believe that the study of the great English poets is just as important to the preservation of the Free World as, well . . . some of these other areas. We value what you do, George. We cherish it."

"Then why do you direct funds from the arts into the applied sciences?" said George Bunn.

"Professor Bunn, it's just temporary," said Charlie Dusenberry mildly. "I guess the applied sciences are sexier right now."

"Fascinating," said Bunn contemptuously.

Charlie Dusenberry wasn't used to anyone's contempt. "To put it crudely, Professor Bunn," he said, "guys like Professor Farris make it possible for us to afford guys like you."

"I see," said George Bunn.

"Well, I'd like to move on now," said Jack Daniels, looking at his watch.

Suddenly Stephen found he had his hand up.

"Dr Daker?"

"Look, um . . . Senate's a decision making body, isn't it?"

"Why, sure it is, Steve."

"Well, this may sound naive, but we never seem to make any decisions. All we do is . . . rubber-stamp things that have already happened. And if the proposal's to expand the applied sciences and squeeze the arts, well that seems like a huge change. Shouldn't we be discussing it fully? And then voting on it? I mean, do we actually have any power at all?"

"Good for you, Daker!" roared George Bunn.

"We surely do, Steve," said Jack Daniels swiftly and sincerely. "Right now, all we're doing is testing the temperature of the baby's bathwater. I really look forward to a full and frank discussion at a later date in Senate."

"And elsewhere, Vice-Chancellor." George Bunn was on his feet again. "I thought I might start the ball rolling with a few letters and articles. *Times, Guardian, THES,* that sort of thing, I'm sure they'd be interested. Perhaps even the *Sun*? 'Double pay for sexy boffins', eh?"

"Hey now, George, hold on there," said Jack, his face showing a flicker of concern for the first time. But Bunn was already shouldering his way out.

"Work to do, work to do. Come to dinner, Daker. Thursday. Bring your wife, or whatever." He turned at the door.

"'Ask you what provocation I have had?
The strong antipathy of good to bad!'"

One part of Lowlands University that remained a source of unproblematic pleasure was the swimming pool. Luxurious, Olympic-sized, it had been built during the first era of prosperity back in the sixties, when there had been some notion of establishing Lowlands as a centre of physical excellence, tempting athletes over from the States, Australia, Japan. All these plans had come to nothing, and now people just had fun in the pool. Even Stephen Daker had fun in it, once Lyn Turtle had saved his life in it and taught him to swim. Now he could manage ten whole lengths without stopping more than once or twice, and all in all he felt very pleased with life as he sat dripping and panting with his feet dangling in the water watching Grete Grotowska, who had come to the pool in search of material for her work-in-progress, a photo-essay provisionally entitled "Vulnerable Flesh".

"What about that one?" said Stephen.

"Where? Oh, yes, I see."

A tall slim fair-haired boy had come out of the changing rooms and was walking up towards the deep end. The first impression he gave was of delicate fragility. He had a long neck, slender ankles and wrists, and no overt musculature. Then you noticed his deep chest and powerful tapering shoulders, and that his thighs only looked slender because his legs were so long. He looked, not to put too fine a point

168

on it, angelic, as he stood at the deep end, rather endearingly dipping one slender foot into the water to test the temperature, and Stephen had a vague feeling that he had seen him somewhere before.

"What a shame," said Grete. "Too beautiful. I can't use him; he'd ruin my thesis."

Down at the shallow end, Bob Buzzard, fearsome in goggles and noseclip, hurled himself into the water and thrashed maniacally up the pool, just as the angel dived smoothly in at the deep end without leaving a ripple. Bob Buzzard and the angel collided in a flurry of arms and legs halfway up the pool.

"What the hell d'you think you're playing at?" roared Bob Buzzard.

"Just swimming, man, same as you," said the angel in a mild Geordie accent.

"Well bloody well look where you're going then!" said Bob, shouldering past him and ploughing on towards the deep end. Bloody plebs getting in his bloody way. Why couldn't they stay on their bloody slagheaps?

Bob finished his twenty and strode into the changing rooms, puffing and blowing. First thing he saw was the pleb. Actually, now you looked at him he didn't look a bad sort of chap. Nice build. Looked after himself. Don't suppose the chap had got in his way on purpose.

"Dr Buzzard man," said the pleb shyly. "Sorry about that, bumping into you like."

"Oh, think nothing of it, old chap," Bob found himself saying to his considerable surprise. "Sorry I yelled at you."

"Ah, I've been yelled at before, man. Seen you in the pool a few times. Powerful swimmer. You keep in shape, don't you?"

"Well," said Bob, flattered. "Can't let the bastards grind you down. Matter of fact, there's something vaguely familiar about you. Hang on."

He reached for his towel, put on his specs, and peered closely at the tall chap. Well, of course. That's what it was.

"You look like that runner fellow, that's what it is. What's his name. Glenn Oates."

"Well I am Glenn Oates, like," said the runner shyly.

"Good God. I saw you on the telly the other week. I thought you were going to beat Cram."

"Aye, so did I till the bugger did me in the last ten yards."

"What on earth are you doing in a place like this?"

"Phys Ed and English. Teacher training, like."

"Well, blow me down. Glenn Oates. Proud to meet you, buddy. I'm a fan. You must let me buy you a drink some time."

"Why aye," said the runner. "I'd like that fine."

Bob Buzzard went out of the Sports Centre feeling highly chuffed. Glenn Oates. Fine fellow. Built like a young god. And not a bit of side about him. Seemed quite sort of lonely in a way, as if he needed a pal. Well, Bob Buzzard would be proud to be a pal of the best middle-distance prospect since Cram. Glenn Oates. Just wait till he told Daphne and the . . . oh, Lord. Still. Mustn't weaken.

Jack Daniels and Charlie Dusenberry were talking about Professor George Bunn. The occasion of the conversation was Bunn's letter to *The Times*, which had been published that morning.

"It don't look good, Jack," said Charlie.

"Hell," said the Vice-Chancellor. "It's just a letter to a newspaper from some crazy old fart."

"Not just any crazy old fart. I've been fielding press calls since eight am. Professor Bunn has become a problem."

"Well," said Jack Daniels easily, "when someone becomes a problem, either you give them something or you take something away from them."

"Right," said Charlie, snapping a pencil. Jack shook his head gently. Charlie was one of the right guys, but he could be a little impatient. He'd spent a year or two problem-solving in San Salvador, and was inclined to favour short cuts of the kind that didn't seem appropriate in Europe.

"OK Elaine, have him come in," said Jack, pressing the buzzer. "And go easy, Charlie, OK?"

Charlie settled down and went with the flow like the good guy he was, even complimenting Professor Bunn on his prose style. Then Jack tried out one or two angles, but the ball just wouldn't bounce right. George Bunn's console didn't light up on the personal incentive aspect, which he called bribery. Nor did he bite when Jack suggested that some special accommodations might be made for the English Department as a whole.

"In return for my promise to keep my head down, eh?" he said, showing a deal more perception than tact. "Sorry, Daniels. My concerns are less parochial than my own department. You're destroying the idea of the university here at Lowlands, and I shall continue to say so, in private and in public."

"George," said Jack Daniels. "I'm getting a little frustrated here." When Jack Daniels let his smile fade, his clear blue eyes looked startlingly cold. "You know, George, I get the feeling that nothing I say is going to strike you right."

"Don't take it personally, Daniels," said Bunn cheerfully. "It's my job to preserve liberal values, it's your job to try to destroy them. Good day to you, gentlemen."

"Guess you're going to have to take something away from him," said Charlie when he had gone.

"Yeah," said Jack. He was thinking he would enjoy doing just that. That guy Bunn had really taken the shine off a beautiful morning. "You know, Charlie, I hate fat boys. All the trouble-makers in this place are fat boys."

"Daker's not a fat boy, Jack."

Jack looked up, frowning.

"You think he's a trouble-maker? Yeah, maybe's he's getting to be. But he doesn't carry the weight, does he? That's what I mean about fat boys. I feel more comfortable with lean guys around me. A lean guy is a hungry guy. Hungry guys handle easy. These fat boys, they're always kinda heavy to throw."

Charlie was waiting patiently. He knew that Jack liked a little bit of metaphysical musing while he was making his mind up.

"OK, Charlie," said Jack, snapping out of it. "How do we can a full professor?"

171

Charlie had researched that one.

"Not easy, Jack. Incompetence won't do it, not in England. Anyway, this guy is competent. Hell, he's famous. Rich, too. Old family money, we can't buy him. We can squeeze his department till he walks out in disgust, but I guess that's going to take too long. I guess it looks like Gross Moral Turpitude."

"What in hell's that?" enquired the Vice-Chancellor.

"University Charter's a little vague on it, but for dismissal it has to be something really bad. Murder, rape, plagiarism."

"Plagiarism, what's that?"

"Jack?"

"Ah, shit, yeah, I know, for a moment there I was thinking it was some kind of sexual perversion. Well, does Bunn do any of that stuff?"

"I don't know, Jack," said Charlie.

"Let's find out, OK?"

There was a short silence while both men considered the George Bunn problem.

"The Great English Poets," said the Vice-Chancellor after a while. "Charlie, which *are* the Great English Poets?"

"Shit, Jack, how would I know a thing like that?" said Charlie. "Uh . . . Shakespeare, I guess?"

There was another long pause.

"Uh . . . Milton?"

"John Wilmot, Earl of Rochester?" said Dr Rose Marie. "I've never heard of him, Chloris."

"Neither had we till this term," said Chloris Jakeman. Chloris Jakeman was a second-year English student, as was her friend and admirer Jo Lentill, and they had come to Rose to complain about their professor. They were unhappy about George Bunn's choice of texts and the way he taught them. Since the beginning of the year he had assaulted them with such grossly misogynistic authors as Pope, Swift, Rochester, and even Cleland, reading aloud with obvious relish long passages of what they saw as the coarsest woman-hating pornography. Not only did he do that, he made them do it too, claiming that only thus could they imbibe the underlying rhythms and resonances. He had made them talk about the stuff. He had made them write essays on it. And he had refused to take seriously their complaints and their suggestions for alternative authors such as Aphra Behn and Mary Wollstonecraft, claiming that these writers were not in the Great Tradition, and promising them with insultingly avuncular good humour that when they were professors and he was an undergraduate again they could choose the texts for him.

They were both sincere in their complaints, and articulate about them, and Rose Marie sympathized with them entirely. She was, in fact, delighted to help them. She had never liked Professor Bunn, who was in the habit of smoking his cigars in the Staff Club Reading Room, and had always affected not to know what her name was on the rare occasions when they had spoken. Moreover, this afforded an opportunity to widen the definition of sexual harassment within the university; indecent assault with a seventeenth-century lyric should quite clearly be included as one of the indefensible ways in which men treated women, when they got the chance. George Bunn was going to get what he deserved at last.

Rose looked at her patients and smiled at them with affection, sympathy, and gratitude. Women were so much nicer to look at than men. Chloris was a mature student, twenty-seven or twenty-eight, at a guess, small but chunky, big brown eyes in a face as smooth and hard as a nut. Large strong-looking hands resting calmly in her lap; she had the rare ability of being able to sit perfectly still. Jo was quite different: lots of curly black hair, a face that was still plump and dimply, not yet set into its adult identity. A long slim fidgety body with surprisingly generous breasts and hips. A natural target for the predatory male. They were both quite lovely in their different ways, and it was intolerable that they should be subjected to such stressful indignity. What they needed was help, and support, and ... Rose was, of course, in love with Grete Grotowska, but that didn't prevent her from responding, on occasions, as a woman, to other women. However. What they needed now was her professional help as physician and counsellor.

173

"I think the best thing would be to make an informal approach to the Vice-Chancellor in the first instance," she said. "I could do that for you if you like. And in the meantime, I'll write you both medical certificates excusing you from attendance at Professor Bunn's lectures, and from writing those essays you mentioned."

"But ... we're not really *ill*, Dr Rose Marie," said Jo.

"You're obviously both very shocked and suffering extreme nervous strain," said Rose firmly. "That's my opinion, Jo, as your medical practitioner."

"Oh, I see," said Jo. She smiled. "Right."

Stephen Daker went for dinner at George Bunn's house, and found that he was having a very good time. He took Grete with him, and she seemed to go down very well with the Bunns. The other dinner guest was Jock McCannon, who was, it appeared, an old ally of the professor's from the Hemmingway years. The food was excellent and the portions gargantuan. The conversation had been erudite, rapid and good-humoured over the first two or three bottles; now it had become more rambling and desultory. Stephen was in fact feeling rather sleepy, sitting as he was nearest to the great log fire that roared in the grate.

"Yes," said George Bunn, apropos of who knew what, since he was breaking a longish but unthreatening silence. "A good man nowadays is hard to find." He held a new bottle up to the light and reached for his wife's glass. "A good woman, too, saving your presence, my dear. My wife is a truly excellent woman."

Stephen felt a little surge of affection, and another of envy. Bunn sounded utterly sincere. It must be good to be married to someone you thought a truly excellent woman.

"Bunn is apt to go on like this when he's on his third bottle," said his wife. "George, it's insensitive to praise your wife in front of other women."

"Is it?" said Bunn, considering this as if it were a new concept to him. "Yes, perhaps it is. Dr Grotowska" – he turned to Grete – "I'm sure you're an excellent woman too."

"Grete, please. Like a cheese-grater," she said. "And matter of fact, I am a rude nasty girl."

"Are you indeed?" said George Bunn with great interest. "I've got some of those in my own department. Dreadful young women, seem to think literature's some sort of branch of feminist politics, hope you're not like that."

"Everything is to do with politics," she told him, and bit noisily into a large stick of celery.

"Oh, Lord," he said in real or simulated dismay. "That's just what *they* say. I tell them to bugger off. Is that wrong?"

"Well of course it is," said Stephen, surprising himself. "Education should be about exchanging views, shouldn't it?"

"I don't want to exchange views with teenage idiots!" said George Bunn, as if he were sending a double-glazing rep about his business. "No one under twenty-five understands *anything*. How old are you, Grete?"

"Twenty-seven," said Grete cheerfully. Stephen couldn't understand why she hadn't hit Bunn yet.

"Well, there you are then," said Bunn. "You're a grown-up. Have some more wine." She grinned and passed her glass. Why did she like him? Why did Stephen like him, come to that? He was like something out of the dark ages.

"Look, George," said Stephen. "It's got nothing to do with age, it's about intelligence. You're talking nonsense."

"Oh, am I indeed?" said Bunn pugnaciously.

"Yes of course you are," said Joan Bunn.

"Man comes to dinner, tells me I'm talking nonsense, who asked this man to dinner?"

"You did," said his wife.

"Did I? Oh. Well he must be all right then. Yes, he is. Remember now, had a go at Daniels. You're a good man, Daker. Bit of a softy, bit of a lefty, but you're all right. Have some more wine."

"Look, can we forget about that and be serious a minute?" said Stephen, who was feeling quite wide awake now and hardly drunk at all. "I mean, what *about* Jack Daniels? He's done some good things. Look, this time last year they were talking about closing down the Medical Centre. They were talking about closing down the whole university. He's changed all that."

"But at what price?" said Jock McCannon, suddenly erupting into consciousness in a shower of breadcrumbs. "At what price, Stephen? Financially we flourish, morally we wither! Bunn, I am weary of these French soft drinks, you wouldn't have a little Scotch whisky about the place?"

Bunn lumbered up in search of strong drink for Jock, who continued: "Make no mistake about it, Stephen, make no mistake, Grete my dear, the Prince of Darkness is alive and well and going about under the name of Daniels!"

"Well, *if* that's true, not literally I mean, but *if* Jack Daniels is really trying to turn the university into some sort of weapons research establishment . . . ."

Stephen found his wrist gripped tight in Jock's hairy old fist.

"Worse than that, Stephen, worse than that. He is sucking the soul out of this university as happily as a wee wain sucks sherbet through a straw. Ah, thank you, George, you're a good fellow." He released Stephen's wrist and set about the Macallan. Stephen tried to remember how he was going to continue. Ah, yes. Got it.

"The thing is, George, you've really got up his nose, haven't you? And we all know he's a man who gets things done. I mean . . . if he's that bad, shouldn't you be worried?"

"What can he do to me?" said George Bunn. "I have right on my side. I lead a blameless life. I run the best English Department outside Cambridge. I teach my classes. I publish my books. I sit quietly in this room, writing my little articles."

"Stark naked by a roaring fire," said his wife.

"Really?" said Grete, perking up. "I find this very interesting."

"Little eccentricity of mine," said Bunn, a touch embarrassed. "Find I think better with my togs off."

"Well, why not?" asked Jock.

"Were it not that we have company for dinner," said Joan, "Bunn would be naked now."

"Hey, listen," said Grete eagerly. "If you feel uncomfortable with clothes on, please undress. No skin off my nose you know: male nude is my special subject."

"It's not a pretty sight, Grete," warned Joan.

"Well," said Grete, "I'm not so interested in the pretty sights. I think the body is an interesting sign; it speaks its own quiet language to us."

"Oh, Lord," said Bunn. "You're not one of those semiologists are you?"

She grinned. "Also deconstructionist, Polish style. I'm sorry, this is bad for you?"

"Suppose we can't all live in the eighteenth century," he said bravely.

She turned to him and looked him straight in the eyes. "Professor Bunn," she said formally, "I would be very interested to see your body and take photographs. I am not a pornographer; this is serious academic study. Please say yes; you would be ideal subject."

Bunn stared back at her in some alarm, unable for once to find the words to express what he was feeling.

"Grete," said Joan, smiling, "he's far too shy. And he honestly is no oil painting."

"Who can say this? Many painters would find your husband a good subject."

"Hieronymus Bosch for one, eh?" said Jock McCannon.

"Yes, and Rembrandt," said Grete seriously. "Francis Bacon maybe, yes? All interested in the wulnerable human body."

Even when unclothed and reclining in the approximate pose of a Michelangelo *pietà*, Jack Daniels's body looked curiously invulnerable. Lightly and evenly tanned, solidly muscled, dignified even in his unbuttoned boxer shorts, he lay with his head in Rose Marie's lap in the soft lamplight of her sanctuary in the Medical Centre, while she stroked his temples.

"Relax," she said.

"Yeah. I just feel, I dunno, kinda strange here, Rose."

"We're the only people in the building. And a doctor's consulting room is the most private place in the world. You do trust me, don't you Jack?"

He smiled. "Yeah. I guess." He came back to an earlier

177

subject. "So: what you're saying, George Bunn gets his rocks off reading dirty poems to innocent young girls."

Rose's fingers moved slowly down from the Vice-Chancellor's temples, over his broad chest and muscular belly, and ventured delicately into the shadowy cave inside his boxer shorts.

"Mmm," she said. "It's a particularly revolting form of exhibitionism. Metaphorically, of course, he's shaking his penis in their faces."

"Yeah, sure, I understand. It's ... kinda conceptual, though. I'd like to have a little more to go to bat with. Guess I'd be happier if he'd jumped a few of them, you know? You haven't heard anything like that? ... Oh, honey, that's good."

"I ... I shouldn't think *he's* capable of it, Jack."

The boxer shorts were straining at the seams and showing signs of distress. Deftly Rose released another popper, and set the prisoner free. The sceptre of the Vice-Chancellor's power stood proudly, regarding them gravely with its calm monocular gaze.

"Well," said Jack Daniels. "I guess we're not all built the same."

"That's certainly true," said Rose, with warm appreciation.

"That guy," said Jack Daniels with conviction, "is definitely a threat to the moral values of the university. No man, however eminent, can flout the values that we all hold dear, the values of the family."

"You're absolutely right."

"Yeah. It's kinda thin, though. Well, maybe Charlie can come up with something else on him. You know, Rose, I really appreciate your input. There's special people and there's very special people, and I guess you're one of the very special people."

"I'm so glad you feel that way, Jack. I get such a thrill from being close to you. The way you let me inside your ... thoughts."

"Yeah, sure," said Jack. "But, I dunno . . . ."

"Yes, Jack?"

178

"Well, gosh ... I guess I'm just a regular old-fashioned guy in some ways. I guess I find myself wanting what every guy wants. Hell, I know we're opening up unique new ways of interpersonally relating, I mean just talking to you is more fulfilling than *balling* some chicks, but .... Listen, Rose. How d'you feel about Trojans?"

"Well," she said. "They were rather naive about the Wooden Horse."

"Ah, no, honey. I guess I'm talking about how I'd like to give myself to you in the fullest sense."

"Yes. I see. Oh, Jack, I feel so vulnerable to you. As a woman."

"You do?"

"I've never told anyone this: when I was very young, I was married for a short time. It was a very ... damaging experience. And when it was over, I made up my mind I'd never let any man inside me again. I never imagined I would ever meet a man who'd make me feel differently, who would be ... man enough to make me feel that ... marriage might still be something I could contemplate. Until now."

The sceptre of the Vice-Chancellor's power, which had been nodding, as it were in quiet approbation, throughout this discourse, froze into immobility.

"Uh ... yeah," said the Vice-Chancellor.

Bob Buzzard was having that drink with young Glenn Oates the runner, and he was having a better time than he'd had in weeks. It wasn't just pride at knowing one of the country's finest young athletes, there was something about the chap that, well, sounds a bit wet, but ... made you feel warm inside. And the chap seemed to take to Bob, too. Look up to him, even. Bob hadn't felt looked up to in years.

"Look, Bob man, running's fine, but it's not everything. All a runner can do is run, like. I mean, you're a doctor, that's really something. Making people better, having that power .... Ah, well, I haven't the brains for it, so there we are."

He smiled at Bob. Chap had a nice smile. Funny how usually you never noticed things like that. Not all that bright, though: why the hell should anyone want to be a GP?

"Let me tell you Glenn, it's not so bloody brilliant. Bloody patients take me for bloody granted. I don't get any recognition. I don't get any gratitude. Just another bloody job."

"No, it's not," said Glenn earnestly. "I think you're marvellous, you, the way you're so modest about it, like."

"No, no. You've got it wrong, buddy. *You're* modest. Not me. You're Oates. I'm Buzzard. You're the star of the track. I'm just a ... Pemberton-Simms, that was his name."

"Whose name?"

"Chap in my house at school. Looked a bit like you. Had that sort of lock of hair that just sort of ... Captain of Athletics when I was just a sprog. Lord, I used to worship that chap."

Glenn's eyes had widened. Good Lord. Mustn't let the fellow get the wrong idea, don't want to alarm him. Good God, how awful if he thought I was a poofter.

"Just, you know, hero worship, you know. Boys' stuff."

"Aye, I know, Bob man."

"I used to hang about, you know, hoping he'd notice me," said Bob wistfully. "Course, he never did. Anyway. How's the training going, buddy?"

"Not so good," said the athlete wryly. "Pulled a thigh muscle in Koblenz last week. Sartorius, like. I can feel it from here to here." He demonstrated from where to where.

"Well, you would," said Bob. Odd how warm it had suddenly become in the half-empty bar.

"That's why I was in the pool yesterday, should have been doing speed work on the track really."

"I see," said Bob Buzzard, deeply moved. "That's really rotten luck. Look here, what else are you getting for it? Intensive physio? Infra-red? Deep-tissue massage?"

"Well," said Glenn wryly. "Have to go to London for that, can't be done man, got me lectures and that, like."

"No need to go to London, buddy," said Bob forcefully. "We have the technology right here at Lowlands. Maureen Gahagan looks after that area. She's on holiday this week, but I'd be happy to sort you out myself. Know a bit about massage. Always had a yen for sports medicine. Why didn't you mention it before?"

"Well," said Glenn shyly. "Didn't want to impose, like."

Lovely blue eyes the chap had, hang on, didn't mean to think that, good straight steady honest gaze, salt of the earth, that's more like it.

"Look here, buddy," said Bob. "You're a special case as far as I'm concerned. Working on you wouldn't be an imposition. It'd be a privilege."

Dr J. G. McCannon, MD, experienced a feeling of privilege as well as puzzlement when he was consulted by the Vice-Chancellor's wife. She wanted a full physical check-up, and Jock summoned up all he could remember of his best Harley Street manners and mores, and gave her the works. This was a pleasure as well as a privilege: Julie Daniels was a fine woman in the full flower of her maturity, fine-boned but strong like a thoroughbred mare. A little on edge, perhaps, but were we not all on edge in these dark days, as he reminded her. Nothing physically wrong with her at all. Hadn't been sleeping well. Jock would give her a little something, and everything would be fine.

"Well, I sure hope you don't feel I've been wasting your time," she said.

"Quite the contrary, my dear," said Jock gallantly. "You're a very fine woman. I haven't examined a bonnier wee lass in a long while."

"Jeez," she said. "If you knew how much I needed to hear something like that."

Jock McCannon knew a cry for help when he heard one.

"Sit down, Mrs Daniels," he rumbled, flashing her a glimpse of his dreadful old teeth. "Spend a few more minutes with a poor old man. I'm very flattered, you know, that you selected me."

"Guess I identified a kindred spirit," she said.

"Will you take a wee dram with me now, Mrs Daniels?" said Jock, whose instinct for some things was very finely tuned. "Bourbon and ice cubes have I none, but straight Scotch whisky I find is a great medicinal aid."

"Straight Scotch is fine," she said, holding her hand out.

Jock poured her a drink half the size of his own monster dose, caught her eye, and equalized the measures.

"Here's looking at you, Mrs Daniels."

"It's just the place, I guess," she sighed. "Lowlands. What a pissant dump. You know?"

"I do indeed, my dear. How can our fragile dreams survive in such a swamp of fear and loathing? But I sense, my dear, something deeper, something more specific than that. Isn't there? You can trust old Jock McCannon."

Julie Daniels was silent for a moment.

"Well, it's Jack, I guess. The bastard's seeing someone."

"Really?" said Jock. "You surprise me. With all his manifold schemes, I'd never have thought he'd have the time."

"Oh, he's always found the time when he wanted to," said Julie. "Modelled his whole style on John F. Kennedy, you know? Yeah, he's got some little Marilyn Monroe shacked up somewhere."

This needed delicate handling. The dear lady seemed perfectly in control at the moment, but he could be dealing with a paranoid fantasy, or he might be about to be sobbed on, and ten in the morning was too early in the day to be engulfed in the tears of a Texan heiress.

"Eh ... what makes you suspect this?"

"Shit, it's obvious," said Julie impatiently, lighting a cigarette. "He always showered a lot, but these days he's in and out of the bathroom so much it's like living with one of those Disneyland dolphins ... and he's always like standing in his shorts in front of the mirror smiling and stroking his tits ... and oh, yeah, this is the clincher. Like he has this routine at night, when we're gonna ball, he kinda walks about the room in his shorts, parading, you know ...?"

"Yes, I think I follow, my dear."

"And then he like pops the poppers ... pop ... pop ... and lets them slide down his legs, then he like catches them on his toe, and kicks them high in the air, and catches them? I used to think that was awful cute."

"Yes, well," said Jock, anxious to make the right

response, "I can see how one would, yes indeed, but I don't understand how this might confirm your suspicions, do you see?"

"Last night he went through the whole performance without noticing he had the shorts on inside out. Yeah. He's getting his pipe cleaned somewhere. And the hell of it is . . . I guess I still love the bastard."

A single tear rolled down her perfect cheek and she dabbed at it discreetly.

"Jeez. I'm sorry."

"My dear," said Jock. "Listen to me. I think your husband is trying to tell you something. The shorts on inside out . . . it's such a blatantly Freudian slip. The man's not usually absent-minded?"

"No, he isn't."

"Well," said Jock. "There you are. He has become entangled with another woman, or fears that he might be. He wants to escape, he wants to end it. He waves his shorts above his head, not in triumph, but in guilt and remorse. A desperate signal. A cry for help. The white shorts of surrender."

"Yeah, I get it!" said Julie Daniels eagerly. "He's had his fun, now he wants out. Sorry, kid, the wife's found out. What a bastard!"

She looked up at Jock.

"Hey, you're kind of a brilliant guy, you know that?"

"You're too kind, Mrs Daniels. Empathy and experience, that's all."

"Yeah," she said, still looking at him, "I bet you've had some of that too. You know what? I should get something going for myself and pay the bastard back, right?"

"Eh . . . you feel this to be wise? Here in the pissant swamp we seem to have moved into a post-sexual era."

"Don't you believe it," she told him. It was clear that on certain matters Julie Daniels spoke with authority. She put her glass down and smiled at him slowly.

"Hey, you know something? I always kinda sparked on older guys."

"Eh . . . my dear," said Jock, somewhat apprehensively.

"If you mean what I think you do ... ten years ago it might have been a different story, but old Jock's been *hors de combat* for many a moon, many a moon."

She was still smiling at him.

"I guess you never met a Fort Worth girl before, Dr McCannon?"

"No, my dear, I don't believe I have."

"Well, honey," she said. "You might be in for one or two surprises."

"Tell you another thing, buddy," said Bob Buzzard to Glenn Oates. "And this is from long and painful experience. Think twice before you get married."

This may seem an odd sort of thing for a man in the waistcoat and trousers of a two hundred quid suit to say to another man dressed only in a jockstrap, while stroking his thigh from knee to groin, but it is not only the Rolf-Reichians who know that intensive deep-tissue massage is a situation which calls up deep and powerful emotional feelings in both client and therapist.

"Aye, well," said Glenn. "No danger of that at present. Ah, that's good."

"Mind you, I'm prejudiced," said Bob. "My wife walked out on me, you know."

"No!" said Glenn, startled, as if astonished at the idea that anyone might walk out on so wonderful a man and doctor.

"Four weeks ago," said Bob bitterly. "After fifteen years."

Glenn sat up on one elbow, his face troubled: massage makes for empathy.

"Ah Christ man, I'm sorry. You must feel bloody terrible, like."

Bob was touched by the chap's simple good-heartedness.

"Well, I can't pretend it hasn't been a slap in the chops. Straight back to mother with the twins, haven't heard a dickybird since. Fifteen years down the plughole, well that's life." He gritted his teeth and grinned courageously at his new friend. "Now, this is the gunge that's supposed to get down to the deep tissues."

He plunged both hands into a large jar of white goo and seized Glenn's thigh high up, near the groin, and squeezed.

"How's that, buddy?"

Glenn closed his eyes and sighed.

"Ah, that's magic. You could teach our coach a thing or two."

"Well," said Bob. "Glad I'm getting something right."

"Why did she go? The wife like?"

"Search me, buddy. Haven't the foggiest. You know I always used to say that apart from Daphne I could never make women out at all. Now it seems I couldn't make her out either."

Glenn Oates sat up on one elbow again and looked at Bob seriously out of his deep honest blue eyes.

"Maybe she didn't understand *you*, like."

"No, no. Nothing deep or devious about Buzzard. Just an ordinary chap who fell well short of her girlish expectations, I suppose."

"Hey, now," said Glenn, laying a strong brown hand on Bob's arm. "You're not an ordinary chap. I think you're bloody wonderful."

In the Senate Meeting that took place next day, Jack Daniels took a little time out to share some thoughts he'd been having about moral values, values of the family. A university existed to create new knowledge, but if that was all it created, then that knowledge was not worth a pinch of soured owlshit. A university should show us how to live as well: offer an ideal model of society, a sense of community. The academic leaders of the university community should dedicate themselves to moral conduct which could serve as a model for others to follow. Morality, personal morality, was the bottom line. Nobody quite knew why he was saying all this, and nobody felt inclined to ask.

"No, it doesn't matter, Grete," said Rose Marie, trying not to let irritation and jealousy leak into her telephone voice. "It's just that *Desert Hearts* is on at the Arts Centre; I thought we might go together."

"Yes, I would like that, but tomorrow night I'm round at George Bunn's house."

"George Bunn? Grete, you have such odd friends these days."

"He is nice man I think. I'm going to make photographs of him, in the nude!"

"Grete. You're joking."

"No. He is a nudist. This is true. In his own house he never wears his clothes! Big fat wulnerable body!"

"Well," said Rose Marie. "That certainly sounds like an opportunity one shouldn't refuse. You must come round to lunch on Sunday and tell me all about it."

In the next Group Meeting of the practice, Stephen passed on Jack Daniels's thoughts on the values of the family, producing a bafflingly powerful reaction from Jock McCannon.

"The hypocrisy of the man! The very values of European civilization are being trampled under the hooves of the Midnight Cowboy, and he has the nerve to tell us to pull our moral socks up when he himself ... I'll say no more, I'm bound by the Hippocratic oath."

"Well," said Stephen, rather puzzled. "Not having a family myself, I'm not in a strong position to lead the discussion. What I recall of family values is mostly to do with moral blackmail, fear, guilt, feelings of inadequacy, silent oppressive Sunday lunches, nightmares about forgetting anniversaries .... I'm sorry."

"No! No!" said Bob Buzzard passionately. "Right on the button, buddy! That's what holds the whole thing together! Take them away, and what have you got? People will start doing anything they damn well like! People will start enjoying themselves, and we all know where that leads!"

"Where *does* it lead, Bob?" asked Rose Marie.

"God knows, I've never had the chance to find out, have I?"

"Till now, perhaps," she said gently.

"Lord, yes," said Bob. "Keep forgetting. Part of my mind still believes she's there, you know, that I'll come home, open the door, twins' computers pattering away like mice in the bedrooms, and there she'll be in the kitchen, meal on the table, all ready to tear me off a strip for some cockup or other. Strange that, isn't it?"

With a loud groan, he clasped his head in his hands.

"Bob," said Stephen. "We all admire the way you're coping with your, er, problems."

"Indeed we do," said Jock warmly. "Eh, Robert, who would that handsome laddie be, who's always wafting round the corridors these days?"

"Handsome laddie? Oh, you mean *Glenn*!" said Bob, cheering up. "Glenn Oates, the middle-distance man."

His colleagues stared at him uncomprehendingly.

"Oh, come *on*. You must have seen him on the box. Ran second in the fifteen hundred at Koblenz? Well, he's had a little bother with his sartorius muscle, and I was able to help him."

"Yes, I'm sure you were," said Rose Marie, her eyes wide and ingenuous.

"He seems very, eh, *attached* to you, Robert. I hope there's no incipient problem there?"

"No, no, Jock. Clearing up fine."

"I meant of the personal kind," said Jock, favouring the company with one of his dark therapeutic chuckles. "The predatory patient syndrome, as I had occasion to remark upon last week?"

"Or even, perhaps" – this was Rose Marie – "the other way round? The over-solicitous doctor?"

Bob Buzzard stared at them open-mouthed.

"Are you off your trolleys? This isn't a *tottie*! This is a *chap*! An *athlete*! And a damn good bloke too!"

His colleagues continued to regard him in the same concerned, sympathetic, therapeutic way.

"Good *God*!" he gasped, finally getting the point. "I've come across some dirty-minded swine in this profession, but you two really take the bloody biscuit! Excuse me, Stephen. I think I need a breath of fresh air!"

He strode to the door, opened it, and his colleagues heard his voice soften as he spoke to someone in the corridor.

"Oh! Hello, buddy. Look, I've had it up to here with this place, let's go and have a pint."

"Fine by me, Dr Buzzard," said the other person in a soft north-eastern accent. The door closed outside.

"Come on in then, Glenn," said Bob much later on that evening, shouldering his way through into the kitchen, kicking aside a few of the cardboard boxes a chap on his own seemed to accumulate. He started to look for the electric kettle, while Glenn stared round him. The kitchen was so full of things it was barely possible to move. All the cupboard doors stood open, there was an ironing board with a shirt sprawled across it in an abandoned attitude, where it had been abandoned, a basket of clean washing, two baskets of dirty washing, a table three layers deep in dirty plates and old newspapers. Well, nothing the matter with any of that. An hour's brisk work would sort the lot out. It was just that it never seemed to be the right hour.

"Bit of a tip, I'm afraid," said Bob, noticing Glenn's incredulous gaze. Glenn had been on bitter shandies all night and was quite alert. Bob had started on best bitter and gone on to Christ knows what later on, and was feeling a bit on the tired side.

"Why aye, it is a bit untidy like," said Glenn tactfully.

"Can't see the hang of this domestic bit. Get things out all right. Can't seem to remember to put them back. God, this is ridiculous. I know that kettle was there this morning."

"And you leave the light burning all day when you're out?"

"Ah," said Bob, tapping his nose. "Labour-saving device. Saves switching it on at night, clever, eh? Oh, God."

Several plates slid off the kitchen table.

"Look, Bob man," said Glenn. "You sit there. Let me tidy up a bit, eh? Best cook and bottle-washer in our flat, me, ask any of the lads."

"No, no," said Bob firmly. "Wouldn't hear of it. Let's both sit down. Have a proper drink."

He found a half-full bottle of Scotch and two not particularly dirty glasses.

"Come on, Glenn. Once in a lifetime won't hurt you."

"Aye, all right then. Seeing as it's you."

They sipped their whisky in silence for a while. Then Bob put his glass down on the table. For some reason his brain couldn't get the message through to his fingers to unclasp themselves from the glass. He glanced up at Glenn, and their eyes met. Somehow this felt oddly unsettling. Bob started to talk without any idea of what might come out of his mouth.

"I could do with a good chap like you about the place. Just till ... and I don't mean just the skivvying. Chap gets. Chap gets a bit. Chap gets a bit lonely. You know."

"Aye, I do. I'd be glad to. If you're serious." Glenn looked serious. What was he looking so serious about? Ah. Suppose it would be quite. No. Shame. Ah well.

"No. No." he said. "Nice thought. Wouldn't do though. Two chaps. Two chaps together. I mean everyone would think we were a couple of. No. Wouldn't do. Not on."

He was finding it a bit difficult to focus on Glenn, so he focussed on his Scotch instead and had another swig of it, spilling some down his chin. When he managed to put it down, Glenn was still gazing at him steadily.

"Ah, come on man," said Glenn. "When are we going to stop pissing about?"

"What?"

"I was hoping you'd take the lead like. I mean I've never been in this situation before, I don't know what to do any more than you do it seems. But, like ... we have to do *something*, though but."

"What are you talking about?" said Bob, utterly baffled, but with a dreadful premonition that something unspeakable was welling up from the depths of the unconscious.

"Ah, look, Bob man," said Glenn tenderly. "You know I love you. I want to go to bed with you like."

"I don't quite understand, Mrs Daniels," said Rose Marie next day in her consulting room. "Isn't Dr McCannon treating you?"

"Oh, sure," said Julie. "I went to see him one time. This time I thought I'd come and see you. That's OK, isn't it? I mean you're like one big happy family?"

"Of course it is," said Rose warmly. "I was just wondering if you'd experienced any ... problems with Dr McCannon. Anything that disturbed you. You can tell me in absolute confidence and privacy, you know."

"That's nice, honey," said the Vice-Chancellor's wife. "No, no problems with Dr McCannon. Kinda weird, but kinda cute. Did he tell you what *my* problem was?"

"Well ... his case notes do tend to be rather brief and cryptic," said Rose, glancing at the grubby note in Jock's file.

"OK, I'll lay it on the line for you. Jack, my husband, is making it with some chick on campus."

"Oh, I *am* sorry," said Rose carefully. "Are you sure you might not be mistaken?"

"No, honey. He's doing something all right. Dr McCannon helped me to look at it right though. It's like Jack's leaving all these clues? Like he wants me to find out? Like he walks in the door on a gale of Estee Lauder, you know? Hey, isn't that what you use, honey?"

"Why yes, it is actually."

Rose found herself laughing nervously.

"Kind of a common scent. I mean, a lot of English women seem to like it. I wouldn't offend you, honey, not for the world. And then, he'd leave his wallet lying round the bedroom, just like a kid in high school, all loaded ready to go with packets of Trojans ... and telephone numbers? I checked the numbers out. I figured that was what he wanted me to do."

"I see," said Rose Marie.

"I feel sorry for those chicks, you know?" Julie opened her purse and lit up a Virginia Slim, and Rose felt incapable of pointing out that the whole Medical Centre, and the Women's Sanctuary in particular, was a no-smoking area. "Yeah. Jack and his chicks. They never bothered me before. The chicks Jack has laid, stretched end to end, they'd reach from here to LA."

"I'm so sorry, Mrs Daniels."

"You don't have to be, honey. I got it licked now. I know I got something for Jack that none of these bimbos will ever give him."

Rose couldn't resist asking.

"And what would that be, Mrs Daniels?"

"Let me give you a clue, honey. It's green, and it rustles, and it sure comes in handy if your taste runs to Mercedes."

"Sorry to disturb you, Jock," said Stephen later that morning. He had put his head round Jock's door to find him peering into a mirror, trimming his moustache with a pair of nail scissors. He was wearing a suit Stephen had never seen before, too. Surely it couldn't be ... a *new* suit?

"Yes?"

"I just wondered if you had any idea what's happened to Bob. He's not in today. And Mrs Kramer can't raise him on the phone. I'm a bit worried. I mean, Bob's never ill, and he has been a bit ...."

"Leave this to me, Stephen," said Jock briskly. "Young Robert needs the care and counselling of an older man. And I feel capable of anything today. The sap is flowing again, my boy. The sap is flowing!"

Grete Grotowska shot a couple of dozen frames of George Bunn naked at his typewriter, then moved him over to the Chesterfield under the window, where, he said, he did most of his reading. After the first five minutes he had lost his shyness about Grete's presence, finding this easy, for she seemed to take his enormous pink bulk as part of the furniture.

"Just sit like normal, whatever you do when by yourself, OK?" said Grete, as she adjusted the lights. "With whatever book you are reading just now, yes?"

"You might improve the shining hour by reading aloud to us, Bunn," said Joan, who was sitting knitting by the fire. George Bunn turned over the pages of the Nonesuch Donne and found the poem he wanted. Grete took a photograph.

" 'Whoever loves, if he do not propose
The right true end of love, he's one that goes
To sea for nothing but to make him sick:
Love is a bear-whelp born; if we o're lick

191

Our love, and force it new strange shapes to take,
We err, and of a lump a monster make.
Perfection is in unity: prefer
One woman first, and then one thing in her.' "

He looked up from the book.

"You forgot to take a snap then," he said.

"I know," said Grete. "I was listening to the poem."

That same evening, Chloris Jakeman and Jo Lentill went to see Dr Rose Marie again. Professor Bunn, they said, had refused to change the essay titles, and had also refused to extend the deadline, despite their medical certificates.

"This is all extremely promising," said Rose. "Now . . . I know this will be very difficult and painful for you, but I think you should confront Professor Bunn as soon as possible. And since he's refused to see you in his office, then you should go to his house and have it out with him there."

"As soon as possible, you reckon?" said Chloris.

"Why not this evening?"

"All right," said Chloris.

"Ooh, I dunno," said Jo. "Go to his house? I'd be terrified."

"He doesn't terrify me," said Chloris sturdily.

"You'd be together, Jo," said Rose. "And there might well be advantages in doing it this way. People are less guarded in their own homes. He might . . . let something slip that would help your case."

Bob Buzzard was slumped over his kitchen table. He had tried to make himself move several times during the last eight or nine hours, without success. Why should he get up? Where could he go? His world had collapsed. The kitchen was a tip, but so was his mind. So was his heart. At least it was quiet. Apart from some drunk who seemed to be stumbling about in his driveway. What? Who could it be? This was an executive estate, they didn't *have* drunks in driveways, except for the odd occasions when Bob himself . . . perhaps Glenn had come back, after all Bob had said to him.

192

How could he face Glenn? *And what would they do?*

The kitchen door opened.

"Glenn?"

"Eh, no, my dear fellow." Bugger me. It was the old fart.

"Take heart, my dear fellow. Old Jock has come to stay with you."

Bob focussed blearily. Yes. It was Jock all right. With two bulging carrier bags. It looked as if he meant business.

"Oh, God," said Bob.

"No need to explain," said Jock, sitting down heavily at the kitchen table and unwrapping a new bottle of Bells. "I have talked with the young man. He's very upset, you know. Very upset."

"*He's* upset! What about *me*? I feel as if the whole world's turned upside down. I mean, I went right out of my way for that chap, Jock. Glenn Oates. England's biggest new prospect. A poofter!"

"Bob, Bob, it doesn't help to categorize people like that."

"And the worst of it is," said Bob, staring wildly at him, "he was a really nice bloke. I mean I really . . . Oh, *God*!"

He buried his head in his arms again.

"Of course he's a nice bloke," said Jock patiently. "My dear man, why should he not be? Listen to me, Robert, these men you call poofters . . . they are just like you and me, we all need love, Bob."

Getting no response, he laid a fatherly hand over one of Bob's. Bob jerked up instantly.

"My God, not you as well!" he said, snatching his hand away.

"My dear man," said Jock with some concern. "Let's not get carried into the realms of paranoid fantasy. Old Jock is here to counsel you through this difficult time."

Bob blinked.

"Ah. Right. Yes. Of course. Appreciate this, Jock. And I'd be happy to have you stay, you know, till . . . ."

"Excellent. And eh, Robert . . . I hope you wouldn't take it amiss, if old Jock were occasionally to entertain a guest?"

Stephen had gone to bed early that evening, not being on

duty, and expecting no visitors; and he was highly irritated when his doorbell rang, and then surprised and pleased to find that his visitor was Grete.

"Go back to bed," she said. "I come and talk to you there."

She told him about the photography session, and talked for a while about George and Joan Bunn.

"They are such nice people, Stephen," she said. "They really love each other, you know."

"Yes," he said.

"I want to say something to you. A thing I have been thinking about, and tonight I make my mind up."

"Yes?" he said, not without some apprehension.

She bit her lip.

"If you want to have sex with me, OK. I think we should try this now."

"Oh, Grete," he said.

"Hey," she said. "Don't look so happy. I think this is going to be one big disaster."

After Grete Grotowska had left his house, George Bunn sat up late in his study marking essays. He made short work of a batch of third-year finalists, not liking what he read at all. The trouble with undergraduates these days was that they made up their minds about texts before actually trying to read them. (The students might have said with some degree of justification that the trouble with George Bunn was that he made up his mind about their essays before he'd got halfway down the first page.) It was with some bafflement that he heard voices in the hall, his wife's, and two other voices, young voices, nothing to do with him, anyway. Half past eleven. Bit late for Jehovah's Witnesses, surely.

"Well, if you're absolutely sure he's expecting you," said Joan outside. "Wait there, please. I'll just tell him you're here."

Then the study door was opening, and Joan came in, followed by two young women. Good Lord. Two of his students. Those two who were always asking for things, and complaining about things. What on earth were they doing here now? And what on earth were their names again?

He got to his feet.

"Miss Jakeman? Miss Lentill?"

Yes, he'd got them right, he was sure. So why were they staring at him like that? One of them, the curly-haired one, he was sure it was Lentill, or Chickpea, or something like that, put both hands up to her face, gasped, and stumbled out of the room. Then the other one followed her out. Extraordinary.

"Oh, *Bunn*," said his wife.

What was *she* on about?

Then he looked down, and understood.

"Oh, Lord," said George Bunn. And then: "Oh, well."

RUST PRESSES ON

Ron has not been out of his cell for a week. He feels like a monk and he smells like a tramp. Everything is going too fast. Everything is out of control. Sometimes he thinks his little room is full of people, dozens of people, sitting jammed together on his bed, shuffling round and round on his floor, pressing against his back and joggling against his elbows as he types. Me, me, me, they murmur. As soon as he gets rid of one of them, another takes up the space. He is beginning to feel like a doctor. He would like to leap lightly from his chair, thread his way invisibly through the silent accusing faces, float away on the breeze like a feather to the car park, and glide away in his frail old Merc. He knows he can't. They're squeezing him too tightly. Now his elbows are pressed so hard against his sides, it is all he can do to move his fingers. There is no way out but through. He loads the tractor feed and switches on. The smooth screen is like a pale spectral bum. Elbows pressed to his sides, pain throbbing in his temples, he types: The Big Squeeze.

– 6

"THE BIG SQUEEZE"

Dawn in the new University of Lowlands. The rubbish van groaning inexorably towards the huge gaunt skips. Two nuns were on one of the skips, fighting with a group of ragged emaciated students over a large sheet of corrugated cardboard. It was a brief and uneven combat, as though a bunch of ragged starlings had challenged two huge glossy crows. There was a flurry of fast movement. One of the students slipped and fell off the side of the skip, hit the concrete, and lay still. And the nuns flapped off with their prize.

They scurried past the sheltered side of the Biochemistry block, where a few more fortunate students had set up little cardboard shacks in the warm alcoves, where yellowish steam emerged from the iron gratings set into the paving stones. Pale faces peered out of tiny windows roughly hacked in the cardboard façades. It had been several weeks since the first students had left the halls and started to sleep rough. The numbers were increasing daily. Rents were up, grants were cut, frozen, or pegged, and the State looked on in blank indifference. The big squeeze was on, and corrugated cardboard had become a valuable commodity.

Sammy Limb, who had never regarded his puny grant as adequate to keep body and soul together, was still managing to pay his rent at Kennedy. He was on night work now, nearly all night nearly every night, freelancing for Express Deliveries on his bike. He needed to finance not only his bodily existence and his academic life, but his legal affairs.

He was suing the University of Lowlands in the European Court of Human Rights, and so far things were looking good. If only he didn't feel so nackered all the time. He'd lost concentration and come off the bike once or twice lately. Nothing serious. Nothing to worry about. Couple of hours' kip before his first lecture of the day and he'd be fine. He waved to the dossers in the shadow of Biochemistry and roared on towards Kennedy Hall.

In his bedroom at Kennedy Hall, Stephen Daker stirred and woke to the sound of Sammy Limb's motor bike. He turned in the bed and looked down at Grete. Little calm cat face. It didn't look fierce at all when she was sleeping. He leant down carefully and kissed her on the pale prominent collarbone, softly, so as not to wake her. She opened one eye.

"Morning," she said.

"Good morning, Grete."

"Have a good sleep?"

"Yes, thank you, Grete, I had a brilliant sleep. Did you have a good sleep?"

She opened the other eye, yawned, grinned, and stretched both her thin white arms above her head. When she did that, her breasts practically disappeared. Stephen liked watching them go, and he liked watching them come back. He kissed one of them and then, on an afterthought, kissed the other one.

"Not bad at all, matter of fact," she said. "After the big disaster."

"I'm sorry it was a disaster, Grete," he said.

"Not your fault. I did warn you. Actually it wasn't quite as bad as I thought it was going to be, you know?"

"Oh ... well ... thank you very much."

"You're welcome, Stephen," she said, smiling. "Tell me ... how was it, for you?"

"Oh, Grete," he said tenderly. "It was ... it was ... well, it was pretty dreadful actually."

They both started to laugh.

"There you *are*!" she said. "I *told* you this! Well at least I didn't go into spasm, eh?"

"No, you were very brave, Grete. It was the way you screwed your face up."

"Did I do that?"

"Yes. And the way you, well, shouted."

She sat up.

"Was I *shouting*?"

Stephen nodded. Grete glared at him.

"Well, so what? You don't like noisy women? You like to make love in total silence, or what?"

"No, no, of course not," he said hastily.

"Well what then?"

"Well," he said, "it was what you were shouting."

"And what did I shout?"

"'Oh blimey this is terrible.'"

"Really?"

Stephen nodded again.

Grete buried her face in the pillow.

"I'm a terrible person. You better jack me in. Better for you, better for me."

Her little cropped head. Her little ears. Her thin neck.

"I couldn't do that," he said. "I'm ... well I'm completely hooked on you, I'm afraid."

She turned her head sideways and opened one eye.

"Bad news, eh?"

"And ... well it is early days yet. We can't expect it to come right all at once. It, well, it takes time."

She sat up, her eyes round and incredulous.

"Oh blimey. You mean you want to try this *again*?"

"Well ... only if you do."

"OK. You have another condom?"

"Grete, I didn't necessarily mean right now."

"You have another condom?"

"Well," he said. "Yes."

"OK," she said grimly. "Start the lovemaking."

She threw herself down flat on her back, kicked the quilt off, spread her legs, and lay rigidly still with her arms out by her sides, her eyes closed, and her face screwed up. Oh, Lord. What was to be done with her? What was to become of them? He couldn't do anything but sit there looking down at her fierce determined little face. Some moments passed, then she opened one eye again.

"Something the matter here?"

"I love you," he said.

Bob Buzzard woke up in a panic, from a dream of tall athletes in little silky pants pursuing him with hoovers and castanets. The sound was coming from downstairs, he realized. Someone was destroying his kitchen. Then he remembered. Of course. The old fart was staying with him. Oh, Lord. Just when you thought you'd reached the bottom you found another six feet of shit to sink into. He braced himself, sat up, held his head on with one hand, and tottered into the bathroom, and after twenty minutes under a head-drilling shower felt strong enough to stagger down and see what the old fart was up to now.

He stopped in the kitchen doorway, unable to move or speak. The place had been totally transformed. No dirty dishes. No piles of old newspapers and overturned bottles. All doors shut, all surfaces glittering. The old fart was sitting at the table looking very spruce for him in a tolerably clean fawn linen suit and a horrible paisley cravat, and a handsome dark-skinned tottie Bob had never seen before in his life was crashing about at the cooker. As Bob stared, she turned, marched over to the table, and plonked a massive plate of fried eggs on toast in front of the old fart.

"Enjoy!" she snarled, and strode back to the cooker.

"Ah, Robert, my dear fellow!" said Jock hospitably. "Come and join us! Breakfast, the best meal of the day, so long since I've enjoyed a proper breakfast! Consuela my dear, this is delicious! Eh, oh, yes, of course. Robert, this is Consuela. Consuela, this is Dr Robert Buzzard."

Bob sat down, feeling a little shell-shocked. The woman turned.

"Is this your kitchen?" she demanded threateningly.

"Yes, it is," he admitted.

"You are a very dirty man! So what do you want for breakfast?"

"Coffee, please," said Bob humbly.

"Coffee! Right!" she snarled into his face. "You want eggs?"

"N-no thank you."

"No eggs! You want toast, you want English muffin, you want corn muffin, you want Danish?"

"No thank you." His head hurt terribly. What he really wanted was for this fierce tottie to go away and stop shouting at him, but he was far too frightened to say that.

"My dear man," said Jock. "You must try something. We don't want to hurt Consuela's feelings, do we?"

"All right," said Bob weakly.

Consuela put one hand on her hip.

"Toast, English muffin, corn muffin or Danish?" she hissed at him in a tone of savage intensity.

"Er, Danish muffin, please," said Bob. Somehow this was the wrong answer.

"No Danish *muffin*! *Danish*! You want *muffin* or you want *Danish*?"

"I want muffin!" yelled Bob, panicking.

"All right! So don't shout!" said Consuela, and went to make the muffin.

"Er, Jock," whispered Bob.

"Yes, my boy?"

"Is she, er, is she your *tottie*?"

"Good gracious me, no. This is *Consuela*. Mrs Daniels, our Vice-Chancellor's wife, was kind enough to lend us Consuela on a part-time basis."

"*One*-time basis!" shouted Consuela from the cooker. "After today, you don't see me no more. Because you are two very dirty men!"

"Ah, no, my dear," said Jock gallantly, "you're far too soft-hearted to desert us. I agree you found us living in a *pissant rathole*, but now you've transformed it, we'll be *very* good in future. Two of the very cleanest men you've ever known, I promise you!"

"Huh!" said Consuela.

"Come on, my boy, cheer up!" said Jock. "You and I are going to have a woolly-assed good time!"

*

201

Everything was looking good for the Daniels initiative at Lowlands University. The funding was coming through for the sensitive research. They had a blank check on the special people. Whitehall was happy. Washington was happy. And why shouldn't they be happy? They were getting it cheap, because Jack and Charlie had gone out and hustled for the co-production money. But now it was time for the second stage. The profile still looked kind of flabby to the co-production people. It was time to look at the plant profitability question. And it was time to take another look at the Arts Faculty.

Jack and Charlie looked at what was left of the Arts Faculty. They had Languages. Hell, everyone spoke American now. They had History, but who needs history? History is a thing of the past. Art History was no longer a problem, because old Perce had opted for early retirement, settled for only fifty-five grand, maybe there *had* been something funny about those Braques in the art gallery.

And then there was English. That was the real problem, because George Bunn was trouble. Charlie favoured going for the throat, even though they didn't really have enough on Bunn. Do it to Bunn and do it to the Department, that was Charlie's view, because he was going to be trouble whether they axed English or not.

Jack Daniels sighed.

"That guy Bunn. He's not a reasonable man, Charlie. It's a shame. Hell, I wish . . . ." He lapsed into silence.

"Yeah?"

"No. Nothing. Crazy thoughts."

"Yeah," said Charlie, understanding. Things had been a whole lot easier in Salvador. He closed the Arts Faculty file and stood up.

"Mrs Daniels well?"

"Oh, yeah, Charlie. She's fine."

"She is?"

"I guess she's finally adjusting to the climate," said Jack. "Like she's finding new interests? Aerobics, she says, and she sure as shit looks well on it. Came home from the class last night, hell her skin was glowing like a young girl's, Charlie."

"That right?"

"I owe that woman a lot, Charlie," said the Vice-Chancellor seriously. "I kinda need to remind myself of that from time to time."

He grinned, that boyish grin that some day was going to take him all the way to the White House.

"Hell, you know I sometimes ... but Julie, well, she's a special person. I guess that's the bottom line."

Minutes of a Group Meeting
Present: Dr Daker (Chair), Dr Buzzard, Dr Rose Marie, Nurse Gahagan

Dr Daker remarked that Glenn Oates had pulled out of the 1500 metres final at Stockholm. Nurse Gahagan asked Dr Buzzard if this was due to groin strain. Dr Buzzard said he had no idea, it was nothing to do with him, because Mr Oates was now on Dr McCannon's list. Dr Rose Marie said that Glenn Oates still seemed to be hanging round the Medical Centre a lot, and that she had noticed that he was weeping. Dr Daker reminded the meeting that all members of the team should be alert for signs of distress in patients; with the approaching exams, the annual suicide season was under way. Nurse Gahagan pointed out that examinations were not the only reason for suicide at Lowlands. Dr Buzzard asked Nurse Gahagan what she thought she was getting at. Nurse Gahagan told Dr Buzzard he could take it any way he liked, at which Dr Buzzard went very quiet, as well he might, God only knowing what he had been up to with that poor boy.

Dr McCannon breezed in fifteen minutes late with no hint of an apology, and informed his colleagues that it was a beautiful morning, a beautiful day, that the grass was as high as an elephant's ass, and that though Lowlands might well be a pissant swamp, fulfilment was still there for those who sought it. Dr Daker asked Dr McCannon if he was feeling all right: something seemed to be happening to his vocabulary. Dr McCannon explained that he had been dipping into the honeypots of transatlantic culture, the better to understand the machinations of the Midnight Cowboy.

Dr McCannon went on to say that that morning he had seen a student living in a cardboard box, and wondered if his colleagues had any light to throw on this. Nurse Gahagan pointed out what any fool could see, that Central Administration had index-linked the rents, and that only those students with maximum grants or large private incomes could now afford to live in hall, and eat, and buy books. Most students were now opting not to buy books, some were opting not to eat. The box people were opting not to live in hall.

Dr Daker expressed his concern at this situation, and said he felt guilty that he had not, as Hall Warden, been assiduous enough in discovering and helping cases of hardship. He would certainly remedy this immediately. He had been rather preoccupied with other matters of late. Dr McCannon said that early morning sexual intercourse could disorientate the best of men, and reminded the meeting of Uncle George and Auntie Mabel, who fainted at the breakfast table, which only served you as a warning never to do it in the morning.

Dr Daker asked his colleagues to be alert for illnesses arising from financial hardship, and there being no other business, the meeting ended at 10.42 am.

"What a terrible job this is," said Bob Buzzard to Maureen Gahagan, as he stood at the sink washing his hands with ferocious thoroughness. "Why did I get lumbered with this one? Old Dickie Dado and Marie Celeste actually *enjoy* examining women. Can't be doing with it myself, Maureen. Nightmare territory for Buzzard. What do they call that fairground ride? Tunnel of Death, is it?"

"Tunnel of Love they called it in County Kerry, Dr Buzzard."

"Don't you believe it," said Bob. "Right, Miss Blackbush. Come out, come out, wherever you are!"

"Brownleaf," hissed Maureen.

"What?"

"She's called *Brownleaf*."

"Really? Out you come then, Miss Brownleaf."

A pale thin student with dark rings under her eyes emerged from behind the screen, tucking her shirt into the waistband of her jeans.

"Come on, sit down there," said Bob. "Well, you're definitely not pregnant, for a start."

"Well, that's something," she said wanly. "I didn't really see how I could be, I mean we always ..."

"All right, all right, spare us the details."

"But I have missed two periods."

"Well you know the reason for that as well as I do, don't you?" said Bob, lunging his jaw at her across the table like an Airedale terrier.

"No, I don't," she said.

"You should take a look at yourself in the mirror, young lady," said Bob severely. "Arms and legs like sticks. You're doing yourself a lot of harm, you know. So why don't you stop all this nonsense and get yourself around a few steak and kidney puddings, you'll soon find your, er, thingies'll be back to normal!"

"Right. OK. Thanks very much, Dr Buzzard," said Miss Brownleaf, in a resigned sort of way.

"Just a minute, Annette," said Maureen.

"Oh, come *on*, Maureen, we haven't got all day," said Bob, who had his finger on the button to bell the next patient already.

"Just a minute, Dr Buzzard, it won't take long."

"Oh, right, fine," said Bob savagely. "Sorry about that Miss Blackbush, thought I was the doctor for a moment but it seems Nurse Gahagan is in charge. Do go ahead, Maureen."

"You get a grant?" said Maureen.

"Five hundred and seventy," said the girl.

"But your parents make it up?"

"Well, Dad says he can't really afford to this year. It's not his fault really. It's terrible in the building trade at the moment."

"Fascinating, fascinating," muttered Bob through clenched teeth.

"And you live in university accommodation?"

205

"Well ... up to now. I do eight hours a week stacking shelves, can't do any more really, not with Finals coming up."

"There you are then," said Maureen to Bob.

"What d'you mean, there you are?"

"Well, it's obvious. She's starving."

"Oh, really, Maureen!" said Bob, exasperated. "Come on! Do us a favour! This is *England*!"

On the same day, Sammy Limb consulted Jock McCannon, complaining of headaches and dizzy spells, which weren't really anything very much, but made it a bit worrying when he was on the bike. Jock confided that he had many similar experiences in the old Riley, which had been quite worrying until he had taken the matter in hand. He had been faced with a choice of cutting down drastically on the Bells or giving up driving, and had opted for the latter course; the stipendiary magistrate being some influence in helping him towards his decision.

"I can't give up the bike," said Sammy. "Deliveries are all I got to keep body and soul together. Better give up the booze, eh?"

"A terrible dilemma," said Jock. "I feel for you, Sammy, I feel for you."

"Oh, I can hack it," said Sammy. "You reckon that's all it is then?"

"Trust me, my boy," said Jock McCannon. "Trust me."

"Oh, I *am* sorry," said Rose Marie. "If I'd had any idea that something like *that* was going to happen, I'd never have advised you to see Professor Bunn at his home. You must have been ... terribly upset."

"Well, it was a bit of a shock," said Jo Lentill bravely.

"Of course it was," said Rose, favouring Jo with a gaze of warm sisterly concern. "And he was ... forgive me ... he was stark naked?"

"Not quite," said Chloris. "He was wearing shoes. And socks. And *sock suspenders*."

"Quite pathological," said Rose, shuddering delicately.

"Um ... I've been thinking," said Jo. "I know he's been down on us all year ... ."

"And forcing his sexist pornography on us," said Chloris.

"Yes, that too ... but exposing himself to us ... couldn't that have been an accident?"

"I'm afraid these things are never accidents," said Rose Marie sadly. "He simply took his chance to inflict the final degradation."

"Yes. Suppose you're right," said Jo doubtfully.

"It's almost certainly not the first time," said Rose. "Many women, you know, feel too shamed and humiliated to report such behaviour."

"Well he picked the wrong ones this time," said Chloris.

A few days later, Jack Daniels let Senate in on the way things were going to go. He gave it to them square-jaw, frontier style. Tall in the saddle. It was not an occasion for the boyish grin. The eyes were visionary, but the mouth was set for realism. As a consequence of Lowlands' success in achieving top league status as a centre for research excellence, he explained to the assembled assholes, he had had to accept a certain amount of rationalization in certain areas, mainly affecting undergraduate intake and staffing in arts and social sciences. Naturally all present courses and commitments would be honoured. The Vice-Chancellor still held to his vision of a Platonic community blending the best of all the arts and the sciences. He was still fighting for that vision, the vision of a Camelot here at Lowlands. But the only way to achieve it was for the university to pay its way, all the way down the line, which had meant taking some very painful decisions. He referred the assholes to the details outlined in Senate Paper 42, and another document which outlined draft proposals on maximizing real estate assets on campus. Jack Daniels, on his best form, could sell shit to sewer rats, as Charlie Dusenberry often remarked, but there was no disguising this package. It was the big squeeze, and everybody knew it. Jack Daniels was all ready for a bumpy ride.

"OK," he said. "I'll take discussion now ... I guess Professor Bunn would wish to comment?"

"No," said George Bunn.

"This sure isn't the George Bunn we all know and love," said the Vice-Chancellor.

Bunn snorted.

"Recently," he said, "I've found Senate a very unrewarding area for debate. I find the press much more receptive. And one or two people from the television. I shall be presenting my views on Sunday week. 'The Destruction of Learning.' Channel 4 at eleven-thirty, I'm afraid, but perhaps one or two of our legislators might be awake."

Jack Daniels and Charlie Dusenberry exchanged glances. Sunday week. They were going to have to do it to him fast.

"Thank you, George," said Jack Daniels. "I think we should hear a reaction from the Students' Union. Harry?"

Stephen looked over with interest to hear what the President would have to say. Harry Pointer was a stocky young man in his mid-twenties, wearing a sharp double-breasted suit. He had attended a number of Senate meetings where matters affecting the Students' Union had been discussed, had listened keenly, made a good many notes, and held a good many whispered conversations with Charlie Dusenberry, but Stephen had never heard him speak before. Perhaps he was shy in the company of so many august academics. Now he rose to his feet, taking his time. Stephen realized that Harry Pointer was not shy in the least.

"Thank you, Vice-Chancellor," said Harry Pointer. He had a North London accent, and spoke quietly at first. "You realize of course that any comments I make now are off the record; I have to be mandated by my members at a general meeting. But I think I'm fairly safe in saying . . . ." and here he gazed round as if picking off targets among the sea of faces ". . . that my Union will be *bitterly opposed* to *every single one* of the measures outlined in Paper 42, and that honouring present courses will not go *any way at all* towards appeasing student feeling. Even the silent majority of head-down hardworking students are now feeling that the *cynical exploitation* of university life has now reached *crisis point*. What we are seeing now is the systematic erosion of this country's educational base, and Lowlands University is leading the assault on civilized values. What's happening in student accommodation is, if anything, a hotter issue. We'll demand full and instant consultation, of course, but that is no way going to satisfy my members. As I say, this is off the record, but I wouldn't rule out *total lecture boycotts*. I wouldn't rule out *rent strikes*. I wouldn't rule out *sit-ins*. My members are not just discontented. They are *desperate*, Vice-Chancellor. I think you've put yourself in line for the biggest outbreak of student unrest since 1968, OK?"

He sat down calmly, took out a small penknife, and began to trim his nails, apparently quite uninterested in any impression he had made. Stephen was impressed, and stirred, not just by the genuine passion of the man, but also by the articulacy and the sheer force of Pointer's oratory. Here were the words that needed to be said, and said by a man who could really bang them in. So why were Jack Daniels and Charlie Dusenberry looking so unconcerned? Surely what they had just heard amounted to a declaration of war?

"Well," said Jack Daniels. "I guess I'd like to thank Harry Pointer for that very frank and helpful input. And of course you'll get full consultation all the way down the line. Harry and I have licked some pretty thorny problems together, and I guess we'll find a way of licking this one. It's a real challenge. But you know what they say ..."

Stephen watched fascinated as the Vice-Chancellor's eyes assumed that characteristic distant-horizon light-out-for-the-territory visionary gleam.

"... when the going gets tough, the tough get going."

"Uh, listen, Rose," said Jack Daniels later that evening, setting down his glass of Wild Turkey. "This is kind of hard to say."

"You can say anything to me, Jack," she assured him softly.

"Well ... I guess we have to stop seeing each other. Julie knows."

"And what Julie says goes?"

Both of them looked down at Rose's ringless hand, which was resting on the Vice-Chancellor's powerful thigh.

"Honey, it's not just that. I guess, you and me ... it was one of those wonderful dreams that had to end. What you've given me. It's meant so much to me. As a man."

"And to me, Jack. As a woman."

"But you know," he said, "a President can't just be a man like other men."

"A President, Jack?"

Jack cleared his throat.

"A Vice-Chancellor, Rose, he represents something more. He's got to be emblematic of the values of the community. And at this point in time we're foregrounding traditional family values."

Rose sighed.

"And extramarital sexual affairs, even the postmodernist conceptual kind, don't quite go with the image?"

"I knew you'd understand," he said gratefully. "And I know I can count on your discretion."

"You've been able to count on it up to now, Jack."

"Yeah," he said. Something in her tone, or was it something about the stillness of her body, made him feel as if he might have wandered into Indian territory.

"You know, Rose," he said cautiously, "I wish I could do something to make you happy."

"But Jack," she said, wide-eyed. "You've done so much to make me happy."

"Dean of Women is still on the cards, if you want it."

"Mmm," she said. "Jack. Don't you feel it would be a forward-looking move if a woman were to become head of the Health Centre?"

So that was it. Hell, he should have expected that one. Bring me the head of Stephen Daker. With all the rest of the stuff he had on his plate.

"Honey," he said, "that's a tough one. And right now we have as much as we can handle with George Bunn and the Students' Union."

"Jack," she said sweetly, taking her hand off his leg, "if you can't manage it, you only have to say so. I don't expect you to perform miracles."

"Hey, now, honey," said Jack, who was in truth feeling

210

more than a little frustrated: here was a chick who, whichever way you looked at it, had passed up her ticket for one of the really legendary All-Action-Spectaculars: what was she getting at now? "Did I say I couldn't deliver? Honey, it's just that sometimes ... miracles can take a little time, you know? You ever know me not to deliver, honey?"

She smiled, and her hand crept back into his lap.

"Why, no, Jack. Sometimes ... well, it's as if you had a magic wand."

"Yeah," said Jack. That was more like it. "And I'm sure grateful to you, Rose ... you showed me some cute new ways to ... Dean of Women *and* head of the Health Centre. That's quite a little goodbye present."

"Just what I always wanted, Jack," she said.

"Uh huh. Rose, I kinda feel like that's two presents, not one. Remind me what it is you're giving me."

"I'm giving you my promise of absolute discretion, Jack."

"Yeah," he said. "I guess."

"And I have something else to give you as well."

"You do?"

"I'm going to give you George Bunn."

Grete Grotowska had come round to spend an evening at Rose's flat, and for Rose it had been an evening which was extremely rewarding in some ways, but less so in others. Rose heard Grete's account of the photography session at Bunn's house. Grete had portrayed it as a wholly innocent, if eccentric, occasion, but there were details which might prove to be extremely helpful. Once the Professor had overcome his initial shyness he had been, in Grete's words, keen as a horseradish, and at the end of the session he had presented her with a bag of toffees, just as if she were a little girl. Men, they agreed, were such odd creatures.

On that same evening, Rose had learnt to her chagrin that Grete had first slept with Stephen on the night of the beagles, the night when she had phoned up Rose Marie in distress, and Rose had turned her away because she was all tied up with Jack Daniels. In other words, on the fateful night, it could have been Rose. But she was somewhat cheered to hear that Stephen and Grete's sex life was a total disaster, a dog's breakfast in bed, as Grete put it. Rose also realized that when Stephen and Grete had first slept together, Grete had still, technically, been Stephen's patient. Promising. And there was enough in Grete's demeanour to give Rose the hope that once Dr Daker had been disposed of, and Dr Rose Marie was head of the practice, Dr Grotowska might see her way to developing a research interest in the Wulnerable Female Body.

Bob Buzzard was on to a new interest too. Freddy Frith had dropped him the word about a possible opening in international medical supplies, nothing to do with rubber johnnies at all, and something he could combine with the day job, do it all from the office, and save on the phone bills. Little Dolly Dado was of course shocked to the core by moonlighting, so most of it would have to be done by moonlight, while Dado was safely tucked up with his Polish tart.

So Bob was a bit taken aback when he lurked into the Centre at half eight in the evening, long after the last patients had gone home, to find Carmen Kramer still fiddling about at the reception desk.

"Evening, Mrs Kramer," he barked. "Don't worry about Buzzard, you just pack up and go home – got a few bits and bobs to tidy up in the Body Lab."

"That's all right, Dr Buzzard," she replied rather roguishly. "I understand. Your special appointment's waiting for you in your room."

"Special appointment? I haven't got a special appointment!"

"No, of *course* you haven't," she said demurely. "I understand. Mum's the word, eh?"

"Good God, it's not my mother is it?" said Bob, appalled.

"No, no, this is madness!" he said when he saw who it was. "Who let you in?"

"Mrs Kramer, man," said Glenn Oates.

"Well she had no business to," said Bob firmly.

"McCannon's the man for you now. Sorry. This isn't on. Bad medicine."

"Ah, come on, man," said Glenn pathetically. "Have pity on me."

"But you're not my *patient* any more!"

Trouble was, he couldn't *help* having pity on the poor fellow. England's best middle-distance prospect was in a bad way. Hair lank, eyes red and puffy, he was sitting hunched up on the couch with his knees up to his chin in a ragged holey T-shirt and a pair of filthy tracksuit bottoms. His feet were bare. Bob couldn't abide scruffiness in any shape or form, but despite the way he'd let himself go, Glenn looked so ... no. That way madness lay. What the hell was he to do?

"This is personal, Bob," said Glenn Oates.

"Oh, my God," said Bob. "Don't you understand, Glenn? That's why I transferred you!"

"Aye," said the athlete tearfully. "I s'pose so. But I thought, like, we could still be friends."

"Oh, God," said Bob, finding that he needed to sit down, legs had gone trembly all of a sudden. "I don't mind telling you, Glenn, this business has shaken me up more than somewhat. I mean, I thought we *were* ... when I think how I ... Lord, it throws a chap's whole life into question."

"Aye, I know," said Glenn softly.

If the chap went on looking at him like that for much longer he'd be blubbing himself.

"No. No. You have to understand. Not on. Absolutely out of bounds. You'll just have to pull yourself together and get on with your life. That's what I've done."

"Oh, Bob man, I've tried, but I can't. I can't run, I can't train, I can't sleep, I can't work, I'm failing me subsid, I'll be out at the end of the year ... please help me, Bob?"

He gulped, and tears rolled down his cheeks. Silently Bob passed across an immaculate white hanky and watched Glenn wipe his reddened eyes and blow his beautiful nose.

"Sorry," said Glenn humbly.

"Look, I ... this is terrible. What's your subsid subject again?"

"English," said Glenn, calmer now. "I thought I was all

right, like, but Professor Bunn second marked my course work, and he said it was balderdash like. Gave it an F. He really has it in for athletes, Bunn."

"Bunn, eh?" said Bob fiercely, grateful for the chance to channel his emotions into the familiar froth of anger. "*That* pompous patronizing slob! He's always seen fit to talk to me as if I were an idiot, for no good reason that I can see. And with a belly like that on him of course he's going to hate athletes. You're being victimized."

"Well, tell you the truth," said Glenn ruefully, "I'm not so good at English, but I hoped I'd scrape through like."

"Listen, Glenn," said Bob. "You're a good chap. Despite ... well. Nuff said. I'll see what I can do about this Bunn business. But as for anything else: forget it, buddy. Out of the question."

Oh, Lord, he was giving him that look again.

"Not even just ... the odd little kiss like?"

"*Absolutely* not!" said Bob horrified. "You've just got to pull yourself together. Get on with your life. Put all that sort of thing behind you. Er, so to speak."

Glenn looked at him silently for a few moments, his lip trembling. Then, "Aye, all right," he said. "I'll try."

Stephen had been most impressed by Harry Pointer's intervention in Senate. Here, clearly, was someone who cared about people as strongly as Stephen himself did, and was actually doing something about it. Stephen felt deeply ashamed of his sketchy grasp of the political situation within the university. Grete had been right. Everything was to do with politics. Rose had been right: illness was a political manifestation as much as a physical one. His job as Warden of Kennedy, which he had seen as a purely pastoral role, was now, he realized, much more than that. He was going to have to take sides: and the first step would be to go and see Harry Pointer. He needed a crash course in the political realities of Lowlands University if he was going to be effective.

He was rather disconcerted to find that the office of the President of the Students' Union was only marginally less luxurious than the Vice-Chancellor's. Harry Pointer sat behind a large desk in what might well have been a four hundred quid suit, with the sleeves casually pushed up to the elbows. A couple of other young men of about Harry's age were lounging about on easy chairs. They both favoured double-breasted suits, too, and one of them had a Crombie overcoat draped round his shoulders. They didn't look like students, somehow: they looked like the kind of people who could get things done for you. They looked, curiously enough, a bit like some of the men in suits one saw lounging about in Senate House. There was a case of claret on the desk, with the name of a smart Pall Mall wine merchant on it, and several opened bottles were dispersed around the room.

"Dr Daker!" said Harry, as Stephen hesitated in the doorway. "Come on in. What can we do you for?"

"Well, if you're not busy," said Stephen diffidently.

"Not really. Just tasting a bit of this claret we're thinking of putting in the Union bar. Pour a glass for Dr Daker, Mal."

One of the men got up and did that.

"Mal Prentis, Entertainments Officer, Johnny Graftin, VP. External Affairs. Dr Stephen Daker. Call you Stephen, all right?"

"Yes, of course," said Stephen. "Cheers."

The claret tasted excellent, rather better if anything than George Bunn's, to Stephen's untutored palate.

"We haven't met before, have we Stephen?" said the one called Mal Prentis genially.

"No, you Union officers must be very healthy people."

"Ah, well, you see," said Harry, "sabbatical post-holders get BUPA, brought that one in my first term of office. Look, Stephen, I have to ask you this, you're nothing to do with that enquiry, are you?"

"No," said Stephen, puzzled. "Er, what enquiry?"

"They're investigating us again," said Johnny Graftin bitterly.

"Oh," said Stephen.

"It's *so* silly," said Harry Pointer. "They know they won't

215

find a single dodgy thing. It just creates bad feeling, yeah?"

"After all we've done for the ungrateful bastards," said Johnny Graftin.

"All right, Johnny," said Harry gently. "He's very sensitive, Stephen. Keep telling him you can't be too sensitive in this job. So, what's on your mind, Stephen?"

"Well," said Stephen. "I should imagine it's the same thing that's worrying you. The systematic running-down of parts of the university, and, well, what seems like the deliberate application of market forces to the accommodation and catering departments. We're actually starting to get students coming into the surgery whose illnesses are poverty-related."

"Yeah, right," said Mal Prentis. "It's shocking, Stephen, shocking." He didn't look or sound particularly shocked, but it was hardly Stephen's place to make judgements. Mal Prentis had probably seen too much injustice and suffering to be shocked any more. He was there to do something about it.

"I feel, well, very guilty that I haven't actively involved myself before."

"Lot of apathy about, Stephen," said Prentis comfortably. "And you're very busy with your doctoring. Know how it is."

"Well, I don't see a doctor's job as narrowly as that," said Stephen. "I just wanted you to know I'm on your side, and I want to do what I can to help."

"Good on you, Stephen," said Harry Pointer. "There's not many like you."

"There's hardly *anyone* who seems to question what's going on," said Stephen vehemently. "And, well, actually, till I heard you in Senate, I hadn't realized just how militant the student feeling has become."

"Have a drop more claret, Stephen," said Mal Prentis.

"Er ... thanks. I mean ... I used to think Ernie Hemmingway was crazy, but now I'm beginning to think that Jack Daniels is just as crazy, in a different way."

Harry Pointer leaned forward. Stephen noticed how thick, hairy and strong his forearms looked.

"I've never thought either of them was crazy, Stephen. Just doing their jobs, that's all. Same as you. Same as me. Jack Daniels is a bit on the sharp side. Doesn't do to underestimate the enemy."

"No," said Stephen, feeling, absurdly, as if he were ten years younger than Harry Pointer, instead of ten years older. "Suppose I'm a bit naive, politically."

"Well, aren't we all?" said Harry generously. "Look, Stephen, I really appreciate you coming over. We'll keep in touch, right? It's good to know we'll have your support in the fight against injustice . . . when the time comes, eh?"

Later that day, Stephen had an unexpected visit. Jeannie McAllister, who had embarrassed him so painfully by writing a profile of him in the student newspaper, turned up unannounced in his consulting room. She seemed delighted to see him again. Though she had only graduated the previous year, she had changed her appearance a lot. She had always been formidably bright, but a bit of a scruff. Now she looked formidably smart, and was clearly doing formidably well. She had a job on a good North London newspaper, and was already freelancing on the side for Fleet Street, and doing a bit for local TV as well. Just research so far, but with luck she would get in front of the camera soon. Her visit, she said, was partly a sentimental journey, partly a little research project. She was trying to put something together about student unrest in the late eighties: was another May '68 looming on the horizon? Stephen surprised her by saying that he thought she had come to the right place, and further surprised her by agreeing to give her some facts and figures on student health and its correlation with student hardship.

"You're not so cagey as you used to be, are you?" she said. "Dr Blue Eyes on the barricades, is it now?" Her mischievous smile was one thing that hadn't changed.

"Well," he said, embarrassed. "Something like that."

"And what's all this about Professor Bunn getting the sack for sexual irregularities?"

"*What*?" said Stephen, astonished. "Jeannie, I don't

know who you've been talking to, but believe me, that's absolute nonsense."

"Ah, well, there goes another story," she said. "I must say it didn't sound like him. It's really lovely to see you again, you know. How's your girl friend, by the way?"

"Well, fine," said Stephen. "I didn't realize you ...." He stopped. She meant Lyn, of course. When was he going to sort out his feelings about Lyn? "Well, Lyn's fine. She's in Hong Kong, actually."

"I see," said Jeannie. "Well, I hope you're keeping out of mischief, Dr Daker."

Stephen would have done well to sort out his feelings about Lyn. That evening, he let himself into his flat, and found Grete sitting on his bed. She did not smile at him or speak to him, and she looked as if she had been crying.

"Grete," he said. "How did you get in?"

"Sammy opened the door for me," she said. "Do you mind?"

"No, of course not," he said. "Look, are you all right?"

"No," she said. "I saw Professor Platt today. My crap department is closing down. Tin handshake for Dr Grotowska. Not very nice, eh?"

"The bastards," he said, feelingly.

"Well, you should know, you're one of them."

"What d'you mean?" he said. She was looking at him as if she hated him. It was awful. It was like being hit in the face. It was worse than being hit in the face.

"You're on Senate, you mean you didn't know about this?"

"Grete, look ... I know Jack Daniels is trying to squeeze the arts and social sciences, but nothing's settled yet. We're going to fight it."

"How do you fight it when the professor takes his money and runs away to Venice? What do you think I am, a dozy bugger?"

"No, I don't think you're a dozy bugger, I think you're wonderful. Look," he said, sitting on the bed beside her and putting his hand on hers. She took her hand away.

"What is it?" he said.

"Nothing for you to worry about. It's all right, Stephen, you don't have to do anything for me. I am known in my field, I speak five languages, I can work in Paris, I can work in Germany, I can even go back to Poland. Lot of bastards there too, but at least you know who they are, eh?"

What was happening? Of course she was upset about the job, but why had she turned against *him*?

"Look," he said. "Don't you *want* to stay here? *I* want you to stay here."

She stared at him coldly.

"No, I don't think so. I think, very convenient for you if I lose my job and go away. I think it's been quite nice for you to amuse yourself with a bit of foreign muffin, till the wonderful girlfriend comes back, and you can have your wonderful sex with her again. Maybe have a good laugh about the rude nasty girl, such a dog's breakfast in bed."

"Grete, what are you talking about? Lyn's not coming back to me."

"So what's all these?"

She thrust a handful of postcards at him. She must have been holding them behind her back all the time. She read aloud from one of them.

"'Keep taking the pills Doc. I am. Love Lyn.' All right, I know, bad to go looking through your stuff, but I was lonely waiting for you, I wanted to look at your things."

"Grete," he said weakly. "They're just postcards. She keeps in touch, that's all."

"I don't believe you," she said flatly.

He didn't blame her. Lyn had always said just enough in her postcards to give him hope that she might come back, enough to feed his yearning fantasies over the first few months, more than enough to give him nagging pangs of guilt more recently ... he really should have worked his feelings out, he really should have written a long letter to Lyn about Grete ... but then Lyn had never given him an address to write to. Excuses. Excuses.

"Look ..." he tried. "I told you about Lyn. I told you I loved her. It was all before I met you."

219

"And you still love her, don't you?"

That was the hard one.

"You don't just ... stop loving people," he said. "But ... it's all over, Grete. She didn't love me enough to stay with me. And yes, that hurt a lot at the time. But not now. Because of you." And that was the truth, or as near as he could get to it, or as much of the truth as he knew.

It wasn't enough for Grete.

"So. If she does come back, what then?"

"Grete, she's not *going* to come back."

"But if she *does*?"

In the end, he had to say it.

"I don't know."

She started to cry, but it wasn't the sort of crying that could be comforted. It was fierce crying, angry crying.

"Oh, yes, I think you know. Hello wonderful girlfriend. On your bike rude nasty person." She was on her feet now.

"Well, I think I save you the trouble."

She said some more things in Polish on her way to the door, and for the first time Stephen was grateful that he didn't understand the words: the message was clear enough. She turned at the door.

"And I tell you something else. Sometimes it's quite easy to stop loving people!"

"This is a University Court," said Jack Daniels, 'convened according to Charter, and presided over by Lord Thickthorn, as President of Council. Its purpose is to investigate allegations of gross moral turpitude against Professor George Bunn."

Jeannie McAllister had not been misinformed. On the day after her visit, Charlie Dusenberry had telephoned Stephen informing him of developments in the Bunn case, and telling him that the Vice-Chancellor would value his input as a member of the adjudicating panel. Though surprised to be asked, Stephen had agreed at once. It seemed unlikely that George Bunn would find any other friendly faces on the panel, and so it had proved. The other two Senate members on the panel were Farris and Brahmachari. Lord Thickthorn, who was chairing the panel, was an enormously wealthy local industrialist whose habitual expression was that of a man who has just discovered half a slug in his doughnut. Now he cleared his throat and glared at George Bunn.

"Professor Bunn, I understand you've waived your right to legal representation?"

"That's correct," said George Bunn.

Thickthorn snorted.

"All right. Go on then, Mr Dusenberry."

"The charges are fully detailed and documented on paper one, three, a through e. One, that on seventeen separate occasions, Professor Bunn sexually harassed female students in his department by reading obscene poems to them, and by insisting that his students discuss and write about these obscene poems; two, that when two of these students, Chloris Jakeman and Joanna Lentill, sought to discuss their objections with them he refused consultation with them and abused them verbally; three, that subsequently Professor Bunn maliciously lowered course work marks for these two students; four, that in the case of another student, Glenn Oates, he altered a final mark from a pass to a fail, so that a student he disliked would be required to leave the university."

Charlie Dusenberry paused and looked around, then read the final charge.

"Five: that when Chloris Jakeman and Joanna Lentill sought to discuss their grievance with him on the 29th of last month, Professor Bunn indecently exposed himself to them."

While the charges were being read out, Stephen saw Jeannie McAllister slip quietly in through a side door and sit down. A moment or two later, one of the men in dark suits went over to her, whispered something to her, and escorted her out.

"All right," said Lord Thickthorn. "Let's see if we can look at these in order. Obscene poems."

"Appendix 1a," said Charlie Dusenberry, and several minutes passed while members of the adjudicating committee, ordinary members of Senate, and witnesses wrestled

221

with the huge wodges of photocopied bumph supplied by the ushers.

Lord Thickthorn voiced the general feeling.

"Well I don't know about the rest of you, but I've read more poetry in the last week than I've read in forty years. Rather rum stuff, too, some of it."

He riffled through the pile, spilling cascades of deathless octosyllabic couplets over the edge of the table.

"Do you deny that you read any of these chaps aloud to your students, Professor Bunn?"

"I do not."

"'Ceilia shits', eh? Did Dean Swift write that?"

"He did indeed, Lord Thickthorn."

"Well, well. No doubt she did."

Stephen found himself beginning to warm to Lord Thickthorn a little.

"And you also made these young women discuss and write essays about them?"

"Yes, of course I did," said Bunn cheerfully. He seemed to have no inkling at all of what a dangerous situation he was in. "Amongst other major eighteenth-century works. And to save you the trouble of more tedious questions, I freely confess that I took pleasure in it; it seems a curious idea that a professor should not enjoy his work. I confess also that I refused to discuss my choice of syllabus with them."

Farris leaned forward.

"Wouldn't you say that that was rather high-handed, Professor Bunn?"

"Yes indeed, I'm sure it was, Farris. Now no doubt you let your undergraduates decide what *bugs* and *germs* they ought to study, well, jolly good luck to you. I'm afraid I take my responsibilities more seriously. Verbal abuse. Yes, I confess to that, called them a couple of silly young women, very regrettable, didn't realize it was a sacking matter. As to the marks I award my students, I'm prepared to submit to the judgement of the external examiners, but I can't see that this court has any competence to question them."

"Hm. Nor do I, I must say," said Lord Thickthorn. "And in any case, both these students were given clear pass marks."

He leant over to Jack Daniels, and in a discreet whisper that reverberated around the courtroom with the crisp clarity claimed for compact discs, said: "Think we might lay aside these minor charges? After all, this is about whether the feller's a flasher or not, isn't it?"

Jack Daniels was better at whispering than Lord Thickthorn, but the room was so silent that most people heard his reply.

"I guess it was felt that the minor elements provided background material relating directly to the major indictment, Lord Thickthorn. And, ah, we haven't really looked at the Glenn Oates allegation."

"Hm. Yes. All right. Go ahead then, Mr Dusenberry."

"I'd like to call Chloris Jakeman, Lord Thickthorn."

Chloris Jakeman was called, and Joanna Lentill followed her; and the whole atmosphere of the hearing was transformed. Both of them were calm, composed, moderate, and lucid. By the time they had finished their evidence, the minor accusations, which had previously seemed absurd, trivial, or both, now formed part of an escalating pattern of abuse leading with inexorable logic to the culminating act of sexual indecency.

"Do you want to put any questions, Professor Bunn?" asked Thickthorn when they had finished.

"No. I've no wish to embarrass either of these young ladies any further," said Bunn quietly.

"So you accept their version of events, do you?" said Lord Thickthorn, when Chloris and Jo had left the court.

"Uninvited visitors to my house must take me as they find me," said Bunn. "They found me naked. In point of fact, I had completely forgotten that I had no clothes on."

This sounded extremely thin, in fact highly unlikely, as Lord Thickthorn lost no time in pointing out. Stephen found himself intervening on George Bunn's behalf to say that he and others knew about Bunn's penchant for domestic nudism, though he knew as he spoke that he too sounded highly unconvincing.

"Really? Seen him naked yourself, have you, Daker?"

"Well, no, not personally, but I do know that . . ."

"Hearsay evidence, I'm afraid," said Thickthorn briskly. It was getting near lunchtime. "All right, Mr Dusenberry, who's next, the other doctor, is it?"

Rose Marie took the stand, avoiding Stephen's eyes, and gave her opinion as a medical practitioner that both Chloris Jakeman and Joanna Lentill had suffered severe nervous and emotional trauma as a result of a series of insults and humiliations deliberately imposed on them by a man who, since he was their professor, was in the position of being able to treat them in any way he wished.

"But surely – that's not a fact, is it? It's just an opinion, isn't it?" said Stephen.

"Professor Bunn has already made it clear that his power to do and say what he likes as a professor is a fact," said Rose. "And my opinion as to the students' mental and emotional state is my expert opinion as their personal physician. If there is another doctor present who has examined my patients, then of course the court should hear that second opinion."

Stephen could think of nothing to say to that. Rose was hesitating, as if on the brink of saying something else.

"Yes, Dr Rose Marie?" said Lord Thickthorn benignly. Clearly she had made a good impression on him.

"Well ... I just thought I should add that another female patient came to me and told me that Professor Bunn had invited her to take photographs of his naked body ... offering her a bag of toffees as an inducement."

"Oh, really, Rose, that's absolute nonsense!"

Lord Thickthorn turned ponderously round and glared at him.

"Dr Daker. Hardly the language of the courtroom."

"I'm sorry, Lord Thickthorn, but really ... ."

"All right, Daker. Are you going to produce this female patient, Mr Dusenberry?"

No, of course he wasn't, but the damage had been done now, hadn't it? Stephen could almost literally see the idea tapping on people's skulls, raising little trapdoors, and crawling in. Even if they hadn't been convinced by Chloris and Jo's convincing narrative, this patient-in-the-head with her bag of toffees completed a picture. Farris pointed out that unless the doctor had fabricated the story, it seemed to him that ... that was when Stephen found himself saying (well, shouting) some very injudicious things about the personal interests of certain members of the adjudicating panel, provoking equally heated reactions from Farris and Brahmachari, and the hearing adjourned for lunch in a state of some disorder.

Jack Daniels came over to Stephen smiling broadly, gripped his arm as if he meant to crush it like a lager can, and said: "Steve, I'm real disappointed. Sure hope you're gonna shape up. I'd really hate to lose you." Then he patted his shoulder, and beamed his warm public smile on the room in general.

"OK you guys. Let's go eat."

Stephen didn't go eat with the others. He had to find Grete. As he ran across the campus past Biochemistry, he saw Jeannie McAllister taking photographs and talking to the dossers of Cardboard City. Then a couple of men in suits came up to her, took her by the elbows, and hurried her away towards Senate House.

"Jeannie!" he shouted. "What's the matter? Look, d'you mind telling me where you're taking her?"

"It's all right, Dr Daker!" she called. "I'm getting an exclusive interview with the Vice-Chancellor!"

Stephen ran on. The Art History block was cool, dark, deserted. God, where *was* she? Stephen came out into the sunshine. Twenty minutes gone already. He had no idea where to look. Then he saw Sammy Limb wheeling his motorbike towards Kennedy.

"Sammy!" he panted. "Seen Grete? Dr Grotowska?"

Sammy stopped and grinned at him rather vaguely.

"Oh. Yeah. She was ... hang on Doc."

He put his head on one side, rubbed it, and gave it a couple of bangs.

"Sammy, are you all right?"

"Oh, yeah, just a bit short of ..."

"Brains?"

"Sleep. Got it. Down by the lake."

"Thanks, Sammy."

"Well, she was about half an hour ago."

Stephen ran all the way to the lake. She was still there, standing facing the water with her back to him. A couple of dogs were frolicking about, barking at the ducks. When Stephen was ten yards away, she turned round. She was not smiling.

"Yes?" she said.

He hadn't thought of what he was going to say, he had only thought about finding her.

"I love you," he said.

"And?"

"My name is Grete Grotowska," she said. "I am a lecturer in Art History. I am authority on the male nude: many publications on this subject. I asked Professor Bunn if I could make photographs of his body for my book. He was kind enough to agree."

She paused and looked across at Rose Marie, who was sitting next to Bob Buzzard at the side of the court.

"I think some people get this story wrong," she said.

"Yes, go on, Dr Grotowska," said Lord Thickthorn. He was looking marginally more human after lunch. He was almost smiling.

"Thank you," she said. "What I saw, and what those girls saw, is the exact same thing. A man in his house, with his wife, without his clothes. A wulnerable human body. If they are shocked, then I am sorry for them. Perception theory teaches us this: we see what we wish to see. The body is a simple sign; we who look at it make our own meanings."

She paused, and looked at the row of men on the panel: Brahmachari beaming benignly, Farris fidgeting uneasily, Stephen desperately anxious, Thickthorn peering sharply at her from inside his rolls of flesh.

"And here we all are now, inside the big suits. Wulnerable human bodies. It's not so terrible to think about, is it? Why are people so frightened of this? Listen: you want to sack Professor Bunn because he makes trouble, do it. But not because of his wulnerable human body."

226

There were a few moments of silence while people thought about their vulnerable human bodies.

"Thank you, Dr Grotowska," said Lord Thickthorn.

She smiled at him.

"You're welcome."

He went on looking at her for a few more moments, then seemed to come to himself. He leaned across to Charlie Dusenberry.

"You don't want to come back to this Oates business, do you? Seems a bit of a side issue."

Suddenly Bob was on his feet.

"Not for Glenn it isn't! He's being thrown out of Lowlands just for spite!" he blurted.

Thickthorn looked at him.

"Sorry," said Bob.

"The case is," said Charlie Dusenberry smoothly, "that Professor Bunn went out of his way to get hold of Mr Oates's papers, and reduced another lecturer's marks from a C to an F."

"Certainly did," said George Bunn. "Work was balderdash."

Jack Daniels cleared his throat.

"I guess in fairness to Professor Bunn we should look into this one."

"Hm. All right," said Thickthorn.

"Dr Buzzard?" said Charlie Dusenberry.

Bob Buzzard got up again, rather less precipitately.

"Glenn Oates is a student of this university, my Lord, and as your Lordship may know, a very distinguished athlete. A really . . . a really excellent all-round man."

"All right, all right, get on."

It was clear that Lord Thickthorn found Dr Buzzard somewhat less interesting to listen to than Dr Grotowska.

"Er, right, your Lordship," said Bob. "Well . . . ."

The door at the back of the court burst open, and Glenn Oates came in, dishevelled and wild-eyed. He was followed by two of the men in suits who were trying and failing to restrain him, and, at a more leisurely pace, by Jock McCannon.

"Bob! Bob! Don't do it, man!"

"Who *is* this?" demanded Thickthorn.

"It's Glenn," said Bob. "Oh, Glenn!"

"It's not right, Bob," said Glenn. "I should never have asked you, it's not fair on you. I don't deserve to pass. It was crap work, I know that. Ah, Bob man, you're really great doing this for me, but it's not right."

He turned to Lord Thickthorn, and said in all simplicity: "He's only doing it because he loves me, like."

"He's mad!" yelled Bob. They were all staring at him. "Oh, my God." He sat down and buried his face in his hands.

"What *is* all this about, Mr Dusenberry?"

Charlie Dusenberry glanced at Jack Daniels.

"I guess the university would wish to withdraw this particular charge," he said.

"I'm glad to hear it," said Lord Thickthorn. "And all the others, if you'll take my advice. I don't mind telling you the whole thing smells very odd to me."

As Charlie and Jack looked at each other, hesitating, Jock McCannon gave a rich throaty growl from the back of the court.

"Eh, Vice-Chancellor?"

"And what can we do for *you*, Dr McCannon?" asked Thickthorn with weary courtesy.

"I am merely a messenger, Lord Thickthorn. Mrs Daniels has been unavoidably delayed, but I gather that she too has some information she feels might be of assistance, about family values, doctor-patient relationships, and sexual mores in the pissant swamp."

"That won't be necessary, Dr McCannon," said Jack Daniels. "It's my very happy duty to say that the university no longer finds any substance in the complaints levelled at my old friend George Bunn. I'm only sorry that it had to come to this, George. But a university has to uphold the very highest standards of personal conduct, and it's necessary that justice should be done, and be seen to be done."

"Oh, absolutely, Vice-Chancellor," said George Bunn. "I understand *exactly* how you feel."

*

228

"You're *leaving*?" said Stephen. "After going through all that? I don't understand it."

Stephen, Grete, George Bunn and Jock McCannon were drinking in the university bar a couple of nights later. It was their first chance to celebrate the outcome of the hearing; after the trial George Bunn had gone straight home to his wife and stayed there.

"I have no wish to haunt the places where my honour died," said Bunn.

"But your honour didn't die," said Grete.

"Thanks in no small part to you, my dear. But it came to me, as I sat there listening ... I *am* an old freak, you know. I am quite out of touch with these people and their concerns. These young women may well be quite right about my taste in literature. I simply have no interest in their opinions. Not a shred of it. A man like that should no longer be teaching literature to the young. So I'm taking myself off."

"But where?" said Stephen.

"My old college at Oxford has offered me a fellowship. The eighteenth century is still alive and well there, you see; I have no wish to watch the Midnight Cowboy drag us into the twenty-first."

He stood up ponderously and drained his glass.

"Thank you, Grete. I appreciated what you said. The trouble is, I didn't understand a word of it. Goodnight."

"Not many of us left, Stephen," said Jock McCannon darkly after Bunn had blundered his way out through the swing doors, bumping into and spilling the drink of a short unsavoury-looking man as he went.

"No," said Stephen gloomily, and then, cheering up: "Well, at least we'll get to read about it in the papers."

"Yes, indeed," said Jock. " 'Prince of Darkness suffers temporary setback. Armageddon postponed.' Well, I have to leave you too. A pressing appointment, as they say: reconstituting the remains of young Robert Buzzard."

He stood up.

"Don't be cast down. Cherish each other. All you need, you know, is love."

Stephen, with some trepidation, was about to embark on

a tentative exploration of the area Jock had indicated, when he was prevented by Jeannie McAllister, who dashed up in a state of high excitement and perched herself on Jock's empty chair.

"Jeannie! Have a drink."

"No, I can't stop," she said. "Just wanted to catch you before I went to thank you for all your help."

"Did you get everything you wanted then?"

"Oh, yes," she said, smiling. "It was brilliant."

"So when's it going to be published?"

She looked puzzled for a second.

"Oh, that! Oh, I've had to leave that for a while, well maybe quite a long while. I've just got a new job!"

"Really?" he said.

"In New York! Television! And I get to be in front of camera! Mr Daniels made just one phone call, he's a fantastic operator you know."

"Yes," said Stephen bleakly. "Congratulations."

"So," he said when she had gone. "What now?"

"Well," said Grete.

They looked at each other seriously for quite a long time. Then she grinned.

"Dog's breakfast? Could you stand it?"

"Really?" he said. "You mean it? I mean, that's what you really want?"

She shrugged.

"Sometimes, I think, you just have to trust someone. You know?"

"Yes," he said.

RUST AND THE SWEET SMELL
OF SUCCESS

Jonathan Powell and Ken Riddington took Ron Rust to
lunch at Julie's restaurant. Jonathan Powell ate frugally and
drank Perrier; Ken Riddington ate heroically and drank
moderately; Ron Rust crammed and swilled down everything
he could get his hands on. He had not expected to get a
second shot at Julie's restaurant. There was a big squeeze on
at the BBC and Rust and his serial were probably due for the
chop. He waited till he was quite full before venturing to ask:
"Why Julie's, by the way?"

Jonathan Powell smiled.

"We took you to Julie's last time, Ron, and you put it in
that libellous little book you wrote. So I thought we'd make
it Julie's again; you see, you won't be able to use it, will you?
A good writer never repeats himself."

"Good thinking, Jonathan," said Rust seriously. "You're
a clever man."

"Love the new scripts, Ron," said Jonathan Powell.

"Really?" said Rust. He was waiting for the but. There is
always a but.

"I, er, thought nobody was supposed to be having it off in
the new series, Ron."

"Nobody is having it off," said Rust.

"Oh, come on, Ron," said Riddington, exasperated.
"They're all shagging like rabbits."

"Well, they're not enjoying it, are they?" said Rust
defensively. "Surely they can have sex so long as they don't
like it."

He bit into the last of the bread rolls.

"Well, it's the weather," he said. "When the weather
perks up a bit my characters always start getting randy. It's
not my fault."

"But honestly, Ron," said Riddington. "Jock *McCannon*?
That's obscene. And all these people taking their clothes off,
how are we going to cast Bunn, for God's sake?"

231

"Not my job, Ken," said Rust. "And I won't write a nude scene for the old fart. You have my promise on that."

"Even so," said Riddington. "Who's going to believe an old man like that . . . ."

Rust put his hand on Riddington's arm and looked him sincerely in the eyes.

"Listen, Ken," he said. "Believe it or not, there *are* a few women who get off on older men. I mean, well . . . surely you must have come across that yourself, now and then?"

"You talk to him," said Riddington. "I can't talk to him any more. He's not rational."

Jonathan Powell was still smiling.

"That's what I like about him." he said. "His mind is totally out of control. Shall we tell him, Ken?"

"Oh, Lord," said Riddington gloomily. "All right. If you must."

"Ron," said Jonathan Powell. "We're thinking about a third series."

Now Rust is sitting in the Groucho Club with Deep Throat, drinking Pils at about a million pounds a bottle. *Rust* in the *Groucho Club*? Yes indeed, he's a member, though none of the staff ever recognizes him, and the other members look at him, if they can bear to look at him, rather as if he were some old alkie who'd collapsed in the street outside and been brought in out of sheer compassion to wait for the knacker's van. How he comes to be a member is like this: a teenage film producer called Amanda Schiff was silly enough to entertain him to tea there once, and Rust thought what a lovely peaceful chintzy haven it was from the fear and loathing in the streets outside. So he joined as a country member (cheaper) and every time he's been there since it has been absolutely jam-packed full of the most dreadful little shits of about twelve or thirteen years old, all in four hundred quid suits, all shrieking at each other fit to bust and spilling their Spritzers all over their Filofaxes.

Still, it must make a change for Deep Throat to get away from the Greeks and Indians he usually frequents: lately he's actually been looking a bit like a lobster bhuna. Actually, now Rust takes a proper look at him, he doesn't strike Rust as looking all that brilliant. Takes too much exercise, of course: doesn't smoke enough. Not a boy any more, he ought to be a bit kinder to himself. And he's a bit on the quiet side tonight. Well that will never do. Deep Throat is his deep throat. Rust needs to get a few diseases from him.

"Come on, mate," says Rust urgently. "What do people die of? Ideally, quick and nasty, not slow and beautiful."

"Fuck me, Ron," says Deep Throat, wincing. "You don't want to know about that."

"Yes, I do," says Rust. "Well, I don't really, but the story does. You haven't given me any nasty medical things lately, and I've *used* everything *I've* had."

"Can't we talk about something else, Ron?"

"*No*. You're a *doctor*. I want you to give me *illnesses*. What's the matter with you, for Christ's sake?"

"Well, I'll tell you the truth, Ron," says Deep Throat. "I haven't been feeling too well myself lately."

"That right?"

"They want me to go in for an op, Ron."

"Well, that's all right, isn't it? I mean, they'll make you better, won't they? What's the matter? What are you looking at me like that for?"

"Are you fucking mad or what, Ron?" says Deep Throat. "They want to give me a general fucking *anaesthetic*. They want to cut me open with a *knife*, Ron." He has gone quite pale.

"Well . . . there's nothing to be nervous about, is there?"

"Of course there's something to be fucking nervous about, you moron. Operations are fucking *dangerous*. Why d'you think they make you sign that fucking form? Because they know there's a fucking good chance they're going to *kill* you, that's why. D'you think the average anaesthetist knows what he's doing, Ron? D'you think it's good for you having your belly hacked open with a *knife*? I'm a doctor, Ron. I drink with these guys. Have you ever met a doctor who wasn't scared shitless of going on the table?"

"You're the only doctor I know," says Rust humbly. "Sorry. I really am sorry."

Rust is aware that the shrieking of the shits in their immediate vicinity has moderated more than somewhat, and that some of the pubescent posers are looking a bit green about the gills.

"Please," says Rust. "I really wouldn't bother you at such a difficult time, but I have to kill some of the buggers off. If I don't, they're going to make me do a third series, and we don't want that, do we?"

"Christ, no," says Deep Throat with feeling. "All right, Ron. I'll give you just one, that's all I can bear for tonight, and then can we please talk about something nice, like big girls' tits?"

"I promise," says Rust.

"All right, then, seeing as it's you. Let's have a little chat about subdural haematoma."

7

"DEATH OF A UNIVERSITY"

Stephen awoke cold and shivering on the pebbled shore of the lake, and saw the black nuns flapping away from him like glossy black crows. The light hurt his eyes. He turned and looked towards the trees. The horses were still there, quietly cropping the sparse and patchy grass. He turned towards the lake again. A black hooded figure sat motionless by a boulder at the very edge of the water, where little waves nibbled at the pebbles. Stephen pulled himself up, and walked stiffly towards the water's edge. Now he could see the chessboard laid out on the boulder. He sat down opposite the hooded figure, who still had not moved. Stephen knew that when the figure did turn, he would see the face of Death. Stephen saw his own hand tremble as he reached out and moved a white pawn. Then the hooded figure turned.

"And the weird thing was, he looked just like Ron Rust," said Stephen. "You know, that Creative Writing bloke. Writes novels and stuff."

"Maybe it was a dream about the Death of the Novel," said Grete Grotowska. "Anyway, I don't like chess. I like games of chance, you know? Always bet more than you can afford to lose, otherwise no fun. Listen. Close your eyes. I want to say something to you in Polish."

He lay back on the pillow, feeling her fingers tracing gentle patterns on his chest, listening to her speaking softly to him in Polish.

"That sounded good," he said, when she stopped speaking. "What was it?"

"Oh," she said. "Just something in Polish."

Sammy Limb, feeling giddy and drunk, wavered towards the crowd in the piazza. Harry Pointer was addressing them through a loudspeaker, standing on the bonnet of a new white Montego. He was speaking with his usual lucid passion.

"*Certainly* we are ready, willing and able to implement a rent strike! But we are a *democratic* union. We believe in *negotiation* from *strength*! We are going to the Vice-Chancellor and we are going to *demand*! Fair rents in university accommodation! No implementation of the pyramid failing policy! Hello, Sammy, pissed again I see."

Mal Prentis and Johnny Graftin moved through the crowd to stand at Sammy's side.

"Who paid for Harry Pointer's Montego?" yelled Sammy.

"Come on, Sammy," said Mal Prentis, taking his arm, "we'll buy you a drink."

They led him round the corner out of sight and hit him a few times until he fell down. Harry Pointer turned the volume up a bit, so that nobody in the crowd heard what they were doing to Sammy. Nobody would have paid much attention if they had heard. People were always hitting Sammy Limb.

"College kids," said Jack Daniels, turning from the window.

"Who needs them, right?" said Charlie Dusenberry.

"Kinda sad, though. I had a good enough time at Harvard. Our fraternity house, the stuff that went down there. You know what the freshmen had to do to get in? Go out and catch a rat, bring him home, skin him, roast him, and eat him."

"That right?" said Charlie Dusenberry. "I've eaten rat. Rat's not so bad."

"The point I'm making, Charlie, this place has no traditions. OK, so we use the pyramid structure to take out half the students in each year. You know, that'll give us the highest proportion of first-class degrees in Europe."

236

"Release a lot of teaching facilities, too. We can turn them over to research and development."

"How about the halls?"

"Yeah," said Charlie, "the letter's gone out to all resident staff and students. New rent scheme, based on market values, index linked."

"Good, I like that, Charlie," said the Vice-Chancellor. "That's a New Deal. No favours, no discrimination. If your money's good, you can be white or yellow or black or tan, we want you at Lowlands."

"I guess in practice we'll be evicting ninety, ninety-five per cent of them," said Charlie.

"Yeah, that figures. Hey, the brochure came through today. Listen to this, Charlie." Jack read from a glossy folder. " 'Lowlands University, a new concept in conference and leisure facilities for business.' Yeah. Pictures look great. Make it clear we're offering a year-round facility, not just vacations."

"Jack," said Charlie, "you don't feel we might be going a little fast here?"

"We're front runners, Charlie," said the Vice-Chancellor. "Front runners have to go fast. Anyway, this is England. If there is trouble, we have the best police force in the world. But there won't be any trouble. Harry Pointer is a sensible guy. You know what I think, Charlie? I think you spent too long in Nicaragua. Come on, loosen up. We're having a ball."

Minutes of a Group Meeting
Present: Dr Daker, Dr Buzzard, Dr McCannon, Dr Rose Marie, Nurse Gahagan

Dr Daker proposed that in view of the greatly increased number of patients there should be an extension of surgery hours. Dr Buzzard said that was no go today as far as he was concerned, he was on court with the Vice-Chancellor at eleven fifteen. Moreover, if the rabble didn't have the wit to come in out of the rain, that was their own lookout. Dr McCannon pointed out that the students were suffering as a direct result of the machinations of the Midnight Cowboy. He was surprised at Dr Buzzard. Dr Buzzard should do his job like a conscientious doctor. Dr Buzzard told Dr McCannon a) that he was no longer head of the practice, b) that we were not living in a bleeding hearts culture any more, and c) to belt up.

Dr Daker said that it was not a question of bleeding hearts; the practice was facing a medical emergency. They were dealing with vitamin deficiencies, malnutrition, severe clinical depression, bronchitis, pleurisy, and pneumonia on an epidemic scale. Dr Rose Marie had even seen a case of what used to be called trench foot. The crisis was the direct result of policies pursued by the administration. Students could no longer afford to eat and buy books. Moreover, however hard the students worked, half of them could expect to be thrown out after the end of term examinations. Dr Buzzard remarked that that would get the patient numbers down a bit.

Dr Rose Marie proposed that Dr Daker should confront the Vice-Chancellor with the reality of the situation. Mr Daniels was a brilliant man, a powerful man, a force for good or for evil. He would recognize another such in Dr Daker. Dr Daker, uniquely, would be able to force the Vice-Chancellor to recognize the strength that lay in gentleness, in caring, in love.

Dr McCannon supported Dr Rose Marie's proposal. As he had occasion to remark on previous occasions, all we need is love.

Nurse Gahagan said that if it wasn't too vulgar a suggestion, what was needed was a bit of hard work from the doctors because the patients were stacked up four deep in the waiting room. And for once, believe it or not, the dozy bunch recognized a bit of sense when they heard it, and the meeting concluded at nine thirty-five.

The doctors dealt with the crisis as best they could, often finding themselves prescribing Complan and protein supplements designed for post-operative and geriatric patients, simply because so many of their patients were not so much ill as weak and undernourished. Maureen Gahagan kept the tea constantly on the brew and handed out jam butties to all who came to her for jabs. But amongst the throng of sad, weak, dispirited students, there were some less routine consultations that morning.

"Sammy, you look like an emblem of our battered dreams," said Jock McCannon. "The fight game is clearly not your métier."

"Yeah, well," said Sammy.

He replaced his dark glasses and peered at Jock through the gloom.

"Allie gave me a bit of a seeing to last night. Oh, yeah, and then I got into a hot political discussion with a couple of Harry Pointer's friends, not my style, that, I'm into litigation, me. I'm taking the university *and* the Union to the Court of Human Rights, *and* I think I got a chance of a result . . . is it hot in here?"

"How are the dizzy spells?" asked Jock.

"Come and go, like . . . quite sort of nice, like dreaming," said Sammy vaguely.

"Sammy," said Jock. "After you came off the bike that time, did they give you an X-ray in hospital?"

"Can't remember, Doc."

"Well," said Jock. "I think you should toddle down there and have one. There's just the faintest possibility you might be wandering round with a hairline fracture of the skull, which might adversely affect your razor-keen forensic skills, if you follow me?"

"Yeah, right," said Sammy. "Cheers."

Jock walked round the desk and put his arms round Sammy's shoulders.

"Sammy, Sammy, you must take care of yourself, my boy. Men like you and me are rare today, men who understand the sovereignty of love and justice. Sammy: we must love one another or die."

"Yeah, right, know what you mean, Doc," said Sammy.

Jock knitted his brows, and reflected.

"Or was it: love one another *and* die?"

*

Bob Buzzard was working well on his new wheeze, Buzzard-Lowlands International Medical Supplies. He had established an excellent supply source through a Dr Hassan in Al Makallah, an old pal from the Jeddah Rackets club, and Freddy Frith had put him in touch with a buyer in Bogota. Everything was fine, except that these bloody *patients* kept getting in the way.

"Robert Buzzard, Buzzard-Lowlands International," he said into the telephone.

The door opened and a patient came in, some awful little type from Admin called Smallcock or something.

"Yes, Dr Corazon, you're speaking to Robert Buzzard in person, and I'm happy to say that everything's in order and in the pipeline. We've been able to locate the goods to your precise specification. Put your tongue out, Mr Smallcock."

"Small*cott*," said the patient.

"Right, let's see your tongue then."

"Not *cock*," said the patient.

"No, *tongue*! *Tongue*! Are you *deaf*? I do beg your pardon, Dr Corazon."

Bob Buzzard took a quick shufti at the awful little admin type's awful little tongue and peered at his eyeballs while continuing his long-distance conversation.

"Oh, absolutely, an impeccably reliable source. As soon as we get your bank draft we'll authorize shipment of the arms and accessories by private air freight c.i.f. Bogota, all documents ahead."

He scribbled a prescription for the horrible little man.

"Yes, that civil war must be a bloody nuisance to you ... oh, jolly good. Pretty quiet here too. Well we're always at your service, give us a ring, we'll give you a quote. We try harder at Buzzard-Lowlands. Ciaou!"

He put the phone down.

"Two of those a day, plenty of liquids, early nights, off you go, Mr Smallcock."

He pressed the intercom button.

"Miss Goitre for Dr Buzzard, please."

"So what is this, with the card?" said Grete Grotowska to

Rose Marie. "I'm ill and I don't know it? You got me frightened, you know."

"Grete, I'm sorry. It ... it seemed to be the only way of seeing you. You've been so inaccessible lately. And I'd like to help you."

"Really?" said Grete curiously. "Not so easy with the Polish disaster person. They are chopping my crap department so I have no job. You have a job for me?"

"You might be able to keep your job here, Grete," said Rose. "I ... I do know Jack Daniels would be sorry to lose you. There's so much new thinking going on: Jack wants to put the emphasis on individual talent, and bypass cumbersome departmental structures. Would you let me see what I can do with Jack?"

"With *Jack*? Hey. You got something going with the *Vice-Chancellor*? You *seeing* him?"

"Grete, you know that's not my style. But I do have his ear. And, well, with Stephen leaving ... ."

"What?" said Grete.

"He hasn't mentioned it? Well, no doubt he would find it difficult to tell you, Grete. There's going to be some restructuring at the Health Centre soon. I think Stephen will be quite pleased to be ... moving on."

"Moving on? What d'you mean, moving on? What moving on? Where? What are you saying now?"

"Oh, Grete," said Rose. "I hoped I wouldn't have to be the one to tell you."

"Dr Daker," said Mrs Kramer over the intercom, "there's a Chief Inspector of Police to see you."

"*What*?" said Stephen. What had he done? Nothing. So who could it be? Bob? Sammy Limb? Surely not Jock?

"Er, yes, all right, I'm free now, Mrs Kramer, send him through."

When the door opened he thought he was dreaming. The police inspector was a woman and she had Lyn's face.

"Morning, Doc," she said.

He found himself unable to move.

"*Lyn*?"

"Well remembered," she said. "Chief Inspector Turtle to you. Accelerated promotion. Good, eh?"

"But . . . ."

"Hey," she said. "It's *me*. Honest. Look."

She took off her Inspector's hat and shook her hair out so that it fell loosely on her shoulders.

"Does *that* refresh your memory?"

Yes, it did. It was Lyn all right. Lyn dressed up as a policewoman for a party. And it wasn't that he'd exactly forgotten how big, how strong, how healthy she always looked, just that the reality of her now was somehow brighter, brighter and clearer. She *was* an amazing-looking person: what had she ever seen in *him*? She was smiling at him. He hadn't exactly *forgotten* that smile, it was just that he hadn't fully retained what it did to him. Weak at the knees. What a brilliantly accurate phrase that was. And looking at her, he remembered some more things: she'd always been amused by him, she'd always found him funny. And he'd always felt just a little bit in awe of her. And she had always, always been in charge. Always taken him over and sorted him out. And now she'd come back to do it again.

"Oh, Lyn," he said.

"On your feet, son," she said, grinning. "Come on."

He found himself getting up.

"Over here."

He had to go over there. Now he was very close. That was her smell. Yes. Oh, God.

"Lyn," he said.

"Come here, Doc."

She took him gently by the ears, as she had been wont to do, and pulled his face nearer, and kissed him briefly but firmly on the mouth. She felt so big, warm, soft, and strong. Then she kissed him once on each cheek. Then she pulled her head back and smiled at him again.

"Right," she said.

"Look . . ."

"Arms go round here, remember? *That's* it. Mmm."

After a few seconds, she took her mouth away from his, and looked at him, frowning.

"Um ..." said Stephen.

"Yeah," she said. "Is there something you'd like to tell me, Stephen?"

They sat by the lake and watched one of the men in blue suits and dark glasses. He was throwing sticks into the water for a couple of Rottweilers.

"I really feel dreadful about it," said Stephen.

"Hey. Listen," she said. "I know how these things happen. Me own fault for going away and leaving you, wasn't it? Tasty bloke like you. And, um ... actually there was quite a bit of stuff I was thinking I'd have to tell you. No need to now, eh? Come on, Doc. Cheer up."

"It's really ... it's really all *right*?"

He couldn't believe it. She was smiling at him. She still cared for him. But she wasn't angry with him. She didn't seem to feel rejected at all. She was so much stronger than him. No. So much better than him.

She was laughing at him again.

"Disappointed?" she said. "You always were one for having a bad time."

She looked at his troubled face for a few moments.

"Tell you one thing, Stephen. I wish you weren't such a one at a time person."

There was a question there all right; there was a definite possibility. If he wanted, he could have *two* wonderful girlfriends. And he still loved Lyn. He would always love her and, and ... he tried to push the ignoble thought away, but there it was ... sex with Lyn had been so much better, so cheerfully, uninhibitedly, uproariously, yes, *easily* ... but no, somehow *not better* than the big disaster with Grete, the dog's breakfast in bed. There it was. That was it. He *was* a one at a time person. And Lyn, who had always understood him so much better than Grete ever would, leaned over, ruffled his hair, and stood up.

"OK, Doc," she said cheerfully. "Didn't come here just to see you anyway. I'm, er ... I'm sort of a police spy. Brilliant disguise, eh?"

"What?" he said. He'd forgotten how quickly she could

dispose of one huge area of life, file it, and move cheerfully on to the next.

"Well, you know," she said. "There's a bit of a buzz going round that something's going to sort of *happen* here that might involve us. No, not you and me. Me and them. The *Force*, Doc. Well, You must be joking, I said. Things *happening*? At *Lowlands*? All right Turtle, they said, you're an old Lowlands lag, go and have a look round. So, what have you all been up to, eh?"

"Blow me down, six-three to Daniels!" said Bob Buzzard. "Not often I get hammered like that, sir!"

"Well," said Jack Daniels complacently, "I like to keep in shape." It was easy to confirm this, because he was, as it happened, stark naked, as was Bob. They had finished their squash game and were about to go for a swim.

"Yes, you certainly *are* in good shape, sir!" said Bob enthusiastically. Oh, Lord. That sounded ... and after that Oates business ... my God, the Vice-Chancellor probably thought he was a raving ....

"Er ... I mean ... I didn't mean to ..." he stammered.

The Vice-Chancellor took his arm firmly but gently with one strong brown hand.

"So are you, Bobby," he smiled.

Bob panicked completely. My God. Not only did the Vice-Chancellor think *he* was a raving ... no, surely not. Surely the VC himself couldn't be a raving ... could he?

"But then on the other hand –" he said wildly.

"Bobby."

"Yes?" squeaked Bob.

"I know what went down just now. On the court. Next time, I want your best game, Bobby. Right?"

A few minutes later, Bob was thrashing down the pool desperately trying to catch up with his Vice-Chancellor. Jack's crawl looked leisurely, almost lazy, but he moved through the water with shark-like efficiency.

"Er ... did you have a chance to ... glance through those ... privatization proposals, sir?" gasped Bob when he got close enough.

"Why, sure I did, Bobby." The Vice-Chancellor surface-dived and came up very close to Bob. Bob felt the electricity in those bright blue eyes, experienced the power of that visionary gaze; awesome at close quarters.

"We like the quality of your thinking, Bobby," said Jack Daniels. Then he tossed the lock of hair back, dived again, and vanished under the green and glittering depths.

The Big Squeeze continued. The new rent scheme went into operation, and most students were unable to pay. The Cardboard City spread beyond the shelter of Biochemistry and straggled across the campus as far as Cybernetics. But most of the students stayed in their rooms in hall, waiting for the eviction, or the revolution, depending on their politics and their temperaments. There were peaceful demonstrations. There were deputations. Nothing came of them. The examination season started, and the dispirited masses trooped into the examination halls to have their fates sealed by the pyramid failing policy. Sammy Limb forgot about going to get his skull X-rayed. Jock McCannon had taken to reading the Bible, and its imagery seeped into the muttered incantations he committed to his rinky dinky little tape-recorder as he wandered by the lake: "And the Lamb opened the fifth seal, and I heard a voice like the voice of thunder, saying; on the twenty-seventh day, when the temples shall burn, and darkness cover the pissant swamp, on that day shall the nuns leave the barren lands for ever, and that day shall be the day before the last day."

"Dangerous mood?" said Charlie Dusenberry, turning from the window. "I don't think so, Harry. I think you're putting me on."

"Straight up, Mr Dusenberry: I don't think we can hold them. We've got nothing to hold them *with*."

"This is the late eighties, Harry. People don't have expectations any more. They're grateful for anything they can get."

"But ... you're not offering them *anything*. I mean ... some sort of easy payment facility, something that *sounds* like a concession. I got to go back to them with *something*."

There was a short silence.

"I guess you could use a bigger car, Harry."

"That is not the *point*. Yeah, well . . . ."

"You like Mercedes? I think they're awfully reliable."

"When are you going to move them out?"

Charlie Dusenberry shook his head, smiling.

"I have to know, Mr Dusenberry. I'm trying to *help*."

"Ten days."

"350 SEL?"

"Maybe."

"I can't promise anything, Mr Dusenberry."

"Neither can I, Harry."

Lyn Turtle spent a good deal of time wandering round the campus, looking at things and talking to people. She spent a good deal of time with Stephen, too, talking about old times, learning to be just good friends. Stephen found this a little problematic, and worried about not feeling guilty, but Lyn gradually laughed him out of it. He talked to her a lot about Grete, but somehow he had not got round to introducing them. As a matter of fact, he hadn't seen much of Grete these last few days. That wasn't unusual: when she was writing something she tended go into solitary for three or four days at a time, only leaving her desk to sleep and eat lonely meals of Polish sausage and pickled cucumbers.

Now he was sitting in the bar with Lyn. It was lunchtime, and they were the only customers, apart from a thin girl sitting with her knees up to her chin, while her boyfriend slept full length on the padded bench beside her.

"Yeah, well," said Lyn. "It looks like the classic revolutionary situation, but it's not going to happen, Stephen. I'm a body language person, and the body language is all wrong. Everyone's gone droopy."

She nodded at the couple opposite.

"Can't see them storming the winter palace, can you? No, I think I've been wasting police time, here, Doc. Apart from seeing you, and that's been nice . . . are you paying attention here, Doc?"

He was staring towards the doorway. Grete was standing there. She was looking very tense.

"That's her," he said. "That's Grete."

He scrambled to his feet as Grete walked towards them.

"Hello, Grete, this is ..."

She walked straight past their table and up to the bar, where she stood with her back to them.

"Double dry white wine," she said to the barman. Her hands were shaking.

"Look, let me ..." said Stephen.

Grete banged money down on the bar and lit a cigarette. She still hadn't turned. Stephen smiled awkwardly at Lyn, who raised an eyebrow. Then Grete turned to face them, her back against the bar counter.

"I'm sorry, I shouldn't have come in here," she said. "I don't know why I did that."

"Don't be silly," said Stephen. "Come and join us."

"I wanted to see you," said Grete to Lyn. "Now I don't feel so good."

"I'm not that horrible," said Lyn calmly.

Stephen pulled out a chair for Grete. She walked over to the table but didn't sit down. Her glass rattled as she put it on the table. Stephen found the need to clear his throat.

"Er, Lyn, this is Grete," he said, feeling ridiculous. "Grete, this is Lyn."

"Wonderful girlfriend meets the big disaster," said Grete. Her lip was trembling.

"Heard a lot about you," said Lyn pleasantly. "Polish, right?"

"Yes, Polish, Polish, foreign and Polish, good for bad times in bed while the wonderful girlfriend's not there."

She began to cough, and stabbed her cigarette messily and violently into the ashtray, managing to knock it off the table. She started to cry, to cry in Polish, crying the same words over and over again. Stephen went to her and took her gently by the shoulders. Lyn thought: he's so tender with her, if I hadn't been so together all the time I could have had some of that.

Grete was still crying and talking Polish.

"Grete, what's the matter?" said Stephen. "What are you saying?"

"Just Polish, Polish, something in Polish, that's all." She pulled away from him. "I'm sorry," she said to Lyn. "You come to take him away, all right, take him away."

"I'm not going to take him away," said Lyn.

"Well, stay here with him. Whatever. They give me the boot anyway. *I* go away."

"Hey," said Lyn. "Hasn't he *told* you? Haven't you *told* her, you daft prat?"

He felt dreadful.

"I didn't, um ... I was going to but it never seemed the right ... I didn't tell her you were here."

Lyn gave him a long level look that made him feel even worse. Then she said: "Look, Grete. He's not going away. I'm going away."

"Not what I hear," said Grete. She had stopped crying now, but her nose was running. She wiped it angrily with the back of her hand.

"He loves you now," said Lyn. "So there you are. You can have him."

"Something the matter with him?"

"Well," said Lyn. "He's a bloody awful swimmer, for one thing. But what it is ... he's jacked me in, you see, because he's fallen in love with you, and I'm just being really really nice about it."

"This is true?"

Lyn nodded.

"This is true, Stephen?"

"Yes, it's true."

Grete sat down, picked up her double white wine, and drank most of it.

"Blimey, now I don't know what to say to you," she said.

"Think we should start again from where you walk in?" said Lyn.

Slowly, Grete began to smile.

"Come on then, Doc," said Lyn. "Empty glasses here. Get 'em in."

The next day, Lyn Turtle said goodbye to Stephen and drove back to Hendon; and at dawn on the day after that, they evicted the students from Kennedy Hall. Charlie Dusenberry used a firm of professional security men, and the operation went like clockwork. Most of the pickets outside were still struggling out of their sleeping bags when the team went in, and there was no violent resistance at all. There was a lot of noise and a lot of panic, of course; a few students suffered minor accidental injuries, and some of their stuff got broken. The Resident Warden made a lot of fuss, but the men had been told to expect that. They ignored him and got on with the job as they had been instructed. They took fifty-two minutes to clear the whole building.

Julie Daniels had happily accommodated herself to Jock McCannon's odd nocturnal habits; she would often slip on a Gucci jogging suit and go out with him before first light to wander round the pissant swamp. Thus it was that Julie Daniels and Jock McCannon were able to watch from the wooded hill above Lowlands as Kennedy Hall was cleared.

"What an asshole," said Julie, finding the *mot juste* as ever. "You know, I never thought he'd really do it. What ... an ... *asshole*. This is just so gross, you know? I'm just so ashamed, honey, this is really Asshole County."

"Truly, my dear," said Jock, "he is the Prince of Darkness."

"My husband is not the Prince of Darkness, sweetiepie," said Julie. "He is just a very mean ambitious Boston Irish asshole, with a Brooks Brothers suit and a piece missing out of his goddam brain. Honey, I can't bear to look at this any more. Take me away, honey. Let's go someplace nice."

Stephen went to see Jack Daniels, who kept him waiting for an hour, then listened with ill-concealed impatience while Stephen, trying to keep as calm as he could, described the plight of the students in his charge as Warden of Kennedy and as Director of the Medical Centre. The Vice-Chancellor looked as boyishly handsome, as vibrant, as confident as ever; but there was something different about him, something that showed in the eyes, as if they were focussed permanently now on that inner vision that drove him, and he no longer saw Stephen as a person at all.

"Steve," said Jack Daniels when Stephen had run out of arguments. "I'm getting a little tired of your attitude. Those students have a choice. If they don't want to live on campus, they don't have to live on campus. I don't see anything immoral in asking for a little financial commitment, a little personal investment in their own futures. I don't know about you, Steve, but I didn't have it so soft when I was a college student. I worked my way through college, Steve, I'm not ashamed of that."

"Yes, fine," said Stephen, "but there aren't any jobs that they can *do*!"

"I'm disappointed in you, Steve," said the Vice-Chancellor, picking up a glass paperweight and hefting it in his hand. "All I hear from you is whining, beefing and bellyaching. You have a positive suggestion?"

"Yes, I have," said Stephen, stung. "Reverse the rent policy. Reverse the failing policy. Subsidize teaching and accommodation out of all these profits we're making."

"See what I mean, Steve? Negative thinking. Negative attitudes. I want positive thinking. Harry Pointer is thinking positive, he's helping us to find solutions, and we're gonna be very grateful to Harry. Think about it."

For a moment Jack's eyes really focussed on Stephen's: it was a moment of recognition.

"You're a real bastard, aren't you?" said Stephen.

Jack smiled.

"I've been called worse than that by bigger guys than you, Steve. It don't mean diddleysquat to me. I'm not doing anything I'd be ashamed to tell my mother about."

He stood up and walked to the window.

"I don't think you're happy here at Lowlands, Steve. You're not coming on like one of the team. I guess we're gonna have to let you go, Steve."

"No," said Stephen. "I'm not leaving."

Jack Daniels came back to the big desk and leaned right across it.

"I don't think you hear what I'm saying, Steve. I want you to get the fuck out of my university. I hear you've been sleeping with your patients, and I don't like that kinda stuff. We go for family values here. So I guess I want your resignation, OK? Because I'd sure hate for you to be ... what do you guys say ... struck off?"

"Bloody well try it!" said Stephen, surprising himself with his own ferocity.

Jack smiled.

"OK, Steve. Just as soon as I find a window in my diary."

Bob was on the telephone, person to person, long distance.

"Well, I can't understand it, Dr Corazon, the crate was flown out yesterday, it should be with you by ... ah, wait a minute, what time do you have there?"

The door opened, and a patient came in, oh God that frightful little admin chap back again, Peter Short was it? Bob pointed to a chair and the frightful little chap sat down.

"Ah! Bingo!" he said into the phone. "Time zones, of course. You'll take delivery at o nine seventeen hours tomorrow morning, Bogota."

He stuck his tongue out at the patient, who took some moments, bloody fool, to realize that he was supposed to do the same. Bob peered at it from a safe distance. It looked horrible.

"Not at all, Dr Corazon. Buzzard-Lowlands are always at your service."

He put the phone down.

"Right, Mr Littledick."

"Smallcott," said the patient.

"You're fine, Smallcock. You're cured. Take yourself off."

"But I'm rather worried ...."

"We're *all* rather *worried*! Try going into the *arms* trade, that'll make you *worried*! Wait till your *wife* leaves you, you'll go *bananas*!"

He leant very close to Smallcott, and shouted in his face.

"Now listen to me, I'll say this just once, it's *nothing* to do with the *size*! It's what you can *do* with it! *Out*!"

A few days later, the examination pass lists went up. In every subject, the list of those who had failed to satisfy the examiners was rather longer than the list of those who had succeeded. Some departments, anxious to show themselves in the vanguard of the new thinking, had failed as many as three-quarters of their first- and second-year students. Sammy Limb did not even bother to look at the Law list to find out whether he was one of the survivors. He pushed his way through the crowd of stunned and shell-shocked students, and tore the Law list down from the notice board.

"We don't have to take it cos it's not legal!" he asserted firmly. "Tear 'em down, and take 'em to court!"

There was a moment's shocked silence, then someone started to cheer. More students surged towards the notice boards, and more of the lists were torn down. Several men in suits converged on Sammy, who began to flail about wildly, continuing to advise his fellow students to tear them down and take them to court. Several scuffles broke out between students and security men. One of the men in suits took Sammy round a corner and hit him several times until he fell down. This time, quite a few people noticed, and some of them hit the man in the suit until he fell down too. It took the security firm about fifteen minutes to isolate the trouble-makers and get the situation under control.

"Commander Gross?" said Charlie into the telephone. "Charles Dusenberry, Lowlands University. We touched base last week? Right .... Well, it's all quiet now. There was a minor incident this afternoon, just a scuffle .... I guess what we anticipate tomorrow is a fair-sized peaceful demonstration. We're getting good intelligence from the Students' Union, and there's a small troublemaking element. I guess a token police presence would be very helpful in nipping any trouble in the bud? ... Yeah, I'm sure that would do it fine. We're very grateful for your input, Commander."

He put the phone down.

"I like this country, Jack," he said. "Make a call like that in Salvador, either you get nothing, or a hundred guys swarm in, stealing the typewriters and tearing people's heads off. British moderation, yeah?"

The door opened and Julie Daniels came in.

"Mrs Daniels?"

"Beat it, Charlie," she said.

Charlie shrugged and went into the outer office.

"I'm leaving, Jack," she told her husband.

"You're leaving *Lowlands*?"

"I'm leaving you, Jack."

He seemed puzzled rather than angry.

"What the hell *for*?"

"Because you're an asshole, Jack. And because I guess I've finally found the love of a good man. Don't be shy, honey. Come on in."

A rather embarrassed Jock McCannon shuffled into the doorway. Jack stared at him.

"What is it with these goddam *doctors*?" he said.

Bob Buzzard was running across the darkening car park with a terrible sense of impending doom. He had been at home in the kitchen trying to coax a cup of tea out of a used teabag (come back Consuela, all is forgiven) when Maureen Gahagan had phoned, saying he'd have to come in to the Centre, this great crate had turned up at surgery and he had to sign for it personally, and would he get a move on because it was filling the waiting room and it had this strange kind of smell on it, oh God oh God oh God please let it not be what he knew it would be . . . .

He burst through the swing doors, and there it was. A four by four by four wooden crate with a zinc lining that was clearly not up to specification because a dark stain was already spreading on the waiting room carpet. And there was Maureen with her hands on her hips and a serve-you-right-Buzzard look on her cheeky face, and a big chap with a clipboard who had to be the driver of the artic standing outside . . . .

"You bloody fool!" yelled Bob. "This is supposed to be in *Bogota*!"

"You want a punch in the throat or what, mate?" said the driver mildly. "Watch your lip and sign here."

Nothing else for it. Bob signed, and the man went.

"No! Wait!" yelled Bob. Too late. "Oh, my God!"

"What's in it, Dr Buzzard?" asked Maureen.

"Arms!" said Bob. He was almost sobbing.

"You're dealing in *arms*?"

"Yes, if it's any of your business!"

"Well I hope they're going to the right boys," said Maureen.

"What are you *talking* about?"

"Ireland, of course," she said. "What else?"

"No, no!" he yelled. "*Arms*! *Arms*! For Bogota University Medical School!"

Maureen screwed her face up in disgust.

"Come on, come on!" he yelled. "We've got to get them in a freezer! There's forty grand's worth there! And they're *defrosting*!"

She stared at him.

"I think you're disgusting," she said. "I'm going home." And she walked past him and out through the doors.

"Maureen! Maureen! You've got to *help* me!"

He collapsed across the crate, sobbing.

It was nearly midnight when the BMW finally weaved its way up the avenue towards Buzzard Mansions. Bob left it in the drive, too whacked to put it in the garage, and walked towards the front door, his knees buckling. And, oh Christ, the house was ablaze with lights, and someone was banging about in the kitchen. Rage gave him energy. He scrabbled for his keys, opened the front door, and came in shouting.

"Right, McCannon, enough is enough! This is my home, not the best little whorehouse in Texas!"

But it wasn't McCannon in the kitchen. It was Daphne. It was his own dear Daphne. And she was standing at the sink, and she was up to her elbows in water, and she even had her dear old rubber gloves on.

"Daphne," he said. The tears rolled down his cheeks.

"Hello, my darling," she said. "Yes, I've come back. And I'll never leave you again. You're an absolute bounder, Robert my darling ... but I just can't live without you."

She turned from the sink and held out her dripping arms, and Bob went to her, and she held him. It was so good to be back in Daphne's clutches.

"Oh, Daphne, Daphne."

"There, there," she murmured, patting him on the back with her rubber-gloved hands.

"I've had such a terrible time, Daphne."

"Well, of course you have, my darling, that was the whole idea," she said. "But everything's going to be all right now."

"Is it Daphne?"

"Of course it is, my darling. Oh, by the way, Mr Dusenberry phoned while you were out."

"Oh, my God," said Bob stiffening.

"He said that the Vice-Chancellor had some *very good news* for you, my darling."

"*Really?*" said Bob, in wild surmise.

"I think that this is really it, my darling. I think we're really and truly getting on with our lives!"

The token police presence consisted of Chief Inspector Lyn Turtle and a couple of minibuses full of constables. They were parked inconspicuously in a narrow service road a few yards from the main lecture theatre, where the protest meeting was taking place. It was a soft option for the blokes. They chatted and played cards and worked out their overtime. Lyn paced up and down by the vans. She was extremely bored.

Inside the lecture theatre Harry Pointer was having a difficult time convincing his members that his stance was militant enough. The hall was packed, the aisles crammed with the unwashed. Even Cardboard City had come out. Bunch of oddballs up at the back; he could see Sammy Limb standing next to that old fart McCannon. What was *he* doing here? A lot of silly buggers playing silly-buggers, taking the piss and trying to shout him down. Very aggravating, but Harry Pointer had come through some hairy occasions in his time, and he was going to come through this one. He had the mike, after all, and he'd made sure he had a bloody good PA system.

"Believe me, I understand the feeling of this meeting and I share it! All the way! But what I say to you is this! What I say to you is this!"

He had bugger all to say to them of course; Charlie and Jack had given him nothing to say to them, but Harry could reel off the content-free rhetoric till the cows went home. They'd get tired of it before he did.

"We've got our lines of communication right! We've got our values right! We're in a meaningful dialogue situation! And we have to keep that dialogue going!"

Now they were yelling at him.

"Jack Daniels is a reasonable man!"

That didn't go down at all well. Harry was getting annoyed.

"You are just being bloody ignorant! Negotiations" – they were yelling even louder now – "negotiations – negotiations are well advanced! We mustn't throw away our chances! This Union has never let you down and never will! Trust me and I'll see you all right!"

Christ, the cows were *laughing* at him now. Someone started to chant something, and others took it up.

> "Harry's got his Merc,
> Harry's got his Merc,
> Ee aye addio . . . ."

"That is a bloody lie!" yelled Harry, losing his temper. "You ignorant lying bastards, I'll see you in court for this!"

They were laughing again.

"*I'm* taking *you* to court, Harry!" yelled Sammy Limb from the back, and they started cheering the little bastard. Soon fix that.

"All right, Sammy!"

Christ, he couldn't hear himself. Some cow had pulled the plug on the PA. Then that old bastard McCannon started up. Fuck me, that man had a voice on him.

"Who do we want for President!"

"Sammy Limb!" they all roared.

"Who do we want?"

"Sammy Limb!"

"This is a democratic Union!" yelled Harry Pointer, but they were coming down the aisles at him now.

"Flash Harry Pointer, out out out!"

Then he and Mal and Johnny were off the platform and Jock McCannon and Sammy Limb were on it, and someone had plugged in the PA again, and they were all cheering Sammy Limb.

Sammy Limb felt funny. Excited, dizzy, and somehow his head was a bit . . . he scratched it, and grinned vaguely. The hall was silent now.

"I don't know what to say," said Sammy.

"May I?" said Jock McCannon. He took the microphone and threw back his head, the light of battle in his eyes.

"Storm the Senate House!" he roared.

They were all cheering.

"Open the files!"

They were all coming down the aisles now.

"Reclaim your university!"

It all happened so quickly that before the policemen could get out of the vans, more than a hundred students were already past them, running fast towards Senate House. The security men at Senate House had had half a minute's warning over the walkie-talkies but no one could find the key to lock the front door in time. They tried to hold the doors shut, and succeeded for about two seconds, then the students surged in. Senate House was occupied.

Half an hour later, the situation had stabilized. There were eighty or ninety students inside the building, and forty or fifty more, with banners, cricket bats, and hockey sticks, guarding the entrance. Grete Grotowska stood with them, her tattered Solidarity banner lending an incongruous air of universality to Lowlands' little local difficulty. A much larger crowd of at least a thousand students had gathered at a little distance, good-humouredly cheering the secretaries who were coming out of the building, some of whom waved back. On the steps, between the two groups of students, were Lyn Turtle and her token group of constables, some of whom were distinctly nervous. Lyn was practising unthreatening body language, chatting with, smiling at and touching the students on the doors, and going down the steps from time to time to talk to the students at the front of the large crowd. It was going to be OK, she reckoned. She was in radio touch with headquarters, and had so far persuaded the Commander to keep the reinforcements, four coachloads of them with riot gear, half a mile away on the perimeter road.

Charlie Dusenberry came out of the building, walking fast with his head down, to massive booing, but nobody tried to do anything to him. The crowd opened up to make a path for him, and he walked away into the gathering dusk.

"Come on, relax," said Lyn to her coppers. "Smile a bit, eh? Everything's going to be fine."

Rose Marie came out of the crowd and walked up the steps.

"I'm a doctor," she said to one of the policemen. "Would you let me through please? There may be injured people in there."

"Hello, Rose, thanks for coming, go on up," said Lyn.

Rose walked up the steps to where Grete was standing.

"Grete," she said.

"I don't speak to you no more," said Grete. "You told me a lot of porkers I think."

"I wanted to help, Grete . . . it was all for you."

"Yes? So now what? You join us, or what?"

Rose looked at the banners and the cricket bats and the hockey sticks, and sighed.

"Oh, Grete. These are just . . . boys' games."

"Not boys," said Grete fiercely. "*People*. Wulnerable human bodies."

"Goodbye, Grete," said Rose. She turned and walked back through the crowd.

Jack Daniels sat quietly at his desk. His eyes were glittering strangely. There were twenty or thirty people in his office. Some of them were ransacking his filing cabinets and some of them were drinking his bourbon. He watched them unmoved, his hands motionless on the desk in front of him.

Jock McCannon and Sammy Limb were drinking the bourbon, sitting on one of the Vice-Chancellor's big squashy sofas.

"Well, Sammy," said Jock. "The hero of the hour. How does it feel, my dear fellow?"

"Feels all right like," said Sammy.

He paused and scratched his head.

"Matter of fact, I feel a bit funny. Got a sort of tingle down me right arm."

"Sammy," said Jock. "You did go for that X-ray?"

"Yeah, sure. Well ... I was going, but the bike wouldn't. Don't worry, Doc, I'll go tomorrow, right?"

"No, sir," said Lyn outside, speaking softly into the radio phone. "It's very quiet now. I know these people, I think it's going to be all right. My very firm advice is you hold them on the perimeter. Got someone here who's going in to talk, I think we'll get a result. Bloke from the Senate, head of the Medical Centre." She grinned at Stephen. "Yes, sir, he seems a sensible sort of bloke to me. Thank you sir." She looked at Stephen. "You're in, Doc."

It was dark outside now, and Stephen and Jack Daniels were alone in the big quiet office. The Vice-Chancellor was sitting rigidly still, his hands gripping the edge of the desk, his brilliant blue eyes alight with conviction.

"I'm not gonna give the bastards anything, Steve," he said. "The way I look at it, a few students are expendable. The way I look at it, *all* the students are expendable."

"You're crazy," said Stephen softly.

"I'm not crazy, Steve," said the Vice-Chancellor mildly, as though correcting some small factual error. "I'm the future, and you'd better believe it. All that crap out there ... all those *people* ... they're irrelevant, Steve. A university is about knowledge and power. Cosmic knowledge. Cosmic power. It's about understanding and controlling the universe."

"Jack," said Stephen carefully. "You've been under a terrible strain these last few weeks. Your marriage breaking up .... I know what that feels like."

259

"I don't give a shit about marriage, I'm talking ultimate values here. You think a university is about being kind to dumb old farts? You think a university is about a lot of middle-class kids getting their rocks off? The university is bigger than all of us. Don't you understand yet, you dumb English bastard? Those kids are *expendable*. *You* are expendable. And ultimately, Steve ... even *I* am expendable."

The silence that followed lasted for over a minute. When he spoke again, it was as if to an irritating pet.

"I'm bored with you now, Steve. Why don't you go and screw yourself?"

The crowd were still peaceful when Stephen stepped outside again. Some of them were holding lighted candles. A few of them were singing.

"Nothing," he told Lyn. "He's not rational. He seems to want ... Armageddon or something."

"Shit," said Lyn. "Sorry, sir." Stephen realized that she still had the line open; a man's voice was talking to her. "No, really, sir, I think it would be counterproductive ... how can Mr Dusenberry assess the situation when he's not here? ... Sorry sir. Right."

She turned to Stephen, her eyes wide and worried.

"Well, that's it," she said. "They're coming in. Minimum necessary force."

Grete had refused to be persuaded to move, so now Stephen stood with her at the top of the steps under the Solidarity banner. Lyn paced restlessly to and fro. Stephen had never seen her look so worried. Her constables were cheering up now though, looking resolute, shifting from foot to foot, glad that something was going to happen. The crowd were laughing and singing. Jock McCannon and Sammy Limb came out through the glass doors and stood next to Stephen and Grete.

"Look," said Stephen to Jock. "You'd better get clear. This is going to be nasty."

"Never!" said Jock cheerfully. "We stand firm, right, Sammy?"

"Right, doc," said Sammy vaguely. He was very pale. Suddenly he looked very puzzled. "Look, sorry, I . . . ."

He fell down and lay very still.

Stephen bent over him and felt for a pulse.

He looked up at Jock, his face white.

"Coma."

Jock spoke with uncharacteristic briskness and economy.

"Had a bang on the head over a week ago. Diplopia and headache today. He just told me he felt tingling down his right side."

"Subdural haematoma?" said Stephen.

"Stephen. He must have had intracranial bleeding all this week. Oh, Sammy, Sammy, I didn't look after you!"

Then they heard the first screams and yells as the police reinforcements charged through the back of the crowd. It was dark, and no one had seen them coming, and no one in the big crowd was facing the right way; the students were wheeling and scattering, many of them falling. "Go go go!" went the riot squad, moving through the crowd at a steady trot. They were very disciplined. Only the people directly in their path got hit, kicked or trampled.

With a great inarticulate throaty cry, Jock picked Sammy's skinny body up and held him in his arms.

"Clear the way, you stupid little men!" he roared. "Let me through with my patient!"

He started to walk down the steps, directly into the path of the oncoming policemen. But on the second step he staggered, faltered, and swayed. His face was suffused with a mixture of pain and wonder. So *that's* what it's like, was his last conscious thought. He pitched face forward down the steps, still clutching Sammy Limb to his chest. The policemen ran right over them.

"Stop! Stop!" yelled Stephen, running down the steps. One of the policemen hit him on the head. He fell down and some more policemen ran over him. The front of the riot squad had reached the top of the steps and were fighting with the students at the doors.

Stephen felt dizzy and sick. A lot of the students in the big crowd had realized what was happening now, and were running towards the steps after the policemen. He was hurting all over. Once he caught a glimpse of Lyn. She was trying to get to him, but she couldn't, shouting at the men but they were taking no notice. Then she pulled off her hat, and took off her uniform jacket. She was crying. He didn't see her after that. He couldn't see Grete at all. He tried to get up, but he found he felt very tired. The police had got through the doors and were in the building now, but the fighting went on. Stephen thought he could see two nuns in the thick of it. They appeared to be fighting on both sides. He wondered if he was hallucinating.

High up in his office, Jack Daniels stared out of the window.

"I have a dream," he said. "No man is an island. I'm talking Plato's Republic. I'm talking Camelot."

And the fighting went on.

By dawn, everything was under control. One or two buildings were still smoking, but all the fires were out now. On the steps of Senate House and scattered at various points around the piazza were abandoned hockey sticks, cricket bats, and a few dozen broken placards and sodden bedraggled banners. One of them bore the Solidarity legend. Here and there on the concrete, dark stains showed up in the growing pale light. They would soon be cleaned up. A couple of police vans cruised quietly round and round the campus roads. The revolution was over.

No one was there to see the nuns leaving Lowlands. They rustled through the silent campus, crossed the perimeter road, and flapped like glossy black crows up the grassy slope towards the wooded hills. At the top of a little knoll they stopped, and looked back towards the bleak squat façade and the thin columns of dirty grey smoke. There were three of them; and one had the face of Rose Marie.

Two years later, Stephen, Grete and Lyn stood on a grassy knoll looking down towards what used to be Lowlands

University. A yard or two from where they were standing was a small white wooden stake surrounded by buttercups. The words on the stake read:

> Jock McCannon, MD
> Sammy Limb
> Died at Lowlands, June 1988

A cold breeze sprang up suddenly, rustling the trees. Lyn, who was wearing only a T-shirt and jeans, rubbed her arms and shivered. Joanna Daker woke up and whimpered, and Grete shifted her balance and joggled her sling till she was quiet again.

"Well, Doc," said Lyn. "Think you're going to like it in Poland?"

"Suppose I am a bit nervous about it," said Stephen.

"You won't notice much differences," said Grete. "Just another desperate country."

Stephen sighed.

"Strange to think that used to be Lowlands University," said Stephen.

"Well, we were there, Doc."

"Bob Buzzard's *still* there," said Stephen. "Head of the Medical Centre. Looking after Jack Daniels and a lot of robots."

"Right up his alleys, eh?" said Grete.

"Oh, God," said Stephen. "It could have been such a good place, you know? It could have been really OK."

Half a mile away down the hill, behind the high security fence with its barbed wire and observation posts, behind the inner fence with its electroacoustic warning and counter-insurgency system, behind the blank windowless concrete walls, three floors below ground level, Jack Daniels is walking down a long quiet carpeted corridor banked with mainframes which glow and flicker in an endlessly changing pattern of light, and hum and chatter to him softly. The one he likes best is right at the end of the corridor. He calls it Ronnie, and he likes to touch base with Ronnie every morning right after moving his bowels.

"Good morning, Jack."

"Good morning, Ronnie, how are you today?"

"I guess I'm fine, Jack," says the robot. "How are you?"

"I'm in good shape, I guess. But I haven't been sleeping so good, Ronnie."

"I'm sorry to hear that, Jack. Maybe you should see the doctor."

"Why, thank you, Ronnie," says Jack Daniels. "I guess I'll do just that."

RUST SAYS GOODBYE

"Well, you've really blown it now, Ron," says Ken Riddington.

"I'm not changing a word," says Rust. "That's the way it's going to be."

They are sitting in Jonathan Powell's office in Threshold House. Riddington looks terrible. Rust has a strange visionary gleam in his eyes. Jonathan Powell is looking spruce and cheerful.

"I think it's heaven on wheels, Ken," he says.

"But he's ... I mean he's killed half his characters. He's destroyed the whole fucking university. I mean how are we going to get a third series out of *this*?"

"Have faith in the artist," says Jonathan Powell. "I've got faith in him. Of course we can have another series, Ron: we'll take it to Poland if that's what you want."

Rust is deeply moved. No one has ever had this sort of faith in him before. But he won't weaken. That way madness lies.

"No," he says. "No third series."

They stare at him.

"But Ron," says Ken. "What are you going to *do*?"

Rust smiles.

"I'm going to be a rewrite man for Sam Goldwyn."

Rust leaves Threshold House for the last time feeling as frisky as a young porker. The traffic howls and thunders round and round Shepherds Bush Green, but that doesn't bother Rust any more. Nothing can touch him now. He skips lightly across the road, and something does touch him. A number 49 bus. It doesn't hit him very hard, just hard enough to spin him into a parked Sierra. He slides smoothly across the bonnet of the Sierra and finishes up lying on the pavement, feeling rather silly. A family of beggars with a pram are looking at him with mild interest. After a moment or two he realizes that he's OK. He gets up. Fine. No damage. Rust is indestructible.

A week or so later, he is not feeling quite the thing. Nothing to write home about. Just a nagging persistent headache and a touch of double vision. He has a vague memory of something Deep Throat once said to him in Groucho's and wonders if he ought to lurk down to the Royal Free and have an X-ray or something.

The next day, he feels an odd tingle all the way down his right arm.